More Praise for *The Dollhouse*

"In her page-turning debut, Fiona Davis deftly weaves the storylines of two women living at the famed Barbizon Hotel for Women.... Davis alternates the chapters between each woman until the twists and turns of their respective storylines ultimately weave together, upping the anticipation along the way." —*RealSimple*

"Davis layers on relationships and intrigue, while building tension through her story structure.... The pace quickens as the story hurtles to its surprising—but satisfying—end. Who said history had to be dull, anyway?" —*BookPage*

"Fiona Davis's debut novel deftly blends the contemporary and mid-century storylines to form a wholly absorbing and entertaining read.... Period fiction mingled with twists and turns that keep the reader engrossed until the very last page." —Bookreporter.com

"Davis's debut novel . . . is a lively one, tripping along at a sprightly clip." —*Kirkus Reviews*

"Get ready for glitz, glamour, and a whole lot of sleuthing." —Brit + Co

"Clever and full of twists.... A story well told." —*New York Journal of Books*

"Sensory and vivid.... A zippy plot and a refreshing focus on the lives of women many would overlook." —*The Dallas Morning News*

"Highly readable, *The Dollhouse* conjures up 1950s New York convincingly. In particular the now-vanished world of the Barbizon Hotel for Women, with its antiquated rules and intriguing array of female personalities and tragic fates, lives on in the pages of the novel in delectable detail.... This is no mere 'chick-lit,' but feminist-inspired entertainment." —Historical Novel Society

"Fans of Suzanne Rindell's *Three-Martini Lunch* will enjoy this debut's strong sense of time and place as the author brings a legendary New York building to life and populates it with realistic characters who find themselves in unusual situations." —*Library Journal*

"Davis delivers a fast-paced, richly imagined debut that's almost impossible to put down."

—Kathleen Tessaro, author of *The Perfume Collector*

"The ghosts of the famed NYC women's hotel come to life in *The Dollhouse*. Davis expertly weaves together the stories of several women who lived in the Barbizon during its heyday in the 1950s, and the broken-hearted journalist who decides to get the 'scoop' on a decades-old tragedy that happened in the building. A fun, page-turning mystery."

—Suzanne Rindell, author of *The Other Typist*
and *Three-Martini Lunch*

"Multigenerational and steeped in history, *The Dollhouse* is a story about women—from the clicking anxiety of Katie Gibbs's secretaries to the willowy cool of Eileen Ford's models, to honey-voiced hatcheck girls and glamorous eccentrics with lapdogs named Bird. Davis celebrates the women of New York's present and past—the ones who live boldly, independently, carving out lives on their own terms."

—Elizabeth Winder, author of *Pain, Parties, Work:*
Sylvia Plath in New York, Summer 1953

"Two coming-of-age stories rolled into an ode to New York City and the young women—of past and present—who have tried to forge lives and careers there. Poetic, romantic, crushing, and soulful."

—Jules Moulin, author of *Ally Hughes Has Sex Sometimes*

THE DOLLHOUSE

A Novel

⤨

Fiona Davis

DUTTON

DUTTON

An imprint of Penguin Random House LLC
375 Hudson Street
New York, New York 10014

Previously published as a Dutton hardcover, August 2016

First paperback printing, July 2017

The Library of Congress has catalogued the hardcover edition of this book as follows:
Names: Davis, Fiona, 1966– author.
Title: The dollhouse / Fiona Davis.
Description: New York : Dutton 1852, [2016]
Identifiers: LCCN 2015044905 (print) | LCCN 2016001580 (ebook) |
ISBN 9781101984994 (hardback) | ISBN 9781101985007 (eBook) |
ISBN 9781101985014 (paperback)
Subjects: LCSH: Women journalists—Fiction. | Older women—Fiction. |
Housekeepers—Crimes against—Fiction. | New York (N.Y.)—Fiction. |
Suspense fiction. | BISAC: FICTION / Historical. | FICTION / Contemporary
Women. | FICTION / Literary.
Classification: LCC PS3604.A95695 D65 2016 (print) | LCC PS3604.A95695
(ebook) | DDC 813/.6—dc23
LC record available at http://lccn.loc.gov/2015044905

Printed in the United States of America
1   3   5   7   9   10   8   6   4   2

Book Design by Cassandra Garruzzo
Set in Bell MT Std

For my parents

CHAPTER ONE

New York City, 2016

She'd forgotten the onions.

After all the preparation, the lists, the running out of work early to finish shopping and buy everything she needed for their special dinner, Rose had forgotten a key risotto ingredient. She checked the pantry, but the basket was empty save for a few remnants of the papery outer layers.

Griff had raved about her risotto soon after they'd started dating, and she remembered how proud she'd been listing off the more surprising ingredients.

"The coconut milk is the secret to it," she'd confided.

"Why coconut milk?" He sat back in the rickety chair she'd bought at the thrift store on Bleecker, his long arms and legs far too unwieldy for her small studio apartment.

"I find it makes the texture especially creamy." She said it lightly, as she collected their plates, as if cooking was easy for her, just another thing she did well, rather than a panic-inducing race to the finish line. "I slowly add the chicken stock and coconut milk to the rice and spices until all the flavors have melded."

"I like the way you say that. *Melded.* Say it again."

She did so, the way she would on camera, her pitch slightly lower than her conversational voice, clear and sure.

Then he'd swept her up and made love to her on her bed with its tasteful handmade quilt. She'd stifled the impulse to sweep it to the side, so as not to have to send it to the dry cleaners tomorrow, and had instead surrendered to the enormity of him, all muscles and sinew, an athlete's body even at forty-five.

She missed the simplicity and the heat of their life back then, before the angry ex-wife and the surly children punctured their co-coon of happiness. Before she'd given up her apartment and they'd moved into the Barbizon condo on the Upper East Side.

Of course, his ex-wife and children wouldn't share her perspective. To them she was the interloper, taking up Griff's attention and love. She checked the clock on the oven. Almost six. If she was fast, she could run out to Gourmet Garage and pick up white onions before Griff got home from City Hall.

Her cell phone rang. Maddy again. The fourth call this hour.

"What, Maddy?" She tried to sound irritated, but laughed before Maddy could reply.

"I know, I know. You don't have *any* time to talk to your best friend right now. You're far too busy doing the dutiful housewife thing, right?"

"Yup. And you're off to the Soapies?"

"Daytime Emmys, if you please. I wish you were coming, Ro. What shoes go with the Michael Kors? Nude or gold?" Maddy's career as an actress had taken off since they'd met in college. Maddy had landed a contract role out of school on a daytime soap opera, and this was her first nomination.

Rose swallowed her guilt at not being by her friend's side. "The nude, definitely. Text me a pic, okay?"

"Any idea what Griff's big news is yet?"

Rose smiled and leaned back on the kitchen counter. "Probably nothing so big, in the end," she lied. "Maybe he's been promoted again? Such an overachiever."

"I don't think so. Do the math: It's been a year since his divorce was finalized, you've been living together for three months, and it's time to set a date."

"He has been acting weird lately. But what if I'm getting way ahead of myself?"

"Trust your gut."

"My gut says something's up. Even though sometimes it still feels like it's early stages. I mean, we haven't even furnished the apartment yet."

The apartment she both loved and hated. Loved for its tall French casement windows, for its Wolf range and spacious closets. Loved for the air of promise it held in its baseboards and crown moldings and Bolivian rosewood floors.

But hated for its emptiness. She and Griff both worked too many hours during the week to take a real stab at furniture shopping, and weekends he went to his house in Litchfield with his kids, his wife off gallivanting with her other divorced friends. *Ex-wife*, she corrected.

So much work needed to be done to make it homey. The wallpaper in the smallest bedroom was covered in tiny climbing monkeys. Delightful as nursery wallpaper but not at all right for Griff's teenaged daughters. The floorboards in the dining room were bare except for the ghost outline of the prior owner's Oriental rug.

Rose often felt like a ghost herself on weekends, sitting in the window seat off the library, staring down at the traffic and pedestrians wandering in pairs below. The sounds of honking and laughter easily permeated their fifth-floor apartment, even when the windows were shut. The neighborhood, Sixty-Third Street just off of Lexington, lacked the character of her old West Village stomping ground, where the trees formed a canopy over the cobblestones. Up here the sidewalks were bare, the avenue crammed with gilded little shops selling white linen toddler dresses and antique maps of Paris.

Rose waited while Maddy grunted into her dress. "Jesus, this zipper is literally unreachable. I need another pair of hands."

"Where's Billy again?"

"Parent-teacher night. He and his ex are having dinner afterward to discuss school options for next year. And if I haven't already mentioned it, I'm quite happy to have a Get Out of Jail Free card for that one."

"I'd be there to dress you properly if I could, you know that."

"Oh, don't worry, honey, I know. I'll text you a pic and you do the same once you get the ring."

Rose hung up, laughing, and padded down the long hall to the master bedroom, where she slipped out of the sheath she'd worn that day. As usual, she'd overdressed. The rest of her barely legal colleagues at the media start-up, all younger by at least ten years, gravitated toward jeans and hoodies. She pulled on a pair of leggings and a soft cashmere V-neck, then touched up her lips in the mirror.

Griff liked to call her his pinup girl, an image she encouraged when they went out together with a shade of crimson lipstick that worked with her pale skin and dark, sleek bob. But lately she'd begun wondering if the color was garish for a woman in her mid-thirties. Like she was trying too hard.

Did a man wonder whether his face was too shiny, his hair curling unreasonably, or if his crow's-feet had possibly deepened overnight? She couldn't imagine Griff giving any of these things a second thought. He entered a room as an agent of change, a man who made the news. Not as the pleasant-featured girl who simply reported it. When she'd worked at the network, Rose wanted to be taken seriously and dressed the part even though her producer wanted plunging necklines. Quiet wardrobe choices aside, Rose was dismissed as eye candy by a big chunk of her core audience—some of whom also liked to tweet nasty comments about her breasts and legs. At least her new job kept her out of the limelight.

The sounds of a horn drifted up through the open bedroom window. Not a car horn, though. A low, mournful longing, followed by the rasp of a drum. She wasn't sure who: Miles Davis was the only trumpet player she could name. Her father had liked to play Dave Brubeck records when she was young, and the memory brought a smile to her face. She'd download some Brubeck to her iPhone and play it when she visited her father this weekend. He'd like that. Or he'd throw the phone across the room. You never knew, these days.

She should get going, but the haunting melody pulled her toward the open window. She leaned on the windowsill, stuck her head out, and listened. The sound drifted up from the apartment below hers but stopped moments later, replaced by a tune sung by two women. One had an edgy alto, like Lucinda Williams. The other was sweet, high, and almost angelic. The juxtaposition of the voices was unbearably beautiful: pain and hope, mixed together. The song ended with what sounded like giggling, oddly enough.

Time to get moving. She needed onions.

The apartment phone rang. Hopefully, Griff was calling to say he was running late.

"Is my dad there?"

Rose still couldn't tell his daughters' voices apart.

"Isabelle?"

"No, it's Miranda." The girl let out an impatient huff. "Is my dad there?"

Neither girl would say Rose's name out loud. Maddening. Then again, they were young and their lives were difficult. Even though Griff and his wife had been separated for three years, divorced for one, Rose had become the touchstone for everything that had gone wrong between their parents. Maddy had lucked out, meeting a man whose kids were four and seven, magical ages when Maddy was simply an extra person to play with, to receive attention from, rather than a threat.

She brightened her tone. "Hi, Miranda. He's not home from work yet. Did you try his cell?"

"Yeah. Went straight to voice mail. That's why I'm calling here."

"Well, he must be in the subway. I'll let him know you called."

No good-bye, just a click followed by a dial tone. Maybe she'd leave the monkey wallpaper up after all.

If Griff was indeed on the subway, she didn't have much time. Rose shouldered her bag and marched down the hallway, into the elevator. After an interminable wait, the doors closed, only to open again one floor below.

A woman stepped forward, wearing white gloves and a beautiful dark-blue straw hat with an ivory veil that obscured her eyes and nose. Her matching coat, far too warm for this time of year, flared out from a closely fitted waist. Only her tentative movements, as if the floor might give way beneath her ivory shoes at any time, and the lines around her mouth and down her neck, belied her advanced age. She clutched the leash of a small dog. Immediately, she turned around to face front. Rose's bright greeting went unanswered.

The fourth floor. When Griff and Rose were looking at the build-ing, the real estate broker had mentioned in hushed tones that a dozen or so tenants were "leftovers," long-term residents of the Barbizon who began as paying guests back when it was a women-only hotel in the last century. Instead of being evicted after the building turned condo, they'd all been moved to rent-controlled apartments on the fourth floor.

The dog barked up at Rose and she leaned over and let him sniff her hand. The veiled lady didn't move a centimeter. The other residents sometimes groused about the fourth-floor tenants, women who lived in valuable real estate without paying the thousands of dollars in monthly common charges that the rest of them did, but Rose felt otherwise. They were here first, and they fascinated her.

What had it been like, when the exclusive address housed hundreds of pretty young girls? Several had gone on to great fame: Grace Kelly, Sylvia Plath, Candice Bergen; the list went on and on.

"I'm Rose Lewin." She couldn't help herself. The woman clearly wanted to be left alone, but Rose's inquisitive nature took over. "I've just moved in, a few months ago. I'm afraid we haven't met."

The woman turned, slowly, her lips pursed into a tight pink line. "Welcome." Her voice warbled with age.

The elevator door finally opened and Rose waited while her mysterious neighbor maneuvered onto the marble floor of the lobby. She walked carefully, taking small, wobbly strides and keeping her shoulders and head ramrod straight. The dog, a terrier of some kind, trotted an uneven staccato rhythm across the floor, as if the coolness of the stone hurt his thimble-size feet. Rose lagged behind them.

The doorman gallantly swept open the heavy front door. "Miss McLaughlin, greetings. And how is Bird today?"

"Fine, thank you, Patrick."

After they passed through, Patrick addressed Rose with a smile and a slight bow. "Miss Lewin. How are you this evening?"

"Fine, thanks. I'm off to the store, back in a moment."

She was still getting used to having a doorman. There was no need to tell him why she was going out, or to make small talk about the weather. Her tendency to do so drove Griff nuts. To him, getting out of the lobby was a mere blip in a long, busy day.

The woman and her dog turned toward Park Avenue, and Rose headed over to Second. Although the store was mobbed, she picked up two onions and a bunch of white peonies and made it through the express aisle in record time.

Patrick was standing out on the sidewalk when she returned, hands behind his back, looking up at the new building being constructed across the street. His stomach stuck out from above his belt buckle and his gray hair lifted in the breeze. She stopped and looked up with him.

"How big is it going to be?" she asked.

"Too big." He'd been working for the Barbizon since he'd arrived in America forty years ago, and she was fairly certain he played up his Irish accent to charm the ladies. "I was thinking about what it was like when our building was the tallest in the neighborhood. Can you imagine? I've seen a photo of it, towering above the brownstones. Now this monstrosity across the street is going to be double the size. We don't stand a chance."

"Everything's tall these days," Rose offered. "But that's probably what they said when our building went up." She'd admired its design the first time they'd come to view the apartment. It was solid, unusual. The building grew thinner at the top, like a brick-and-sandstone wedding cake, the terraces decorated with grand Moorish arches.

"Patrick, when did you start working here?"

He turned to face her, eyebrows raised in surprise. She gathered that few residents asked him personal questions. "Back in the seventies. Things were very different then."

She liked the way *things* came out as *tings*. "Do you know many of the older residents?"

"The ladies? Of course. I know them all."

"What about the woman who left a little while ago? The one with the dog."

He smiled. "Miss McLaughlin. And Bird. Odd woman."

A woman with buttery blond hair clopped toward them, carrying several packages. Patrick left Rose's side and scuttled over to her. Rose checked her watch. She really should get upstairs, not stand around chatting, but Patrick quickly reappeared. "Can I get you a taxi, Miss Lewin?"

"No, no." She waved her hand in front of her. "I was hoping you could tell me more about Mrs. McLaughlin."

"*Miss* McLaughlin." He was about four inches shorter than she was and he lifted his ruddy, round face to hers. "I don't like to talk too much about the other residents, you know."

Patrick loved to talk about the other tenants, but Rose put on a serious expression and nodded.

"She's from way back, the fifties, that was when she first moved in. Came here to go to secretary school."

"She seems like an interesting woman, the way she dresses and all."

"Not many friends in the building. Management can't stand her. She kicked and screamed when they said she had to move from her apartment down to 4B, with the rest of the longtimers. Threatened to call her lawyer. But never did. In the end, I helped her pack up and move. She's a retired lady, couldn't afford proper movers, and I was happy to do it. She always remembers me at Christmas with a card and a small token."

Apartment 4B was the one directly under theirs. The one with the music. "That was very kind of you, to help her move."

"Terrible story, what happened to her."

Leave it to Patrick to bury the lead. "What happened?"

"There was a skirmish up on the terrace."

"A skirmish?"

"Yes. I can't say what happened exactly. She was up there with one of the maids. It was a hotel back then, not like today, employed a big staff. Anyway, the two girls got into a fight and the maid fell to her death."

"Good Lord. That's awful."

"I know. I remember I talked to one of the older porters when I first came on the job. I noticed she always wore a veil, never saw her without it. I said, 'Why does the woman always cover her face?' He told me she can't stand to be seen, ever since that day."

"Why is that?"

A family of tourists interrupted them, asking the way to Bloomingdale's. As if he knew Rose was on the edge of her seat, Patrick spent quite a while explaining the best route and recommending a decent bistro in the neighborhood. She really had to get upstairs. If they ended up ordering in dinner, the mood would be all wrong.

Rose was waiting for the elevator to descend from one of the high floors, when Patrick reappeared by her side.

"Anyway, like I was saying. Poor Miss McLaughlin. The old porter, you know, the one I mentioned I spoke with, he said she was going to secretarial school. She was one of the innocents who came from the boondocks, not knowing anything, and she got caught up in all kinds of trouble."

"What kind?"

"That I couldn't tell you." He rubbed his temple. "But in the skirmish, as they called it, she was cut."

"Cut?"

He made a motion from the corner of his forehead down through the opposite eye. "Cut. With a knife."

Her stomach turned.

"She was left disfigured, horribly scarred. Poor, poor Miss McLaughlin." He closed his eyes. "Hasn't once shown her face to the world again since."

The elevator door opened and Rose stepped inside, suppressing a shudder.

She should have never asked.

CHAPTER TWO

New York City, 1952

The woman behind the desk at the Barbizon Hotel for Women looked up in confusion. "McLaughlin? I'm afraid we don't have anyone here by that name."

"But I'm not here yet, I've just arrived." Darby bit her lip. If only Mother had come with her, she wouldn't be in this situation. If Mother had come, she'd be telling the clerk to go back and check her records, that she'd sent a letter off last month stating that Darby McLaughlin was arriving on the fifth of September and enclosing the three letters of recommendation. Then she'd turn to Darby and tell her to stop biting her lip.

She bit her lip harder and tasted blood.

The woman wore spectacles that made her eyes look unusually round, and Darby couldn't help but widen hers in sympathy.

A group of five or six girls her age flounced through the lobby, and Darby could have sworn she heard one of them making a hooting noise. The lady behind the counter appeared not to have noticed.

"You've just arrived, you say?"

"Yes, I just arrived from Ohio today, and my mother, Mrs. Saunders, made the reservation ages ago. I'm to be here through June."

The idea of getting back on a train and returning to Ohio was daunting. Grand Central Terminal had frightened her to bits, the hordes of people walking this way and that, knowing exactly where they were headed and why. She had stood close to the big clock and clutched her suitcase, trying to get her bearings as if she were standing on the deck of a giant ship. The floor even seemed to sway ever so slightly under her black patent leather pumps.

Then she spied the sign for taxis and hurled herself toward it, bumping into people and apologizing furiously. Before she had a moment to watch the city whizzing by in the cab, she was dropped off in front of the Barbizon Hotel and found herself standing in the cool, cavernous lobby. The dark wood of an intricately carved balcony loomed over three sides, offset by bright white walls. Lush palm plants stood guard against the columns.

All she wanted, after the overnight train ride, with its fancy dining car and linen tablecloths, was to go to her room and lie down for a moment. To collect herself from the onslaught of sensations. And now they said she didn't even have a room.

She knew no one in the city, no one at all. The Barbizon Hotel for Women was her only hope.

The clerk returned from a back room, clutching a white piece of paper. "Saunders is the name it was filed under."

She breathed out a sigh of relief. "Yes, that's my stepfather. Mother took his name after she married him. But mine remained McLaughlin."

The owl-eyed woman threw Darby a largely indifferent look. "Well, I have Saunders here, miss. Do you want me to change it?"

"Yes, please."

"Good enough. Wait here and Mrs. Eustis will be with you shortly."

She had no sooner sat on the hard bench than the woman appeared. She was what Darby's mother would describe as horsey: a tall, solid woman with an aquiline profile, wearing a navy suit that sported a floppy fabric corsage. Darby stood and shook her hand.

"You look exhausted, Miss McLaughlin. I hope the trip wasn't too arduous."

"No, not at all. I quite enjoyed it," lied Darby. "Trains are terrific." Mother had handed her a book titled *The Art of Conversation* at the train station, and she'd dutifully read through it because the cover promised a "fascinating new way to win poise, power, personality." *Make your rejoinders positive!* it had decreed.

Mrs. Eustis gave a curt nod. "Come with me and I'll show you to your room. You're on the fifteenth floor, and I think you'll find it quite accommodating."

The elevator doors opened. Darby tried not to stare when a young girl in a uniform yanked open the interior gates for them to enter. Mrs. Eustis indicated for Darby to step inside. "Male visitors must be signed in and are only allowed in the public lounges. The safety of our girls comes first."

The elevator girl rolled her eyes and Darby suppressed a smile. As they trundled up, Mrs. Eustis ticked off the pertinent information in such a rush that Darby was certain she wouldn't remember a thing. "Meals are served in the second-floor dining room. The hours are posted in the lobby, but you can always pop in to pour yourself a cup of tea or coffee. Socials are held every Thursday evening in the West lounge. Anyone found sneaking a man up into the private rooms risks expulsion. You may use the pool, gymnasium, and squash courts in the basement from eight o'clock in the morning to six o'clock at night. At the top floor you'll find the sky terrace and solarium. You're en-rolled at Katharine Gibbs, is that correct, Miss McLaughlin?"

The elevator door opened and they stepped down a narrow hallway. "Yes, ma'am. I'm due to start classes Monday."

"Very good. I'm afraid there were no vacant rooms on the floors where the Gibbs girls are housed. You'll be here, with girls who work for Eileen Ford."

"Like the cars?" Darby asked. She imagined all the secretaries learning the names of automotive parts.

"No, not the cars." Mrs. Eustis let out a frustrated sigh. "Here we are."

She stuck a key into a doorknob and opened the door. The long, narrow room smelled of mustiness and hair spray. Darby touched the surface of the bureau, happy to discover it wasn't sticky with residue.

A twin bed hugged one wall, with a small wooden desk and chair squeezed against the foot of it. The bedspread sported a garish poppy design, as did the curtains, which hung down almost to the floor, making the window appear longer than it actually was. A scuffed wingback chair, too small to curl up in, was wedged into the corner opposite the desk.

"No pets are allowed, no fish, no turtles, nothing of the sort."

Darby wasn't sure where she'd get a live fish in the first place. Did they have stores for such things in New York City? Of course they did. They had everything.

"You look quite dazed. I say, are you all right?"

"I'm fine, Mrs. Eustis."

"Very well, then I'll leave you be. Most of the girls on your floor are out on a trip to the Museum of Natural History today, so you'll find it rather quiet until they return."

Darby hung up her dresses in the closet and put away the rest of her clothes. She placed her brush and comb on the top of the bureau and lay on the bed, unsure of what to do next, and fell into a deep, dreamless sleep.

A girl's scream woke her. The noise was high-pitched and terrifying, and Darby sat up quickly. With a sinking heart, she remembered she was in the middle of a strange city, alone. Out the window, the sun had disappeared behind the horizon in a dull haze, lending an otherworldly glow to the rooftops and water towers.

The scream dissolved into helpless laughter as the racket outside her door increased. The Ford girls must have returned from their outing.

Darby got up and brushed her hair, then put on her favorite dress for courage. It was a creamy cotton that buttoned right up to the neck and had short, cuffed sleeves. The dress flowed out from the belted waist, from which dozens of images of closed umbrellas and parasols hung down among the many pleats. The varying shapes and colors made her smile whenever she looked down.

In the mirror, her face had a sallow cast and her brown hair hung limply in the heat, making her ears seem bigger than normal. The Ear Beautifier that Mother had ordered and insisted she use nightly hadn't made them any less pronounced. Still, the dress was awfully pretty.

Taking a deep breath, Darby ventured into the hallway.

A gorgeous redheaded girl stopped mid-stride. "Well, hello."

Darby stuck out her hand. "Hello, I'm Darby McLaughlin." She plastered a bright smile on her face.

"Darby, I'm Stella Conover. I haven't seen you before." Stella stood several inches taller than Darby and had the tiniest ears she'd ever seen.

"No. I'm here for secretarial school. From Ohio. Just arrived today. For a moment they didn't have my reservation, and I figured I'd have to turn around and go right back. But then they found it. They'd put it under my stepfather's name instead of mine. He's Saunders; I'm McLaughlin."

She was babbling. This was not at all what *The Art of Conversation* advised.

"Well, I'm glad it was sorted out." Stella took her by the arm. Maybe Darby hadn't sounded idiotic. "I love your dress, by the way."

Stella brought her to an open door. Inside, six or seven other girls lolled about while one read out loud from a fashion magazine. When Darby appeared, they all stared up at her.

They looked as if they'd drifted right out of the pages of the magazine. One wore a bright-red lipstick that showed off her perfect bow lips, while another had a tousle of golden curls. Their clothes were tailored and crisp: embroidered white blouses atop pencil skirts, rayon dresses in colorful stripes. A bevy of princesses holed up in a high tower. Even though she'd be turning eighteen in three months, Darby felt more like an ankle-biter in the presence of such beauties.

"Ladies, this is Darby; she just arrived today for Katie Gibbs." Stella pointed to each girl, their names tripping off her tongue. "We're all with Eileen Ford, the modeling agency."

That explained it. She was terribly out of place, like a panda in a room full of gazelles.

The girls said hello, and the one with the magazine, named Candy, invited Stella and Darby to join them. Darby tucked herself into the corner, eager to deflect any attention.

"I was just reading the newlywed tips from *Mademoiselle.* Do you read it, Darby?"

"Of course." Well, not exactly. Mother bought the latest issue for her every month, and Darby would pretend to leaf through it.

The willowy models, with their knowing gazes and impossibly tiny waists, intimidated.

"Anyway, here is the advice, ladies. Number one: 'Comb your hair and wash your face before breakfast and put lipstick on before you put the coffee on.' Number two: 'Never touch your husband's razor or tidy his desk.'"

"Ugh, I wouldn't want to touch his razor." The blonde tossed her head and grimaced. Even while making an ugly face, she was pretty.

"Number three: 'The first time your baby and your husband call you at the same time, go to your husband.'"

Darby imagined a baby crying its head off in hunger, while the husband needed help looking for a missing sock. Didn't seem right.

"Number four: 'Don't compete with your husband.' And finally, number five: 'Remember that marriage is fun.'"

The girls clamored to comment, the words tumbling out.

"I comb my hair before coming downstairs anyway; that wouldn't make much difference to me."

"And I'll have a nurse to see to the baby, so I'll be free to mind my husband."

"What do you think, Darby?"

Candy stared at her. This was a test. She needed to respond with an air of élan and a witty comment. If she did, she'd make friends for life, and these girls would ask her to be a bridesmaid at their weddings and invite her to their baby showers and they'd exchange letters, remembering their time together in New York City when they were young and the world was ahead of them.

"I don't plan on marrying," Darby said.

Candy's jaw dropped open. She fiddled with the pearls around her neck. "Ever?"

"That's why I'm here, to go to school and learn how to earn my own wage. I don't want a man to support me." She remembered the look on Mother's face, both stricken and triumphant, when Daddy had passed away. The other girls stared at her, dumbstruck, and she tried to explain. "A woman shouldn't have to depend on a man."

"Right. Maybe you prefer to depend on a woman instead?"

"I'm not sure what you mean."

Candy's eyes shone with a menacing glee. "You really don't know what I'm talking about?"

"All I'm saying is that I plan to make enough money to support myself. Isn't that what you want? Isn't that why you're here?"

Candy cackled. "No, sugar. I'm looking to find the richest man I can. Don't be a nosebleed."

Before she could respond, Stella announced it was time for dinner, and the gaggle sprang up and trotted out the door. The magazine fell to the floor and Darby carefully picked it up and laid it back on the bed.

She'd said the wrong thing. She smoothed her umbrella dress and followed them down the hallway.

⌒❧⌒

The clattering of dishes and lively chatter rebounded around the dining room, which was as fancy as any restaurant Darby had been to, with crisp white tablecloths and an art deco chandelier of Odeon glass hanging from the ceiling. Darby followed Stella like a lost puppy, trailing behind the one person who'd been kind. Stella filled her own plate with broccoli and a spoonful of mashed potatoes, but Darby was famished and asked for an extra chicken filet. Her girdle would be tight afterward, but she didn't care.

"Now, tell me, where are you from in Ohio?" asked Stella once they'd sat down at the table filled with their hall mates.

"Defiance." *Keep your answers short and sweet; don't drone on.*

"What an original name for a town. Much better than Granite Falls, anyway—that's where I'm from in North Carolina." Stella took a dainty bite of potato and continued. "It's strange they put you on the same floor as the models, though. The Gibbs girls are up on sixteen and seventeen." She put a hand on Darby's arm. "We're happy to have you, of course."

"Why, thank you. Happy to be had." Wrong. Stupid. Stella threw her an odd glance.

Darby wished she were at home, cuddling her dogs while Mother cooked, enjoying the few quiet hours after school and before Mr. Saunders came home. She'd brought several books with her, including her beloved anthology of Shakespeare's plays, and part of her wanted nothing more than to run up to her room and lose herself in *Twelfth Night* or *Cymbeline*, imagining the stage sets and costumes in her head as she read.

"I'm sorry, I'm out of my element here." Darby fiddled with her cutlery as tears pricked the corners of her eyes.

"There, now." Stella lowered her voice. "I felt the same way before I settled in. Granite Falls doesn't even have a bus depot, so you can imagine how overwhelming this was for me when I arrived."

For the first time, Darby noticed the other girl spoke with a soft Southern lilt. Her voice was musical, like a song.

"I like your accent."

"Thank you. I try to play it down—the modeling agency thinks it makes me seem unsophisticated."

"How can they say that? It's beautiful, like a melody."

Stella drew back, pleased. "That's so well put. You should be a writer."

"You're kind, but I can't waste time daydreaming. I'm here to learn to be a secretary. Mother used all of the insurance money she got when Daddy died to get me here. I won't have another chance."

"I see," said Stella. "And where would you like to work once you're through with Katie Gibbs, Little Miss Serious?"

Darby smiled. "Funny, I hadn't thought that far ahead." The din was nice; it offered them a cocoon of privacy.

"Well, I think you should aim high. You could be the secretary to a top businessman, to someone who runs a publishing house or a fashion line. Someone who'll appreciate a girl who has a way with words."

"That sounds like a dream. But we don't have any such people in Defiance."

"So don't go back to Ohio at all, then. You can stay here in New York City."

"Oh, no, I couldn't do that."

"But why not?"

Darby wouldn't dare explain why. That she'd miss her dogs too much, and Mother would be left alone with Mr. Saunders and his moods and temper.

"Did you hear what happened last year?" Candy addressed the entire table, cutting into Darby and Stella's conversation.

"No, what?" asked Stella, turning away from Darby.

"I heard one of the girls jumped to her death from the fourteenth floor."

"Hush, Candy. That's just a rumor and you know it."

"No, it's true." Candy stared right at Darby. "One of the doormen told me all about it. Said they covered it up so the papers wouldn't find out, just shoveled up the body and sent it home to wherever she was from."

"Awful!" The girls' protests rang out.

"We're not supposed to know. And apparently another girl used a gun to shoot herself in the head in her room several years ago. Her ghost still walks the halls, half of her head gone."

Stella pushed away her plate. "Lord, Candy. I'm still eating. You could at least wait until bedtime for such gruesome stories."

"She wasn't a guest editor or a model, I know that much. Probably a Katie Gibbs girl. You better watch out, Darby."

The room began to spin.

"You don't look very well," said Stella.

"I'm fine." Darby wiped her mouth with her napkin and offered up a weak smile.

"You know, I have a powder that would be perfect for the shine on your nose." Stella again, saving the day. Bored with the line of conversation, the other girls turned away. "I'll give it to you when we go back to our rooms. Would you like that?"

"I would like that very much. Thank you." Embarrassed, Darby patted at her cheeks with her napkin, hoping to tone down the oily sheen that had haunted her since she was fourteen. She was way out of her league with these girls: ugly, uninformed, and dull-witted. How many dinners would she have to sit through before she could return to Defiance? September through June, ten months, seven dinners a week, four weeks a month: two hundred and eighty, minus some for the holiday vacations.

Back in her room, Darby threw herself facedown on her bed and silently wept into her pillow. She had just wound down when a knock sounded on her door.

"Darby, I brought your powder. Pond's Angel Face; it's to die for." Stella stepped in and closed the door behind her. "Why are you sitting in the dark?"

Darby sat up and wiped her eyes. "I want to go home, Stella. I don't want to be here."

Stella joined her on the bed and put her arm around her. She smelled of vanilla, and Darby couldn't help but lay her head on her shoulder. Stella didn't flinch, as she might have, and this small kindness almost set off another round of tears.

"There, there." Stella reached around with her free hand and tucked Darby's hair behind her ear. "You'll settle in soon enough."

"Do you really think there's a ghost?"

"No. I think Candy's a first-class brat. Don't let her get to you. You're a Barbizon girl now; you're one of us."

The dull panic that had clutched her heart since she'd left Ohio loosened, just a little, and Darby let out a deep, sad sigh.

CHAPTER THREE

New York City, 2016

The risotto was simmering nicely by the time Griff arrived home, and the scent of the peonies drifted in from the foyer, where Rose had placed them in a glass vase. He popped his head into the kitchen and she smiled up at him. "Well, hello, stranger."

Her heart flipped as it always did when she saw him, even after three years together. His eyes, which were the color of seawater, had a laserlike intensity that made politics the obvious career choice. That or terrorist interrogator. She'd seen both men and women turn into pools of mush before him. To be the object of his affection was flattering.

He gave her a quick kiss. "Gotta change out of this suit. Just give me a minute."

"How did it go today?"

"The mayor's got me digging into the latest housing scandal, leaving me to figure his mess out."

As the first deputy mayor of the city of New York, Griff was in charge of everything the mayor threw at him. Rose sympathized, having experienced similar chaos in the television studio.

While he changed, she poured two glasses of his favorite Burgundy. After a gentle stir of the risotto, she lowered the burner to a simmer, covered the pot, and joined him in the living room.

Griff reached for his glass of wine and took a large sip, then sank down into the sofa, staring into the black void of the TV screen.

"The risotto needs another ten minutes." She rubbed his leg with her hand. "You okay?"

"I'm fine. I have some interesting news."

"Let's hear it."

"On my way out the door, the mayor stopped me and suggested I run for office when he's done with his term."

Griff had talked about running for mayor down the road, when he had more political capital and experience behind him. But that was supposed to happen far in the future. If Griff ran and won in the next election, she'd be the first lady of New York City in less than two years. The idea rattled her. The scrutiny would be horrible, Page Six of the *New York Post* every day. "Wow. That's a huge leap."

Griff gave a shy smile. "He thinks I have a strong chance, that people are looking for a fresh candidate—one who isn't imbedded in the system."

Whatever happened, they'd manage. She threw her arms around his neck and kissed him. She loved the way he seemed surprised by his success, and he truly was. Just a good boy from upstate who happened to be brilliant at his job.

"Probably best not to think about it too much yet." Griff dismissed the idea with a wave of his hand. "There's so much to accomplish before then."

"Of course."

His eyes were more sunken than usual, and she wondered if he might be coming down with something. She curled her legs under her and snuggled in for closer inspection. Usually when they met up in the evening, she liked to entertain him with the latest exploits of her ridiculous twentysomething boss. When Rose's job at the network had ended in a spectacular flameout, Griff had encouraged her to take a pay cut and work where she could write about culture and the arts, her first loves. She took a job at WordMerge, a media start-up with an admittedly terrible name, one that tripped on the tongue when uttered aloud.

"Today, Tyler asked if I'd cover some new strip club in Brooklyn that offers farm-to-table food and microbrewed beer. It's called Au Naturel. Can you believe it?"

Griff nodded. "Very hip. Are you going to do it?"

"I'd rather not. I'll let one of the assistant editors have it."

"Why all the fluff all of a sudden?"

"I think the board is pressuring Tyler to attract more advertisers. And right now that means finding readers who only eat organic at strip clubs and are willing to drop two hundred bucks on a pot of beard-grooming cream."

Griff smiled, but it didn't reach his eyes. "Could be a great story."

"You're kidding, right?"

"Hey, sometimes you have to do certain things to please certain people. Then you get what you want."

She sat up, surprised. "I guess so. Still." She checked her watch. "The risotto should be ready. Are you hungry?"

"Um, not yet."

Usually he came home ravenous.

"Okay, we can wait a few more minutes, no problem. You'll never guess what I learned from Patrick today."

His brow furrowed. "Patrick?"

"The Irish doorman."

"Right."

"I shared an elevator with one of the longtime residents, a very odd, elegant old lady who wore a veil that covered her face. She lives in the apartment right below us. Turns out she was involved in an incident on one of the terraces way back when. She was cut on the face by a maid, who then fell to her death."

"Huh."

He was far away, not even listening to her.

"Anyway, what a story, right?" She ran a finger around the lip of her wineglass. "And your daughter called, looking for you."

He snapped back to attention. "Which one?"

"Miranda."

He leapt up with a smooth leonine grace. "I'll call her back now, before dinner."

His footsteps echoed against the stark walls as he retreated into the bedroom. He didn't seem like a man on the verge of proposing. Or maybe he was behaving so strangely because he was nervous.

Swigging down another mouthful of wine, she looked out the window at the brick facade of another building filled with people who were aging and fighting and making love. The thought was oddly comforting.

Griff's murmurs were unintelligible. She wandered to the kitchen and gave the risotto an idle stir before adding salt and pepper.

"Can we talk for a moment?"

He was suddenly beside her, looking serious.

"Of course."

He led her back into the living room and they sat back down. As he reached into his pocket, she gripped her palms tightly together, trying to remain calm. The time had come. He was so anxious, her heart went out to him.

He pulled out his cell phone and turned it off.

Griff never turned off his phone. He'd put it on vibrate, maybe. But not off.

"You've been so good to me," he said.

"Of course. And you've been good to me." Her words came out robotic, an automatic response.

"Rose, I love you so much."

Her mouth went dry. She was reminded of the first time she'd ever presented the news: the countdown to going on air, the fear of doing something stupid or saying the wrong words. Like then, she reminded herself to breathe and loosened her shoulders, letting the tension flow out of her. She hoped he'd get to the point quickly, put her out of her misery, proposal or no.

"Talk to me, Griff."

"I've been speaking with Connie lately, about the girls, and we've been really worried, particularly about Miranda."

Not the response she was expecting. And the use of *we* was troubling. Not *we* as in Rose and Griff, but the prior *we*.

He continued, one jean-clad leg jiggling furiously. "I do want to get married. I do."

The sentence should have been a simple declaration. But the two words tagged on at the end changed everything, acted as a hinge, a doorway to a different meaning entirely. She waited for the next part of the phrase, the one that would turn it on its head.

"I think I have to go back to them."

Her head swarmed with confusion, her thoughts like bees whose hive has been destroyed. "Go back to Connie?"

"Not Connie, exactly. The girls. I realize what I've done to you is a terrible, terrible thing. I love you and I always will."

She held perfectly still and scrutinized his face. His eyes were wide, innocent, an open book. But his pupils dilated with fear, dark wheels barely encircled with green.

"And I love you." She continued to play by the script, waiting until she had surer footing.

"But my family needs me right now. The girls are a mess. Miranda's been suspended from school again. Connie can't handle her alone. "

"I'm so sorry, but maybe you shouldn't make any impulsive decisions right now. Let's furnish this apartment so you can spend more time with the kids here. I'll help. You don't have to go there every weekend."

Every weekend. He'd told Rose that Connie stayed with friends when he went to the house in Litchfield to spend time with the girls. But maybe she'd been there as well, luring him back, sleeping with him, making him miss the comforts of home and hearth. While Rose had been left sitting in a half-empty, three-bedroom condo, playing the patient girlfriend when she wasn't putting in ten-hour workdays.

She'd taken a huge cut in salary to join WordMerge. How was she going to pay for her father's care now? Her despair simmered into a dull anger.

The smell of burning rice snapped her to attention.

In the kitchen, she yanked the pot off the burner and turned off the gas. The bottom of the risotto was burned, and the pot would have to be tossed. How would she be able to buy a new one, never mind an entirely new set of cutlery, dishes, furniture? The list went on and on.

Griff came up behind her and rested his hands lightly on her shoulders. The pressure was soothing. Maybe this was temporary insanity.

She turned around and his hands slid to her hips.

"Do you think that maybe you're panicking here?" she asked. He dropped his head and pressed his forehead to hers. Her heartbeat slowed ever so slightly, more like R & B than speed metal for the moment. "Miranda will be fine; you need to give her time. Think of everything we have together."

"That's just it. We do have so much, such an amazing connection. But I have to do this for my daughter."

"But you're divorced. Who goes back to their ex-wife? It's insane."

"You can stay here for as long as you need to, while I work the details out. I'm as confused as you right now."

Fuck the risotto. Fuck his sad-dog face and soft words that covered up the fact that he was dumping her. Fuck him.

On her way out the door, Rose picked up the vase of peonies from the foyer table and threw it down the hall, sending shards of glass skittering across the rosewood floor.

⌒∞⌒

"He's an asshole."

Maddy tossed back the last of her bourbon and followed it with a defiant shake of her blond head.

Rose nodded but couldn't speak. She kept waiting for a flood of tears to come, now that she was safe in a Hell's Kitchen bar with her best friend, away from Griff and his lies and betrayal. Her mind was working like some kind of supercomputer, circling around her father, her finances, her future, then back again to Griff, but she was in a daze, perhaps still recovering from the shock. They made quite a pair in the dive bar, Rose dressed in the casual uniform of an Upper East Side power wife, the part she thought she'd been auditioning for, and Maddy in a strapless lilac gown, looking as if she'd just descended from a horse-drawn carriage.

"Looking back now, he has been sort of withdrawing the past few weeks. I just didn't know why." Rose took a sip of her bourbon, and for a fleeting moment the liquid's slow burn provided a distraction. "Thanks for meeting me. I know this was supposed to be a fun night for you, not a sob fest."

Maddy yanked up the bodice of her dress. "I lost, anyway. To Missy Lake. Her fake boobs were bigger than mine. Typical. I knew I should have gone up a size."

"Stop. You don't want to look like a Real Housewife." Maddy and Rose had bonded the first day of speech class at college, when the professor had encouraged the students to open their throats wide, as if "you're swallowing the Empire State Building." Maddy, a beauty queen with champagne-blond tresses, had burst out laughing, as had Rose, and they'd been tight ever since. Even now, if they passed the landmark building in the backseat of a cab, they'd lose it, unable to speak for several minutes.

"So tell me what the clues were."

Rose sighed. "He called less and less, just to check in. At one point, he said he had a conference call and went into another room, but his tone wasn't right; it wasn't work. He was talking to Connie." Anger and confusion welled up in her stomach, and she thought she might be sick.

"He's a dick." Maddy rubbed her friend's back and signaled the bartender for another round.

"He's worried about his daughter."

"You're being too nice. Who leaves his girlfriend to go back to an ex-wife? He encouraged you to give up your apartment and move in with him. You gave up your apartment for him."

The loss of her cozy studio apartment, sunny and equipped with a working fireplace, a true find in this city of overpriced hellholes, cut into her like a knife. Someone else lived there now. She'd given up the one thing she'd been most proud of: a rent-stabilized West Village studio. The perfect artist's garret, at the top of a set of narrow, creaky stairs.

"I'm homeless."

"No. He told you that you could stay at the condo as long as you needed. You're not homeless."

"A few months ago, I started having a recurring dream. That I was looking for an apartment in a strange neighborhood I'd never been to, somewhere kind of dangerous. The apartments were dirty, desolate, and I woke up in a total panic. Then I looked around and remembered how safe I was, lying next to Griff, and tried to put it out of my head. I knew. I knew all along."

"You can always stay with us, you know that. I promise Billy and I won't throw things at each other when you're around."

Rose smiled at the memory. "That was some New Year's Eve party."

"Don't worry," said Maddy. "We make up as hard as we fight." She waggled her brows.

"That's the difference between you and me. My work life feels crazy enough without having to come home to any madness. Griff and I love each other. Our sex life is great. He makes me laugh, he's so supportive. Calm seas, no drama."

"Sounds suspect to me."

"Well, we care about each other." The words hung in the air.

Maddy gave Rose a sideways glance and swirled the liquid in her glass. "You always have a place to crash. You know that, right?"

"I do. Thank you. Though sometimes I'm convinced I'll end up a deranged old lady wandering around the city, looking through trash cans."

Panic welled up. This was real, it was happening. Griff was leaving her.

"Please, don't cry. Have another drink."

"Fuck, Maddy. How am I going to do this?"

"You will manage the way you always have, brilliantly. Look at when you started working for the network. You were an intern one day, and the next you were reading the news."

"First of all, that's not quite accurate. And second, every other newscaster on Channel 7 hated me for moving up so fast." Their catty comments still stung.

"True. But that just made you more determined. And now you've dumped all the stupid hairdos at the network for something more serious. No more talking head. You're running the show."

"Tyler, the preteen despot, is running the show."

"For now, but wait until WordMerge is bought by a big fish, which you know is going to happen. Then you'll be right back on top."

"You're very optimistic. In the meantime, my salary's been cut in half. And you're rewriting history. I got tossed out of network news. I didn't move on voluntarily. I'm thirty-five and all washed-up. In more ways than one."

"Stop that. I'm going to pee. Don't go anywhere."

Rose looked around the room. Who were all these people working at jobs they thought were important and then going home to someone they loved and hoped loved them back? How did anyone ever survive it, knowing that their story was just a single beam among millions of flashing lights? That no one mattered much at all, when it came down to it. Rose was unimportant, inconsequential, a face in the crowd. Petals on a wet, black bough, according to Ezra Pound.

Maybe Griff's panic could be contained. The pressure he was under, from the mayor, from Connie, must be intense. He would change his mind, once they talked again. She'd fix this, and everything would go back to normal, a simple blip in a long, loving relationship, one they'd laugh about on their honeymoon.

CHAPTER FOUR

New York City, 1952

Stella cornered Darby as she stuck her key into her door. "Where on earth have you been all day? Better get yourself changed, Defiance: We're off to the theater and dinner and you must come."

Darby had hoped to avoid the gazelles. Earlier that morning, she'd read quietly in her room until they left on yet another outing, and then she slipped out through the lobby without making any eye contact. From there, the day improved. She walked each street between Central Park and York Avenue, going east and then west and then east again, until she reached Fifty-Third Street. She ate a quick bite at a cafeteria, then continued on.

The grid pattern made her feel safe, and as she walked, her shoulders dropped an inch or two. She began looking up at the buildings instead of down at the sidewalk, and eventually a dizzying amazement replaced the buzz of dread.

But now her feet throbbed, her calves ached, and all she wanted was a long bath.

Stella cocked her head. "You look exhausted."

"I was out walking, seeing the city."

"Do you feel a little more at home now?"

Darby nodded. "Funnily enough, I do."

"New York has that effect, doesn't it? I love it now. Can't imagine living anywhere else."

Darby wasn't quite at that point yet, but she agreed there was a kind of magic to it. "The city makes sense, though not in the way I expected. I studied several maps before I came, but it's different when it's three-dimensional."

"Huh. You're an odd little bird, aren't you, Darby?" Stella put her hands on her hips. "Anyway, we're one short for a show and dinner afterward, and I need you to come."

Darby's right eye gave a twitch. There was no saying no to Stella. She'd been far too nice. Plus, her beauty was captivating. Staring at her was a pleasure, and Darby could only imagine the effect she had on men. "I'm not sure. I wouldn't know what to do."

Stella laughed. "You sit back and enjoy yourself, silly. I'm seeing a boy named Thomas, and he has a friend Walter, and I promised I'd bring someone for Walter tonight. I'd lined up Mary—you haven't met her yet, but you will—but she's come down with a chill and refuses to join me."

Darby started to shake her head, and Stella quickly continued on. "Don't worry, we're a group of ten, so it's not like a true date. Just some friends going out for a night on the town; won't that be delightful?"

Her first impulse was to make up an excuse, any excuse, to avoid going out with the gazelles and their beaux. But then she imagined the letter she'd write to Mother tomorrow, providing all the details of what they ate and where they went, the witty conversation that flowed back and forth. Mother would be so proud. Sometimes you have to push through your fears, she'd advised, just as Darby had done today walking about the city.

She changed into the umbrella dress and combed her hair. Stella had given her ten minutes to get ready and meet them in the lobby. Darby chatted with the elevator girl the entire way down, explaining that she was going out to the theater and dinner with her girlfriends.

Her heart sank, though, as soon as she spied Stella and the other girls. They wore fancy evening frocks, jewel-toned dresses made from taffeta and silk. Stella looked like a princess, in a sequined, black lace bodice over a bouffant skirt made of tulle, so airy and light it seemed as if she might float off at any moment. Darby was a farm girl in comparison.

Before she could turn to run back upstairs and hide beneath her bed, Stella swooped her up and planted her in a taxi, and then they were funneled into the theater lobby. There was no time for introductions with the boys, as they were all running late, and the curtain rose as soon as they took their seats. The musical was wonderful, and for a giddy moment Darby was transported to old Siam, where women with hoop skirts waltzed with exotic foreigners. After, they walked as a group to the Café Brittany on Ninth Avenue. Darby didn't speak much, but she didn't have to, for the boys were all trying to outdo one another with jokes and teasing.

"Darby, this is Walter." Outside the restaurant, Stella dragged over a slightly pudgy boy whose cheeks were dotted with red spots. He looked her up and down, then reached out his hand.

"Pleasure to meet you, Darby."

Darby held up a gloved hand and gave him a firm but elegant shake, just as Daddy had taught her.

Walter laughed. "You're a spirited girl, I can see that. Where are you from?" He held the door open as she walked through into the foyer.

"Defiance, Ohio."

"Well, look at that. I'm an Ohio boy myself. From Cleveland."

He smiled broadly, exposing pink gums. She liked the way his almond-shaped eyes lent him an air of mischievousness. He must've been a sweet-looking little boy, before the acne ravaged his skin.

They sat down next to each other at a large, round table covered with a red-checked tablecloth. Darby tried to catch Stella's eye, but her friend's body was angled toward Thomas, the tall, blond boy sitting next to her. Thomas laughed at something Stella said, then draped his arm on the back of her chair, curving his hand around her bare shoulder. Stella moved in closer. When Darby finally caught her eye, she winked.

Walter ordered their meals, which was a relief. The first course, escargot, was slippery and rich.

"Oh my."

"Too much for you? I'm disappointed—I thought you'd enjoy it."

"We don't have this kind of thing where I'm from. But there's something compelling about the taste. I'm not certain whether I love it or loathe it, to tell you the truth."

He laughed. "I like you, Darby; you have a unique perspective on the world."

She'd have to remember that for the letter tomorrow. "Well, thanks."

"And how do you like living in the Dollhouse?"

"The what?"

"That's what we boys like to call it." He gestured around the table. "The Barbizon Hotel for Women, packed to the rafters with pretty little dolls. Just like you."

Darby glanced at the other girls. She didn't look like them, not even close. He was trying to be kind. Not that he was a movie star himself, by any means.

She swallowed the last snail and turned to him the way Stella had done to Thomas. "And what are you doing here in New York City?"

"I'm working as a sales representative for International Mutoscope."

"Sounds like you're a spy."

He grinned, pleased. "No, nothing of the sort. We make the Voice-O-Graph. You may have seen it in Times Square."

She shook her head.

"It looks like a telephone booth. You pick up the phone inside, put in your money, and record whatever you want: jokes, a story, whatever. You wait a couple of minutes and then a record pops out, of whatever you've said. The thing's wild, I tell you; it's going to change everything."

In his excitement, a drop of spittle had landed on her arm. She stayed still, not wanting to embarrass him. "How will it do that?"

"It's your actual voice. Why send a letter or a card anymore when you can make a recording and mail it off to your grandmother for her birthday? Or let your family know how you're getting on? They can replay it whenever they like. It's like sending along a piece of yourself."

"What an interesting job you have. I wonder if they'll be hiring secretaries by the time I'm done with my course."

"If so, I'll put in a good word, I promise you that."

She'd hardly been there for two days and she already had a potential job referral. Imagine that! She'd include that in the letter as well.

After dinner, they wandered up Broadway to the edge of Central Park. Even though the hour was late, people streamed along the sidewalks, women clutching the arms of their husbands, clacking along on high heels. Carriages drawn by patient, bored-looking horses lined Central Park South. One of the animals snorted as they walked by and Stella jumped.

They were lagging behind the rest of the group, but Thomas pulled Stella closer to the horse and insisted she pet its nose.

"No, I can't!"

Darby stepped in. "It's nothing, really. They're lovely and feel like velvet. Here."

She took Stella's wrist and guided it up to the horse's face, between its eyes. "My grandfather had horses, and they like to be stroked."

Stella's date nudged Walter in the ribs and guffawed.

"Stop it, you two," Stella demanded.

"Hey, step away from there." The driver came out from behind the carriage. "He's a biter."

Before he'd finished the sentence, the horse tossed its head. Stella leapt away and narrowly missed being nipped on the soft skin of her forearm.

"He'll chomp off your hand, girly. Don't you know to ask first?"

A blush of shame fell over Darby. She'd been showing off and had almost gotten Stella hurt.

Stella rubbed her arm, and Thomas was immediately at her side, fuming. He turned to Darby. "You're a lucky one. If Stella'd been bitten, she wouldn't be able to work next week. You need to think before you do something so rash." He rubbed the inside of Stella's arm gently.

Darby didn't bother to point out that it was his idea in the first place.

"Sorry, Stella."

"Don't be silly. I'm fine."

"It's nearly curfew; we should be heading back."

"We don't want to get you ladies home late." Even though Thomas spoke in a mocking tone, Darby was relieved by his words. Until he added, "Let's cut through the park."

"Do you think that's wise?" Darby hated the sound of her voice, so plaintive. But Mrs. Eustis had advised against venturing in after the sun had set.

"Walter and I have the situation well in hand."

Walter offered Darby his arm and she took it. They headed in at Seventh Avenue and followed the street as it curved east.

"The path that lets out onto Fifth Avenue isn't far," Walter offered. "We'll be back out in civilization in no time. Don't be nervous."

The sound of the wind rattled in the trees, and the dim lamplight illuminated a small circle of road at a time.

"Hopefully, we'll outnumber any marauders," Darby joked.

"That's my girl."

Thomas moved toward a rocky outcropping on their left, pulling Stella along with him. "We're going to climb to the top so I can show Stella the view. You can come up if you like."

"No, thanks." She didn't want to be climbing anywhere right now. She wanted to be back at the Barbizon.

Stella took off her shoes and handed them to Darby. "Hold these for me. I'll be right back."

"Are you sure that's a good idea? You might cut your feet."

"Thomas says the view is gorgeous." She winked and clambered up after him.

Walter shrugged. "I guess they needed some time alone. Hope you don't mind. We can sit here and wait. Or head back now."

She couldn't imagine leaving Stella behind. Walter took off his jacket and laid it down on a nearby boulder, gesturing for her to sit.

"Thank you." She shoved her hands under her legs, tightening the dress around her like a mermaid's tail.

Walter's side touched hers and she shivered. "Would you rather wear my jacket?" he asked.

"No, this is fine."

In the darkness, his breathing quickened and she heard him lick his lips.

"Thomas is desperately in love with Stella; she's all he talks about."

"She seems quite taken with him as well."

"So tell me about yourself, Darby."

"Not much to tell. I have two dogs, Judy and Josephine. They're chocolate Labs. I live with my mother and her husband."

"What happened to your father?"

Strange. Most people avoided asking the question outright. No one in Defiance ever asked about Daddy, even before he'd died, when he'd been terribly ill for months and months. After the private funeral, Mr. Saunders had not tolerated any talk of the man who'd come before him. In a way, it had been a relief.

"He passed away. Cancer."

"Sorry to hear about that." Walter stared at her, his eyes glassy in the darkness. "My mother died. When I was born."

"My sympathies, Walter." Words were inadequate; Darby knew that much. "Did your father ever remarry?"

"No. It's been just me and my two older brothers. I hate both of them."

"My stepfather's fairly difficult as well."

"Has he ever broken your arm? That's what my older brother did. On purpose." An edge had crept into his voice, one that unnerved her.

"No, no broken bones. He's just a bully, I suppose."

"Hey, what do you say I kiss you?" He licked his lips again.

When she spoke, her pitch came out higher than normal. "We don't really know each other yet, Walter."

"Come on, just one kiss."

"No, thank you."

"Do you want to know how he did it?"

"How who did what?"

Walter took one of her arms and bent it behind her back. "How he broke it. Like this." He leaned in close and his breath was on her cheek. "Kiss me or I'll break it."

Darby tried to pull away, but the twisted arm prevented her from putting any distance between them. "Walter. Stop, that hurts."

"They always fix me up with the ugly one, but they really pulled a mean trick on me this time."

"What?" Darby's heart beat wildly. His tone reminded her of Mr. Saunders, menacing and whiny at the same time. "Please, stop."

He pulled her arm a little more and she yelped.

"I'll break it, I swear. The least you could do is to kiss me. It's dark enough that you don't have to see me and I don't have to look at you. The two freaks."

"I'm not a freak. You're not a freak, Walter." He was going to kill her, rape her. Would Stella hear her if she cried out?

He leaned in close. "Kiss me."

She did so, a fast touch of the lips. He let go of her hand only to encircle her with both arms and smash his mouth into hers. She pushed away with her palms, hating the doughy feel of his chest and the rancid taste of his tongue.

"Stop!" She tried to cry out, but he muffled her with his mouth. His hands clutched at her body, her breasts and between her legs. If she didn't do something, he'd be on top of her and she'd be pinned beneath his weight.

Too late. He pulled her down off the rock. She lay on her back, panting, and he kneeled up and began undoing his belt. She only had one chance.

The dirt was gritty beneath her hands, loose. She grabbed two handfuls and flung it into Walter's face. He cried out, and she bent her knees and kicked hard with both feet into his groin. He flew backward, rolling on his back with his hands cupping himself. At first he didn't make a sound, until a high-pitched cry turned into a bellow.

There was no time to search for Stella's shoes. Darby turned and ran, screaming out Stella's name. She followed the road until it curved back out of the park, where there was light and people and safety. Her umbrella dress was torn and dirty. Stella was still in the park, possibly in danger, but Darby couldn't go back in and look for her. As she ran to the hotel, she looked for a policeman or a police car in vain.

"You've missed curfew." Mrs. Eustis sat in one of the lobby chairs, a clipboard in her hands. "And you're a mess. Not a good way to begin your stay here at the Barbizon, Miss McLaughlin."

"I was with Stella, we were . . ."

"You were what?"

If she told her what she and Stella had done, they'd both be in trouble. And she couldn't do that to her only friend.

"We got separated. I'm sorry, I got lost."

"Stella came back fifteen minutes ago. You should have stayed closer to her and you wouldn't be in trouble now."

Stella was back already? "Yes, ma'am."

In the elevator, the same girl was working the gates and the lever. "You okay? You look like you had a tough night." She had shiny dark hair and a Spanish accent. Her brown eyes scanned Darby's face.

"I'm fine." Darby tried to wipe her nose with her fingers, as a dam of tears threatened to break through any moment.

"Use my handkerchief," offered the girl.

"Thanks. I'll get it back to you."

A couple of girls dressed in bathrobes and curlers stared when Darby emerged from the elevator.

Stella popped out of her room, toothbrush in her hand, and paused for a split second before coming forward.

"Where did you go?" Darby whimpered, detesting the weakness in her voice. "How did you get back so fast?"

"We didn't see you when we came down from the rock. And I couldn't find my shoes anywhere in the dark. Where did *you* go?"

"That boy—Walter—attacked me in the park. I missed curfew."

Before Stella could reply, Candy emerged from the bathroom and scrutinized Darby closely. "How did she do?"

Darby blinked with confusion. "What do you mean? How did I do what?"

"Walter, right? Did he try to get up your skirt? He tried the same thing on one of the other girls last week."

Darby turned to Stella, looking for clarification.

Stella raised a pale hand to her neck. "I didn't know any of this. You've got to believe me."

Candy piped up. "He's an ass. But he's my cousin, so you better not say anything."

"I don't understand." Darby balled up the handkerchief in her fist. "Why would you set him up with me on purpose? He tried to hurt me."

"My, my, so dramatic," Candy tsked. "He didn't hurt you at all. You're standing here talking to me, right? So he got a little randy and tore your dress. It wasn't all that great to begin with."

Darby began to weep. She knew she should hold it in, return to her room, but the sobs came fast, wrenching sounds that erupted from her very core. She dropped her chin to her chest and wrapped her arms about herself, totally alone. The girls stared and Stella took one hesitating step toward her, and then backed quickly into her room.

She was a failure. The letter to Mother was ruined, as was her favorite dress that was really an ugly dress. Tomorrow first thing, she'd pack up and leave for Ohio. This was what happened when you tried to live a larger life.

A voice boomed down the hallway. "That's enough. Leave her alone!"

Darby looked up as the elevator girl stormed toward them. She must've watched the entire scene.

"Come with me." She took Darby by the arm and spit on the floor, her saliva just missing Candy's furry slippers.

Shocked, Darby allowed the elevator girl to lead her away as Candy yelled down the hall at them. "You'll have to clean that up, Esme, you guttersnipe."

The girl yelled something back in Spanish that Darby couldn't understand.

Not that it mattered. New York City had beaten her down already. She hadn't even lasted two days.

CHAPTER FIVE

New York City, 2016

The WordMerge office was housed in a seedy block in the mid-Thirties, far west of Broadway, next to a McDonald's and a gas station that primarily served taxi drivers. Rose had walked over from her Lexington subway stop in an effort to clear her head, but ended up feeling damp and sweaty in the morning heat. Her mind whirled with what she would say to Griff next, what she should have said last night. So many unspoken possibilities. She clung to the idea that she could change his mind with the right sentence, the right phrase.

"Pitch meeting in my office in ten minutes," Tyler announced as he whizzed past the editors' desks.

After he slammed the door shut to his office, Rose moaned out loud. "Anyone have anything juicy?" she asked no one in particular.

"God, no." Jenna, who sat in the cubicle next to her, rubbed her eyes. "I bet you do, though. You're the queen of pitch meetings. I just wish some of your glitter would rub off on me."

In fact, Tyler shot down as many of Rose's ideas as anyone else's. But by now she knew there was no point in correcting Jenna.

The rest of the office, all ten of them, were bright young things.

She'd figured, when she'd arrived three months ago, that she'd be treated like anyone else, but of course her notoriety had preceded her. The other reporters often turned to her for advice, and three asked her to be their mentor her very first day. Which was ridiculous since all of them were more capable than she was. Maybe not in writing skills, but they were faster and far more adaptable in an environment that valued speed and flexibility.

When Rose worked in television, there'd been a sense of camaraderie, as the producers and editors worked through the night on a story and chugged coffee outside the editing suites. WordMerge exuded an entirely different energy. The two girls who sat on either side of her wore earphones most of the day, nodding in time to the beat, like sunflowers bobbing in the wind.

Tyler emerged once again. "Turns out I have a call with the Coast in ten minutes. My office, let's go."

Being pushed around by a grizzled news producer was one thing, but having a baby-faced neophyte do it was harder to take. She joined the others and trooped into his small office. He preferred having meetings here, versus the large conference room down the hall that they shared with an app design company. The employees squeezed into corners, perched on the windowsill, and several leaned against the walls. Rose snagged one of the few chairs.

"As you know, we're here to save journalism, one story at a time."

She hated when he started out with this speech. It was so forced and saccharine. Better to save the rah-rah for potential investors.

"I want to hear the best you've got. But keep in mind: Right now, we need stories that will go viral, stories that fly, even if they don't have the same substance we'd want in other circumstances."

"Wait, I'm confused." Rose should keep her mouth shut. But she couldn't help herself. "You've always said you wanted quality reporting most of all. If you want viral, we might as well do cat videos, right?"

Tyler was happy to confess that he'd earned a master's in journalism from Stanford on a whim, as a way to kill time until his trust fund matured. But in his preferred version of the story, he was a changed person by the time he graduated, inspired to save a dying profession from itself. WordMerge, he promised, was the answer, offering old-school reporting in a form that would appeal to modern readers. The guy was a complete prick and endlessly self-impressed, but his pitch was a winner—he had wooed Rose and many others with passion and tenacity. And yet the boy wonder was on edge these days, worried. How much of his investment had he blown through already?

No one spoke for a few tense beats.

"No, Rose. No cat videos. I'm talking about a piece about a soldier with PTSD who overcomes it with the help of his gluten-free diet. Or something about the Peruvian tea everyone's drinking in order to find a higher plane of consciousness. It's becoming clear that we need to marry news and entertainment to get ourselves off the ground."

The other staffers murmured their approval.

Rose tapped her pen on her notebook. The others all carried iPads. She might as well have brought an inkwell and feather. "Look, I'm all for originality. But I thought we were staying away from trendy pieces."

"We were, last week. But I need to increase page views. I'm meeting with some potential backers and I want to show them we have the click-throughs to grow into a major news hub. Any ideas?"

Jenna piped up. "How about two investment bankers fighting for custody of their pet iguana?"

"Iguanas aren't photogenic. Neither are investment bankers, for that matter. Next."

"Or I could do something on the influx of young Mexican immigrants. We're talking kids, crossing the border alone."

"I like that. Find me a kid who crossed because they wanted to be on reality TV. Something with a twist."

"Are you kidding?" Rose leaned forward. "That's impossible, and strange."

"I'm not saying that exactly. I mean something along those lines. You know what I mean, right, Jenna?"

Jenna nodded.

"What do you have for me, Rose?"

Normally, she'd have a dozen possibilities at her fingertips, but she was so addled from lack of sleep, nothing clicked in.

Tyler sat back in his chair and began orbiting, as they all liked to call it, using a small white rubber ball suspended by a thin string from the white ceiling tiles above his desk. When he got irritated, he'd fling it in wide circles around the room, catching it as it flew by him, then sending it back around. Anyone close by was forced to weave and duck to avoid getting hit.

"Have you ever heard of the Barbizon Hotel for Women?"

Every female intern and editor nodded. Rose smiled. Sylvia Plath hadn't died in vain.

"What about it?" Tyler asked.

"Back in the day, it was the place to stay if you were a single girl in New York City. Turns out there are a dozen or so older women who still live there—they were grandfathered in after it went condo. I could do a story about what their lives are like now."

"I'm sorry, but why does *our* audience care about a bunch of old ladies?" Tyler swung the ball so violently, Rose was worried it would break free of its tether.

He had a point. Why should WordMerge readers care about relics from another century who still wore white gloves to walk their dogs?

Because she recognized a kernel of her own life in theirs, and so would other women. The pitch came to her in a flash. "There's one with a terrible scar down her face. She was stabbed by a maid in the 1950s, apparently. The maid then fell to her death from the terrace. I could talk to her, use her tragedy to draw readers into the story."

He stopped the ball in mid-flight and looked at her with interest. "How bad's the scar?"

"Um, I'm not sure. She always wears a veil."

"Get her to show her face, get photos, video, and we'll do something about the tragedy. We'll revisit it, and then find something that's happened today to set against it. Find that model who got slashed in the eighties. We can compare and contrast."

A truly ghastly idea. But Rose knew better than to say so. "I'll see what I can do."

"Excellent. And bring in Jason for visuals."

"Jason?"

"Freelance video guy. He'll be able to guide you so you don't get all mushy on me. Let's go, who's next?"

Rose sat back, annoyed. At least he'd finally stopped flinging that ball. And she'd gotten the green light.

After Tyler gave his usual, annoying dismissal ("Back to your cubes, warriors!"), Rose went downstairs and picked up a cup of coffee from the lobby store. She headed outside, south down Tenth Avenue, and checked her phone. Nothing from Griff, not a text, not a voice message. The morning roar of the traffic was deafening, so she turned east onto a quieter cross street and dialed.

"Rose."

She was surprised he'd picked up, after the way she'd stormed out last night, spending a few hours with Maddy at the bar before returning to a Griff-less apartment. She had to give him kudos for facing the music.

"Griff, we have to talk." Everything she said was preprogrammed, the litany of sentences passed on through time when one person rejected another.

"I know, and we will. I am so sorry about this."

"Why do you have to go back? I had no idea; you didn't give me any warning you were unhappy."

He sighed. "It's not like that. I realized it's not about my happiness. I am happy, happier, with you. But until the girls are more stable, I can't leave them. We think Miranda has a serious illness."

"What do you mean?"

"It's very possible she has bipolar disorder. We're trying to find out more."

"I'm sorry." She couldn't argue with him. Sicknesses of the mind were just as terrible as those of the body, no different from cancer. Like her father, spiraling out of control, getting worse every day. "What are you going to do?"

"We're finding a treatment center for her. It's complicated, and that's why I have to be around right now."

"Do you think, once the crisis has passed, you might come back? That we could pick up where we leave off?"

"Perhaps. If you want that. I don't know if you'd want that by then."

"Neither do I."

Of course she would. Why kid herself? She'd invested three years in their relationship, and letting go wasn't easy.

"God, Rose, this is torture. I know I keep saying this, but I'm so sorry to do this to you."

His voice was heavy, sad. If only he'd confided in her, told her what was happening. She knew Miranda was difficult, but assumed it was typical teen drama. A passing my-parents-ruined-my-life-by-getting-divorced kind of thing.

"I just wish you'd said something sooner. I might have helped."

"It's not for you to fix. It's for me and Connie."

Rose checked her watch. She should be getting back. "Can we keep on talking?"

"Of course. I'm going to Albany with the mayor for a few days. We'll talk when I get back."

Back in her cubicle twenty minutes later, Rose's phone rang. Maddy calling for an update. She whispered a quick rehash of her conversation with Griff.

"You're out of your mind." Maddy was never one to hold back. "You need to be getting angry, not acting like an understanding suck-up."

That hurt. "I'm not sucking up." Rose ducked her head down, hoping for a smidgen of privacy. "He's going through something awful, just like me and my dad. If I'm calm and reasonable about the situation, he might come to his senses later."

"Do you really want a man like that?"

"What, one who cares for his children? Yes, in fact, I do."

"Plenty of men get divorced and care for their children without having to go back to their ex-wives. It's more than that. He's giving you the sympathetic version because he knows you'll fall for it."

If she were Maddy, she'd toss Griff off the nearest cliff, but his actions weren't so cut-and-dried in Rose's mind. Griff was a man with a sick child, desperate to make her better.

A sharp pain seared along her scalp, the beginnings of a bad headache. Maddy had a point, Griff had a point. She didn't know what to think.

"I'm not prepared to blow it all up yet. And I don't think he is, either." She rubbed her temples with her thumb and ring finger. "Please, Maddy, I need your support. Neither of us has kids, so we can't really know what's going on in his head."

"Touché. I have enough stress from my sweet baby stepmonsters, never mind dealing with genetic offspring. But promise me you won't wait around for him for too long. You deserve better."

Rose promised and hung up, then lost herself in the research for the Barbizon story, a welcome distraction from her troubles.

∝∾

The apartment was as desolate as ever when Rose finally made it home. Griff's suits, the ones he wore every day, were missing from the closet, his sock and underwear drawers empty and left half-open.

She flung herself on the bed, hoping for a good cry, but when no tears came, she got up and sat by the window. Would it be better if she tossed the rest of his suits out onto the street below?

No. She needed to bide her time, let him return to Connie and see how awful it was, then allow him back with certain provisions. They had to get married, buy furniture, see a counselor. She mentally checked off a list one by one. If only she'd hired an interior designer to furnish the damn apartment in one fell swoop. Perhaps if he'd felt more settled, or even financially invested, he'd have stuck around.

At the very least, then she'd have a nice place to stay, for a while. Instead of this tomb.

It was all she could do not to climb under the covers and go to sleep, turn off her brain for a moment. But she had to keep her job, which meant putting on a brave face and charming the woman downstairs. She rummaged through her bag for the letter she'd written at work, explaining who she was and asking for a short interview. She knew she'd have to earn Miss McLaughlin's trust first, and she didn't want to scare her off.

After swiping on a coat of fresh lipstick and smoothing her hair, she grabbed the envelope and her keys and took the elevator down to the fourth floor.

The dog, the one named Bird, barked furiously when she knocked on the door of 4B. She heard a muffled voice tell him to be quiet and the shuffle of steps. She stood back, trying to look as friendly as possible, the envelope tucked behind her back. But the door didn't creak open, not even an inch.

She knocked again. "Miss McLaughlin, are you home?"

Nothing.

She put her ear to the door. She had the uncanny sensation of a presence lurking on the other side, but the older woman wasn't moving a muscle.

"I'm Rose Lewin. I live upstairs. I was hoping I might be able to introduce myself."

She waited. The woman didn't even say hello. Rose should have come down saying that there had been a leak in her apartment and she wanted to make sure it hadn't seeped through her neighbor's ceiling. That would have gotten her in the door, at the very least. She was off her game. Normally, that type of thinking would have come instinctively.

She had to reach her somehow.

"I'm so sorry to bother you. I would love to say hello. I'm something of a historian-slash-journalist, and I'd like to find out about what the Barbizon was like back in the fifties. In fact, I'm doing research for an article."

The dog gave a sharp yip, but was quickly silenced.

"Okay, well, sorry to have bothered you." Unbelievable. The woman was standing a few feet away, behind her closed door. Who behaves that way?

"I'll slip a note under your door. I hope you'll take the time to read it. I'd love to get your help with the project. I'll stop by again later."

She slid the note under the door and waited, half expecting it to shoot back out.

"I'm off; have a good night."

Back at her apartment, she poured a large glass of wine and curled up on the sofa. She needed this story. It was the first pitch she and Tyler had agreed on in ages. The woman in 4B was an enigma, living alone with her tiny dog in the same apartment year after year. How did she fill her time? Did she have family nearby? Did she have someone close to her she could rely on?

A faint sound came up through the open window. The music again. Rose perched on the windowsill, wine in hand, and listened as her curious neighbor played the same sad, sweet love song over and over.

CHAPTER SIX

New York City, 1952

The elevator girl hit the light switch in Darby's room and closed the door behind them. "Ignore the giraffes; they're a nasty bunch."

Darby stared at the girl. Esme, they'd called her. She was about her height, with velvety brown eyes accentuated by the severity of her hairstyle, which was pulled back in a tight bun.

"Giraffes?" she croaked, wiping her eyes with the handkerchief.

"All long necks, loping along like prey. Just hoping a big lion will attack, if you know what I mean. A big, manly lion."

As she talked, she walked behind Darby and unzipped her dress. Darby allowed it to pool at her feet and stepped out of the circle of fabric.

"I'll have this washed and mended and it'll be fine. Don't worry about that." Her accent was crisp, slicing through the air.

"Where are you from?" Darby couldn't help asking.

"Manhattanville. Puerto Rico before that. I'm Esme, by the way. Do you know where Manhattanville is?"

"I'm Darby. And no, not exactly. Sounds very pretty."

"No, *chica*. Trust me. Stick to the East Side for now. You just got here, right?"

"Yes." Profound misery enveloped her once again. She was surrounded by girls who were nasty, when she hadn't done anything to inspire their wrath. Or had she? Was there some code or password she'd missed out on? During high school she'd preferred novels to her classmates: They were in every way easier to read.

"Don't start crying again. That's what those girls like. You gotta toughen up."

"I just want to go home."

Esme stood quietly for a moment, then led Darby to the bed and sat her down. "The city is scary at first, even for these girls. For me, too. When I got off the plane from San Juan, I thought I'd freeze to death. Snow, ice, everywhere. My aunt told me that when she first got on a subway, she tried to find the cord to make it stop, like you have on a bus, right?" She swore under her breath and Darby couldn't make out the word. "You'll get used to it, don't worry. You gotta decide what you want out of it. Don't let them trample you."

"I imagined them as gazelles, the girls." Darby smiled, in spite of herself. "I like giraffes better."

"That's the way. Laugh it off. And put in a request to Mrs. Eustis to switch floors. You should be with the other Katie Gibbs girls, not with these monsters. They're the messiest of all the guests here at the hotel. Leave their stockings and girdles all over the bathroom, not caring who sees what. It's disgusting."

Darby didn't mention that spitting was fairly disgusting behavior as well.

"Thank you for helping me, Esme. That was nice of you."

"Sure thing. I figured you weren't like them."

"Clearly not; just look at me. My dress is all wrong, my hair. You can take the dress and burn it, for all I care. I'll never wear it again." She still tasted Walter's breath and tongue, the feel of his hands on her.

"It's a little dullsville, to be honest. Why umbrellas?"

Her response caught Darby off guard. "I thought it was an interesting pattern."

"You need to get glamorous. Umbrellas aren't glamorous."

"You don't understand. I'm going to be a secretary. Secretaries aren't meant to be chic."

Esme walked over to the window and yanked it open. She sat on the ledge, repinning the maid's cap on her head. "Why limit yourself? I don't. I'm going to be a famous entertainer. I'm auditioning this week for the American Academy of Dramatic Arts. I'm gonna make films and have fans swoon over me."

Darby studied Esme with renewed interest. She'd never seen anyone with her kind of accent as a major film star. In the background, sure, but not like Judy Garland and Katharine Hepburn. They didn't talk or look like this girl.

"I know, you think I'm not the right type. But I can do proper, and I can do fiery. I'm going to show them when I audition. I'll knock their socks off."

"What kind of thing do you have to do for the audition?"

"I'll be performing a monologue from *Romeo and Juliet*. By Shakespeare."

An ambitious choice. "How exciting."

Esme grabbed Darby's bathrobe where it lay on the armchair and tossed it to her. "Hey, we should go out sometime this week. I can show you the best places in town. The real ones. Not the stuck-up supper clubs."

Darby wasn't sure how to respond. Mother would never approve of her hanging about with one of the maids from the hotel. The uncertainty must have registered on her face, as Esme shrugged and stood. "You don't have to. I'm sure you'll be busy with your school stuff."

Darby hated the idea of rebuffing the only person, besides Stella, who had shown any kindness to her. Then again, look what Stella had led her into. She had to keep her distance, be careful. "But thank you for the invitation."

"Sure. Here's what I recommend: Talk to Mrs. Eustis, and stay away from the giraffes. Good luck."

Darby wanted to say more, to reach out in some way and let Esme know how much she appreciated her help and kind words, but Esme closed the door with a quiet click before she could utter a word.

⚬◈⚬

Mrs. Eustis had promised to look into a room transfer for Darby, but four days later, she hadn't heard back. Darby's routine consisted of getting up early, before the other girls rose, running in and out of the bathroom as quickly and quietly as possible, and then heading off to class at the Katharine Gibbs School. The first day, the school director had listed off the qualifications for Gibbs graduates, including a strong work ethic and a respectable background. When she added that graduates were known for having a "natural physical endowment," Darby could have sworn she looked right at her, and not in a good way. What the heck did that mean? Pretty? Buxom? She'd pulled her shoulders back and sat up straighter.

The classes were tedious, for the most part: typing, shorthand, communication, and spelling tests. She'd already received bad marks for having a run in her stockings, and another for slouching. She missed her English teacher from high school, who'd assigned short stories and Russian novels to be analyzed in great detail. Learning to type and memorizing Gregg shorthand symbols were deadly boring in comparison.

By Thursday evening of her first week, she was frustrated. And hungry. She'd waited until all the other girls left before going down to the Barbizon dining room, and missed dinner by five minutes. She was staring longingly at the menu posted outside the doorway when Esme walked by, carrying a mop and bucket.

"Esme?"

"Miss McLaughlin." Esme nodded in her direction but kept walking.

"Wait." Darby dashed after her and put a hand on her arm. Esme's expression was pleasant but not warm. "I wanted to say thank you for everything you did for me last weekend. You really helped me out there."

"I'm glad." She put the bucket down. "Are the giraffes leaving you alone?"

"So far. And I asked Mrs. Eustis for a transfer and she's working on it. In the meantime, I try to work around their schedules. I'm in school full-time now, so it's easy." She didn't mention that she was dreading the upcoming weekend, when she had nothing at all to do. If she sat inside her room the entire time, she'd go mad, she was sure of that.

Esme nodded in the direction of the dining room. "You miss dinner?"

"I did. So busy with homework."

"Do you want me to get you a roll or something?"

Darby clutched at her stomach. "Would you? I'm starving. Could you do that without getting into trouble?"

"I'll meet you up in your room. Be there in ten."

As promised, Esme showed up with several slices of bread tucked into her laundry basket, along with a small jar of raspberry jelly and a knife.

"Oh, this is wonderful, thank you! Do you want some?"

"No, I'll just fold some sheets here while you dine, if you don't mind."

"Go ahead." Darby sat at her desk and slathered the jam on the bread. "May I ask about your audition?"

Esme gave her a wide smile. "It was great. I had it yesterday, and they'll let me know in a week or so."

"Tell me, what was it like? Were you nervous?"

"I'm never nervous. I think they were, though. The minute I opened my mouth, you could see they weren't expecting a Puerto Rican to apply to their fancy academy. All the other people auditioning talked right. But I did my speech and the judges flipped."

"I'm so excited for you. I couldn't imagine doing such a thing. What courage you have."

"Courage is easy when the other choices are folding sheets and dealing with guests all day. When you want to get out of a situation fast, you get courage."

"It must be difficult, dealing with so many girls."

"It's a dirty, nasty job. But to make up for it, I do something beautiful at night."

"What's that?"

"If you like, I'll show you. Come out with me. I finish at nine thirty."

"I couldn't. I'd miss curfew."

"You can easily sneak in the back way. I'll show you how."

"That's awfully late, isn't it?"

"Did you have other plans?" asked Esme.

Darby swallowed and tore off another piece of bread. "Not really."

"Have you been out since last weekend?"

She hated to admit she hadn't. It had taken all her energy to get to school and back each day, and although the other girls in her classes were friendly enough, she'd been too skittish to try in earnest.

Esme didn't give her a chance to respond. "C'mon, Darby, live a little. Come out with me tonight. I'll meet you outside. Don't be late." She walked over to Darby's small closet and opened it, pulling out the black brocade dress she'd last worn at Daddy's funeral. "And wear this."

When Darby walked out of the Barbizon at nine thirty on the dot, Esme ran toward her, squealing. She'd changed into a bright red taffeta dress with a delicate scalloped trim around the neckline. Her hair, unleashed from its updo, fell in gentle curls around her head. She looked more fashionable than any of the girls on Darby's floor.

As the cab ventured into the East Village, the street scene changed. The buildings were no higher than six stories, the sidewalks dirty with cigarette butts and crumpled newspapers. Darby almost gagged at the smell of urine as she stepped out of the taxi, but she followed Esme along a narrow alleyway between two buildings to a tiny, treeless courtyard at the back of the one of the tenements.

Esme smiled up at a black man smoking a cigarette outside a doorway and dragged Darby into the darkness.

"Where are we going? How do you know where to go?" Darby asked.

"I work here some nights as a hatcheck girl. Good tips, and it's a wild scene."

"What is it, exactly?"

"The Flatted Fifth. A jazz club. All the greats come here, after they've played at the posh places on Fifty-Second Street. It's gritty and grubby and the best."

She agreed with the first two adjectives. They walked through a tiny kitchen, where a cook stared hard at them as they breezed by.

"What are you doing, Esme?" he said. "You know he doesn't like it when you bring in nonpayers."

Esme thrust out her chin and put a hand on her hip. "Sam, meet Darby. Darby, this is Sam. He thinks he runs the place, but he doesn't. Right, Sam?"

The cook scowled back. "If he catches you, you'll get fired, Esme."

Darby stared at him. While none of his features was remarkable on its own—the nose too large, the edges of his eyes sloped downward—he was oddly handsome, with a perfect dimpled chin. He looked to be in his mid-twenties but had a boyish frame, all long limbs and sharp points.

He turned back to the oven.

"Manners, Sam. I'll have to talk to your dad about that." Esme didn't wait for a reply but pulled Darby farther into the bowels of the building, pushing past a swinging door.

They were in the basement of the tenement. The low-ceilinged main room was packed, a mixture of blacks and whites, young men and women posturing and smoking and talking over one another.

Esme squeezed Darby's hand. "We're waiting for Stick Hawkins. They say he's coming tonight, but you never know with that cat."

Stick? Cat? Darby looked at Esme, perplexed.

Esme laughed. "Don't worry, you'll catch on."

Darby wasn't so sure. The place was frightening, and she scanned the exits, wondering which was the quickest way out in case there was a fire or a fight. All these people pressed together, in the smoke and darkness, made her heart beat faster and her mouth grow dry in panic. She wanted to run away, go back to the lonely safety of her room. But she couldn't bear another night of tossing and turning and ruminations.

"You look like you're about to be sick." Esme's eyes were animated, slightly mocking.

"No. I'm fine. What do we do now?"

Esme pulled her to a table with a couple of free seats. A waiter wearing a long white apron, a white shirt, and a thin black tie whispered something in Esme's ear. She touched the inside of his wrist with her finger, laughed at what he'd said, and ordered them a couple of whiskey sours.

"Now we drink. You'll feel braver if you aren't sober."

The noise level in the room astounded Darby. Even though two walls of the room had been draped with Moroccan rugs to absorb the sound, they weren't very effective. The two other patrons seated at the rickety table didn't bother interrupting their loud conversation to acknowledge them. Darby took a sip of her drink and glanced around. The decor was minimal at best. One long wall consisted of exposed, chipped bricks. Behind the stage, old playbills had been plastered up as a kind of backdrop, their corners curling and frayed. A layer of dirt, grease, and cigarette ash covered the floor.

The audience began to complain, calling for Stick and slow-clapping. Finally, four musicians stepped onstage. One slid in behind a set of drums and took a seat, another hooked a saxophone to the cord around his neck, while the third heaved a bass upright. A trumpet player stepped up to the microphone.

"Sorry, Stick's not here yet," the trumpet player announced.

The audience booed, but the musician was undaunted. He held up a hand above his eyes, blocking the lights, and looked out into the audience. Beside her, Esme sat up tall, as if a jolt of electricity had suddenly passed through her.

"Where's Esme?" the man called out.

Esme turned and smiled at Darby, and suddenly she was up onstage, adjusting the mic and smiling out over the crowd.

"I know you want your Stick," she purred into the microphone, "but stick with me for now, all right?"

The audience gave an interested grumble. Then Esme began to sing. Her voice was edgy and low and at first Darby strained to hear, worried that Esme wouldn't be able to fill the space. But after a crescendo at the end of the second verse, she let it rip and her voice soared out.

Esme had a smooth, sexual presence onstage, her hips moving in time with the music, and her shoulders responding a moment behind the beat, in a slinky, slippery motion. When she finished, the crowd clapped and whistled. Darby hoped she'd sing more, but a movement at the front door caught her eye. A man sauntered through the tables, shaking hands and nodding. Stick had arrived. Esme quickly jumped off the stage and slid back into her seat.

"You're so talented, Esme," said Darby. "You can really sing."

"Wait until you hear this. My singing is nothing compared to this guy's playing."

A few moments later a waiter came over with a couple of drinks. "From the gentleman over there." He pointed to a man sitting alone two tables away, his table an isolated island in the middle of a sea of people pontificating and gesticulating wildly, cigarettes in hand.

Darby took a sip of her drink. A martini. She'd never had one before, and only knew it from the shape of the glass.

"Don't do that." Esme grabbed the drink from her hands, spilling some on the floor.

Darby was too surprised to speak.

"Trust me, you don't want to take anything from that guy."

"Why?" She stole a glance in his direction. He watched them, an amused expression on his pockmarked face. His eyes were enormous, like a basset hound's, with dark bags underneath. She'd never been sent a drink before and was unsure of the protocol.

"He's an undercover cop. Named Quigley. He's always sniffing around, trying to find out what's going on."

"Is something going on?"

"Of course not. It's folks drinking and listening to music. What harm is there in that?"

"Then why is he here?"

"The cops are all over the jazz clubs, looking for horse. If you take a drink from him, he'll think you're willing to talk, and all the musicians will hate you."

Darby didn't understand what she meant. "Looking for a horse?"

"No, *chica*. Heroin."

"Oh."

"A lot of the musicians say that it's the only way to channel the music. If it worked for Bird, they want to do it, too."

The names were like a secret code. "Who's Bird?"

"Charlie Parker, alto sax player. Got the nickname when he made his band stop a car on the way to a gig so he could chase a chicken. Ate it for dinner that night."

"Have you ever done horse?"

Esme looked at Darby as if she were crazy. "Are you kidding? I have bigger things in my life than dozing off."

"Then how does it help the musicians?"

"It makes them more creative, gives them ideas while they solo, I guess."

Darby looked over at the policeman again. "Does everyone know that he's a cop?"

"Sure. It's a game we all play. We pretend not to know; he pretends that we don't know. My guess is he just likes the music. But you don't want to encourage him."

Stick sat on the piano bench and counted off the beat. He wore a scraggly beard and a shiny black suit. While the other musicians played, he rocked back and forth for a minute, then got up and started to dance a kind of jig, one hand on the top of the piano. Finally, he dashed back to the bench, and his hands slid across the keyboard, barely touching the notes, while his loafered feet tapped out a beat of their own on the floor. The sounds were strange and haunting. Fast, furious playing that sometimes sounded wonderful, and at other times off-key.

Darby took another sip of her whiskey sour and almost choked as Stick performed a set of arpeggios so fast his hands were a blur. When he finished, the audience rose to their feet, demanding more.

⚮

The next song featured the horn player, and the sound came out thick and sad. When he seared out a solo, the intonation penetrated into Darby's body, like a musical bullet. She was reminded of the sound of the wind the night before Daddy died. A thermal had risen in the afternoon, the first strong, warm breeze after a long winter, smelling of mud and new growth. By the evening it was howling around the house.

"God sweeping away the cold," Mother had said, to no one in particular.

Darby heard Daddy moan in pain upstairs, and she looked up

from reading her book at the kitchen table. "Do you think we should give him something, or call the doctor?"

"Nothing to be done. The doctor can't help him. I can't help him."

The last time Daddy was on the road, Mother complained about his absence, then turned on him viciously when he returned home and announced that he'd been fired. In a quiet moment, Darby asked him what happened. "I'm too likable," he'd replied. "The boss considered me a threat to his job. And he was right."

That winter, before he'd weakened, he bought a used sailboat and took to restoring it in their barn. Mother was aghast at the expense, and Darby could hardly blame her. The only water was the Maumee River, which wound its way through town. No one sailed there, too many rocks. Why buy a boat that you could never use?

Whenever the atmosphere in the house crackled with tension, Darby headed into the barn. Together she and Daddy planed the plywood hull, breathing in the scent of wood chips and varnish and shivering in the drafty space. Or she stuffed putty in the screw holes, then sanded them smooth while they compared their favorite Shakespearean characters. His was Falstaff. Hers, Cleopatra. When a waltz came on the transistor radio, he would grab her and they twirled around the barn together, and as the music ended, he'd bow low and call her Lady Darby.

His last night alive, Darby sat with him, reading aloud from *Henry V.* After he stopped breathing, she placed his hands on top of his chest like she'd seen in the movies and woke Mother at dawn with the news.

Mr. Saunders came calling for Mother shortly after. As soon as they married, he began taking digs at Darby. Most evenings she snuck out to the barn and sat in the unfinished boat and read, remembering Daddy's whistle and the way he'd laughed and praised her handiwork. Until one day she came out to discover Mr. Saunders had smashed the boat to bits with an ax.

The trumpeter took center stage again. His knifelike sound pierced into Darby's armor, the one she'd worn since Mr. Saunders had moved in. Darby breathed deeply, her whole body vibrating with the music. Her stomach turned, the bitter taste of alcohol still on her lips, and she stood and stumbled her way out the back door. She knelt down, squatting on her haunches in the most unladylike way.

"You okay?" Sam stood in the doorway, looking down at her. A halo of light shone behind him, so she couldn't read his expression.

"I don't feel well." Darby took a couple of deep breaths. "Must be all the smoke."

He disappeared inside. She'd made a fool of herself. Not that it mattered, of course.

He reappeared holding a cup. "Drink. You'll feel better."

She'd expected the harshness of black coffee, but instead her tongue came alive with a sweet, spicy flavor. Milk and sugar and something else.

"What is this?"

"Cardamom tea."

"It's delicious." She took another sip.

"The cardamom spice comes from the forests of India and is good for lots of things, including digestion, hiccups, even bad breath."

She placed a hand over her mouth. "Do I have bad breath?"

He laughed. "I have no idea what your breath is like. I just figured you might be ill."

"The music, the trumpet." Her explanation sounded so silly, even to her.

"Like you're being chopped up into pieces, right?"

She looked up at him in amazement. "Yes. I couldn't control my thoughts. Is it always like this?"

"Only with the best musicians."

"I liked it, I loved it, when they all played together and it made sense. But most of the time it didn't."

"You'll understand after you've listened to enough bebop. It's like learning another language. It's all a muddle at first, but then it rings clear."

Darby wasn't so sure.

"What the hell?" Esme poked her head out the doorway.

Darby passed the cup back to Sam and smiled. "I didn't feel well."

"Did Sam give you one of his mojo potions?"

For some reason, the question hurt. Darby wished she'd been the sole recipient of his special tea. Even though that was silly.

Esme helped her to her feet. "Come on, let's scram."

Darby was suddenly reluctant to go, but it was late.

Back at the Barbizon, Esme brought her in through the employees' entrance at the side of the building, and they hugged quickly before Darby began the long climb up to her floor. She trod lightly, staring down at the steps, which is why she didn't see the couple kissing on the third-floor landing until she was almost on top of them. They were pressed up against a tile mosaic, all blues and greens, some kind of lush underwater scene. Stella's mermaid-red hair stood out against the background.

"Sorry." Darby glanced away and attempted to maneuver past them.

Stella yelped in surprise and craned her neck around her date's head.

"Oh, Darby, you gave me a fright! My friend Paul and I were just saying good-bye. But I'm glad to see you. I've been meaning to catch you and apologize. About the other night."

"Okay." She slid by them. The last thing she wanted to do was discuss the evening with Walter. But Stella untangled herself from her date and stepped out onto the landing, closer to where Darby stood.

"I'm impressed, you breaking curfew," said Stella, flashing a conspiratorial smile. "You have a bad streak, too, don't you?"

Darby considered the idea. She was sneaking in late after visiting a jazz club in a seedy part of town with one of the maids from the Barbizon. This was not what Mother had envisioned for her.

But she didn't smile back.

"Yes, I guess I do." She turned the corner and kept on moving.

CHAPTER SEVEN

New York City, 2016

Rose jumped into a cab and gave the driver an address on the West Side, shaking off the effects of another sleepless night. She was running late, but the morning traffic had eased and the taxi sliced through the park at a high speed. Her father's nursing home was way over by the Hudson River, an old brick building surrounded by sleek glass high-rises.

His room was empty.

"Where's my father, Regina?"

The Jamaican nurse laughed and shook her head. "He's trouble, that man."

"No, he's a doll. And you know it."

"I'm afraid not." The smile stayed on her face, but Rose couldn't tell whether she was kidding. "You best go to the breakfast room. Maybe you can get him up and out of there. If not, we're gonna have to call in the big guys."

Her father sat at a table near the window and stared out across the water. She recognized the bushy eyebrows and handsome profile at once, but the rest of his body seemed to belong to a stranger. She had a sudden memory of him pushing himself away from the dinner table after a big meal, balancing on the back two legs of his chair and patting his round belly. All the extra padding had disappeared over the past five years, as his mental state had become less agile. The high school math and science teacher who scribbled out calculations on napkins during dinner had slowly faded away. He didn't even remember how to hold a pencil.

She put a hand on his bony shoulder. "Dad?"

He dropped his head to his chest and puffed out his cheeks.

"I came by to say hello. Do you want to take a walk?"

"I want breakfast."

She looked up. The staff was clearing tables. "Did Mr. Lewin get breakfast this morning?"

One of the aides nodded. "Ate it all. He want more?"

"Dad, do you want more?"

"No."

His doctors had said he was depressed, a common side effect of the medication that kept him calm.

She waited, hoping he'd show some animation. He turned his face up to her and she caught her breath. A bruise covered his right temple, purple and blue hues vivid beneath the thin skin. "Stay here. I'm going to talk to Dr. Mehra, all right?"

The nurses paged the doctor, who trotted briskly down the hall. Rose had liked Dr. Mehra, as he had a gentle manner but didn't dance around the truth.

"What happened to his head? He's hurt."

Dr. Mehra blinked. "Didn't they call you?"

"No."

"He became belligerent last night, wanted to go outside. He slipped as they were getting him back to bed and hit his head on the safety rail. Not hard, he didn't lose consciousness."

"But hard enough that it's badly bruised."

"I examined him last night and again this morning. We see no signs of concussion."

"How could you tell? He's not responding to anything I say."

"Actually, we should sit and talk; do you have time?"

The pit in Rose's stomach grew bigger. She didn't have time. Tyler would be asking where she was by now, but he'd have to wait.

The doctor led her into his office. "We need to talk about the possibility of placing your father in the dementia unit."

"Why? He needs to be looked after, but he's not that bad. He can walk and feed himself still."

"He knocked down another patient last night as he was trying to get out."

Rose sat back and gripped her hands together. "Was the other patient hurt?"

"Fine, nothing broken. But he's a danger to others."

Rose mulled over the possibilities. "I wouldn't want anything to happen to someone else because of him. I'm just wondering if this is a one-time thing. He's been so docile."

"You may need to reframe your thinking. He's in a decline, and it's only going to get worse. We ought to move him sooner rather than later, for everyone's sake."

"I see. And how much more does that cost a month?" The question was crass, but pertinent. Before, Griff's money would have provided a cushion for emergencies like this. No longer.

"You'll have to talk to the billing department. They'll be able to answer all of your questions."

She shook his hand. "I will. Thank you."

By the time she got back to her father, he was dozing in the big armchair in his room. She touched the bruise lightly with her finger and straightened a lock of his gray hair that had fallen over his forehead. She imagined him waking up and chatting with her, suggesting they head to their favorite diner for a cheeseburger.

But she knew the truth: That was the past, a little girl's wishful thinking. He was lost to her more every week.

⁓≫⁓

The fourth-floor hallway at the Barbizon was eerily quiet.

Rose tried Miss McLaughlin's door again but didn't get an answer or even a yap from Bird. She was probably out walking the dog. Several other residents opened their doors a crack, before shaking their heads and declining to speak further after she'd told them she was a journalist. Another, a large woman in her seventies, had a coughing fit and said she was too ill to speak.

Strange. Rose had figured these women would be bored and lonely, eager to speak about the minutia of their lives. In fact, they treated her like a pain in the ass.

A wreath of ivy encircled the peephole of the farthest door. Rose knocked and waited.

"Who is it?" cried a hoarse voice.

"My name is Rose Lewin. I live on the fifth floor. I'm a journalist, working on a piece about the Barbizon Hotel for Women."

The door opened and a strong-featured woman peered out. "You live here?"

"Yes, just one floor up. I moved in a few months ago." She didn't add that she'd be moving out shortly.

The woman looked her up and down. "You want to talk to us crones?"

The harsh term took her by surprise. "I'd like to talk to you, if you have a moment."

The woman shook her head. She had dyed red hair cut in a flattering pixie. "No, thank you. Read *The Bell Jar*, read her poems. I've got nothing to add."

"I take it you've been approached by the media before?"

She waved her hand dismissively. "Please. Everyone wants to know about Sylvia Plath, the guest editors, the drama. I don't know why. That was years ago, over and done with. But every few years, we get another gal like you, wanting to know the 'real story' of what happened to her here."

No wonder the other women of the fourth floor weren't willing to talk to her.

"I'm not interested in Sylvia Plath," Rose said. "I want to know more about the place, from your perspective. What rules you had to abide by, what your life was like, that kind of thing."

"Huh." The redhead made a face. "I can't tell you how often we get notes passed to us from the doorman—from journalists, from tourists, from lonely teenagers—asking if we knew Sylvia the Great and Greatly Wounded."

"Even though she lived here only a month, I guess the tragedy outshines the facts."

"Exactly. Who do you work for?"

"I work for a media company called WordMerge."

The woman gave a throaty laugh. "That's a terrible name for a business."

"Trust me, I know."

"I'll talk with you, but I only have twenty minutes before I have to go see my doctor. You can come in and have some tea if you like. I just boiled the water."

Rose followed her inside, surprised at the stark contrast to the renovated units. The apartment was small and dark and needed another coat of paint. Or rather, several layers of paint needed to be scraped off first. The moldings that ran along the ceiling and around the windows were shellacked with latex. Deep grooves marred the dark wood flooring. The kitchen featured a shiny avocado-green refrigerator and matching oven, left over from the seventies.

Rose tried not to stare at the outdated decor as the woman poured out two cups of tea. "My hope is to talk with each of the fourth-floor residents, compile an oral history. I think we take for granted so much that happened between then and now."

"You mean 'we' as in women?"

"Exactly."

"No one cares. Trust me. Everyone moves on, there's nothing new to write about; it's all been covered. Move on to something more interesting."

"Like what?"

She stopped and put her hands on her hips. "How do I know? You're the journalist, sweetheart."

A wild yapping erupted from another room, and Bird tore down the hallway toward them.

"Damn dog. I thought I'd closed that door."

"Is that Bird?"

The woman studied Rose closely. "You know Bird?"

"Miss McLaughlin and I talked just the other day." Not exactly a lie. Rose talked, and Darby McLaughlin listened. "I'm Rose Lewin, by the way." Rose stuck out her hand.

"I'm Stella Conover. But like I said, I only have twenty minutes." She rubbed one arm. "My nerve pain is acting up again. I recognize you from the news show. You don't work there anymore?"

"No."

"Good. You all looked like a bunch of idiots, sitting around yapping just like Bird here. Hope that doesn't offend you."

"Far from it. I think you summed up the job perfectly."

Ms. Conover handed her a mug. "Although it was terrible the way they forced you out. Especially since you were right about Senator Madden all along, that sleazebag. Embezzling money from senior citizens. You're the hero, in my book. You and Gloria Buckstone."

Rose remained silent. She'd learned by now there was no point in setting the record straight. After all, she'd benefited from the assumption that she was an aggressive journalist with a righteous cause. It had landed her the job at WordMerge.

"Come into the other room. And I'm only doing this because you're a fellow resident."

"Of course, and I appreciate it."

They ventured into the living room, where two south-facing windows filled with plants served as the focal point, along with an oversize couch.

"It's not grand, but in New York, it's a steal."

"I'm sure." Rose sat down on the couch, sinking in so far her knees rose above her hips, and tried not to spill her tea. "So kind of you to do this, Ms. Conover." She placed the cup on the table beside her and took out a notebook and a pen from her bag.

"Oh, please, call me Stella."

"Stella. When did you come to the Barbizon?"

"Back in 1952. I was scouted by the Eileen Ford agency. I worked as a model for ten years, and then became a muse of sorts for the designers, if you know what I mean."

Rose blinked.

"I made the rounds. Let certain men take care of me for the pleasure of having me on their arm. Don't be squeamish. Figured it would lead to other Cinderella-type things like in the movies, but no such luck. I did well, though. I made enough to take care of myself."

"I see." If all of the women were as forthright as Stella, the piece for WordMerge would be terrific. "What was it like when you first arrived? I understand men weren't allowed above the first floor?"

"The rules were strict. I remember coming down in slacks one day and the matron on duty, this dour woman, told me to go right back upstairs and change. I couldn't cross the lobby in pants, only a skirt. And this lasted through the sixties, mind you. Seems so silly today."

"What about the girls who went to secretarial school?"

"Right. The Katharine Gibbs girls. We always felt so smug when we saw them dressed in their gloves and hats for class. They had their own floors and we didn't interact much. The place was like a beehive with all these tiny rooms off long, dark hallways. Lively, though, everyone had a great time. J. D. Salinger used to show up at the café on the ground floor, hoping to pick up one of the models."

"Did you date J. D. Salinger?"

"No, not my type."

"This is exactly what I'm looking for; the history is fascinating." She tapped the notepad with her pen. "You know, I've tried to reach some of the other women on the floor, but they don't want to talk, it seems."

"Old biddies, the lot of them." She let out a husky laugh. Her profile was aristocratic, with a high forehead and strong nose. Rose could very well imagine her dressed to kill in the cinched, girdled fashions of a bygone era. "When it was still a hotel, they used to sit in the lobby all day commenting on the other guests like a Greek chorus. After it went condo, loitering was discouraged, so they withdrew to the fourth floor."

"What about Darby McLaughlin; did you know her back then?"

Stella paused for a moment, then seemed to choose her words carefully. "She was an odd duck at first. We had an uneasy beginning, but we eventually reached a kind of detente. Darby went to Gibbs, then worked as a secretary for the same company for years and years until she retired." The radiator began to clank. "Oh, dear God, I keep telling the super to come up and turn the damn thing off already, but he's too busy kowtowing to the rich tenants. Don't be offended."

"No, not at all. What kind of company did Miss McLaughlin work for?"

"Some button shop on West Thirty-Eighth Street. Only retired five or six years ago, old goose."

The clanking continued. "Do you want me to turn the heat off?"

"No, it involves taking all the plants off the windowsill and lifting up that shelf they sit on. It's the least he can do, for the little I ask of him."

"It must be strange to see the building change so drastically."

"Everything changes. I couldn't care less. I have my little slice of New York City and that's enough for me."

"You said you were good friends with Miss McLaughlin?"

"I didn't say that. But we help each other out, now and again. I'm taking care of Bird while she's away."

The news surprised Rose. "Where did she go?"

"God knows. This morning she seemed upset, asked me to watch Bird while she's gone for a while, and that was that. Said she had some business to take care of. Whatever that means. What kind of business can an eighty-one-year-old woman have? Said she'd be back in three weeks."

Rose's hopes fell. Tyler wouldn't be happy. "Does she often go on trips?"

"Rarely. Can't think of the last time she left town. Like I said, she was in a hurry. You said you talked to her?"

"Yes, we were going to set up a time to speak further. Were you here when she had the accident?"

"How did you hear about that?"

"One of the doormen. He was very respectful," she added quickly.

"Patrick. Biggest gossip in the building." Her voice became quiet, eerie. "I can't help you out there. Darby's private. She doesn't talk much about it."

"Do you remember the name of the maid who died?"

Stella let out a low whistle. "Can't forget her. She was a wiseass. Esme. Esme Castillo was her full name. After it happened, it was all the girls could talk about for weeks. The hotel kept the scandal quiet, never even hit the papers." She stared at Rose through narrowed eyelids. "Is that what you want to write about?"

"No, not if she's uncomfortable. I would like to talk to her, though, about other things. Do you think you might explain what I'm doing the next time you see her?"

"You seem like a nice enough gal. I'll see what I can do, but you shouldn't hold your breath. Darby's probably the last of the old-timers you'll get to open up. After the accident, she closed herself off. Like a curtain coming down at the end of a play."

Rose left her business card with Stella and took the stairs up one flight. On one hand, Miss McLaughlin's sudden exodus put her story into a tailspin. On the other, Stella's story would make an epic profile and might keep Tyler at bay until she returned.

Exhausted, she passed out on the couch until the ringing of her cell phone woke her up out of a heavy, black sleep. She hurried to it, hoping maybe it was Griff. Instead, Stella's voice crackled across the line.

"I need your help."

"Sure, Stella, what can I do for you?"

"Get my apartment key from Patrick and take Darby's dog."

"I'm sorry?"

"My doctor put me in the hospital for tests. Apparently it's my heart, not my nerves. They think I'm having some kind of a heart attack or something."

"I'm so sorry. What can I do?"

"What I just asked. Take care of Bird while I'm away. Patrick will give you the key."

"I'm happy to help, but Miss McLaughlin and I barely know each other."

"Darby doesn't have many friends, so that's nothing new. You live in the building, and I can track you down if you steal anything, not that we have anything to steal."

"I won't steal a thing, I promise."

"If he runs out of food, there's more in Darby's apartment. Her key is on my kitchen counter. He's a good dog, won't poop on your rugs or anything like that. Darby's instructions are on the kitchen counter."

Rose tried not to sound too excited. Once Miss McLaughlin found out she'd stepped in during a crisis, she'd have to talk. Assuming she wasn't too pissed off. Either way, Rose was just being neighborly, and it was an opportunity to move the story forward and connect with the primary source. "Okay, get well soon and let me know if there's anything else I can do for you."

"Enjoy being young. That's what you can do for me."

CHAPTER EIGHT

New York City, 1952

So this was what a hangover felt like.

Darby wanted to curl back in bed and wait for the pounding in her right temple to subside, but that wasn't what a Katie Gibbs girl did. No, a Katie Gibbs girl gets up and goes to work no matter how ill she might be, knowing that her boss depends on her punctuality. Or at least that's what the typing teacher said as Darby slunk to her seat five minutes after the other girls had arrived.

"Punctuality and presence. If you're not there to answer Mr. Blake's phone, he may miss a very important call, one that the entire organization depends on. Would you want to be the girl who causes a business crisis?" Mrs. Allen peered at Darby through thick-framed glasses, like a scientist staring into a petri dish. "Darby McLaughlin. You are late."

Darby's stomach churned. She had never been late a day in high school. As a matter of fact, she'd always arrived early, terrified of standing out.

"I'm sorry. I got lost, but it won't happen again."

"You got lost?"

Thankfully, the girl who sat next to Darby raised her hand, and Mrs. Allen was momentarily distracted.

"Yes, Maureen."

"Mrs. Allen, who is Mr. Blake?"

"Mr. Blake is the name of the first boss I ever had. I learned much from him, so I use him as my teaching tool." She glared in their direction. "Any other questions?"

"No, ma'am."

She turned away from Darby and began handing out sample letters. Darby slid hers into the stand at the right of the gray Remington typewriter and wished her eyes weren't so blurry. She had taken a terrible risk, going out with Esme. No more taking reckless chances. She'd experienced two sides of New York City, the snooty and the subversive, and from now on, her studies would take precedence.

Mrs. Allen turned on the record player and they began typing in time to a slow march. By the end of a couple of months, according to Mrs. Allen, they'd progress to the Ringing Anvil March, typing forty-seven words per minute. Upon completion of the course, they'd be up to fifty-five. The music helped, flowing through Darby like water and making her fingers dance on the keys. At the end of the class, Darby was pleased to be one of the only students whose letter was deemed "mailable." Her desk mate, the girl named Maureen, had also done well.

As they walked to the next class, Darby tapped her on the arm. She had thin blond hair that looked almost white, and pale blue eyes. A pretty girl, but Darby's mother would probably have described her as big-boned. "Thank you for distracting Mrs. Allen. I thought she might expel me there and then."

"Happy to do it. I heard that one girl in her class went to put in a new sheet of paper after she made a mistake, and Mrs. Allen tossed her out on the spot."

"That's the last thing I want."

"It's only until June, and then you get the advantages of lifetime placement. They'll find jobs for us that'll last all the way until we get married."

"Or die."

She hadn't meant for the words to seem so harsh, but Maureen flinched.

Darby was quick to explain. "I don't mean that we'll die right away, just that some of us may not get married."

"I know." Maureen offered up a pout. "That's so sad."

Unfortunately, Mrs. Allen was seated behind the desk of their next class.

"How did she get here so fast?" whispered Maureen in astonishment.

"She probably flew on her broom."

Maureen giggled, and Darby smiled, too.

Mrs. Allen peered up at the two of them over her glasses. Obviously, a Katie Gibbs girl was not permitted to share a joke with a friend. "Darby, your hair is touching your shoulders. You'll get a demerit for that."

Darby patted at her hair, trying to tuck back the one errant lock. "I'm sorry, Mrs. Allen."

"Very well, be seated and we'll begin." She stood and pointed to the black phone that sat on her desk facing out, the cord curled up neatly. "This is your first class in phone etiquette. Since Katharine Gibbs founded the school in 1911, we have adapted to the changing times. As you can imagine, back in the early days, there were no phones. But they've become a vital instrument in the modern secretary's tool kit. As such, we have found it necessary to train you to use them properly."

The phone was identical to the one Darby had back home. Not that anyone ever called for her. She'd picked it up one day and heard Mother talking on the extension to a friend, listing all of Darby's faults. Too studious, too inward-looking. A wallflower who'd never attract a man. Mother sighed several times and Darby could tell from the tightness in her voice that she was about to cry.

"Now that Arch is gone, I have to make something of that girl," she'd said. "And I have to do it all myself, since she doesn't lift a finger to better herself. Her books are all she cares about. I'm ashamed to have her walking around town, with that hair and that slump in her spine. Mort wants her out of the house as soon as school is over."

Darby waited until Mother and her friend decided her fate, off to New York City and the hope of being a career girl, before hanging up the phone softly and going to her room.

She knew she was missing something that nearly every other girl possessed: She rarely felt light or silly or flirtatious. Only with Daddy had she ever shown that side of herself. He and Mother had been the best-looking couple of their set, and both were so stylish that Darby could hardly say which of them was more beautiful. But Mother was fiercely protective of her clothing and her coiffures, always pushing Darby away, fearful that embraces would leave her wrinkled and stained. Daddy was different. He often reached for Darby and all her smudges, pulling her onto his lap and tickling her until she felt like Jell-O. Later, when she grew older, he would wrap an arm around her shoulders whenever they were in adult company that made her nervous. He liked to whisper jokes into her ear and together they would make private fun of Mother's snooty, brainless friends.

"Miss McLaughlin, please come up to the desk."

Darby jumped. She'd been lost in thought. What had Mrs. Allen been talking about? She looked at Maureen, who gave her an encouraging smile.

Darby walked to the front of the room.

"Keep your head up as you walk; don't look at the floor."

Darby obeyed, pulling her shoulders back.

"Very well, sit at the desk. When I say 'ring, ring,' you pick up and answer."

Darby did as she was told. "Hello?" Her voice came out faint, as if she were at the end of a long tunnel.

"No, no, no. Weren't you listening?"

"I–I'm sorry."

"Obviously not. Repeat after me: 'Mr. Blake's office. How may I assist you today?'"

Darby did, but it wasn't enough.

"Louder."

She repeated the words.

"Now make it friendly. Put a smile in your voice."

Before she could attempt another round, she was cut off. "Don't actually do it. I said put a smile in your voice, not on your face. No one wants to see you grinning like an idiot all day."

Tears sprang into Darby's eyes. *The Art of Conversation* had said to overenunciate your consonants while speaking on the telephone. Or was it your vowels? The other girls stared at her uneasily, knowing they would get similar treatment but relieved not to be the first. She had to get this right. To prove to Mother that she could. She'd mastered biology and chemistry in school, earning straight As in every class. Surely, she could pick up a phone and answer it.

Esme's face popped into her head. She imagined Esme onstage, bellowing out a song at the top of her lungs.

She took a deep breath. "Mr. Blake's office. How may I assist you today?"

The words rang out confident and bright, friendly but business-like. Perfect.

Mrs. Allen's overly plucked eyebrows rose in surprise. "Well done. You see, it's not really that difficult. You may sit down now."

As she did so, she gave a quiet thanks to Esme.

⌐◈⌐

The dining room was almost empty when Darby poked her head in that evening before entering, ready to retreat in case any of the Ford models still lingered. But the only other occupants were Maureen and two other Gibbs girls Darby remembered from class. Maureen marched over before Darby could pick up a tray.

"Darby, we're getting together to drill each other for the business communication test. Wanna join in?" She introduced her friends, twins named Edna and Edith, who wore matching ponytails tied with purple ribbon.

Darby was about to decline when she caught the sound of high-pitched laughter from the end of the hall. Candy was coming. "Sure."

The seventeenth floor, though identical to the one where Darby and the Ford girls were housed, exuded warmth and welcome. Every door was wide-open, and cheery hellos rang out as they passed by. Even the cubist wall sconces that lined the hallway seemed to shine brighter.

In Maureen's room, Darby took a seat on the bed, which was

covered with a pretty quilt instead of the garish Barbizon-issued coverlet, and opened up her folder. She could use the extra time studying, that much was sure, even if her stomach was growling.

Maureen began reading out loud from her notes but stopped mid-sentence.

"Listen, it's Benny Goodman!"

From another room came the tinny sound of a transistor radio playing the "King Porter Stomp."

"Dance with me, Edith." Maureen held out her hand.

Edith checked in with her sister. "We don't dance in Lubbock."

"Don't dance in Lubbock? Who's ever heard of such a thing?" Maureen crooked a finger at Darby. "You know the Lindy Hop, right?"

Darby had loved being swung across the floor at the high school dances, although her only partner was the librarian's lanky son, who had perpetually sweaty palms. "Sure, I guess."

Edith and Edna sat on the bed, legs tucked under them to offer up as much floor space as possible in the narrow room. Maureen shoved her chair under the desk as far as it would go. "Quick, before the song ends."

They lightly touched hands and Darby let Maureen take the lead. For being such a stocky girl, Maureen was surprisingly light on her feet, and they twirled and jigged until Darby lost her footing and fell on the bed in a fit of giggles.

But Maureen wasn't finished. "Everyone on your feet for the Lindy. No excuses."

After fifteen minutes of practice, even the twins knew the basic steps and they danced in pairs, humming the tune out loud and bumping into one another with clumsy delight.

Finally, exhausted from the effort, they sprawled on the floor, reluctant to return to studying. Darby let out a soft sigh. If only she'd been assigned to the correct floor to begin with, she might have had a brighter start to her New York life.

Edith shoved her notebook with her foot. "I can't stand doing four hours of homework every night. I should've stayed in Texas. My head hurts from remembering the shorthand symbols, and the pads of my fingers ache from typing. It's inhumane, the way they treat us."

Edna patted her leg. "Remember what Mother said: If we follow the rules and work hard, we'll look back at our time in New York with pride."

"And maybe marry our handsome bosses," added Maureen.

Darby cringed at the thought. "If that's the goal, then what's the point of learning shorthand?" She didn't mean to sound snappish, but the lack of dinner was getting to her.

Maureen turned over onto her stomach, chin resting in her hands. "What I hate is watching all the models go out on dates every night, dressed in silks and pearls, while we're stuck inside. They're all so beautiful. I hope there'll be some boys left over for us."

"Don't you ever go out at all?" Darby asked.

"Sure. We went to a film matinee on Saturday and saw *A Streetcar Named Desire*. Have you seen it? Marlon Brando acts like a beast for the whole thing but he looks completely divine."

"True," Edith tittered. "But he's not nearly as handsome as Montgomery Clift."

"How about you, Darby? Who's your dream date?"

"Me?" She laughed. "I'm too intimidated by the idea of a movie star to even imagine it. And I'm not much better with real people, if you want to know the truth. I met an actual living, breathing boy last night at a jazz club, and I could hardly put two words together."

Maureen sputtered before getting the words out. "A jazz club? Not truly!"

An electric tingle flew up Darby's spine. "Sure. It's downtown, on the Lower East Side. They play bebop, and it's a real bash." She hoped she sounded casual and sophisticated.

"Can you imagine what Mrs. Eustis would say if she knew you went to a jazz club?" said Edna. "She'd explode."

"I came back after curfew as well. Snuck up the back stairs."

Their awestruck reaction pleased Darby to no end. She described the club, the patrons, the music, in great detail, emphasizing the elements of danger and mystery. And Sam she turned into a dashing hero, with a chiseled profile and piercing eyes.

When she'd finished the description of her daring night out, omitting the fact that a maid from the hotel had been her companion, she made excuses and hugged the girls good-bye. All the dancing had made her too jumpy to sit and study.

Down the hallway, a familiar silhouette disappeared into the stairwell. Darby called out Esme's name, but there was no reply and no sound of footsteps, either. She must have been mistaken.

Dashing down the two flights back to her floor, Darby hummed the Lindy tune out loud, no longer afraid of walking the gauntlet of the hallway back to her room.

The Ford girls had nothing on her.

CHAPTER NINE

New York City, 2016

Miss McLaughlin's dog had quite the bitchy personality. He liked to pee only in certain locations in Central Park, which he eagerly led Rose to, straining against his leash as if he were pulling an eighteen-wheeler behind him. And if another dog approached too closely, particularly one that looked like him, scruffy and brown, he'd bare his teeth and lunge.

The first time he did it, Rose jumped in shock and apologized furiously to the other dog owner, who glared back at her.

"It's not my dog," she'd said. Bird had recovered quickly, throwing her a look of maniacal glee before trotting off with his tail held high.

The key to Miss McLaughlin's apartment lay on Stella's kitchen counter, but Rose hadn't touched it yet, only gathered up the bag of the dog's food and headed upstairs with Bird. The ethics of the situation were murky, to say the least. As a reporter, she would be entering a potential source's apartment without prior approval.

But the woman wasn't a source yet. And Rose was beginning to doubt she'd ever agree to be. Just a batty old lady with a penchant for drama. All Rose was doing was taking care of a neighbor's pet during a time of crisis. If she found herself having to enter Miss McLaughlin's apartment in order to fulfill her duty to Stella, that wouldn't violate any professional boundaries, would it?

Early the next morning, Bird woke her up with several insistent yelps. Bleary-eyed, she stumbled around the block with him, wishing she'd been able to have a cup of coffee first. Upon their return home, as they were entering the building, one of the doormen stopped Rose.

"Looks like Mr. Van Doren is back from his trip."

Griff had returned. "He's home?"

"Just came in a few minutes ago. I told him you'd be right back."

As she unlocked the door, she called out his name.

"I'm here, in the living room."

Relief surged through her. He was back. She was pissed he'd put her through the anguish of the past four days, but it was hard to simply turn off the attraction. She'd missed him.

He stood by the window and gave her a smile.

"Griff, how are you?" She put down her keys and stood there, as awkward as a teenager. The dog bounded into the room, excited to have another person to boss around.

"Who's this?" Griff's brows knitted in concern.

"A neighbor's dog, who was being cared for by another neighbor while she's away. But she had to go to the hospital, the second neighbor, that is. So I'm taking care of him until she's released." Enough, already. Stop babbling and let him take the lead.

Griff kneeled down and held out his hand. Bird trotted over and took a sniff, then allowed him to scratch his neck. If the dog could have purred, he would have. Of course Bird loved Griff. Griff charmed everyone.

She sat on the arm of the couch and crossed her arms. "What's going on?"

"I'm fine, we're fine." He stood up and put his hands into his pockets.

"Miranda's doing better?" she ventured.

"We found a place for her, a school that we hope will help. And a therapist."

"That's good news." She straightened her shoulders, hoping to look strong and determined.

His face crumpled. "I miss you."

Her heart twisted in pain, but a small part of her lit up with triumph. He was miserable. She wished she could read his mind and know what was lurking there, instead of feeling it out, syllable by syllable.

She walked over to him and held him close. He was the first man she'd loved in a grown-up, serious way. He buried his face in her neck and sobbed. After a minute, he stepped back and wiped his tears with the meaty pad of his palm, like a little boy.

He sat on the window ledge and pulled her down beside him and rubbed her arm. "I'm sorry—this is so hard."

"I know." Or did she? "What is?"

"There've been some changes since the last time we talked. I hadn't realized Connie had already made plans."

An icy shiver shot down her spine at the sound of the woman's name on his lips. "I have no idea what you're talking about, Griff."

"I spoke too soon before. It turns out that we need to be in the city, as part of Miranda's treatment."

"Still, I have no idea what you're saying." As a politician, he was good at being obtuse. But he'd never used his evil powers on her before.

He stopped rubbing her arm and looked away. "You'll have to find another place to live."

He wasn't coming back. And he was kicking her out. Shit.

"No way. You said I had some time, right?"

"I'm afraid not. The school and the therapist are here in the city, and Connie wants to move in right away."

Panic rose up in her throat, a bilious, terrible taste. "She wants to move in here?"

"It's what's best for the family."

He was echoing his wife. His ex-wife. She imagined the woman saying it as he got into his car to drive into the city, leaning in to give him a good-bye kiss.

"You're saying that I have to move out, now?"

"Not now, not exactly, but in a few days. She's having some furniture delivered."

He stopped short and she could see him watching her reaction, hoping she had missed the irony. But Rose hadn't missed it. And she was halfway to rage already.

"So now you're decorating the place? After months and months of being too busy, you're letting her swoop in and take over." The anger was a giant relief. She'd been wondering why she'd felt little other than numb panic about Griff's defection. But the enormity of what he'd done, and had been doing behind her back for the past few months, suddenly hit hard. In a strange twist, her fury was evidence of the enormous loss of him in her life.

"I am sorry, Rose." He shook his head.

"Goddammit, Griff. You're letting her take over your life again. Is that what you want? Maybe that's what I should have done, furnished the fucking apartment without any input from you. Then maybe you'd still be here."

"It's not about the furniture; it's about the kids."

"No, it's about your life. How are you going to be a good father when you're back in what you yourself called a 'toxic relationship'? Think of yourself, of us. We had so many plans."

He nodded. "We did. I love you so much, but maybe I'm too old to start another relationship."

Connie's words again, she was sure of it. Yet he'd admitted he still loved her. She softened her tone. "Where am I supposed to go?"

"What about Maddy's? Until you get yourself straightened out."

She couldn't believe it. "How about you put me up in a hotel until I figure things out? You can't toss me out on the street, not after you're the one who insisted I give up my place."

He'd begged her to live with him. They had been at a rooftop bar somewhere in SoHo, music and bodies and heat, and all she wanted was to have him near her, as close as possible. It was all she could do to not wrap herself around him while they raced in a cab back to her place. She was still attached to that version of Griff, and not ready to accept Griff 2.0. How could someone change so suddenly?

"I didn't realize at the time how ill Miranda was. I'm doing this for my daughter. At least until she's well."

"But you see the situation you put me in, don't you?" She counted it out on her fingers. "Because of you, I gave up my apartment and took the WordMerge job along with a salary cut. And now I'm learning my father needs a higher level of care."

"I'm sorry about your dad. I really am. But you can't put your job move on me. You said you were sick of television, ready to do something different. I encouraged you, but you were the one who made that decision. Not me."

She wasn't going to quibble over semantics, but his interpretation of events was pretty damn self-serving. Taking a deep breath, she tried again.

"I'm going to run out of money fast, Griff. What the hell am I going to do?" Her throat closed up, constricting when she wanted to let out a roar.

"Connie insists on holding the purse strings." He sighed. "But let me see what I can do. I know I owe you that much."

Oh, Lord. If Connie was already running their joint finances, Griff was well and truly gone. Rose's tamped-down rage surged again.

"Get the hell out. I don't want anything from you. You're a liar, Griff. A fucking liar, a cheater, and a terrible human being."

The futility of her words washed over her and she ran to the bedroom, slamming the door behind her. She waited until she heard the closing of the front door before she let the sobs wash over her.

⌘

Two days later, Griff texted Rose to say Connie would be heading over that evening. Rose left work early and packed her clothes into four suitcases, along with her toiletries and shoes, while Bird watched from his perch on the bed. If she had to pick a word for the expression on the dog's face, it would be *bemused*. As if he knew all along it wasn't going to work out with Griff, and perhaps if Rose didn't expect so much out of life, she wouldn't be in this situation. All Bird needed was some food and water and three good walks a day. Why did Rose ask so much?

Before Griff came into her life, she'd been independent and strong, and she refused to let him bring her down now. She'd crash at Maddy's until she could find an affordable place, ask Tyler for a raise to cover the additional expenses, and take care of herself. Too bad the door had closed firmly behind her when she'd left the network, with its high salaries and generous benefits. Otherwise she might have considered going back.

She sat cross-legged on the floor and stroked Bird. Instead of lying down like most dogs and exposing his stomach, Bird remained on his haunches, his front legs pressed primly together. "Don't worry, you'll be back home before you know it." Bird sniffed the air and sneezed.

Rose became exhausted just thinking about relocating to Maddy's apartment, which was as chaotic as Griff's was minimal, with crayons and Barbies scattered everywhere. Never mind the strain of putting on a brave face in front of Maddy and her family each day. And, of course, she had to worry about Bird's behavior, too. Hopefully, he wouldn't nip at the kids.

She wished she had a real home to go to. A place in Connecticut maybe, on a tree-lined street where her parents would greet her with a hug and a homemade meal; then she'd go up to her room, which was just as it was when she'd left. Maybe she'd meet their handsome landscaper and fall in love, and realize that small-town life was for her. After several wacky misunderstandings, they'd fall into each other's arms and marry in the backyard.

Instead, her mother had left their Upper West Side brownstone one day while Rose was in first grade, never to return home again. Her father said that she'd gone on a long trip. By the time Rose knew to ask for details, she'd gotten used to their quiet existence together, cooking a simple dinner, reading before lights-out. Later, in high school, he informed her that her mother had passed away in Arizona somewhere, from a drug overdose. By then she was an apparition anyway, more theoretical than real, and Rose tucked the information away in the dark recesses of her mind.

Life with her father was filled with routine and order. She read Austen and the Brontës over and over, and although she never admitted it to anyone, she used to wish she'd been a lady's maid in the 1800s. Rose enjoyed Saturday mornings when she gave their apartment a good cleaning, knowing that she had full control over the five small rooms, while the rest of the world loomed so large and noisy outside. If she were a maid, she'd know what was going to happen in five years, or ten, the same thing, day after day. Lighting coal fires, cleaning gowns, going to bed exhausted and then doing it over again. All oddly comforting. Funny how far that was from the life she would have had with Griff, one half of a power couple taking Manhattan by storm.

On Saturday nights, Rose and her father went out for dinner at the local diner, where she ordered the open-faced turkey sandwich, which came with mashed potatoes and gravy and a big helping of cranberry sauce, and her father would get a Reuben. On a napkin, he tested her in algebra, making silly faces out of the symbols. And when she moved out, off to college and then to a shared apartment with friends in Chelsea, they still met for dinner at least once a week. Until the day the school called her, worried about his dazed manner during a sophomore chemistry class where a student had almost been burned during an experiment. Then tests, and the sad knowledge that he would soon lose every last memory. He apologized to Rose, over and over, sorry to be a burden on her. She held his hand and promised to take care of him. And she would.

Unfortunately, as the synapses in his mind frayed, he spent most of his savings, buying things he didn't need online and sending money to strangers. She moved him to the assisted-living community and sold their apartment at the bottom of the market, paying off his debts with the bulk of it. When Griff came into her life, he brought a renewed sense of hope with him. Everything always turned out fine for Griff, so why not let some of his optimism and confidence rub off on her as well?

Her head began to ache and a familiar aura shimmered wherever she looked. Outside, a flash of lightning was followed by a giant clap of thunder that made Bird jump and run into her lap, shaking. Sometimes when the barometer changed suddenly, the pressure in her head would grow until the inevitable migraine took her out of commission for the next twenty-four hours.

If she didn't do something soon, get somewhere, she'd be stranded with a dog and four suitcases in the pouring rain, unable to focus or even speak without throwing up.

She scrambled to her feet and grabbed two suitcases and the leash and stumbled to the elevator. But instead of pressing the lobby or even the taxi button, she hit four. Stella's apartment was quiet, the only sound the hum of the refrigerator. Miss McLaughlin's key was on the counter and Rose snatched it up. For the first time she noticed a series of photographs that lined the wall between the bedroom and living room. All in black and white, showing Stella in different clothes, different poses. In one, she stood in a shirred strapless bathing suit and cocked one hip toward the camera, her hair falling in shiny waves to her shoulders. Stella had been a beautiful woman.

Outside Miss McLaughlin's apartment, Rose fumbled with the lock, worried that someone would open up their door and demand to know what she was doing. She let the dog inside, placed the two suitcases in the narrow foyer, then headed back upstairs. She left the key to Griff's apartment next to the mail that had accumulated, then returned to Miss McLaughlin's with the last of the suitcases.

The apartment was the same layout as Stella's, but faced north and seemed much smaller. The living room held a mid-century, angular couch, one chair, and a simple walnut coffee table. An old record player sat on a small writing desk, and a bookcase lined one wall. Bird lapped up the last of the water in his bowl in the hallway and curled up on one corner of the sofa, clearly at home.

What was she thinking? She wasn't. The migraine was getting worse, growing steadily on the right side of her head, just behind her eye. Miss McLaughlin wasn't expected back for two and a half weeks. If she went to Stella's and the woman returned home from the hospital, she'd have to explain, and she didn't want to explain anything at the moment. She just needed a day or two to collect herself, figure out a plan.

Squinting through the throbbing in her head, she filled a glass with water and took a couple of sips, then lay down on the sofa with Bird snoring softly at her feet. As the room whirled around her, she gave in to the pain, thankful for a place where she could suffer in silence.

Four suitcases and a dog that wasn't even hers. It was all she had left.

CHAPTER TEN

New York City, 1952

Darby's heart soared when she received the envelope with Mother's familiar, elegant handwriting. She'd stifled memories of home ever since she'd arrived, afraid to think too much about her room, her beloved old house, and the screened-in patio where she'd sat with her dogs and read. Mother wrote with her usual reserve, making no mention of Mr. Saunders, and encouraged Darby to work hard and do well. However, at the bottom she'd drawn a detailed picture of the two dogs lolling in the grass. Darby knew this was Mother's way of saying she was missed, and she carefully taped the letter on the wall above her small desk.

She'd apply herself and make Mother very proud, and go home for Christmas break with perfect marks. With a sigh, she returned to her homework for her secretarial accounting class, a soporific mess of figures and columns. Her favorite class so far, and the one in which her scores were consistently above average, was typing. While she typed, she remembered how Stick's fingers had flown along the keyboard, as if they were independent of the rest of his body. He wasn't thinking about the individual notes but the whole phrase. And Darby found when she looked at sentences, the whole thoughts, of the practice test, she made fewer mistakes than when she focused on the individual letters. Her fingers were becoming more nimble.

A knock at the door broke her concentration. Esme poked her head in, then quickly came in and closed the door behind her.

"I don't have much time. Eustis is after me. How about we head downtown again?"

Darby hadn't seen Esme much the past week, and part of her had been relieved. She proved to be a strong distraction, one that Mother would definitely not condone.

"I can't, too much work to do."

"The other girls giving you any more trouble? I've been stuck in the laundry room all week, couldn't get away."

"No, they ignore me completely now, which is fine with me. It's a relief not to have to pretend to be polite."

"So come downtown. You owe me, right?"

The strange phrase surprised her, but she held firm. "Sorry, not tonight."

"Sam asked about you the other night."

"Sam?" Darby knew exactly who he was.

"The owner's son, cooks the food."

"What did he ask?"

"Why I brought you down there. He seemed protective. Don't you think that's sweet?"

Darby imagined he was more scornful than sweet, after her silly reaction to the music. "I really shouldn't."

"That's too bad." Esme dropped her chin to her chest and shrugged one shoulder. "Because I'd love to have someone to celebrate with. But I guess not."

Darby jumped out of her chair. "You got into acting school?"

Esme nodded and Darby gave her a hug. "Congratulations! I knew you'd get in."

"But that's not all." Esme glowed just like the Ford girls, even in her maid's uniform with its dull black dress, black stockings, and silly white cap.

"What's going on?"

"I am. The owner of the club, Mr. Buckley, said I could go on before the headliner tonight."

Darby grabbed Esme's hands. "That's wonderful. How did you manage it?"

"He was holding auditions the other afternoon, right before my shift. I asked if I could give it a shot, like a real singer, and he said fine. You could say I blew his socks off. I'll have a full band behind me and even a backup singer."

Her excitement was infectious. How could Darby resist?

As they walked from the train to the club, Esme took Darby's hand in her own and swung it merrily. They got off at Union Square and headed south down Fourth Avenue, past a cluster of used bookstores, their wares spilling out onto the street in uneven stacks. New York was a town of surprises.

Darby gave her hand a quick squeeze. "So now you'll be going to acting school, working at the Barbizon and at the club. How will you manage?" Darby thought of her own schedule of classes, which seemed paltry in comparison.

"Mrs. Eustis said she'd arrange my schedule around my classes. She's not all bad."

"How did you find the job at the club in the first place?" Darby asked.

"My aunt knows the owner."

"Did your aunt come with you from Puerto Rico?"

"No. She was here already. I wanted to come. Santurce was too small a *barrio* to hold me."

"Santurce?" Darby rolled the word around her in mouth.

"My father had a store there. Sold all kinds of things, candy, plantain balls, and when I was really young, my father had money and we were treated with respect. But things got worse quick. The store kept being robbed and my father lost it, lost everything eventually." Esme dropped Darby's hand. "There was no other work, so we all came to America, to live with my aunt."

"How old were you when you moved?"

"I came here five years ago, when I was fifteen. Now I live in the same building with the people who worked in the fields, the *jíbaros*. All filthy."

So Esme was a member of the privileged class in Puerto Rico. That explained her brashness. She wasn't like any of the other maids at the Barbizon, who avoided eye contact and scuttled down the halls. "What does your father do now?"

"He helps out our building's super, when he feels like it. But he can't fix a thing, never was good with his hands. That's why I have to make it big on my own. I'm not one of these *arrimados*."

"Sorry?"

Esme laughed. "People who can't take care of themselves, free-loaders."

The girl was to be admired. Darby's circumstances weren't nearly as dire, and all she wanted was a decent job. Esme, who came from a completely different culture, wanted to act, sing, become famous. Was she tenacious? Or deluded?

Perhaps a little of both. Darby held her breath as they walked by a man lying facedown on the sidewalk, but even so, the smell of alcohol and grime permeated her nostrils.

"But what about you, Miss McLaughlin? What's your story?"

Darby shrugged. "My father died three years ago. My mother remarried, and it's not a very happy marriage."

"Was she happy before?"

"I guess not. Mother is one of those women who always want more. More friends, more respect from those friends, more clothes. She's hard to live with. Daddy traveled a lot for work; he sold paper. We were never rich, though, and I don't think he measured up to her standards. She was pretty mean to him."

"What about your stepfather?"

"Mr. Saunders? No one measures up to Mr. Saunders."

They turned into the alleyway and Darby was relieved not to have to go into further detail.

⸎

The Flatted Fifth, which was so mysterious and dark after midnight, looked every inch the nineteenth-century tenement building it was under the harsh glare of the overhead lights, with a cracked linoleum floor and a ceiling darkened by decades of cigarette smoke. The first night, with Esme, Darby had been overcome by panic, imagining a nasty man grabbing her and dragging her into the shadows. Funny how innocuous the club looked now.

Esme yanked her across the floor. "I gotta do a sound check. Will you sit in the back and make sure my mic is loud enough? The drummer thinks he's more important than anyone else onstage."

Darby placed herself at the table near the back of the room as

Esme assembled her musicians onstage and they ran through two numbers. Esme's voice was deep and low and she sang right to Darby, who beamed with approval.

As the musicians discussed the intro to the next song, a man's voice rose from the back of the club.

"This isn't your kitchen, remember that."

Sam's voice answered. "No one's out there, if you haven't noticed. We have no orders to fill and we're ready for tonight. This is only an experiment."

"No experiments. Not at my club. Keep it simple."

"Don't you at least want to taste it?"

"I don't like that kind of food. You're in America. Fucking idiot."

The kitchen door swung open and a tall, sullen-looking man with slicked-back hair and bushy eyebrows raged through, the scent of cloves and pepper whirling in the air behind him. Darby breathed in deeply, and jumped when the door swung open again and Sam appeared.

"Dammit," he muttered.

Darby looked up, embarrassed. She couldn't pretend she hadn't overheard the exchange. "Hi," she muttered.

"Oh. Hi." Sam wiped his forehead with the corner of his apron. He wore a white shirt that was open at the neck, and had rolled up his sleeves, revealing a soft coating of blond hairs on his forearms.

"Why are you turning red?" Sam asked.

She put her hands to her cheeks. "It's hot in here."

"Sorry you had to hear that. That's my dad."

Mr. Buckley. Considering his foul mood, she hoped he'd still allow Esme to sing tonight. "Whatever you're cooking smells wonderful." She meant it, but she also wanted to make him feel better.

"It's in the trash now, unfortunately."

"Too exotic for the Flatted Fifth?"

"We wouldn't know unless we tried, but he's unwilling to do anything new."

"Where did you learn to cook like that?"

"In the army. I was stationed in Southeast Asia."

Darby didn't know how to keep the conversation going. Her knowledge of the world was limited to Defiance and small sections of New York City. "How wonderful."

"Not really."

Thankfully, the band started up again, this time with a pretty black girl standing a few feet to the side of her. The girl was rail thin and wore a bright slash of red lipstick. Her eyelids fluttered open and shut as she swayed to the music.

When Esme hit the chorus, the girl came in a few beats late. The harmonies were simple, but she didn't seem to be able to hold the notes long enough and was ever so slightly off-key. Darby's shoulders rose, an involuntary reaction to the atonal interval, while Sam let out a low "sheesh."

Darby hummed the harmony under her breath, hoping to correct the girl by osmosis, but Esme stopped halfway through. "Tanya, you're falling asleep up here. Stay with me, okay?"

The second attempt wasn't much better. Tanya looked as if she were going to be sick.

"What's wrong with her?" Darby asked Sam.

"She's high."

Tanya put her hands to her head and began listing to the left.

The bass player dropped his bow and reached out to break her fall, but she still landed with a loud thud. Sam raced up to the stage to help.

Esme stomped over to Darby while the girl was carried off by the bassist and drummer. "I knew she wouldn't make it. This is my big night and she's ruined it."

"You can still do the song. You sound terrific."

"The final number's supposed to rev everyone up. I can't rev without a backup singer."

Sam, who was headed back to the kitchen, stopped in front of her. "Darby can back you up."

Esme looked up at Sam, then at Darby, her eyes wide.

Darby laughed. "He's joking."

"I'm not, I heard you singing the right notes. Not loud, but the right ones."

She shook her head. "No, I can't. I don't sing."

"I just heard you."

"Okay, I sang in the chorus at school, but I never did anything for real."

"Backup isn't for real; you just stand there and do it." Esme sang a phrase, her hands stretched out to Darby.

No matter how badly she wanted to help her friend, Darby knew her place, and it wasn't onstage at a nightclub. She pictured the audience laughing at her, the same way the Ford girls laughed at her.

"I'll embarrass you, Esme. You'll do fine alone."

"Sing." She started in again.

"I can't."

Sam punched her playfully in the arm. "Sing under your breath, then. Like before. Just to prove to Esme that I'm not crazy."

His touch startled her. She put a hand over the spot where his knuckles had hit her upper arm and rubbed it gently. Darby sang along, quietly, her voice hesitant but on pitch.

"Yes. You've got to do it. You do that three times, whenever I do the chorus, and you sway your hips a little, and that's it."

"My hips don't sway."

"Come with me."

Esme dragged her down the hall and opened a door.

"Welcome to the green room." Esme swept her arms around as if they'd entered a parlor in Versailles. A couple of raggedy couches lined the walls, one of which was taken up by the prone Tanya, who snored softly. A small table tucked behind the door held some cups and a pot of coffee. "This is where the cats hang out before each show."

"Why is it the green room? It's not green."

"No idea. That's just what they call it. Wait here a moment."

Darby sat on the couch opposite Tanya, her knees pressed tightly together and her hands on her lap. She didn't want to look like a baby in front of Sam. And she only had to sing three choruses. She'd pretend she was back at school at the end-of-year concert, surrounded by other girls. If she did that, she might be able to do the song without falling over like Tanya.

Esme reappeared carrying her purse, the contents of which she poured out on the floor by Darby's feet. An array of cosmetics, from lipsticks to powders, scattered about like Christmas tree ornaments.

"Where did you get all these?" asked Darby.

"Whenever a giraffe leaves something behind in the bathroom, I swipe it. It's like when customers at the Flatted Fifth leave a tip for the waiters."

"Won't the girls notice?"

"Nah. They get all that stuff for free, anyway."

Esme knelt in front of Darby and twisted a bright orange-red lipstick out of its casing.

Darby bit her lip.

"You're right, it's too orange. Try this." Esme replaced it with one that was a softer shade of coral.

"Mother said I don't have a face for cosmetics."

"The only requirement for wearing cosmetics is to have a face, and you have one, as far as I can see."

"It won't help." The same words Mr. Saunders had said when Darby and Mother had come back from shopping for Darby's "city clothes."

"I like a challenge. Your face is plain, but sometimes that's the best kind."

Esme smoothed a cream over Darby's eyelids and filled in her eyebrows with some kind of stick. The wand of mascara was frightening, but Esme told her to look at the ceiling and then the floor while she covered her eyelashes in black goo.

She grabbed a wide comb next. "Not done yet." Darby tried not to wince as her hair was combed backward from the way she normally did it, then flipped to one side and combed back again. "Now look."

A mirror hung crookedly above the table holding the coffee. Darby stood up and stared. Her eyes, defined in black, appeared bigger than they actually were. Her hair puffed up a couple of inches above her scalp, a triumph over gravity. A plastic taste leached into her mouth from the lipstick.

"I look so different."

"You look pretty."

Darby wasn't so sure. "Mother would be horrified. I look like one of those girls."

Esme's grip on her shoulders tightened. She put her face next to Darby's and looked at her in the mirror with a quiet tenderness. "For ten minutes of your life, forget about your mother. You will be one of those girls, the ones who fool around and don't care and get into trouble. But it's all an act. I know you're a good girl. I'm a good girl. We do it for the audience, 'cause they got hunger for girls like that."

The pretense and bravado fell from Esme's face, replaced by a look of desperation. "You have to do this for me. One song, three verses, that's all I'm asking. No one will know. Please."

Underneath the rough voice and confidence, Esme was scared as well. Not scared of change, like Darby was, but scared of staying put, staying unchanged.

The place where Esme touched her bare skin tingled, the beginning of an illicit thrill that shimmied down her spine. Could she be a bad girl? Esme refused to define herself as a hotel maid. And maybe Darby didn't need to define herself as a boring secretary. At least not tonight.

"Okay. I'll try."

Esme squealed and hugged Darby close. "Go out there and get a seat at a table up front. I'll call you up when it's time. And act like you're having fun."

"I'm not swaying my hips."

"Okay, don't sway, just sing. Keep the mic a few inches away from your mouth, not too close, not too far, and look at me if you get scared."

Tanya moaned again.

"Should we do something for her?" Darby asked.

"She'll be fine. She got herself into this mess, and she'll have to get herself out. Buckley will make the busboys dump her in the gutter if she's still here at closing." She turned back to the mirror. "Off you go. I'll see you under the lights of stardom."

When Darby emerged from the green room, the club was three-quarters full. As directed, she took a table near the front. The stage was steps away, but she'd have to be careful getting up there so as not to fall or hike up her dress too high.

The undercover policeman whom she'd seen the first time walked by her table and gave her a nod, staring at her two beats longer than what was considered polite. In fact, several of the men at the nearby tables held her gaze, or tried to hold her gaze, before she looked away. A hot rush of shame traveled through her, from her forehead to her feet. Did they think she was a prostitute, sitting alone?

But so what if they did? They'd see soon enough that she was part of the show. She hummed the notes under her breath, imprinting them on her memory.

Finally, Esme's name was announced and she bounced up to the stage to stand in front of the center mic. Darby nodded along with the beat and clapped at the end of the first song, but her mind was racing, her heart pounding faster than it ever had. A dry stickiness spread over her tongue, a combination of the lipstick and fear.

"And now I'd like to call up Darby McLaughlin to join me." Esme's voice thundered across the room.

A sprinkling of claps covered the endless walk onto the stage. Darby positioned herself behind the backup singer's mic. Esme counted off and launched into "The Bluest Blues." At one point, she looked back at Darby and gave her an encouraging wave of her hand, which Darby knew meant that she should stop standing like a statue and move in time with the music. She bobbed her head, the best she could do under extreme circumstances.

She couldn't see a thing out in front of her with the bright lights shining down from the ceiling. It was as if a black fog hovered just beyond the foot of the stage, and she welcomed the darkness, the inability to see people staring back at her.

Esme swiveled her head around. Darby had missed her cue. She joined in, shocked by the loudness of her voice, then pulled back from the mic a couple of inches, remembering Esme's advice. The first chorus was over before she'd even had time to think.

She was prepared the second time, and matched Esme note for note. The bassist raised his eyebrows and gave her a solemn nod. By the third chorus, she had relaxed enough to let her shoulders dip from side to side in time with the beat. Esme finished with a flourish, holding the last note with no vibrato, a muscular sound that lifted the audience to its feet in appreciation.

"I want to thank everyone," Esme said over the clapping, then listed the band members one by one. "And especially Darby here, who stepped in at the last moment and saved the day for us. Let's give her a special round of applause."

Darby curtsied. As if she were a debutante at a ball. Then turned beet red at her mistake. They trailed off the stage, Esme accepting the accolades of the patrons as though she were Cleopatra on the Nile. At the back of the room, Sam stood next to the door to the kitchen, still in his apron, staring at her. He put his hands to his lips to let out a loud whistle, which soared above the clamor. Darby gave a little wave before a press of well-wishers trying to get to Esme blocked her view.

When they finally got into the green room, Esme turned around and gave Darby a huge hug. She smelled like cinnamon and fresh laundry, unlike any woman Darby had ever known. Then again, she was unlike any other woman she'd ever known.

"You did it, Darby. We did it."

Darby could only nod, unable to say out loud what she was feeling, a mixture of relief and giddiness.

From the couch, Tanya snored on.

CHAPTER ELEVEN

New York City, 2016

Twelve hours after the migraine struck, the pain finally passed. Rose had spent the entire night on the couch, raising her head for a sip of water only once, trying to breathe through the nausea in her gut and the pounding in her head. Now relief flooded through her body, and everything she usually took for granted, like sunlight and the sound of construction and traffic outside the windows, she welcomed with what could almost be called joy.

The apartment smelled yeasty and stale. She opened the windows and took a shower before heading out with the dog. Bird seemed as happy as she was to be outdoors, and didn't charge any of the other dogs they passed on the narrow pathways in Central Park.

Rose made sure to enter and exit through the building's service entrance, where the doormen were unlikely to engage her in conversation. When she turned down the hallway to Miss McLaughlin's apartment, a woman with a walker clomped her way, stopping to let out a phlegmy cough.

As Rose drew closer, the woman regarded her with suspicion, one bushy gray eyebrow raised. "Who are you?"

"I'm the dog sitter for Miss McLaughlin."

"Where'd she go?"

"I'm not sure. On vacation."

"Darby never goes on vacation."

"She'll be back in a couple of weeks. I'm Rose." She stuck out her hand and the woman gave her a limp handshake.

"Alice Wilcox."

Bird sniffed the legs of her walker.

"Have you lived here long?" asked Rose.

Alice laughed. "I came to the hotel in the sixties. Long enough."

"And do you know Miss McLaughlin well?"

"Nope. Keeps to herself. But I don't like that dog. Barks too much. 'Specially when she comes home after midnight."

"Does Miss McLaughlin often stay out late?" Seemed strange for an octogenarian.

"Sure does. She goes out in the evening, dressed all fancy, and returns home at one A.M., sometimes. Damn dog barks when she comes home and it wakes me up. I've talked to her, but she just nods in that weird way of hers. Not very neighborly."

"I'll try to keep the dog quiet for you."

As they chatted on, Alice eventually recognized Rose from the news and agreed to be interviewed for the WordMerge story.

Maybe this wouldn't be so difficult after all.

Rose thanked her and stuck the key in the lock of Miss Mc-Laughlin's front door. Instead of continuing on to the elevator, Alice turned around and clomped slowly back. "I'm doing my laps," she said by way of explanation.

Rose nodded and ducked inside.

As she made coffee, she heard voices in the hallway and stuck her ear to the door. The doors were cheap, not like the ones in the renovated apartments, and the conversation rang clear.

"Who are you?" Alice appeared to have resumed her guard duty.

A young woman's voice explained that she was Stella's grand-niece, Susan, and she was picking up some of her things. Stella would be staying with her and her husband in New Jersey while she recuperated.

Rose stepped out into the hallway and introduced herself. Susan wore dangly gold earrings, skinny jeans, and a friendly smile.

"Stella asked me to take care of a neighbor's dog while she was away," Rose explained. "How is she doing?"

"She'll be fine. She thought it was something to do with her nerves, but it was a heart condition. They caught it early, thank God, but she needs to take it easy. I'll be stopping by to get her mail and water her plants. Since I work in the city, it's easy enough."

"Tell her I said to get well soon, and that I'll take care of the dog in the meantime."

Rose retreated back into the apartment and leaned against the door. She shouldn't be in here; she was risking the story, her job. Miss McLaughlin might even call the police when she found out. But she hadn't stolen the key. Stella had given it to her, then an emergency had come up. And who else was going to take care of her damn dog?

The ceiling creaked above her. Griff must be home, with Connie. They were probably wandering through the apartment, figuring out where their divan would go, how quickly she could replace the king-size bed. Rose had been reduced to a memory. She wanted to throw her head back and scream at the ceiling, release all her pent-up anger at him for not knowing his mind better, for having fallen in and out of love so quickly. She should have been more wary of him, but he was a force of nature. It was part of what made him so good at his job. She'd been sucked in by his charm.

In any case, she was alone. She'd end up like Darby, living in a cave, no family left to worry about her or care for her. When sad-old-lady Rose, homeless and ancient, hobbled down the street, young women would look away quickly, worried that her fate would be theirs. She'd add a catalog of physical pains to her mental anguish until she petered out, unceremoniously.

Jesus, she sounded pathetic. She gave herself a good mental shake and resolved to think positive. It'd been a week since Griff had blown up their life, and who knew what the future held? She didn't do herself any good sulking around like a petulant teenager. Back in high school, when she'd flung herself facedown on the couch after getting a less than flattering haircut, her father had drily observed: "At least you have two arms and two legs."

And that was still true today. She was healthy and strong and it was time to buck up.

In the kitchen, Rose poured hot water into a mug. Darby had only instant coffee in her pantry, and no matter how many spoonfuls Rose put in, it tasted watery. She wandered over to the small bookshelf and studied the spines. Several historical romances, along with a couple of biographies. Old LPs by jazz greats like Charlie Parker, Dizzy Gillespie, Sarah Vaughan, and Thelonious Monk filled two entire shelves.

A silver-framed photograph on the highest shelf caught Rose's eye. She reached up and moved it into better light. It was a black-and-white studio portrait, the kind they did back in the fifties, of a young woman with glowing skin and lustrous hair. She was pretty enough, but her eyes were truly astonishing. Large and liquid, almost alive. Even though Rose knew it was silly, she shifted the frame from side to side to see if the girl's gaze would follow her, like an old portrait in a haunted house.

To Darby, with love was written on the right-hand corner in loopy cursive letters. Rose removed it from the frame and turned it over, but the back of the photograph contained no clue to the identity of the sitter, nor the year taken.

The photo had been placed upon a large tome that lay on its side on the top shelf, too big to fit upright. At first glance, it looked like an old photo album or scrapbook, with a black leather cover marred with scratches and scuffs, and a gold clasp on the side. She carried it with her coffee back to the couch and curled up with her legs underneath her. The clasp opened with a satisfying click; the pages inside were wafer thin, brittle with age.

The first page had *Sam Buckley, 1952* written on the top right-hand corner, as well as a hastily written inscription.

> *Darby, stay where you are. Once the coast is clear,*
> *I'll find you and we'll make our escape. Keep this as*
> *proof that I will come back for you. Love, Sam.*

Rose traced the writing with her finger, her pulse racing. She'd been right to trust her instincts. There was a compelling story here, no question.

Inside, the book was set up like a diary, with dates on the top right of each entry. But instead of words, drawings of various plants and seeds and strange Asian characters covered the pages, along with names Rose had never heard before: *annatto, noomi basra.* Like a chant from yoga class. The pages were worn at the edges and as fragile as ice shavings.

Every so often a familiar word caught her eye: *turmeric, fenugreek, chili.*

The book contained a list of exotic spices, with adjectives describing their essence. Halfway through, the writer had started to create blends of spices, along with descriptions that made her mouth water: *Crush rosemary, lavender, and fennel. Roll in goat cheese or sprinkle on lamb.*

Who was Sam Buckley and why did he keep such a meticulous record on the subject of spices? She went to her computer and googled the name, but it was too common, even if she narrowed the search field by including the word *spice*. The book was obviously a keepsake, as Darby had never cooked with it. No grease stains or spills marred the paper.

A pocket in the inside back cover held a number of loose papers. One was an ancient menu from a place called the Flatted Fifth. The entrées were banal. Bourbon for ninety cents, imported brandies for ninety-five cents. Cheeseburger, chili, fries. No lavender-rubbed goat cheese here.

Also inside was a small vinyl record, about six inches in diameter, with the words *Esme and Darby* scrawled across the paper sleeve.

The maid.

Rose opened the portable record player and put on the record. The turntable spun into motion and she stepped back and enjoyed the scratchy silence at the very beginning of the recording, like the quiet crackle of a fire. Giggles followed, and then a girl's voice rang out, soon matched by another, higher voice. The same song Rose had heard from her apartment, before Griff had shown up and blown her life to bits.

Even though the recording was rough, the girls' voices worked well together. The harmonies, now familiar to Rose's ear, were perfect and lilting. A moment of silence fell once the last note drifted off, followed by the bookend of giggles.

She played it again and went back to her laptop. Who was Esme, other than a maid who died under horrific circumstances, with no fanfare? She'd searched for the name online, with no luck. The past was a black hole.

The record was in beautiful condition, not a scratch on it. Rose returned it to its sleeve with the care of an archivist and tucked it back into the pocket of the book.

⌧

"And why should I care?"

Rose sighed. Tyler had been in a foul mood all day, and she'd tried her best to avoid him. This was not the time to ask for a raise, no matter how much she needed one. But he'd sought her out on his own, calling her into his office after lunch and lobbing question after question about the Barbizon story. She was certain they had an interesting story on their hands. He wasn't easily convinced.

"Because Darby McLaughlin is a link between the way women were treated in the 1950s and the way they are now."

"Meaning what?"

"Back then, they were supposed to get married, have kids, maybe work part-time if at all. Even the girls who came to New York City only did so to learn a skill until they found Mr. Right."

"Like most of the girls I know." He held a pen under his nose as if it were a mustache, curled up his lip to support it without any hands. "Just kidding."

Rose took two deep breaths to keep from losing her temper. "Darby's story is part of the fabric of the city, one we don't want to forget."

"What did she do with her life that makes her so unforgettable?"

There was no way to spin the answer to that question. "According to a neighbor, she worked as a secretary for the same company until she retired."

He tossed the pen down on the table. "So it's sad, pathetic. What's the draw?"

"It has the bones of a juicy airport novel. A good thriller." She leaned forward. "I want to find out what happened when the maid, Esme Castillo, slashed her. Why were they fighting? And what other intrigue went on behind those walls? I've uncovered evidence that Darby was trying to escape some kind of dangerous situation."

"Huh." Luckily, he didn't press for more details. "What about the video element?"

She'd hoped he'd forgotten that part. She never liked video, even when she was working for network news. Being in front of a camera changed people. When she carried only a notebook and pen, maybe a small recorder, her sources stayed relaxed and said things they might not when a camera was stuck in their face. Not to mention all the time it took setting up the lights and sound. By the time the camera was rolling, they tended to offer up careful, canned sentences.

"I haven't heard from the freelance video guy you mentioned yet. What was his name?" She stalled, glanced down at the notebook on her lap.

"Jason Wolf. Hold on. I think he's in the office today."

Tyler lumbered to the door and hollered. "Gina, is Jason in?"

A minute later a broad-shouldered man in his early forties strolled in. He shook Rose's hand, his bear of a paw enveloping hers, and settled on the sofa, one leg crossed over the other knee, arms wide along the back. His eyes were a brilliant, elegant blue, but the rest of him looked like an aging college rugby player.

He wore an old army jacket and sneakers, a combination that usually worked only on Brooklyn hipsters, and tossed her a satisfied smile. "Rose Lewin, from Channel 7, right?"

"Right."

"I remember your piece on the rats in the Hudson."

The story had gone viral soon after the network aired it, shots of rats scrambling along the crumbling piers, set to classical music. The producers thought the sound track would "elevate" the story. They were rodents, for God's sake.

"Not one of my most favorite clips." She grimaced. "One of the reasons I was glad to leave television."

"That and the controversy." Tyler, chiming in. "We were lucky to snag Rose right after she resigned. 'The woman who brought down Senator Madden.' Our investors love it."

Jason didn't say a word, just lifted one eyebrow.

Rose flipped through her notebook, eager to move on from the topic. "Shall I fill you in on the Barbizon story?"

"Please do." The words carried a trace of teasing. Other women probably found it charming, and there was an unmistakable air of masculinity to him that boys like Tyler wished they had.

She checked her notes and dove in. "The building was built in 1927 as a residence for professional women, with around seven hundred rooms. The whole idea was to create a private club-type building for women—only men's clubs existed before then—and this one included perks like a gym and a pool. And it wasn't like you could just show up and check in. Hotel guests had to supply three character references."

"Isn't this the place where Sylvia Plath went nuts?" asked Jason.

She took a deep breath. "Not exactly. In 1953, Sylvia Plath stayed at the Barbizon for a month while working as a guest editor for

Mademoiselle magazine. After she went home, she tried to commit suicide, and then wrote about her experience in *The Bell Jar*, referring to the Barbizon as the Amazon Hotel."

"That needs to be in there." Tyler's voice pitched up, a sign of excitement. "You can shoot B-roll of book covers, old photos, that kind of thing."

Jason jiggled his leg. "Fading out on a shot of her gravestone?"

"I don't think we need to focus so much on Sylvia Plath," interrupted Rose. "It's been said and done. Old news. We want to focus on the women who are living there now, who have seen it change from an exclusive women's hotel to a condo. How their perspective mirrors the changes in New York City, how it relates to women today."

"I like that." Jason looked up, surprised.

"Besides, there are many other famous, accomplished women who lived there as well. Liza Minnelli, Candice Bergen, Joan Crawford."

"Lots of good stuff here," said Tyler. "But what about the lady with the scar?"

"Huh?" Jason turned to her for clarification.

Rose spoke up. "One of the women who arrived at the hotel in the early fifties now lives on the fourth floor, in one of the rent-controlled apartments that house a dozen or so women like her. She was involved in some kind of skirmish way back when, and was cut on the face, while one of the maids fell to her death from a terrace."

"Now, that's interesting. Will she talk to you about it?"

"She's away at the moment, but I think I have an in."

Tyler piped up. "Rose lives in the Barbizon."

"Is there any kind of conflict of interest?" Jason asked.

"Not that I can see." She didn't mention that she was sleeping on Darby McLaughlin's couch, without the woman's knowledge. She'd find a rental soon enough and, hopefully, Darby would be so grateful that Rose stepped in to take care of Bird that she'd agree to be interviewed. At least that was the way it played in her head.

"I think you'll make a good team." Tyler stood, dismissing them. "Jason has been out in the field for a long time, working in war zones, so I'm guessing this chick-lit story will be a breeze for him, right, man?"

Tyler's attempt at male bonding was met with another raised eyebrow from Jason. "Yeah, right."

"Great. Let's try to wrap this up by the first week in July."

Three weeks away. It'd be close. She nodded and walked out of the room. Jason followed her to her cubicle and leaned against the partition, hands in his pockets.

"So what's next, Ms. Lewin?"

His overly formal tone annoyed her. As did Tyler's "chick-lit" comment. "I have to make some more inroads with the ladies on the fourth floor. I'll need a couple of days. In the meantime, I've found some information about Darby McLaughlin."

"Which one is she?"

"The one with the scar on her face."

"The one who's out of town, and you haven't lined up yet, even though Tyler thinks she's the focus of the story."

"Right." He was quick, obviously. She continued on. "You see, there's this book of spices."

"A what?"

"A scrapbook of descriptions of spices from 1952, with mementos and things like that tucked inside. I'm going to dig in a little deeper, see if I can find out some more background. Darby didn't create it. Someone named Sam Buckley did, but she saved it all these years."

"What makes you think this scrapbook is important?"

"There's an inscription inside that mentions waiting until the coast is clear and then they'll make a run for it, that kind of thing. My guess is it has something to do with her accident."

"How did you get it?"

"One of the neighbors had it." Another lie. "Do you want to see it?"

"Sure."

She'd wrapped it in plastic and placed it in her bag on her way out the door that morning, hoping to find the time to study it further. Jason leaned over her desk and leafed through the pages. He fingered the delicate material with a gentle touch. "It's beautiful."

The magic of the drawings and scribblings was undeniable. "Even better, smell it."

He leaned in and sniffed. "Powerful. Like walking into a Moroccan bazaar. Amazing, after all these years."

"And if you look in the back, there's an old menu to some jazz club. We could re-create that time period in the story, focus on 1952, what it was like to be a woman in New York City."

"You seem to be very caught up by this Darby woman."

"I am. She has this air of royalty about her, but not in a pampered way. More like she's a force to be reckoned with, like she makes her own weather."

"Superstorm Darby?"

She couldn't help but laugh. "Sure. Kind of like that." She needed Jason on her side, if only to back up her ideas with Tyler.

"How many ladies are left?"

"Ten. One's in the hospital, but I know she'll be happy to be interviewed when she's out. Another has already given me the green light. Give me a day and I'll see if I can line up some more. It's going to be slow going, as they're all pretty reclusive."

"Okay. You call the shots."

Rose nodded and put away the book.

If only she did.

CHAPTER TWELVE

New York City, 1952

Stella stood just inside Darby's room, biting her lip.

Darby had assumed the knock at her door was Esme, hoping to get some time away from Mrs. Eustis and chat, and was surprised to see Stella. For a few seconds, neither girl spoke. Then Stella heaved a deep sigh and placed her hand just inside the doorframe.

"Darby, I know you're angry with me," she said. "I should probably let things lie, but I can't stop thinking about what happened with Walter in the park. I feel so awful. I want to make it up to you."

Darby didn't want to be reminded of that evening. "If you're worried I'll tell Mrs. Eustis that you were sneaking boys into the hotel, I assure you I won't."

"No, of course I know you wouldn't do that." Stella gave a dismissive wave of her manicured hand. "I was just hoping you'd come with me to the afternoon tea and fashion show. Please."

Saturday's list of events included a showing of coats and hats in the solarium. Anyone with a bit of sense would know that fashion shows weren't for girls like Darby. But she had no desire to speak such humiliating words to Stella.

"I have too much work to do," she said instead. That much was true, anyway.

Stella lowered her voice. "I don't want you to think I'm like the other Ford girls. I only hang around with them because the agency likes us to be seen together." She paused and offered Darby a wicked smile. "Plus, they attract all the best boys. But today you can meet my dear friend Charlotte. I think you two'll get along swimmingly."

"Why do you think that?"

"You remind me of her. She's in publishing, smart as a whip, speaks her mind. And though she comes from an upper-crust family in Boston, she isn't at all a snob. She's on the twelfth floor, with some other career girls."

Career girls in publishing. The words enticed.

Stella jumped on her hesitation. "You'll enjoy it, I promise. And if you don't, you can leave anytime."

True. It wasn't like she'd be trapped in the dark with a groper. She nodded.

Up on the eighteenth floor, the day was sunny and clear, rendering stunning views across the city through the solarium's glass walls. The length of the space had been made into a kind of runway, with wrought iron chairs placed along the walls, while a trio played classical music at the back. Stella waved at a striking-looking girl who had saved a couple of seats. There was only time for quick introductions before Mrs. Eustis stepped up onto the raised platform at the top of the runway.

"Thank you, girls, for coming to our fall fashion show at the Barbizon Hotel for Women. Today you'll get a sense of the styles for the upcoming season and have a chance to add to your wardrobes without even leaving the residence. How exciting is that?"

"God forbid we venture into the real world and buy something inappropriate," Charlotte murmured into Darby's ear.

Mrs. Eustis continued on. "As guests of the hotel, we encourage you to take full advantage of everything New York City has to offer. Fun and fashion are at your fingertips daily."

"Excellent use of alliteration." Charlotte again.

"As long as we don't get fingered by the fun," added Stella.

Darby almost choked as she turned a gasp of laughter into a cough and drew Mrs. Eustis's disapproving look.

"I hope you'll enjoy the show, and if there are any items you find particularly compelling, you may put them on your account. And now, let us begin."

The back doors opened and a dozen or so lithe women drifted down the aisle to the platform, where they each performed a slow turn. A cream felt cloche covered in matching cutout flowers garnered nods of approval, while a wide-brimmed scarlet hat, perched on the top of a model's head like a flying saucer, drew polite applause. The show finished with a bang: a heavy black coat made of a fabric covered in tight black curls—the announcer called it poodle cloth—topped by a small-brimmed hat with a black ribbon that stiffened into a peak at the front, like a sculpture of bird wings extending to the sky.

After, as they were herded to the lounge for tea, Darby examined Charlotte and Stella more closely. Stella wore a daffodil-yellow afternoon dress that softened her figure, while Charlotte's knit one-piece hugged her angular frame, with its sharp shoulders and long torso. To be perfectly honest, Charlotte was far from attractive, with small dark eyes and a crooked nose, but her lips were luscious and carefully drawn in with oxblood-red lipstick. A severe pageboy hairstyle framed her rather chipmunklike cheeks.

Darby had never seen anyone quite like Charlotte before. In Darby's world, girls were either plain or pretty. Charlotte was in a category all her own.

In the center of the lounge, delicious-looking hats in different styles and colors had been arranged on a long table, like cakes in a bakery. The models floated around the room, stopping briefly to allow residents to caress the fabric of their sleeves.

"Come on, let's each choose a new chapeau." Charlotte barged over to the table, and Stella and Darby followed. "I like this one." She lifted up a shantung straw sailor hat.

"You won't be able to use that in the winter very often," said Stella.

"We'll be heading down to Palm Beach again for Christmas, and it will do nicely, thank you very much." She leaned down and signed the chit. "Now you."

Darby pointed to a simple pillbox with a mesh veil. "Maybe that one?"

Stella shook her head. "No, you're far too pretty to hide your face. How about this?"

The hat, a sleek black velvet beret, stood out from the others for its dark elegance. Charlotte picked it up and angled it on Darby's head. "Ideal. *That in black ink my love may still shine bright.*"

Darby smiled. "Sonnet 65."

Charlotte stepped back, looking pleased. "You are a surprise, my dear. Where did Stella say you're from? Iowa?"

"Ohio."

"Right. Well done. This hat is yours."

"And I'm putting it on my account." Stella grabbed the chit before Darby could take it. "Consider it a gift of friendship."

"Oh, I couldn't."

But her protests were ignored. Stella chose a navy bonnet with a poppy snood, and while the hats were being wrapped in tissue paper and placed in boxes, the trio retreated to a window seat.

"Stella said you're in publishing." Darby carefully took a teacup and saucer offered by one of the maids.

"Yes. I'll be a top editor one day, just you wait." She winked one of her beady eyes. "I'm planning to discover the next Carson McCullers."

"Are there many jobs for women where you work? Other than as secretaries, I mean."

"My dear, there are more and more women choosing what books we read every day. I work for Samantha Plowright, who was at *The New Yorker* when Shirley Jackson got discovered."

"Really? I just loved 'The Lottery,'" Darby said. "Is it true Jackson received hate mail after it was published?"

"She did, mountains of it. Signs of a literary triumph, if you ask me."

Stella made a face. "I knew you girls were well suited. Books and quotes. I'm exhausted."

"Yes, it's too bad I'm off to London next week." Charlotte took a sip of her tea, her lips staining the rim of the china. "Otherwise I'd invite you over to the offices to meet Mrs. Plowright. She'd love your quiet charm."

Quiet charm. That's what she had. Darby knew she was grinning like an idiot, but she couldn't help it. "You're going to London?"

"Yes. Mrs. Plowright insisted I accompany her for a couple of months. So many fascinating authors coming from Europe these days. But when I'm back, we'll have lunch and talk books."

"I'd love that." Darby took a deep breath, scared to ask. "How does one become an assistant editor?"

Charlotte laughed. "Mrs. Plowright is an old family friend. It's all who you know. At the moment, my job consists of making Mrs. Plowright tea and shuffling papers about, but she lets me read every manuscript that comes across her desk and offer up my thoughts. It's a hoot."

"Maybe once my course is done at Gibbs, I'll apply for a secretarial position at your firm."

"You? In the secretary pool? Don't be silly. As I said, it's all who you know, and now you know me. Aim high."

More girls gathered around, chattering and laughing, Charlotte always the center of attention. Darby studied her closely, the way she held herself, the way the side of her lip curled up when she was about to laugh.

But she'd ignored her homework for too long, and once her hat was packed, she said her good-byes and received three cheek kisses from Charlotte—right, left, right—and a quick squeeze of the arm from Stella, who offered to walk her to the elevator.

"You forgive me for that evening, don't you? For what that nasty boy did? Your poor dress." Stella sounded truly contrite.

"I do. Thank you for introducing me to Charlotte."

"Isn't she a gem? You never know who you're going to meet here. Now that you're living in the greatest city in the world, anything is possible."

Of course that was Stella's perspective. With her beauty and steady work, she had an independence Darby envied. "If you're a model, maybe."

Stella swung to a stop. "It's not easy for any of us girls, no matter what we look like or where we're from. That's why you absolutely must take advantage of your time here, where you can observe the big bad world from the safety of the Barbizon, and plan your attack accordingly. It's up to you to pick and choose who you want around you." She paused. "It's too bad Charlotte's off to England, but I'll make sure we all go out for lunch together the moment she's back. It's the least I can do."

"I look forward to that very much."

"In the meantime, remember what I said about picking and choosing carefully." Her lips pursed. "The maid you like, for example."

"Esme?"

"Yes. Promise me you'll be careful."

Darby blanched. "Because she's a maid? She's much more than that; you'd see that if you knew her."

The elevator arrived and Stella touched her cheek gently before turning back to the gaggle of girls.

Esme was on duty. She yanked open the gate and gave Darby a sharp look before letting her in. Darby said a cheery hello and stood at the back, tucking the hatbox behind her.

"You were with the giraffes?" Esme pulled the lever, and the elevator descended, slower than normal.

"Only Stella. She invited me to the fashion show. She said she's sorry for what happened that night."

"I bet." Esme chewed on the inside of her mouth and stared forward. "I'm surprised you want to spend time with her, after what she did to you."

"It wasn't really Stella's fault."

"So she says."

"Esme. What's wrong?"

The elevator came to an abrupt stop between floors. Darby placed one palm on the wall to steady herself.

"I'll tell you what's wrong. The girls make fun of you and treat you like a *monstrua*, a freak, and then you're off drinking tea with them? Doesn't make sense."

Darby's heart began to pound. "These were mostly career girls."

"Career girls. Huh."

"I don't understand why you're angry with me."

"Don't you?" Esme hissed. "Maureen, Stella, Candy. They're all the same. Living here makes girls mean. They start thinking they're better than everyone else. Don't let that happen to you, too."

"Of course not." To her relief, the elevator began moving once again, but something still unsettled her. "Was it you in the hallway when I visited Maureen? I could have sworn I saw you there."

Esme looked away. "You were making such a racket, laughing and enjoying yourselves. I would've stopped to say hello, but I had to get back to work."

Esme felt left out, and Darby didn't blame her. Here she was trapped in a metal box for hours, wearing a drab maid's uniform, while Darby could come and go as she pleased and had a brand-new hat. No wonder she was upset.

They finally reached the fifteenth floor, but Darby didn't walk away, unwilling to leave Esme when she was so obviously distressed. "Thank you for worrying about me. I promise I won't turn mean. And let me know when we can go to the Flatted Fifth together again."

"Yeah." Esme's mouth stayed in a tight line, but her eyes gave away her pleasure.

Darby nodded and stepped off the elevator. She gave a little wave and watched as Esme's face, framed by the glass oval in the door, disappeared from view.

CHAPTER THIRTEEN

New York City, 2016

Six out of ten interviews booked.

"Not bad for a hard day's work." Rose smiled down at Bird, who gave her the evil eye.

She refilled his water bowl and he slurped it down messily, then slunk off to his usual place on the couch.

The minute she'd woken up that morning, Rose had showered and dressed, and snapped Bird's leash onto his collar. But instead of heading outside, she'd sat on the sofa, waiting for the elevator's bright ring or the slamming of a neighbor's door, and then sprinted with Bird to the front door.

She and Bird would pop into the hallway and cheerily greet whichever neighbor was making her way out. When the neighbor inquired about who she was, she stopped and chatted, mentioning that she was helping out Stella with Darby's dog while she was away. Luckily, Stella had made many more friends than Darby over the years, and the neighbors responded with sympathetic clucks and expressions of gratitude. Most had recognized her from the news and, after she mentioned that she was doing a story on the elegant lives of the Barbizon ladies, four had immediately agreed to do a sit-down interview within the next two weeks. In one case, the woman had gone on at length about Sylvia Plath, whom she'd seen once in the lobby, before Rose could impress upon her the idea that she was interested in her own story. Blushing, she'd readily agreed.

After each chat, she'd taken Bird around the block and back into the apartment, where she'd lain in wait for her next victim. She'd also reached out to Stella, who'd sounded annoyed at being stuck in New Jersey but relieved to hear that Bird was doing fine, and had agreed to be interviewed next week. Including Alice, that made six interviews lined up. Poor Bird was exhausted, and she'd given him a long ear-scratch for his troubles.

Her phone rang. Jason.

"I'm in the neighborhood; why don't you show me around the building?" He didn't even bother saying hello.

Rose's mind raced. He would have to see the building at some point, particularly if they were going to get the women on camera in their apartments. And she'd have to get permission from the management company to film B-roll in the public spaces. Video sucked. If she were writing a piece for *The New Yorker*, she wouldn't have this problem. Ten thousand words, maybe a few photographs. But at WordMerge, even if it aspired to be a site for narrative writing, images and video were required. No one could be bothered to use their imagination anymore.

Since it was Saturday, Griff and Connie were probably up at the house in Litchfield, so she would be less likely to run into them. "Okay, but we can't film today."

"Fine. Just show me the place so I can figure out what we'll need."

She arranged to meet him at the service entrance. He wore the same army jacket and jeans, looking like a war correspondent on his day off. Which, of course, he was.

"So this is the place, huh?" He looked up and squinted in the bright sunlight.

"Yup. Follow me."

"Whatever you say, boss."

She brought him inside, past the porter who worked the door on weekends.

"How's Mr. Bird's stomach?" he asked. He was a young kid, new to the doorman's union and eager to please.

"What?"

"You've been in and out all morning. Figured he'd eaten something that wasn't agreeing with him."

"Right. Little guy's got the runs, but he's doing much better now, thanks."

She entered the stairwell.

Jason's heavy steps trudged behind her. "Three questions."

"Shoot."

"Is Mr. Bird a bird, do birds get the runs, and why are we going up the back way?"

She reached the second-floor entrance. "Mr. Bird is a dog I'm dog sitting, I don't know the answer to question number two, and we're going up the back way because it's a more direct route to where I want to take you."

She led him down the hallway and pushed open the door to what the real estate agent had called the lounge, a public space that ran the length of the building.

Jason gave out a low whistle. The room remained a showpiece of the art deco era. Cream ceilings and walls contrasted with the polished mahogany floor, and love seats and sofas had been arranged in tableaux over geometric-patterned rugs. A black baby grand piano gleamed in the center of the room. Hardly any of the residents used the lounge, as far as Rose could tell. It had an air of sterile elegance, the walls dotted with black-and-white photos of some of its more famous residents.

"This is one of the public rooms, back then and still today." She hugged her arms to her chest. She would have sworn the air still held the weak scent of perfume and cigarettes.

He took out his phone and shot some rough video, as well as several photos. "We should do the interviews in here. How many do you have lined up so far?"

"Seven." She included Darby in her count, even though she probably ought not to assume.

"Nicely done."

"Thanks. But keep in mind, this is a print story first and foremost."

"Print is dead. Or seriously ill, at any rate. Your story is going online, with video elements."

"I didn't mean print like paper." She hated how flustered he made her. "I meant that the words come first, then the visuals."

"What do you have against video?"

"Nothing. I just prefer long-form writing. Where the writer tells the story, visually, using words. I think we rely on images far too often these days. No one can be bothered to learn about any subject in depth, because it's all about the images. There's no intricacy."

He rubbed the back of his hand over his mouth, as if he were suppressing a smile. "But what about images of events that rile people up, make them want to improve the world or change things? What about Hurricane Katrina, or Abu Ghraib? Do you think readers would have reacted the same way without the photos, the video?"

"Those images summed up the story in a way that caused outrage, no question. But what about when you're dealing with a subject that has multiple layers?"

"Give me an example."

"Watergate. What one photo could explain the ramifications of political corruption in the White House?"

"I'm sure I could think of something."

She'd backed him into a corner, but there was no reason to make enemies today. He'd be frustrated soon enough, once he realized how flimsy her hold was on Darby. "Anyway, thanks. I figured I was the only one working on a Saturday."

"Just let me know what I can do to help."

The offer was unexpected, and for some reason, her eyes burned with a rush of emotion. She shrugged her bag up on her shoulder and looked around. "I think we're good here. There's not much else to show."

"Where did the maid fall from?"

"It was called the sky terrace in all the old articles on the building, but now it's part of someone's apartment. I'll work on that as well."

"In that case, let's take a quick look around the lobby, then I'll buy you a coffee so we can brainstorm some ideas." He paused. "If you have time, of course."

Griff had to be in Connecticut. She made a silent prayer as they took the stairs down to the lobby. "You've seen the black-and-white photos of the lobby from when it was first built, right?"

"I have. Lots of palm fronds, if I remember correctly."

"They went in a different direction when they renovated. Not a frond in sight."

She breathed a sigh of relief that Patrick wasn't on duty. He didn't typically work weekends, and he was the only doorman who would ask about Connie's takeover.

Jason stood in the center of the lobby's marble floor and looked around. "I kinda miss all the original details, that grand balcony, for instance."

"Yes, they basically stripped the place of all its character when they went condo, in my opinion. Not much to shoot."

"Could be a great before and after. Once you've gotten permission, of course."

"Of course."

A loud voice reverberated across the room. "We'll want to make it a rush. Priorities are the bed and the dining room table. And the credenza. You agree?"

In a small alcove off the lobby, two women sat side by side on a sofa, staring down at some cut sheets laid out on the glass coffee table. The woman facing away from Rose and Jason had a single streak of gray that began, Rose knew, at the middle of her forehead and ran the length of her thick brown hair. Once, Griff had proudly recounted how he'd forbidden Connie to dye the streak when it first appeared in her twenties. He'd sounded so proud of the fact that she didn't look like all the other wives. A toxic combination of jealousy and panic threatened Rose's fragile composure.

She turned around and pointed to the revolving door. "We should go."

He followed her in silence until they got out onto the street. "Problems with your neighbors?"

"Exactly. One of the more difficult residents."

She led him to a coffee shop on Lexington, her heart still pounding from the near miss.

They chose a booth near the back and ordered coffee. Jason tapped the edge of the table with his index finger. "So how did you get into journalism?"

"In high school I worked on the paper. Then I majored in journalism in college. I loved collecting facts and then making a story out of them. The perfect combo of science and art. How about you?"

"I thought the outfits were cool. You know, those flak jackets with all the pockets."

She couldn't help but laugh.

"I'm only half kidding."

"I'm not surprised. So let's talk about the structure for the story." She fished for her notebook in the bottom of her bag. "I figure the text will start with the history of the place, then mention the denizens of the fourth floor."

"*Denizen;* fancy word."

"Resident, then."

"No, I like denizen."

Why was he toying with her? She couldn't get a good read on this guy. "I'll mention Darby McLaughlin's story in the opening, but then jump to each woman's story, in the order of when they first arrived. We'll cover the changes over time through their voices. At the end, I'll circle back to Darby and reveal what happened to her. We'll include extras like on-camera interviews, shots of the place past and present, that kind of thing."

"Very nice. Won't get you the Pulitzer, though."

"What's wrong with it?"

"There's no injustice, no quest. It's a boring feature."

"I prefer to let the story reveal itself, rather than try to define the narrative immediately. It's all about asking the right questions." She pushed her coffee to the side. "For now, I'm interested in learning more about these women's lives, what they wanted when they first came to the Barbizon, and whether they got it."

"They obviously didn't get it. You're talking about a bunch of cat women who never moved, never had families. Otherwise they wouldn't still be there."

She sat back and crossed her arms. "Do not call them cat women. Okay?"

"Fine. What should I call them?"

"This kind of thing drives me crazy." Her words came out short and sharp. "Did you know there are dozens of terrible names for old women? Crone, cat lady, hag, battle-ax. But there's no male equivalent. Instead, old men are the roosters of their retirement homes, flirting with the scores of women left behind, considered valuable commodities."

"So that's how you think of older guys? Like inanimate objects to be traded around when the girls get bored? How un-feminist."

She was in no mood to be teased. "What about the fact that women have been no more than possessions for centuries? No man, no safety. No man, no honor. No man, you die. Thank God I live in a time and place where women don't need husbands in order to survive."

She should have stopped talking, stayed professional, but she couldn't help herself. "Did you know the Barbizon used to be called the Dollhouse? Can you get more objectifying than that? As if these women were simply playacting until the magical powers of marriage turned them into living, breathing people. I want to humanize them, include photos of when they were young, descriptions of what their lives were like. Just because they don't look fresh-faced anymore doesn't mean they aren't the same people inside, that they've lost their worth as human beings. You can simply call them by their names."

"Okay, okay. You made a good point. Several, in fact." He leaned forward on his elbows. *"An old woman rises toward her day after day, like a terrible fish."*

She was surprised. "So you read Sylvia Plath's poems. Don't call them terrible fish, either." She paused. "Have you read *The Bell Jar?*"

"Finished it yesterday. Look, I get what you're trying to do. I do. But we need more of a story."

"I'll get it, I promise." She wanted to get him off the subject, wrap this meeting up. "Tyler said you did war documentaries, is that right?"

He leaned back and ran his hand over his head. His torso was broad, but not overweight, and his hands were solid.

The corners of his mouth turned up. He'd caught her staring at him. "Yes, I did some work with the children in Iraq once a reasonable peace had been achieved. We brought together Kurdish and Arab kids, divided them into mixed groups, and had them create their own documentaries about their lives. Then we did a documentary about their documentaries."

"Pretty amazing."

"It was good." His stare unnerved her.

"I'm sure it was. Why did you stop the international work?"

He rubbed his face with one hand. "My mother got sick. I had to move back to New Paltz to help her out until she passed."

"I'm sorry. My dad's sick. That can be really devastating."

"Sure can."

They sat in silence for a moment.

"Do you want to go back to what you were doing?" she asked.

"Eventually. Not right now. I'm picking up work here and there, freelancing for now."

"Well, this shouldn't be too tough. Interviews, B-roll, and we're done."

"Speaking of going back to what you were doing, why was Gloria Buckstone reinstated at the network but you had to leave? You were both proved right in the end after all. Madden was as crooked as a three-dollar bill."

She hadn't been right.

Rose fiddled with the spoon on the table, stalling for time. When a source had sent her bank statements that supposedly showed Senator Madden was skimming money earmarked for state nursing homes, she'd known it was a huge get. With the senator's unstoppable popularity, the story had explosive potential, the power to take Rose's career to the next level. Except something about the documents themselves felt off to Rose. She'd begged her superiors to wait until she had further proof of Madden's crimes before taking the news to air. At the time, Gloria Buckstone was Rose's friend and mentor, and unfortunately, she was also her boss and desperate to have a big exclusive.

In the end, Rose's protests fell on deaf ears. When it turned out the bank statements were, in fact, doctored, the whole thing became a massive PR disaster for the news desk. Luckily, the loss of face lasted all of a week before a different whistle-blower came forward with irrefutable evidence of the senator's wrongdoings. Now all anyone remembered was that Gloria and Rose had broken the story first.

Everyone thought she was a renegade, fighting to get the truth out. But if it were up to her, they'd never have run the incorrect version in the first place.

"I left because I missed writing too much," she said. Always a handy excuse. Made her sound intellectual. The waitress tossed the check on the table and Rose snatched it up, relieved by the interruption. "Allow me."

Outside in the sunshine, Rose considered her next steps. First off was to find the button store Stella had mentioned, and see if she could get some more color on Darby's life.

Jason shrugged his backpack over one shoulder and stood, legs spread wide. He looked like an urban lumberjack. "How is it working for Tyler?"

She considered the question. Best to be ambiguous. "Interesting."

"He's the nephew of one of the guys I worked with in Iraq. Comes from a lot of money."

"So he says. Money buys power."

"That's true. Stupid name, WordMerge."

Rose nodded. "It's impossible to pronounce without laughing. My boyfriend said it's . . ."

She stopped.

"What does he say?"

"Nothing, it was silly. I don't want to be bad mouthing the boss, not cool."

"I'm a freelancer; what do I care? I shoot the video, cash the check, and move on."

"Must be nice."

"You should try it."

"Can't afford it."

"Do you miss network news?" His eyes searched her face, as if he were trying to suss her out. "I always wondered if there was more to the story than came out."

"Nope, that's it."

He swung the backpack to the other shoulder. "Ah. Anyway. You didn't deserve what happened."

"Thanks, I appreciate that."

"And Tyler is lucky to have you."

Ever since the debacle, she'd hated running into people in the business, knowing they'd gossip about their encounter within ten minutes. "I'm doing what I like now. Writing, I mean. Happy to leave the shooting to experts like yourself. It's what I should have done all along." Even to her own ears, her tone was brusque and dismissive.

"Right. Got it." He turned to go. "I'll see you on Monday."

He strode away, head held high. Here she'd been complaining about the lack of collaboration at WordMerge but couldn't have a normal conversation with the first person who seemed to know what he was doing. In any event, what did it matter? She'd probably never work with Jason again; he'd be off to Iraq or Iran or somewhere, shooting footage that put her features to shame.

No, that was the wrong way of thinking.

She'd do whatever it took to make this story work.

❦

Samson Button Shop on West Thirty-Eighth Street sported a black-and-white checkerboard floor, and walls covered with every style and color of button imaginable. The overall effect was slightly psychedelic, and only by focusing on one section at a time could the details be fully appreciated: big black plastic buttons, rose-shaped ones made from silk, others that glowed with a metallic sheen.

Determined to find Darby's former place of business, Rose had googled "button stores" on Thirty-Eighth Street and been surprised at how many were still in existence. The garment district, once a bustling rectangle of New York streets, where pedestrians fought for sidewalk space with workers pushing clothing racks from factory to showroom, was now a burgeoning home for trendy high-rise hotels and tech start-ups, but a dozen or so stalwarts held on. Rose had made her way west from Fifth Avenue while scanning the storefronts, popping into all those that sold buttons.

"May I help you?"

A thin man with a large belly strode over. He wore jeans and an untucked shirt with disappointing white plastic buttons down the front.

"I was wondering if a Miss Darby McLaughlin used to work here."

"Of course. Is she all right?"

"Yes, she's fine. She's an old friend of my mother's." If she didn't lie, she'd never be able to get any information from this man without him wanting to talk to Darby first. And there was no time for that. If anything, the debacle with Gloria Buckstone had toughened her up. Or twisted her ethics. Depended on how you looked at it. "We've only just found each other on Facebook. Luckily, too, as she needed some help with Bird."

He smiled. "Ah, Bird; she brought him by a few years ago."

"She's not as mobile as she used to be, and she asked me to come by and say hello since I was in the neighborhood."

The man laughed. "Excellent. Tell her that Stanley Junior is in charge, and all is well."

"I will. How long did she work here? Seems like a long time."

"Well, she started in the fifties. Kept showing up, day after day, year after year, until she retired five years ago. "

"Did she sell buttons?"

"No. Never wanted to be in the front of the store. She did our books, kept records, acted as a secretary for my father. Sweet lady."

"Very sweet." Rose ran her hand through an open box of ebony-colored buttons. They clattered like pebbles. "Very private, though. She never takes off her veil."

"Always kept her face covered here at work, too, at least above her nose. I knew she'd been in some kind of accident, but since I grew up with her, I never questioned it. Or if I did, my father shut me up soon enough."

"Right. Well, she'll be happy to know that you're still going strong."

"I don't know about that. We sell most of our stock online these days. I'm looking into the possibility of getting out of the bricks-and-mortar part of the business."

She looked around the room. "Do everything online? That would be a shame."

"Another piece of New York City gone with the wind."

Stalling for time, Rose selected six coffee-colored buttons that looked like round chocolates, good enough to eat.

"Good choice." Stanley Jr. brought them to the register and wrapped them in tissue paper. "These will liven up a fall or winter jacket. Very stylish."

As he rang up the purchase, Rose pressed on. "What kind of person was Darby when she was younger? I only ask because she's such a grande dame now. Curious how she was in her youth."

"She was careful, wry. Ate a tuna sandwich for lunch every day, year in and year out. She didn't mind if I played near her desk. In fact, I think she liked it. She had a great sense of humor, loved to play practical jokes."

"Jokes? Really?"

"Sure." He shrugged, thoughtful. "She may have kept to herself because of what happened to her, but she's no stick-in-the-mud.

Darby is a tough cookie. She has class, style. Swagger, almost. An elegant mystery, my father liked to say."

Rose placed the buttons in her bag. "Does Darby have any family or anyone close to her? My mother is hoping she's well taken care of these days but doesn't want to be rude and ask her outright."

"Not really. She complained about her neighbors quite a bit, said they were way too nosy for her taste."

No surprise there.

"But her young friend seemed like someone who would look out for her."

Rose stopped in her tracks. "What friend?"

"Young girl, in her teens. Stopped in a few times. Lovely girl."

"Do you remember her name?"

"Allie, Abby, something like that."

"Her last name?"

He shook his head. "I'm sure Darby mentioned it when she first introduced me, but I don't remember."

"And she never said who she was, how she knew her?"

"Gosh, no. Darby was pretty tight-lipped about everything. The girl made her happy and seemed nice enough, so I didn't push."

"Right. Well, thanks for your help. And the buttons."

"Sure thing. Tell Miss McLaughlin I said hello when you see her."

"Will do."

CHAPTER FOURTEEN

New York City, 1952

Darby watched as Esme readied the hatcheck room, which was really an old closet with a Dutch door, for the evening rush at the Flatted Fifth. When Esme had encouraged Darby to come down to the club earlier that day, she'd quickly agreed. She'd put on the dress Daddy always liked, a black-and-white polka-dotted cotton with a pleated full skirt, and pinned the new black beret on her head so it tilted dramatically to one side.

"Tell me, Esme, what's acting school like?" she asked.

Esme thrust out her chin. "I'm learning to talk right. Check it out: 'If you like peanuts, you'll like Skippy.'"

She sounded like a movie star, with no noticeable trace of an accent. "That's amazing. They teach you television ads?"

Before she could reply, two men walked in the front door and stood in front of the hatcheck. Neither removed his coat.

Esme stiffened. "Club's not open yet."

"We're not here for the club. We're here for you." The taller man spoke with a growl. "You need to work harder, Esme."

"Not sure what you're talking about. I can only check as many coats and hats as come in."

"You know exactly what we're talking about. Come along and let's have a little talk in the back."

Darby opened her mouth to call for help, but Esme put her fingers to her lips. "Shush. I won't be long. All part of the job. Gotta keep the goons happy."

They walked off into the club, and Darby wrapped her arms around herself. She was debating what, if anything, to do, when the front door slammed shut behind her.

"Where's your friend?" Mr. Buckley stepped into the foyer and shook the raindrops off his hat.

Darby whirled around and stared up at him, dumbstruck. His height, authority, and demeanor reminded her of her stepfather. "You mean Esme?"

"You look like a fish. Close your mouth."

She did.

"So where is she?"

"She stepped away, just for a moment."

"She's fired if she doesn't get back here when we open in ten minutes. It's pouring out there, and I can't have everyone sitting in their wet coats during the show."

If Esme lost her job, she wouldn't be able to pay for her acting classes. "I'll do it. I'll cover until she gets back."

Twenty minutes later, Darby was near tears. The men and women coming into the club had piled their coats on the small divider without waiting for tickets. A couple even tossed their umbrellas at her as she frantically tried to keep up with the onslaught. The air smelled of wet wool and underarms, her skirt clung to her legs, and her hair was plastered to her skull. Even worse, she'd had to shove the beret into her purse after it'd fallen onto the muddy floor. She'd never be able to sort this mess out, and every coat looked exactly like the others. Mr. Buckley would fire Esme and never let her sing again. And what if Esme was in terrible trouble right now? Who were those men?

"You look like you just took a bath."

Sam appeared, holding a coffee cup in his hand. He leaned back on the opposite wall and took a sip.

"Esme was taken away." Darby could hardly get the words out. "Two men. I'm not sure where they went."

Sam seemed unperturbed. "Don't worry; that Esme can take care of herself."

"But they seemed awfully angry."

"All bark and no bite. Everyone's a tough guy downtown."

His laconic manner put her slightly more at ease. "And someone just threw an umbrella at me. Threw it." She grabbed a hanger and stuffed a coat onto it. "They're a bunch of animals."

"If it makes you feel any better, they don't treat the waitstaff much differently. Or the musicians, if they see them in the street. Up on-stage is one thing, but the magic is gone in the light of day."

"I don't know how Esme handles this night after night. I'd go crazy."

"You sounded great the other night, by the way."

"Thank you."

"Seriously. Esme's voice is like velvet, but yours is silvery, like a nightingale." He scuffed one foot on the floor.

As she paused to catch her breath, the enormous pile of coats slid off the divider and landed in a mad crush on the mud-stained hall-way floor. She and Sam stared in dismay at the mound of fabric, then burst out laughing.

He placed his cup on a nearby table, and reached down and lifted the pile in one fell swoop. "Open the door."

She did and stepped to the side. He handed her a coat and she hung it on a hanger, placed it on the rack, and shoved them together to make more room. They kept at it, over and over. The motion reminded her of the slam of a typewriter carriage return at the end of a line.

"Why aren't you in the kitchen?" she asked.

"They're fine in there, they don't need me."

"But you're the cook."

"They're just making simple stuff—peas, fries, and chicken liver sauté. Nothing they can't handle."

Every so often, their fingers would touch during the handoff of the hangers, and he was close enough that she could pick up the scent of fryer oil and clove on him. An interesting mix, and not unpleasant.

To her embarrassment, he noticed her sniffing the air. "I hope I don't reek."

"No. You smell like clove. Reminds me of the holidays."

He smelled his forearm. "I've been working on a new recipe. Steak with a mixture of clove, turmeric, and honey."

Her mouth watered. She hadn't eaten anything since a Danish from the Barbizon coffee shop that morning. "Sounds lovely."

"We'll see."

"Will you put it on the menu?"

His laugh was harsh. "Not if my father has anything to do with it. He doesn't want anything that tastes 'weird,' in his words."

"So you found out about combining spices in the army?" She liked hearing him talk. And it was much easier to have a conversation when they were both focused on the coats.

"Right, in Southeast Asia, working as a cook. I had to use what I found."

"And what did you find?"

"So much. There are ten tiny islands clustered in the Banda Sea that used to be the only source for nutmeg and mace. And the oldest clove tree in the world is located on an island called Ternate in the Molucca Sea."

"How old is it?"

"They estimate between three hundred and fifty and four hundred years old. It even has a name. Afo."

"Afo." Such an exotic word. "What did it look like?"

"It's tall but lifeless, with some bare branches. I saw it when we took over the island from the Japanese at the end of the war."

"I can't imagine what that must have been like for you." To go to islands at the other end of the world, to visit dead trees and learn about history that went back so far in time, was unfathomable.

He shrugged. "In the beginning, lots of guys were complaining about the food. The rations were pretty horrible. But then I began experimenting with what the local folks used. I started adding spices to everything we served: eggs, fish, meat. Even desserts. Some of the guys hated it, of course, but they were idiots. Everyone else raved. They gave it a chance. Although, to be honest, the soldiers didn't have much of a choice. Unlike my father."

His rush of words surprised and flattered her. He thought she was someone worth talking to. She hung up a coat and surreptitiously smoothed her hair behind her ears. "Has he tasted any of your experiments?"

"No."

"Well, I'd like to."

Esme appeared, looking flushed but unhurt. "Sorry, D." She startled when she noticed Sam. "What on earth are you doing in the hatcheck girl's closet?"

"Helping out your friend, here, who was helping you keep your job."

Esme's eyes grew wide. "You are the most wonderful *amiga* in the world, Darby."

"Well, we didn't do a very good job. I have no idea what coat goes with what person. And what was with those two men? Are you okay?"

"I'm fine." Her voice was steely. She didn't want to talk in front of Sam.

He took the hint. "I'm heading to the kitchen. Darby, come back and visit me when you're through. I have something to show you." He sauntered off, hands in his pockets.

Darby pulled Esme close and lowered her voice. "What was that? Who were they?"

"Just some guys who think they can tell me what to do."

"What did they mean, you have to work harder?"

"Stupid stuff. They have a deal with all the businesses in the neighborhood. They offer protection, and in exchange the owners let them skim off the top. Which means they're always pushing me to do certain things, you know, for the customers. To bring up the tips."

"Mr. Buckley makes you do that?"

"The girl before me did, so everyone thinks I should, too. But they don't know who they're dealing with. I'm not a cockroach they can step on." Esme reached into her handbag and pulled out a switchblade with a silver handle. "See, I can take care of myself."

"A knife? You need a knife? Why don't you tell Sam what they did? Maybe he can help. Reason with his father somehow?"

Esme gave out a bitter laugh. "You got a lot to learn, girl. A lot to learn." She shooed Darby out of the tiny room and fitted herself inside. "Go see your man. Maybe he'll give you a taste of something sweet."

The steamy front entrance to the club was nothing compared to the junglelike humidity of the kitchen, where the line cooks banged pots against the stove and yelled at each other over the steady drone of the ventilation system. Sam led her to the grill, where a chunk of marbled meat sat on a plate. Burgers sizzled over the fire, and he used a spatula to rearrange them and make room before placing the steak in the center.

The flames flared up. "Here, smell this." He held a small white dish to her nose, filled with yellowish powder. The color reminded her of the maple tree outside her window at home, after the peak of autumn had past, a burnished mustard. The smell was bright and savory, a mixture of toast and turmeric.

"You see, I rub the steak with it and let the meat rise to room temperature." His eagerness was that of a young boy. She wished he'd had a father who would take him under his wing and tell him he was doing well, the way Daddy had done when she'd disappointed Mother yet again.

Once the steak had cooked to his liking, Sam let it sit for several minutes and turned his attention to what the rest of the kitchen was doing. He had an air of authority about him, speaking to a waiter in clipped tones to correct an order, before turning to a busboy to help him lift a tub of dishes into the sink.

He returned to her side and poked the steak with his finger. "Not quite yet. Esme said you go to secretarial school, is that right?"

She didn't want to be reminded of her uptown life. "I do. It's awful."

"Why?"

"I'm a terrible secretary. Or I'll make a terrible secretary. I wish I could do something creative, like this."

"What would you do?"

Charlotte's offer still tantalized, but there was no guarantee she'd remember making it, or even meeting Darby, when she returned. "I really don't know. Is it ready yet?"

He cut into the steak, its juices running red onto the wooden cutting board. "Try this."

The texture of the beef mingled with the spices and sent her mind racing, the same way the jazz music had done that first night. Flavor flooded her palate, first savory, then a strange flowery bitterness, before the spices amalgamated into a final burst of clove.

"Astonishing." She wanted another bite and another.

He fed them to her, laughing at her voraciousness.

"Sam, I've never tasted anything like this. It reminds me of what it's like in the fall back home. I don't know how to explain it."

"Do you want it explained?"

"I do."

"Then follow me." He took off his apron and grabbed her hand. She took it, eager to see where he was going to lead her but reluctant to leave the juicy steak behind.

◦≪∞≫◦

Sam walked quickly, darting through the crowded streets and pulling Darby along after him. Below Houston, the streets ran in every direction, and she had no idea where she was. The rain had stopped, so she wasn't wet, but she felt naked without a coat. Sam didn't seem to care, just forged through the crowd.

She didn't even have her purse, having left it with Esme. Sam turned around to check on her, puzzled at her distress.

"Where are we going?" She tugged at the Peter Pan collar of her dress.

"I can't tell you; it'll be a surprise. But if you liked the steak, you'll love this."

Maybe he was taking her to dinner at a restaurant that served curries and other exotic foods. She hoped she'd be able to eat what was served, that it wouldn't be spiced innards or something too gooey.

He stopped at a nondescript building where laundry hung limply from the fire escapes. The sign on the door was written in unfamiliar characters, the number 12 the only symbol she could recognize. Even stranger, the window was blacked out.

They stepped inside and she was assaulted by the scent of a thousand spices. Almost every surface was covered with wares. Barrels were heaped with dried red chilies, their skins shiny and bright. Open boxes of colorful powders and strange seeds lined the floor, and the shelves on the walls held jars filled with dried plants and stems. Years of foot traffic had grooved the narrow aisles. Sam shouted a loud hello. From the back, a voice called out in response. She couldn't identify the accent, but the sound was deep, with the reverberations of a double bass.

At first she wanted to run back out into the damp evening air and sneeze a dozen times, but eventually her nostrils adjusted to the olfactory mayhem.

"Where are we?"

"The Kalai Spice Emporium."

"Wow. It's a little overwhelming."

"At first, sure. But with the right teacher, it all begins to make sense. This store is my own personal Katie Gibbs."

A loud argument broke out in the back room, and Darby looked at Sam for reassurance. He smiled down at her. "It's nothing. It's the way Mr. Kalai communicates. You'll see."

A young man shot out the door of the back room and walked quickly out to the street.

"Good riddance."

The voice came from nowhere, startling her. She turned to see a bespectacled man in a black dress shirt and pants standing in the inner doorway, staring intently at her. The angularity of his square forehead offset his round cheeks and bulbous nose, and his brown skin was shiny with sweat. He took out a handkerchief and wiped his brow. "Who's this?"

"Mr. Kalai, this is my friend Darby McLaughlin. From the club."

Sam had remembered her surname. "Mr. Kalai, it's a pleasure to meet you." She offered up her bare hand, embarrassed at her lack of gloves, but he didn't seem to mind.

"You want more spice?" he asked Sam.

"No. I tried the Banda mix tonight. Worked well."

"Good, good."

"Mr. Kalai learned the art of spices through generations of his family. He's descended from the sultan of Ternate."

"The island with the tree?"

Mr. Kalai's smile wasn't warm. "The one with the tree."

"I want to show her what a nutmeg looks like," said Sam. "Do you mind?"

Mr. Kalai shook his head. Sam opened one of the jars and scooped out an egg-shaped piece of fruit. Mr. Kalai handed him a knife and he cut the fruit cleanly in half before giving it a twist. Inside was a brown seed covered with thin red veins. "The nut, when dried, makes nutmeg, and the red stuff becomes mace. It's the only tropical fruit that makes two different spices."

She touched the delicate webbing around the seed. "I had no idea."

Mr. Kalai took the fruit out of Sam's hand. "When the spices were first discovered by the other countries, ships bearing all kinds of gifts arrived at my island. The sultan had a crown made from hundreds of jewels, big as your fist, and four hundred women in his harem."

Darby blushed, relieved when Sam spoke up.

"Then the Dutch took over and killed every man over the age of fifteen."

"When did this happen?"

"Almost three hundred years ago."

"But here you are carrying on the tradition."

Mr. Kalai nodded. "Sam's a good boy. Take a look around, but then I'm closing up. I have business outside."

Sam reached up to one of the top shelves and brought down a thick book. "I'm working on a compilation of everything I'm learning here. Take a look."

He rearranged some of the jars on the countertop to make room. The pages were crisp and she leaned down close. "It smells like the shop."

"Everything in here smells like the shop, including us by now."

She leafed through the pages while Sam explained. "I'm keeping track of each spice, where it came from and its history." He pointed to a drawing. "Like here, the Egyptians used cassia for embalming the dead."

She wrinkled her nose. "Yet it has such a pretty name."

"It's delicious, a type of cinnamon, and good if you have stomach problems as well."

"I'm impressed. What are you going to do with your book?"

"I'd like to open a restaurant eventually. I'm meeting the right people through Mr. Kalai, working on a way to get myself out of the Flatted Fifth."

He closed the book and placed it up on the shelf with care. When he turned around quickly, she stepped back, aware that she'd been standing too close.

"Thank you for coming down here with me," he said.

"I'm impressed. And hungry."

"I'll make you something back at the club. In the meantime, taste this." He scooped a dark powder out of one of the jars and poured a tiny amount into the palm of his hand. He dipped one finger in and held it up. "Open your mouth and stick out your tongue."

"Should I close my eyes as well?"

He laughed. "Sure, if you want."

The gentle touch of his finger on her tongue was enough to make her knees wobble, but then a robust bittersweet sensation overwhelmed her taste buds.

"Great, right? It's Mayan cocoa."

"Sure is." She opened her eyes. On the wall behind him hung a small cracked mirror. Normally, she avoided mirrors, and she wasn't expecting to see herself. In her reflection, her cheeks burned bright red against her cauliflower-colored skin, and her hair stuck up at all angles, except for one section that was plastered across her forehead like a toupee.

Mother was right; she was an ugly girl.

What was she doing? She stepped away from him. "We should go back to the club."

"Of course. Hopefully, the kitchen isn't on fire by now."

They walked out into the night air, where a cool breeze had replaced the heavy, humid air with a touch of crispness. The few times he tried to start a conversation, she murmured one-word replies, hoping he wouldn't look at her.

"Is something wrong?" he asked as they neared the club. He swallowed twice.

"No. Nothing. Just tired, I guess."

"I hope I wasn't too forward, taking you to the emporium. I thought you might like it, is all."

He thought he'd done something wrong. When all along she was the one feeling stupid. She rushed to set him right. "I loved it. I really did. And meeting Mr. Kalai." She lowered her voice. "It's funny, when I lived in Ohio, I would read about extraordinary, eccentric characters in books and plays, but I couldn't imagine them in real life. Then I came to New York."

"Where everyone acts like they're the main character of their own book."

She laughed. "Between you and Esme, I'm seeing a whole side of the city I didn't even know existed."

"You seem like a nice girl." He held the door open for her. "Funny to see you with Esme."

"Why do you say that?"

He shrugged and looked inside the club. She could tell he was itching to get back to his kitchen. "She's a handful, that's all."

First Stella, now Sam. "I'm not sure what you mean. She helped me a lot when I first got here, tried to make me feel at home. You saw how she got me onstage. I'm not normally like that."

"Oh, Esme pretty much always gets what she wants. She's too in love with herself to take no for an answer. You, on the other hand, are sweet. Innocent. That's all I'm saying."

Darby pressed her lips together and nodded. Sam was trying to tell her something, in the nicest way possible. Esme was special and Darby was not. And while he might enjoy Darby's friendship, it would never be more.

CHAPTER FIFTEEN

New York City, 2016

Rose almost didn't pick up her cell phone when she saw Maddy's name. She'd gotten to work early and spent the quiet hour, before anyone else arrived, finishing up a book on the history of the Katharine Gibbs School, written by a former teacher. To think that the venerable Mrs. Gibbs began educating women for positions in business, where they were less than welcome, before women even had the right to vote. Fierce.

"Where have you been hiding?" Maddy's voice was mocking but held an undertone of worry. Rose had left her a message after the migraine broke to tell her that she'd be dog-sitting for a neighbor for a few days, but they'd played phone tag ever since.

"Sorry, I've been swamped at work."

"You doing okay? And any news from Griff?"

"Nothing from Griff. I assume he's too busy reconstructing his nuclear family."

Maddy guffawed. "God, he's such an asshole. I told you not to date guys with old-man names. 'Griffin Van Doren.' Jesus."

In spite of herself, Rose laughed. "I remember. Who could have predicted that just this once you'd be right?"

"Ha-ha, very funny. So when are you coming by? And which neighbor are you dog-sitting for, anyway? I thought everyone in the building was unfriendly."

That was true. After she and Griff moved in, she'd expected a couple of the neighbors to stop in and say hello. But none did, and even if she ran into one or two waiting for the elevator, they weren't very enthusiastic. "It's one of the older ladies who's lived there forever, since it was a women's hotel. I'm doing a piece on her and the other women for work."

"Do you really want to stay in a stranger's apartment? It'd be fine to bring the dog with you. The kids would love it."

"I'm not sure how much the dog would love the children, to tell you the truth. He's a feisty old guy." As she spoke, the decision to stay in Darby's apartment, at least for the short term, solidified. It provided privacy, access to the women, and peace and quiet. She'd be out before Darby came back and no one would be the wiser. "Don't worry, his owner returns in two weeks, at which point I'll be moaning with self-pity on your couch."

"Something to look forward to. So how's your dad?"

Rose pressed her knuckles into her forehead. A couple of the other reporters had arrived and she lowered her voice. "He was moved yesterday. I stopped by; he seems like he's adapting."

Indeed, her father hadn't made a fuss. His eyes had been blank, his jaw working back and forth with nervous energy. The dementia ward had lavender-colored walls and locked doors. A large black carpet had been placed in front of the elevator. One of the nurses explained that most patients in the ward were reluctant to step on it, thinking it was a dark hole, and that kept them from trying to escape.

How awful, to have a pit placed between you and freedom, or the world as you remembered it. She was sure her father remembered snippets of their old life. Before she'd left, he'd asked if she'd done her homework and called her Rosie, as he used to when she was a teenager. Then he'd burst into tears, mucus running down his nose and chin. No matter what she'd said, he wouldn't be calmed, until the nurse kindly suggested she leave.

Maddy let out a sympathetic sigh. "You're really getting spanked, aren't you? What can I do to help?"

"I wish I knew."

"Do you think Griff would've gone back to his wife anyway, even if Miranda was okay?"

"Maybe." Connie was a powerhouse of energy, well matched to Griff's temperament. Together they could run a small country. "I don't know what to think anymore. How's the soap business?"

"Trashy. The other day, I had to do a postcoital scene with Robert Hanes-Sterling. He tried to play footsie under the sheet, until I scraped his shin with my toenails. I think I made him bleed."

"That's truly disgusting."

"And that's why they pay me the big bucks. Tell me more about the story you're working on."

"There's a group of elderly ladies who live in rent-controlled apartments, who've been there for years and years. One goes back as far as 1952."

Maddy whistled. "The Sylvia Plath era."

Plath again. "Sylvia Plath was only there for a month. These other women are the heart and soul of the place. They've seen the Barbizon change drastically, and seen New York City change drastically, too. Their stories should matter to us."

"I like the way this has you all worked up. Surprised it got approved, though."

"Barely squeaked by, and only because Tyler wants to sensation-alize it. One of the ladies has a pretty tragic history. That's why I'm dog-sitting for her, to find out more."

"Is that kosher? I mean, in terms of journalistic integrity and all that?"

She preferred not to answer the question. "Coming from someone who gouges the legs of her coworkers."

"Right. I think he went to get a tetanus shot once we wrapped."

"As well he should."

"Are you sure this isn't some weird kind of masochism, staying at the Barbizon when Griff and Connie are there together?" Typical Maddy, like a dog with a bone. "Why put yourself through that kind of torture?"

"It's only temporary."

"So you're not using it as an excuse to stick around, hoping he'll want you to come back to him?"

She hated to admit it to herself, and she sure wasn't going to ad-mit it to Maddy. "Of course not. This is a combo of helping out a neighbor and getting some work done." Time to change the subject. "It's all going to be fine, especially if I can find a way to deal with the video producer I'm working with."

"Why's that?"

"He's a tough guy, shot documentaries in the Middle East, that kind of thing. Probably feels this job is beneath him."

"Then tell him to go back to Afghanistan or wherever."

"His mother fell ill and passed away, so I guess he's biding his time for now. I understand that concept."

"Is he cute?"

Rose rolled her eyes. "Please. He's not my type. I feel like Snow White with her dwarf Smirky."

Maddy laughed. "Well, hang in there. And we're ready for you anytime. There's a bottle of Pinot in the fridge with your name on it."

The sound of throat clearing made her look up. Jason stood on the other side of her cubicle, one arm draped over the partition.

From the expression on his face, he had heard every word.

⚮

Rose studied Jason's face, trying to figure out her next move. One side of his mouth curled upward and he looked amused, entertained even. But when their eyes met, he blinked once, and she knew he was covering his dismay, putting up a front.

She hadn't meant to hurt him; she'd been joking with Maddy, trying to get her off her back about the Griff ordeal. But her joke was nasty.

"You hungry?" Jason asked. "Because I have an apple back at my desk."

She leaned forward in her chair, hands gripping the edge of the seat. "I'm sorry, that was awful. It's my friend Maddy. I didn't mean . . ." She trailed off, hoping he'd say something to stop her from groveling. But he just stood there.

"Just checking in to see if you need me today. I finished another piece early and have the rest of the morning free."

She had to find a way to make this up to him, to smooth things over. Especially if they were going to work together for the next few weeks. "I was going to head downtown, check out the location of that old jazz club, the one with the menu tucked into the book of spices."

"The Flatted Fifth?"

"Yes, exactly. It shut down in the seventies. But I wanted to see the building it was in. You could film it and we could use before and after footage." The idea was lame, but she hoped he'd say yes.

"Not very dynamic."

"No. But it's all I have for now. Will you come?"

He nodded. "I'll get my equipment and meet you in the lobby."

They took a taxi down. The cabbie drove like mad, braking suddenly and accelerating aggressively, which didn't allow for much conversation. Rose gripped the hand strap above the window to avoid careening into Jason, all while filling him in on her visit to the button shop.

"This young girl might be Darby's only real friend, from what I can tell. I'd love to find her."

Jason raised his eyebrows. "Well, we know her name begins with an *A*. Shouldn't be too hard."

The taxi pulled up to a stop at a five-story building on Second Avenue. The gray stone facade was filthy, as if it had been rubbed with a giant piece of charcoal, and graffiti marred the front door. At ground level stood a French bistro.

She pointed to the restaurant, which had a CLOSED sign in the window. "That's where the club used to be."

Jason shot some exteriors, then knocked on the glass door.

A young woman appeared, looking harried and tired. "We're not open until five tonight."

Rose explained who they were, adding that they were researching the location of an old jazz club from the fifties. The minute she said WordMerge, the woman's face lit up. "Of course, I love WordMerge. If you want, come on in and look around. The shell of the place is the same, but everything else has been renovated."

The brick walls had been recently whitewashed and big windows looked out onto the street, making the space seem larger than it actually was. Jason pulled up a black-and-white photo on his phone, showing the interior of the club during a show. Men in suits and ties and women with coifed hairdos were tightly packed into the space, practically on top of one another, while a sax player stood at the edge of a low stage. Without the windows and white-washing, the space had been dark and seedy.

"It looks like the stage was here, and the entrance around here." Jason pointed out the locations. "I can take some interiors if you want."

"Sure, why not." Rose turned to the woman. "Do you know if anyone in the building has lived here a long time? They'd have to be pretty old by now, in their eighties." It was a stretch.

"There's Mr. B. He comes in for a steak frites every Wednesday, before it gets too crowded. Nice guy, talks about the old days. He's the one you want to talk to."

"Do you happen to have his contact info?"

"No, but he lives in apartment 5D. If you buzz him and tell him that Nicole said he should talk to you, he might let you up. Or you can come back on Wednesday and catch him here."

The name on the buzzer for 5D said BUCKLEY.

Jackpot. Maybe Sam had been living a ten-minute taxi ride from Darby the past fifty years. A rush of adrenaline surged through her.

Rose hit the buzzer and waited. Nothing. "He's got to be an old guy; we'll give him time."

"You're the boss."

She turned to him. "Look, I'm really sorry about what I said before. I don't think I'm Snow White, I assure you of that. And you're not . . ."

Again, she couldn't finish the sentence.

He did. "A dwarf?"

"No. Of course not."

"Most dwarfs would take offense at the comment, by the way. They like to be called little people."

"It was just an expression." Sweat prickled her neck. She really didn't want to have this conversation. "I didn't mean it."

"Whatever you say."

God, he was frustrating, always with that stupid smile. "But you do smirk." She couldn't help herself. "You're smirking now."

"No, I'm not. I'm smiling. You're getting all bent out of shape and I'm enjoying it immensely."

"That's the definition of smirking."

He laughed. "Point taken. Am I smirking now?"

She couldn't help grinning. "Yes! You are."

"Hello?"

The voice was crackly, although it was hard to tell if it was from the intercom or the person speaking.

Rose leaned in. "Mr. Buckley? Nicole downstairs suggested we try to reach you. We're doing research on a news story about the Flatted Fifth and she said you might be able to help. My name is Rose Lewin and I'm with my colleague, Jason Wolf. Would you be interested in coming down and talking for a moment? We'd be happy to take you out to coffee nearby."

"I can't come down there. You come up here."

Rose looked at Jason and he nodded. "Let's go."

The stuccoed hallway smelled of rotting vegetables, and the once colorful tile floors were edged with brown grout. When Mr. Buckley finally opened the door to his apartment, Rose was shocked at the contrast from the building's public spaces. Sunlight streamed through the windows and the place was inviting and well kept.

"Come on in. You're reporters, you say?" Mr. Buckley walked

with a cane. He'd once been a tall man, but now his spine curved painfully forward. He had a gray beard and wore thick-framed glasses that overpowered the sharp angles of his face. He looked them both up and down before leading them to the sitting room.

"We are; we appreciate your time. We're interested in finding out more about the people who frequented the Flatted Fifth in the early 1950s." Rose sat on a scarlet couch dotted with garish saffron-colored pillows. Jason sat beside her and took out his camera.

"Do you mind if I record the interview?" he asked.

Mr. Buckley eased himself into a rail-back armchair upholstered in a nubby green fabric and nodded. "Fine with me."

Jason nudged Rose and she followed his gaze. The entire wall of a hallway was filled with shelves of vinyl records, thousands of them.

"Can I take a look?" Jason asked Mr. Buckley.

"Go right ahead. My collection. Pretty much everything you need to know about the bebop era of jazz. The library at Lincoln Center asked me to leave my collection to them when I go. Nice to think of all those Juilliard kids getting a taste of what real music is like."

"Are you Mr. Sam Buckley?" Rose couldn't help herself.

"Sam?" His face clouded over. "No. I'm Malcolm."

Rose silently kicked herself. If she pushed him too hard, she might very well scare him, as she'd done with Darby.

"This is your album." Jason held a cover with black graphics over a photo of a drum kit.

Mr. Buckley grinned. "That it is. I toured and played with the best of them. Until I got hooked on the hard stuff. Not an easy life, when you're always on the road. Easy to turn to whatever makes you feel good."

Rose took out her notebook. "Heroin?"

"You got it. Went down the same path as Monk and Parker. I

didn't die, so I'm not famous. Could've been, though. Later, I found steady work as an arranger."

"Maybe it's better to be unknown and alive than famous and dead?" she said.

"Not so sure of that." He looked down at the thick, arthritic joints on his hands. "It's tough getting old when everyone else is gone. What's your report about?"

"It's an article, with some video as well. It's basically about the Barbizon Hotel for Women and what it was like to be in New York City in the fifties and sixties."

"How did you hear about the club?"

"One of the women who lives at the Barbizon has a menu from the Flatted Fifth. I understand the club was once owned by a Mr. Cornelius Buckley. I assume you're related?"

"Cornelius was my dad. My older brother, Sam, was the cook."

Rose tried to stifle her excitement. "Sam Buckley. Right. We found a book he compiled, of various spices and recipes. Dated from 1952."

"Not surprising. He learned about that from his time in the war, all those fancy spices and things. My dad always put him down, didn't want a cook for a son; he wanted a musician. My asthma kept me from being drafted, which meant I could focus on the drums. For a time I was the golden child. Until I washed out."

"Can I put this record on?" asked Jason.

"Sure thing."

She shot Jason a look, annoyed he'd changed the subject, but his back was turned to her as he fiddled with the stereo. The drums came loud and fast, the beat hard.

Malcolm's face lit up. "You picked a good one. Dizzy and Charlie Parker at Birdland in 1951. Classic bebop."

Rose listened carefully. From the look on his face, music was the key to getting Malcolm to open up. Jason had already figured that out.

"What makes it bebop?" she asked.

Malcolm laughed. "Bebop was all about speed and virtuosity. Back then, everyone was used to swing, right?" He waved his arms in the air. "Dancing around, all that. The greats, like Thelonious Monk, Dizzy, Max Roach, they started exploring a different take on the music. Listen here."

The trumpet solo screeched up into the higher register, and although it always found its way back to the chord, at times the sound seemed strident, off-key.

Rose said so out loud and Malcolm nodded. "Yup. Not what you expect. It's aggressive."

Jason spoke up. "Bebop made what sounded like the wrong notes the right notes."

"You've got it, kid. That's it exactly."

Score one for Jason. Maybe he wasn't so annoying after all.

Rose could hardly wait for the song to finish to ask her next question, but she did, so that the noise wouldn't interfere with the taping. "Is Sam still alive?"

"Don't know. Haven't heard from him in years." He didn't look at her while he spoke. "Where did you get his spice book?"

"From a Miss Darby McLaughlin. Is that name familiar?"

He blinked a couple of times before answering. "Nope. But why don't you just ask her how she knew my brother?"

"She's incapacitated at the moment."

"Huh."

"The notebook is a work of art, full of information and drawings. Sam wrote in the front that he gave it to her for safekeeping, as proof of his love. The message implies they were in danger. I'm curious to know more."

"Can't help you there. I was touring most of the time; didn't make it back much until Sam had taken off."

"Do you know why he took off?"

"My dad said he ran into trouble and had to leave town fast. Last I heard, he was out in California." He pulled at his earlobe. "Anyway, he's a private guy."

The use of present tense was interesting. How did he know, if he hadn't seen him in years? "Do you know anyone named Esme Castillo?"

He squinted his eyes as if he were conjuring up a vision. "Esme. She was the hatcheck girl at the club before I went on tour. Good voice. Pretty, too."

Esme was the missing link between Darby and Sam. She worked in the hotel and at the Flatted Fifth. "Do you know what happened to her?"

"Who, Darby?"

"No. Esme."

"Right. They say she fell off a building and died. But I don't know much else."

They continued talking for another twenty minutes, as Malcolm told story after story about his life as a jazz musician at that time. But whenever Rose tried to get him to tell her more about Sam, he clammed up.

Malcolm knew more than he was saying. He was protecting his brother for some reason. She was sure of that.

Outside, she let Jason carry on for a while about Malcolm's extensive music knowledge. "He's like a walking encyclopedia about bebop and hard bop and that entire era."

"He really is. But I wish we'd found out more about Sam. Was it just me, or did you get the impression he knows where Sam is?"

"Definitely. He wouldn't look at you when he answered. We'll have to circle back to him, gently nudge him into opening up to us."

"Hopefully, by our deadline. Thanks for diverting him when he was about to clam up."

"Hey, I'm just the guy behind the camera. You were great with him, by the way, once I saved your ass."

A jolt of pleasure ran through her at his praise, along with a spark of guilt for what she'd said about him earlier. "That means something, coming from someone who's covered wars. Thank you."

"It's just the truth, Rose. You should think so, too."

CHAPTER SIXTEEN

New York City, 1952

Darby vowed to avoid the Flatted Fifth after the strange spice expedition with Sam. She still cringed with embarrassment each time she remembered the sight of her disheveled face in that mirror. Before she'd gotten a glimpse of herself, she'd imagined they were a pair in one of the romantic movies that played in Times Square, dashing around town breathlessly together. But instead of Natalie Wood, she'd looked like a drowned rat.

In an effort to wipe her memory clean, she threw herself into her classes at Katie Gibbs, making sure to show up on time and well rested. Once, she forgot her gloves on the way there, but she ran into Maureen outside the building, who gave her one of hers. They walked past the monitor, each clutching a folder with one gloved hand, the bare one buried deep in a coat pocket, and sailed through. Even if Darby had gotten off to a rocky start, she still had months left to prove to her teachers that she would make an excellent secretary. And she would.

She'd also successfully steered clear of Esme for nearly a week. But this morning, her friend was back on elevator duty and she'd talked Darby into meeting for lunch at Hector's Cafeteria on Fiftieth

Street. The restaurant was packed when she walked in, and Esme waved at her from the back of the buffet line.

"You made it." Esme handed her a tray and they shuffled along the stainless steel counter, which ran almost the entire length of the restaurant. Esme took a bowl of pea soup and a grilled cheese sandwich and Darby did the same.

The line ground to a halt while the servers refreshed the desserts.

"Where have you been?" Esme cocked her head at Darby. "Sam was asking about you."

"I've been too busy with school. Mother wants me to stay focused."

"Come on. You gotta whoop it up once in a while; otherwise you'll end up miserable, working for a boss who makes passes at you but won't leave his wife, and spending every Christmas and Valentine's Day alone. Is that what you want?"

Darby had to smile. "No. I don't want that. But I do have to support myself and this is the only way that's viable. You should be at the club; you're an entertainer. That's what you want to do with your life. For me it's too distracting."

"Why, because Sam is after you?"

Her heart jumped every time Esme mentioned his name. She remembered the way he'd looked at her after she'd bitten into the steak, the way his finger tasted on her tongue.

"Sam's not after me. He's excited about his cooking, that's all. He was happy to have someone to share it with since his father doesn't approve."

Esme looked about the room, holding up the line even further. Darby nudged her forward. They picked up two éclairs for dessert and paid, then made their way to a table in a corner. Esme took the chair facing the restaurant. "A friend of mine might be stopping by. I have to keep an eye out for him."

Darby accidentally bumped into the table next to them, earning dirty looks from the older ladies seated there. "What friend?"

"Someone from acting class." Esme put her napkin on her lap and dug into the soup. "Delish, right?"

"Very."

"Listen up, I have a way for both of us to make some extra money. You interested?"

Perhaps she meant the extra "customer service" jobs they'd discussed at the Flatted Fifth, ones that promised greater tips.

Esme laughed. "Don't worry, I know what you're thinking and I'm not talking about that. Next Thursday night, Annie Ross is playing and they need two backup singers. People liked it when we sang together, and Mr. Buckley says we've got the gig if we want it. We each get twenty dollars. What do you say?"

"I couldn't. I'd be too scared."

"What's there to be scared of? We'll rehearse together. I'll be standing right next to you for the gig, and then we go home richer. You've got to do it."

"What about Tanya?"

"Disappeared. She was just a junkie anyway."

"But I have to focus on my schoolwork."

"You'll have all weekend to do your schoolwork. This is my stepping-stone to fame and fortune. Without you, it'll be a disaster. We work so well together, everyone noticed."

"You can find someone who's much better, I'm sure."

"It's not about that. It's about the way we sound together." Confusion wrinkled Esme's forehead, her bright red mouth set in a pout. "You really don't want to?"

Darby didn't know how to make her understand. "You're destined for something big, I know that. But I'm not. Why pretend? I'll only embarrass myself."

"You need to change the way you look at things. Why settle for your mother's sad little picture of you? Who cares what she thinks?"

Esme's words rankled. "You don't know my mother, or what we've been through."

"I know that she wants to turn you into a bore. When you should be enjoying life, enjoying being a beautiful girl in Manhattan."

"First of all, I'm not beautiful. Second, it's better to be a bore who can support herself than to throw everything away on a whim. Mother had to marry Mr. Saunders to survive. Her only skills are gossiping and playing tennis. She had nothing to fall back on. What will you do if everything collapses underneath you?"

Esme's eyes were fierce. "I'm scrambling to make a living, so I know what it is to work hard and take care of myself. If I don't become a star, I guess I'll be a maid at the Barbizon the rest of my life."

"No!"

"You got that right."

Darby blushed with shame. She had no right to assume anything about her friend. Coming to New York City from Puerto Rico was completely different from her posh train trip East. "You've got a point. You work hard. What have I done? Graduated from high school. That's it. You're glamorous and you can sing and act. You can probably tap-dance, too, am I right?"

Esme wasn't so easily placated. "Why do you hide from everything that life is throwing at you right now? You can make some easy money, and instead you want to stay uptown and practice typing. You have until June, and then my guess is you're going to run back to your mother and work as a secretary at the local high school or something like that."

She didn't want to mention Charlotte's offer after the fashion show. Esme would get upset, and by the time Charlotte returned from London, she'd probably have forgotten all about their exchange anyway. "Mother wrote and said she'll be able to get me a job in Cleveland, working for some businessman Mr. Saunders knows. It's in the sanitation industry, apparently."

Esme threw back her head and laughed, causing the old ladies sitting nearby to tut-tut at them. She pretended to be typing. "Dear ma'am, I'm sorry our toilets have been backing up on you. I assure you that your sewage is our foremost concern."

"It's a steady job." Darby scooped some custard out of her éclair with her finger. Esme's teasing hurt. "Or maybe I'll go into publishing."

Esme grimaced. "Don't be stupid. Either way, you're stuck behind a desk all day. There's my friend. I'll be right back."

Esme crossed the room, sashaying with every step, and sat down across from an older man, maybe in his thirties, with tightly cropped hair and a rumpled brown suit. He spoke hurriedly, barely moving his mouth. Esme reached into her purse and handed a small parcel to him, which he glanced at before tucking into his jacket pocket.

She was back at the table a couple of minutes later.

"Who was that?"

"Guy from my acting class. Wants to do a scene with me, but I'm not so sure."

"Why did he come all the way here to meet?"

"He wanted the notes from our scene study class. He missed it last week."

"What kind of notes?"

Esme picked up her éclair and took a big bite, the custard oozing out the other end.

"That's indecent," Darby said, giggling.

"Anyway, his name is Peter and he's too old to be going to acting school. Kind of creepy, didn't you think?"

"I guess so. Is there an age limit on acting class?"

"Nope. Especially with the soldiers; we got lots of those."

"Is Peter a soldier?"

"No idea. You have a lot of questions. Now it's my turn. What about Sam?"

"What about him?"

"He likes you. He took you to see his mentor, Mr. Kalai, right?"

"He did." A cold sweat rose up her neck.

"Aren't you the lucky girl? Maybe when Sam's brother comes back, we'll double-date."

"Sam has a brother?" She was surprised he'd never mentioned it.

"Drummer. Very talented. Mr. Buckley thinks the world of him and lets him do whatever he likes. He's off on tour now, but he promised to take me out when he returns. Can you imagine, you and me as the Mrs. Buckleys?"

"But your career comes first."

"It does. And don't ever forget that. Hey, I just thought of something to convince you to sing with me."

"What's that?"

"Finish your dessert and I'll show you."

❧

Hordes of people had descended upon Times Square for the Wednesday matinees, and the girls were forced to walk in the street to avoid being separated.

"Like a bunch of cows this time of the week," yelled Esme. "Being herded into their stalls for milking."

Esme grabbed Darby's hand and pulled her close. She'd narrowly missed being sideswiped by a yellow cab. Darby stifled the urge to put her hands to her ears, overwhelmed by the noises. Honking, screeching brakes, and giddy conversation swirled around her. She clutched her purse to her side and held Esme's hand tight as they cut through the throng like ants tunneling through sand.

Once they were inside a double glass door, the noises were just as loud, only different. Arcade games blasted tinny music, and high-pitched bells rang at irregular intervals.

"What are we doing here?" Darby stopped in her tracks, refusing to go any farther. "I have a class to get to."

"The Playland arcade; it's famous. Come on, this won't take long."

At the very back of the arcade, nestled in a corner, was what looked like a blue phone booth. VOICE-O-GRAPH was printed on the outside in cursive letters. The side was emblazoned with MAKE A RECORD HERE, PLAY IT ANYWHERE.

The memory of the boy in the park, Walter, swept over Darby. He'd worked for this company, had told her about the machine that recorded sounds. She didn't want to step foot in the thing.

"It's a kind of recording studio, a tiny one." Esme stopped and posed beside it, twirling her wrists and presenting the booth as if she were one of the girls hawking washing machines on television ads.

Darby laughed. Walter wasn't anywhere near this place; she had no reason to be afraid. "What are you going to do?"

"I'll drop in a quarter, and then we sing into the telephone. Once we're done, a record drops out the bottom."

"So you want to sing into it?"

"I want us both to sing. We'll do 'Lover, Come Back to Me.' Then I'll play it back for you and you'll see what we sound like, what you sound like. Come on, it'll be fun." Esme popped open her purse and held up a shiny quarter with her gloved fingers. "Follow me."

They squeezed into the booth and Esme slammed the door shut behind them. Inside, the air was still and quiet, a relief after all the commotion. A regular telephone handset was attached to the machine with a black wire, with instructions printed in block letters at eye level. Esme dropped in the quarter and picked up the handset. "You ready? Come closer."

Esme wrapped her free arm around Darby's waist and pulled their bodies together, as if they were conjoined twins. The red light turned to green and a nervous laugh escaped from Darby's lips. Esme sang the first line and Darby joined in, their eyes glued on each other. With no band behind them, the timing was slow, languid. Darby took her cues from Esme as Esme's fingers tapped the beat on Darby's side. As the seconds ticked by, the outside world faded away. Stenography, Sam, the girls at the Barbizon, none of that mattered anymore. Esme's face was just inches away. The button turned red in the middle of a line and they both stopped singing at the same time, then burst out laughing.

"That was ridiculous," said Darby. "And fun."

"I told you." Esme didn't release her grip on Darby. Unexpectedly, she leaned in and gave her a quick kiss on the lips.

Darby drew back as much as she could in the cramped space. "Esme."

"Sorry, you looked so beautiful as you sang, I couldn't help myself." She reached up and touched Darby's face, her fingers soft as they ran over her jawline and up to her ear.

Darby stood frozen in place as the feathery tracing of her ear sent tiny shock waves down her body. The gesture was innocent, almost childlike, and Esme gazed at her with her lips slightly parted. Their breasts touched when Esme inched closer and this time Darby didn't pull away. She wanted to soak up the essence of this woman, this human gravitational force who had pulled Darby into her orbit.

The sound of the record dropping into the knee-level slot broke Darby out of her trance.

Esme reached down and grabbed it, then held the recording up, one arm still around Darby's waist. "Now we're going to go and listen to it."

"Where? I don't have a phonograph."

"No, but I know someone who does."

Darby was dying to hear the recording, she had to admit. But when she realized what Esme had planned, she wished she'd gone back to Katie Gibbs instead.

"We can't go in there. What if she's there?" whispered Darby, as they stood outside Candy's room at the Barbizon. Esme held the master key in her hand, inches from the doorknob. Darby hadn't spoken to Candy since the awful night when Esme had come to her aid.

Esme knocked. "Laundry delivery."

No one answered.

"It'll only take a minute."

She let them in and closed the door softly behind them. Darby's heart pounded; she didn't want to hear the recording this badly. If they were caught in another girl's room uninvited, she'd be kicked out of the hotel and Esme would be fired. And she was still confused by what had happened in the booth.

By the time she opened her mouth to say something, Esme had opened the phonograph on Candy's desk. She snapped on the record and dropped the needle.

The sound was soft at first; then Esme turned a dial and their voices rang out in the tiny room.

"Too loud," warned Darby.

Esme turned it up even louder. "Just listen."

Esme's voice was as Darby had always heard it, smoky, strong, and low. As if her throat were made of the finest sandpaper, roughening up her breath as it traveled from her lungs. Darby's own voice, which she'd always believed to be too reedy, softened the tone. The individual strains melded into one voice, Darby's harmonies pure and on pitch.

"It's beautiful." Darby nodded. "You were right. We're good together."

"Because your voice is gorgeous."

"Thanks."

Outside, a door slammed. Esme grabbed the record, handed it to Darby, and closed the lid of the phonograph. They huddled by the door, listening for sounds of activity.

"I'll go first, wait here," directed Esme. "When I give you the signal, head to your room. I'm on duty, so I'm going straight to the basement."

Darby nodded.

"But you'll sing with me, right? You promise?"

As if she had a choice. Would Esme have kissed her if she hadn't wanted her help? The sensation of her lips lingered.

"I will. I promise."

CHAPTER SEVENTEEN

New York City, 2016

The evening after the talk with Malcolm, Rose opened a bottle of wine and worked her way through Darby's bebop collection. The recklessness of the music matched her mood. She rummaged through the drawers of Darby's desk while a Sarah Vaughan record played in the background.

The top drawer contained receipts and ancient office supplies, including a pad of carbon paper. Nothing to provide any inkling of where Darby had run off to. The red light on her answering machine stayed unblinking, no new messages.

Before Stella had gone into the hospital, she'd implied that Darby rarely traveled anywhere. So why had she left in such a rush now? She'd left behind no clues at all.

Rose yawned, the wine kicking in. She grabbed the top issue of *The New Yorker* magazine from a stack piled up under the desk and carried it to the couch. She'd find a story she'd never usually read, a profile of a sports hero or something like that, and drift off to sleep. But the corner of one page, near the front of the magazine, had been turned over. The jazz listings. In fact, Darby had circled several of the week's events, and placed a couple of exclamation marks by two. Both were tributes to old bebop heroes. Rose worked her way through the rest of the issues and every one was similarly marked. Circles, exclamation points, and short notations in the margin. Darby had certainly stayed on top of the latest performances. Which explained her late-night forays.

The ladies would make excellent subjects, but she needed Darby's contribution to make it sing. Darby would open up to her, she was sure of it. Even Bird had warmed up to her presence. She looked down at him now, wheezing into her armpit, and a wave of melancholy washed over her. What she was doing was wrong, stalking the back stairways of the Barbizon like a crazy woman. She wasn't hanging around the building because of the research or the dog.

She couldn't bear to sever the last tie with the man who'd broken her heart.

But enough was enough. The next day at work, Rose spent most of the morning scouring the real estate listings for a reasonable rental. The prices were a shock, a reminder of how long ago she'd moved into her apartment in the Village, and how quickly the cost of living had risen. Even apartments out in the farthest corners of Brooklyn were unreasonable, considering the fact that she would be paying for her father's room and board at the same time.

She'd stopped by a couple of days ago and been alarmed by the change in him. He tried to get up and open a window three times, waiting until her gaze was averted to the book she was reading aloud from. He jumped up with the swiftness of one of those dancers in the old movies, but when he couldn't manage the lock, he pounded on the glass and tried to roar. The sound came out strangled.

Rose quickly called for the nurses and they resettled him in the chair, but in her heart she knew what he wanted to do. He wanted to leap out the window, replace the antiseptic environment with freedom and the feel of the wind. It was what she would have wanted to do as well.

"How's the Barbizon project going?"

Tyler stood at the doorway to his office.

Rose minimized her browser, hiding the apartment listings from view. "Fine. We've got some footage and started in on the interviews."

"Make sure it's not depressing."

"Sure thing."

After he'd slammed his door shut with more emphasis than necessary, Rose turned back to her monitor.

Two of the real estate listings up in Washington Heights might work. The photos were nice enough. The rent was high, but if she took some extra freelance work, she could manage it, just barely. Something to ask Jason about.

She made calls to the real estate agents and left messages. Good. She was on her way.

After transcribing Malcolm's interview, she looked up at the clock. Early afternoon. The best part of being a journalist was you could always use the excuse of research when sitting at a desk became unbearable. And if walking Bird in the park on a glorious summer day, thinking about the ladies of the fourth floor, counted as research, so be it.

Bird seemed pleasantly surprised when she showed up at the apartment and took him off to the park. During this time of day, the river of motion on the park's main road was constant, with cyclists weaving around horse-drawn carriages, pedicabs, and spandex-clad joggers. Somehow, all the different speeds and methods of conveyance managed to work together. Every so often, a family of tourists on clunky rental bikes broke the trend by going clockwise, the mother looking panicked, the father grimacing, kids ducking their heads in embarrassment. The cyclists on road bikes, who considered themselves the top tier of park users, hollered out in annoyance as they whizzed by.

Today the park seemed to be filled with couples walking hand in hand. Before Griff, she'd dated several men, boys really. Some were charismatic at first, then grew tiresome. Or grew tired of her. But Griff was an adult, successful in his career and respected by the maître d's of the fancy restaurants he took her to.

One evening early in their relationship, they'd taken a leisurely stroll together past the Boathouse, the restaurant perched over the lake in the middle of Central Park. Griff admired the building out loud, and she admitted she'd never been inside. "Too many tourists," she said, laughing. "Who else would be willing to pay so much for a tired piece of steak?"

"We are," he answered, a boyish smile lighting his face. And with that, he dragged her through the double doors, and they drank two bottles of wine while watching the rowboats idling on the pond. A terrible thunderstorm sprang up, as if on cue, while they shared profiteroles for dessert. While the thunder roared and rain poured against the glass walls, he kissed her and told her he loved her.

He'd been the driving force in their relationship, and she was only too happy to enjoy his attention. Slowly, she gave up her identity, leaving her apartment and her job for what she assumed was the next step in her life. Marriage, supporting a husband who had political aspirations. Then he blew it all to bits.

She reached the terrace that overlooked the boat pond, with the restaurant off to the right, and the enormous angel sculpture spurting white water into Bethesda Fountain in the plaza below. A group of teenagers splashed each other with water and shrieked, the girls covering their heads, all black fingernails and long legs. One of the teens was louder than the others, more physical with the boys. Rose stared hard before she recognized the girl. One of Griff's daughters.

Miranda had stared out at her every morning upon Rose's waking, from the photo on top of their bedroom bureau. In it, taken several years ago, Miranda wore a salmon-colored silk dress with ruffles along the top. Rose had admired it for its retro feel, like the disco dresses from the seventies.

But today Miranda sported a T-shirt cut in horizontal strips, revealing a black bra underneath. Rose pulled her sun hat down low and moved along the balustrade until she could see the girl's face. Her skin was pale and smooth and her hair cascaded down her back in thick curls, like a damsel in a romance novel. Even from this distance, Rose could tell her makeup was heavy, with thick black lines around her eyes and lips the color of blood. Griff must hate it. He'd never liked when Rose came home from work wearing pancake makeup from the broadcast. After a while, she'd been sure to take it off in her dressing room instead of waiting until she got home.

A couple holding hands wandered into the frame of her vision and it took a moment for her to realize it was Griff and Connie, coming from the direction of the Boathouse. She knelt down fast, under the pretense of petting Bird. He was panting and needed to be in the shade. She'd forgotten how close his tiny body was to the waves of heat emanating off the concrete sidewalk.

She crossed the street with the intention of heading south along Literary Walk, which was lined with shady elms. Anything to get away from the sight of Griff and Connie together. But as she passed the stairway that led to the tunnel underneath the Seventy-Second Street transverse, she paused. Scooping up Bird, she took the stairs quickly, clutching the handrail. The tunnel had an arched ceiling, and was a coveted spot for street musicians who took advantage of its excellent acoustics, the sound reverberating around the tiled walls.

Today, the area was empty and dark, a perfect hiding spot. The column and the contrast in light kept Rose hidden from view.

Griff and Connie stopped in their tracks when they spotted Miranda. From Rose's vantage point, the tension in their faces was palpable. They murmured to each other like spies working undercover, and then Connie called out to Miranda in a high, sharp voice. The girl turned her head in their direction and all animation fell from her face. Rage briefly crossed over her pretty features before disappearing. Griff's low baritone carried across the plaza but not clearly enough for Rose to catch what he was saying. He let go of Connie's hand and surreptitiously rubbed his palm on a pant leg.

Once Miranda stood before them, Connie put her hands on her hips and thrust her neck forward. She seemed to be berating Miranda, before Griff interrupted her with a dismissive motion of his hands.

Rose tried to tamp down the elation building up inside her. He'd only returned home out of guilt. And his attempt at reconciliation looked rather rocky.

They were coming undone, and Rose was embarrassed for all of them. For the daughter, who was probably confused by the coming and going of the adults in her life, and for Griff, who was a loving dad but unequipped to handle a daughter with a strong agenda of her own.

Without warning, Miranda threw her phone at Griff's feet. It clattered to the ground, bouncing twice. She stared down at it for a second, stricken at what she'd done, then ran off. Connie's face contorted with anguish, and Griff put a hand on her back, but the gesture was automatic, not driven by a need to comfort.

For the first time since Griff had given Rose the terrible news, hope glimmered, followed by a wash of shame. The family was hurtling toward disaster. But the sooner he figured out that being with Connie wouldn't help their daughter any more than being apart, the better. If anything, they seemed to be botching the reconciliation completely.

For the past week, she'd imagined Connie had transformed the apartment into a warm, comfy respite. But a brilliant interior design would never make it a happy home for Griff's family.

What if his misguided attempt at patching things up failed? She imagined him begging her to come back to him, promising the moon.

Could she ever again trust a man who had turned her life upside down?

❧

Stella's grandniece lived in an imposing brick house in Fort Lee just off the highway. Rose could hear the endless whoosh of cars on I-95 as she and Jason got out of the cab.

Stella guided them into the toy-strewn living room.

"It's a pigsty, but I can't say anything because I'm the grateful aunt, happy to be taken in." She eased herself into a recliner and gestured for them to take a seat on the sofa. The only sign of her illness was a hollowness in her cheeks and a slight wheezing. "Mind you don't sit on a Lego. You'll get a bruise for days."

"I take it you're eager to get back to the Barbizon," Rose ventured.

"You bet. They say another few weeks and I'll be good as new."

Rose briefly ran through the various interviews she and Jason had lined up, and Stella's eyes widened with astonishment. "I'm surprised you reached so many of us. You must be very persuasive."

"I think they agree with me that the history of the Barbizon makes a great story."

"Right. Well, what do you want to know? We only have an hour until Susan and her kids get back from ballet lessons or welding class or wherever the hell they are."

Rose looked over at Jason, who nodded. The camera was rolling. "So many different kinds of women stayed at the hotel. How did they all get along? Or did they all get along?"

"God, no. It was a strict class system. Models were on top, then the guest editors for *Mademoiselle* and the others who were in publishing. The bottom tier was for the Gibbs girls."

"Why is that?"

"The goal was to catch a man as soon as possible. Sure, we all paid lip service to the idea of working and making our own money. But it was just pocket money. Our parents took care of the bills until we were handed off to Prince Charming."

"The competition must've been fierce."

"You bet. The boys were tiered as well, handsome and rich was a top catch. The Ford girls expected the full package, but as you moved down the food chain, you might settle for an egghead with cash, or get swept off your feet by a dashing poet."

"Where did you go on a typical date?"

Stella clapped her hands together. "Oh, the choices were endless. Dinner at the Drake, where the roast duck was to die for, or Café de la Paix at the Hotel St. Moritz. Dancing at the El Morocco until late. Broadway shows, the ballet."

"Did you ever head downtown to the jazz clubs?"

"Downtown? Not so much. We tended to stick to the ones on Fifty-Second Street. Those downtown ones, as well as the ones way up in Harlem, were off-limits for the Ford girls. They were considered seedy and full of dangerous elements."

Too bad. She would have loved Stella's take on the Flatted Fifth. "I assume you were pursued by a number of suitors."

"Got that right. But I made a huge mistake. Decided to have a ball, enjoy myself, play around. By the time I was twenty-three, I was no longer a good girl and no longer young. Can you believe that? Twenty-three. That's a baby these days. Still, I don't regret a thing."

"What about the Gibbs girls? Weren't they there to find good jobs?"

"Secretaries fell into two categories: the dowdy type who wouldn't threaten the wife, and the bombshell who looked good behind a desk or, even better, on top of it."

Rose stifled a laugh so as not to screw up the audio. "What category would Miss McLaughlin fall into?"

"Dowdy, for sure. At least at first. But she began to blossom. Who knows how far she might have gone." Her voice trailed off.

The opening was exactly what Rose had been hoping for. "If she hadn't had the accident?"

Stella nodded.

"Do you remember when it happened?"

"Halloween 1952. Some things you never forget." She shifted in her chair and changed the subject, and Rose didn't press. She bided her time, asking questions about the characters Stella had met over the years.

"I had a friend, Charlotte Foster, who was strangely beautiful, though not about to get on the cover of *Vogue*. Charlotte did well for herself. She didn't mess about with any marriage nonsense, and I have to say I think she was right. Focus on your job, do what you love, and get on with your life."

The words resonated. Rose had done so early on, getting a coveted internship out of college and plowing through the office politics. But somewhere along the way, she'd reverted to a 1950s paradigm: Griff had become the center of her world.

She snapped back to the interview. "What happened to Charlotte Foster?"

"Ended up working at *The New Yorker*. She never married, from what I heard, never wanted to. Died in her sixties, while hang gliding in the Alps. What a way to go."

Stella's sharp memory and deadpan delivery made the time fly by. Exactly an hour after they started, the sound of a car pulling up in the driveway signaled the end of the interview.

As they began packing up, Rose broached the subject of Darby again. "Did Miss McLaughlin ever have a young friend who visited? A girl?"

Stella eyed her uneasily. "Yup. I saw them meet up a few times outside the building. Darby never bothered to introduce me, but that was her way. Most of the other women think she's a bitch, but I like it. She doesn't waste my time, and I don't waste hers."

"So you don't know the girl's name?"

"No." She cocked her head. "But once I heard the girl call Darby something odd. Christina, Tina, something like that. I said to Darby later, 'What, you got a new name?' Darby told me it was a private joke."

On the way back to the city, Jason chuckled.

"What's that for?" asked Rose.

"I can't help but wish I'd been born back in the day. Stella was one hell of a firecracker. She must've driven the boys wild."

An unpleasant twinge ran through Rose. Jealousy. Of an eighty-something-year-old lady? No way.

She shook it off. "The more we dig into Darby's story, the stranger it becomes. What's with the girl calling her Christina?"

"Maybe that's her alter ego, a crazy, martini-swilling lady of the night."

"I wouldn't rule it out at this point. I wish we could get Stella to dish out more details on the day Esme fell. She knows more than she's saying."

"You saw how she closed down. She's not going to go there."

"Ditto with Malcolm on Sam. I've tried to reach him a couple of times since our interview. Radio silence."

Jason sighed. "So far, all we know is Darby was planning an escape with Sam, Esme fell, and Darby ended up living at the hotel for decades."

"Maybe Esme was in love with Sam and they battled it out on the roof?"

"Does that make the mystery girl the love child of Darby and Sam?"

"More like the love grandchild." Her head spun with possibilities. "Lots of questions."

"And no one is willing to talk."

"Not yet." Rose stared out at the Hudson River as their taxi cruised over the bridge back to the city.

CHAPTER EIGHTEEN

New York City, 1952

"Close your eyes."

Darby did as Esme instructed. She'd arrived at the club a bundle of nerves. They'd rehearsed in her room at the Barbizon the past week, whispering the harmonies so no one passing by could hear, and even adding some dance steps. For a time it had been a joke, a lark. But late tonight they were scheduled to sing backup for Annie Ross after she headlined at Birdland. Waking up early to get to class on time was bad enough, but Darby's lack of concentration had become more than evident at Gibbs. This morning she'd gotten another warning for her constant tardiness, and in the afternoon's post she received a harsh letter from Mother demanding accountability for her poor grades. The head of the school wrote in the comments that Darby seemed "befuddled and unmotivated," and Darby's mother had underlined the three words in a heavy black pen, adding an exclamation point for further emphasis. She was not pleased.

"Now open them."

Esme stood before her in the green room of the Flatted Fifth, holding up two silver dresses, one draped over each arm. The material was slightly shiny and cut on the bias.

"Who are those for?" Darby dreaded the answer.

"For us. For tonight. We'll make a splash wearing these under the lights. No one will even notice Annie Ross."

Darby fingered the silky material. "Where did you get them?"

Esme blew through her lips. "Phooey. I thought you'd be squealing with joy. The lady my aunt cleans for gave them to her. You know those Park Avenue types. She said neither one fit and she was going to toss them out."

"Why wouldn't she return them?"

"Who knows, who cares? Here, try it on."

Darby slipped behind a screen set up in one corner and slid the dress over her head. It gently curved around her hips before narrowing around the knees. The neckline offered a hint of cleavage and emphasized the smooth line from neck to shoulder. After Esme changed, too, they stood together in front of the full-length mirror.

She laughed. "We look like twins."

The door to the green room opened and Sam appeared.

"Wow."

Darby blushed. "Esme found these."

He stepped back and whistled. "The joint is going upscale tonight, I can see that much."

"You know it." Esme winked and turned her back to Darby. "Unzip me. I've got a few things to do before showtime and I don't want to get it dirty."

"And grab an apron while you're at it," said Sam to Darby. "My father's away tonight and I'm going to change up the menu. I could use some help."

"Is that a good idea?" Esme shrugged the dress off and Darby stifled a gasp. To his credit, Sam turned to face the door, shielding his eyes with his hand.

"Yowza. Warn a guy before you disrobe. Of course it's a good idea. Like the dresses. We've got to elevate our clientele's taste, make the club stand out from all the others. And tonight's the night." He turned his head in their direction, still keeping his eyes covered. "Please, Darby?"

"I should stick with Esme." She shivered when Esme stepped behind her and unzipped her dress.

Esme's breath was hot on her neck. "Sure, she's free."

Darby wished Esme would stay out of it. There was no need to embarrass herself further in front of Sam.

Before she could make up an excuse, Sam spoke. "Thank you. I'll see you in a few."

After he'd left, Esme changed into slacks and a blouse and grabbed her purse. "Hang up the dresses so the musicians don't sit on them or use them to clean their instruments. I'll be back."

"Where are you going?"

"Out. No questions. Have fun cooking with Sam; you'll be domesticated in no time."

"But, Esme, I have to tell you something."

"What? That you're in love with a cook? Your mother won't be pleased."

Darby wished Esme would calm down for one second, not be so flippant. "She's already not pleased. She sent me a letter saying I had to pull myself together at Gibbs or she'd be very unhappy."

Esme eyed her warily. "What does she mean, you have to 'pull yourself together'?"

"I can't come here anymore. I'm tired when I show up to class the next day. And I can't do shorthand nearly as fast as the other girls. I'm falling behind."

Now she had Esme's attention. "Don't let me down now, Darby. We're just getting started here. If you quit, it won't be nearly as much fun. And Sam would pout, I'm pretty sure of it."

"That's just it. I shouldn't even be thinking about Sam that way. That's not why I'm in New York."

"He's obviously got a crush on you."

"Do you think so?" She let her mind wander for a second, before biting her lip hard. "No. That's a dangerous path. I don't want to marry anyone."

"Who said anything about marrying? You can enjoy a kiss or two, right?"

Darby remembered the disastrous night in the park. And her kiss with Esme in the booth. One had disgusted her. The other, she wasn't so sure about.

Esme shrugged. "Fine. Look, I have to go. Help him in the kitchen, or don't, but make sure you're ready by the time we have to go on." She took her hand. "This one time. Promise me?"

"I promise."

The kitchen staff's pace had reached a feverish pitch by the time Darby walked in. The busboy was rubbing some powder from a bowl on a pan full of chicken pieces, and Sam stood in front of the burners poaching juicy pink shrimp. Instead of the usual smell of fryer fat, fragrant odors circulated around the small space.

"What's that?" she asked, pointing to the small bowl beside him.

"Verbena, thyme, and sage." He held it up to her nose. "Smell."

The scent reminded her of climbing the hills behind their house in the spring. A moan of pleasure escaped from her lips.

"I'm going to add it to the shrimp, and serve that instead when someone orders boring old shrimp cocktail."

"Won't the customers be angry?"

"We'll see. Hopefully, they'll be hungry enough to try it without sending it back."

"What will your father do when he finds out?"

"No idea. Probably fire me."

She couldn't tell if he was joking.

Acting on Sam's orders, she laid out shiny white plates as Sam supervised the modified menu. She prayed she wouldn't drop anything or say something stupid.

"Here's what's on the menu for tonight: Instead of fried chicken, we have a spiced roast chicken with satay sauce. Lamb burgers with cumin and garlic instead of the usual burger, and so on and so on."

"I hope your experiment goes well," teased Darby. "Because if not, Esme and I and the rest of the musicians will be facing an angry, hungry crowd tonight."

"I'll do my best. Once I heard my father would be out of town, I went straight to Mr. Kalai's shop. We can always run for it and hide out there until things die down."

She laughed at his teasing, but she could tell he was worried. Uptown, this type of cuisine might go over, but down in the East Village, late at night, the regulars could be surly, drunk, and quick to rebel.

About a half hour later, the first set of orders had been filled. During the lull, Sam cleaned every surface he could. Even though he was smiling and joking around, Darby could tell his nerves were on fire.

The door to the main floor opened and one of the waiters returned, carrying the burger on the plate. He laid it down carefully on the counter and stepped back.

The burger was practically untouched; only one bite had been taken.

"Table six said he didn't like this. Wants fries instead."

Sam rubbed his face with his hand. "Dominic, fire up the fryer." He picked up the plate and dumped the unwanted burger in the trash.

"Sorry, Sam." Darby meant it. "These folks aren't the crowd you should be cooking for. You need to be uptown, in your own restaurant."

"Right. As soon as I get rich, I'll take care of that."

"Everyone in their right mind loves your food; don't let one customer get to you."

He smiled. "I won't. When I was in the war, I started getting requests from the sick soldiers, the really sick ones, for something that reminded them of home. I'd start by asking lots of questions about where they were from, what the soup their mother made tasted like, that kind of thing, and then I'd create a spice blend just for them. Whether they lived in Rhode Island and their families were originally from Portugal, or maybe from Mexico but living in California, I'd work in the kitchen until I had something that clicked. And you should've seen the look on their faces. Even if they'd lost a leg, or were blind in one eye, for a split second it was like they were home. I loved doing that. I want to keep doing that."

"And you will. Just maybe not tonight."

The kitchen door swung open again. Another waiter, another couple of plates.

But they were empty.

Not a crumb was left on either.

"What did they order?" asked Sam, his voice breathless.

"One chicken and one shrimp. They want more. The chicken wants the shrimp this time and vice versa."

Sam and Darby stared at each other, then he whooped with laughter and grabbed her, swinging her around. His build was strong and hard and she clung to his neck, their faces inches apart.

"They liked it."

She let go and stepped backward, off balance. "You'd better get cracking."

The next hour flew by, with orders pouring in as word spread that the food was different, tastier.

Before she knew it, Esme swooped in, telling her to change.

"We only have twenty minutes. Hurry!"

Annie Ross perched on the green-room couch, drawing on a cigarette and nodding as they dashed behind the screen. She was thin, with a close-cropped hairdo and elfin eyes. Not what Darby expected at all.

"I'm scared," Darby whispered. Her legs shook as she pulled the dress over her head. She'd been diverted from her stage fright by helping out Sam, but now the fear crushed her. "I'm not sure if I can breathe, never mind sing."

"Pretend. That's what they teach us in acting class. Pretend and you'll believe it soon enough."

She didn't trip getting up onto the stage. Darby gave herself a mental pat on the back for that minor accomplishment. Ross looked at the drummer and then launched into the first number. Darby followed Esme's lead and moved her hips right, then left, then snapped her fingers. Verse, chorus, verse, chorus, bridge, chorus. Song one was done.

As she began to relax, she was able to look out over the audience, her eyes adjusting to the lights. Sam stood in the back, his arms crossed, grinning widely. Starting tomorrow, she'd happily dedicate herself to spelling tests and punctuation drills. But tonight had been worth it, if only to watch Sam's culinary triumph.

She shook a hip and snapped her fingers and smiled.

⁕

Darby meant to head home as soon as their set was over, but by the time the bar cleared out, it was almost four in the morning. The busboy had placed the chairs upside down on all the tables except one, where she, Esme, and Sam sat with several of the musicians and toasted one another.

The air smelled of marijuana and sweat. Darby sat back, enjoying the banter of the musicians as they teased and flirted with Esme. Sam had taken the seat next to her, one foot crossed over a thigh, his hand barely touching the skin below her neck as it rested on the back of her chair. She resisted the urge to shiver every time he moved his thumb ever so slightly over her flesh.

He'd made burgers for the musicians and they devoured them with relish.

"Damn, this is good." The bass player wiped his mouth with his napkin. "Reminds me of the South."

"No, this is Chicago-style. I can't figure out what's in it, but it's like what they do there."

Darby smiled over at Sam. The spices affected each taster differently, as if personalized to reflect his childhood, his mother's cooking, their favorite meals.

"He's got to open his own place," said Darby. "Don't you think?"

The men nodded. "I'd come by every day I'm in town."

"So?" The word was slurred, Esme's eyes heavy-lidded and un-focused. "When are you going to break free from your father and do it?"

"It's not so easy," said Sam. "But I'm working on it. I have plans."

"You've got to put it into action, Sam. That's what I'm doing. I'm clawing my way to the top if I have to. Nothing and no one will stop me."

"I am putting it into action. I have a benefactor."

"Mr. Kalai?" asked Darby.

"Yes. He's going to help me out when I'm ready. He says not yet, though."

"Mr. Kalai is a powerful man." Esme raised her glass. "Good benefactor to have. Right, Sam?" She winked at him, then downed her drink. "And what about you, Miss McLaughlin? If I'm going to be a famous singer and actress and Sam is going to own his own restaurant, what's your big plan?" She stood up, swaying to an imaginary beat.

Esme already knew the answer and was trying to make Darby look ordinary, unambitious.

"Not everyone has to have a grand plan," said Darby.

"That is so true. You could be more than a typist, though. Don't you agree, Sam?"

Sam put his hands in his lap. "People should do whatever they want to do."

The lateness of the hour made Darby bold. "My hotel is full of girls who want to be someone famous. Movie stars, models. And most of them are really struggling, from what I can tell. Not every-one who dreams of fame gets there."

Esme's lids fluttered open. "Sorry, I'm being awful. Come dance with me."

She reached out and grabbed Darby's hand and pulled her up.

"I don't want to dance." But Esme pulled her close and began swaying, and rather than fight it, Darby relaxed into her touch. She was exhausted and slightly tipsy and didn't want to argue.

Eventually, their group disbanded, the musicians heading to the green room to collect their instruments.

"I've got to go. I have a test tomorrow." Darby grabbed her purse from the floor.

"We're all going out to Minton's," said Esme. "You have to come. Might as well stay out all night, right?"

"No more, I can't take it. You go; you're enjoying yourself."

"I'll put Darby in a cab," offered Sam.

Esme trundled off, giggling and silly, while Sam signaled for Darby to stay put. "I have a surprise for you."

He locked the front door behind the departing revelers, and Darby followed him back into the kitchen.

"I really have to get going. I was supposed to get up early and practice."

"What's the test on?"

"Business methods."

"Sounds boring."

"Is boring."

"Well, this isn't."

He yanked open the icebox and pulled out a bin with the word *vanilla* on the outside.

She couldn't help herself. "Isn't vanilla ice cream the definition of boring?"

"It's not ordinary ice cream." He twisted off the top of a small jar and sprinkled a finely ground powder onto a plate, then rolled a scoop of ice cream in it. "Taste."

She opened her mouth and let him feed her a spoonful. The texture was slightly crunchy, with hints of tart lemon. A groan escaped from the lowest part of her belly.

Sam broke into a huge smile. "That was the reaction I was hoping I'd get."

"You're amazing. What is it?"

"A blend of crystallized honey and some spices from the Middle East."

She opened her mouth again and was rewarded with another spoonful.

Sam took his thumb and touched the corner of her mouth, then put it into his own. "Tastes even better that way."

She opened her mouth again, the cold metal of the spoon against her tongue contrasting with the tang of the ice cream against her palate. This time, Sam rubbed his thumb along her bottom lip, and reflexively she opened her mouth to draw it inside. His gray eyes reminded her of the color of the East River on a cloudy day.

He slid his finger along the bottom row of her teeth and she darted her tongue out to touch it, a whirlwind of flavors swirled on that one patch of skin. Her breathing was ragged and she held herself perfectly still, afraid to move an inch and break the spell.

His other hand went to her hip, lower than what was decent if they'd been dancing together. An unwelcome image of Sam and Esme popped into her head. Had Esme stood in this spot, had Sam touched her lips? Esme was far, far prettier and more outgoing than Darby. Any man would be drawn to her.

She stepped back, exhausted and confused.

Sam placed the spoon in the bowl. "Are you okay?"

"Sure. Fine."

"Can I kiss you?"

He didn't wait for an answer, instead placed his hands on either side of her face and drew her to him. She lifted her head and he paused for a moment, gazing down at her. "You're beautiful."

"Not really."

"No, you are. I mean, onstage, all dressed up and with makeup, you look like a movie star. But I like you like this."

"Plain?"

He shook his head. "Plain? Why would you say plain?"

"I'm not fancy pretty. Or even pretty."

"To be honest, most men don't like fancy pretty. The hairdos are sticky, the makeup thick. I like you like this. When I touch your skin, I'm actually touching you."

She'd never thought of it that way. In Defiance, all the women wore makeup and had their hair done once a week.

He ran his hands through her hair, and her scalp tingled. "A guy gets tired of all of the fakery and perfume. I want a girl who's real, like you. And one who tastes like you."

"What do I taste like?"

"Let me see."

His lips were on hers, but they weren't wet and messy like Walter's. He didn't dive into her mouth with his tongue but waited for her cue.

She parted her lips slightly and gasped when their tongues met. She still had the taste of the spiced ice cream in her mouth, and his lips retained the hint of the bourbon he'd been drinking.

The kisses grew deeper; she moaned ever so slightly and he echoed her sound. Dizzy with desire, she wrapped her hands around his neck and pulled him to her. He inched the shoulders of her dress lower and lower until it slid down around her waist, then undid her bra with a flick of his fingers. She looked down, embarrassed.

"You're lovely." He slid his hands down from her shoulders and cupped her breasts, which fit perfectly into his hands. He touched the nipples with his tongue and she shivered. "Do you like that?" he asked.

She had to close her eyes to process the mixture of pleasure and pain that coursed through her body as he pinched them slightly, followed by a gentle bite of his teeth. The hem of her skirt inched up, past her stockings, as his hands ran up along the side of her legs. When his fingers hit the patch of bare skin near the garter, she ached for them to move inward, parting her legs. She opened her eyes to find him crouched down, his lips following the glide of his fingertips closer and closer to where she ached most.

He stood suddenly, one hand cupped between her thighs while the other lightly grasped her neck and pulled her to him. She yielded to the pressure of his lips and while his tongue swirled around hers, his index finger circled the most sensitive part of her sex over the silky fabric.

A spasm shot through her, short and sharp. "We should stop," she said.

"I want to please you."

"I've never done anything like this before. I don't know what to do."

"You don't have to do anything."

He turned her around so she was pressed against the countertop, her hands braced against the metal, fingers splayed. He was unrelenting with his touch, sliding his finger underneath the fabric and dipping it deep inside her, then returning back. His other hand pinched her nipple and the nerves collided against each other like a double lightning strike, meeting in her solar plexus until the sensation was unbearable. He had her trapped, and she loved the feeling that he was in control of her body completely. The electricity grew until she convulsed, her pelvis rocking back and forth with pleasure.

This was not at all what she'd expected from sex. She'd heard Mr. Saunders and Mother late at night, and Mother's stifled crying afterward. The enormity of what she'd done with Sam hit her like a gunshot. Sobered by the release, she pulled up her dress to cover her bare breasts and yanked down the hem.

"I should go."

"Wait, Darby. Don't."

"I've never done anything like this before. I don't know what to do, or how to do it."

"You did just fine." He smiled. "I liked touching you."

She relaxed slightly, and he pulled her head to his chest. His heartbeat was going as fast as hers. "But I can't do this. It's not safe."

"I understand. We don't have to do anything else."

She looked up at him. "Why do you like me?"

"I saw you singing onstage and it was like you were shining up there. You weren't pretending to be a singer, or crying out for attention from the crowd." He took both her hands in his and placed his forehead against hers. "There was the song, your voice, and your body. The combination was beautiful and that was when I decided I had to kiss you."

She was quiet for a moment, stunned.

"And it helps that you like my cooking."

Maybe she didn't have to be scared after all.

Darby took the back stairs of the Barbizon two at a time, as light as Fred Astaire. At the landing with the mural, she came upon Stella untangling herself from a boy with jet-black hair and crooked glasses.

"Darby, wait. Arthur here was just leaving. I'll walk up with you."

Stella kissed the boy on the lips and then pushed him away from her. Bewildered, he lost his balance and tipped precariously on the top step, catching hold of the handrail just in time.

Stella put her hand to her mouth and giggled. "You're so silly, Arthur. Be careful now." Her Southern lilt was more pronounced than usual.

As the two girls tromped up together, Stella threw one arm around Darby's shoulders. "And where are you sneaking back from?"

"The Flatted Fifth."

She made a sour face. "That jazz club?"

"Yes. You should come sometime. It's quite a scene."

"Right."

Her lack of enthusiasm rankled. "I mean it. You get lost in the music and the rhythms; it's like being hypnotized."

Stella paused at the next landing and slid off her red stilettos. Fuschia-colored toenails gleamed under her stockings. She picked up her shoes and continued climbing. "I take it you were with that maid tonight."

"I was with Esme, yes."

"You really ought to expand your horizons."

A prickle of sweat ran down Darby's back. "Why? Because she's a maid? She happens to be a wonderful person—and she's a talented singer, too. I have no doubt she's destined to be a star."

"She's roped you right in, I see."

Darby's legs, so weightless at the start of her climb, now felt like lead. "Why do you dislike her so much? Is it because she works at the hotel? Or that she's from another country?"

"Neither. But I've heard rumors."

"What kind of rumors?"

"That she's bad news."

Candy immediately came to mind. "Right. Because she doesn't let the guests walk all over her and treat her like a slave. I respect her for that. And I like her."

Stella raised her eyebrows but didn't respond.

"Meanwhile, you're on the back stairs with a different guy every weekend." Darby didn't care how snappish she sounded. "You shouldn't judge someone else's character."

"I have a plan, and I'm perfectly up front about it. I'm not so sure about Esme's intentions, about why she's always skulking after you."

"Because we're friends. Friends spend time together; it's not skulking." Exasperated, she changed the subject. "What exactly is this plan of yours?"

Stella brightened. "I'm looking for a man who can afford my expensive tastes and drive me wild. Not easy. What I want takes work and the right connections. You see, Thomas—the boy from the park—goes to the same college as Paul, who you met last month in the stairwell. Now, Paul comes from money but is dumb as a box of hair. But he introduced me to Arthur, whose father runs a shipping company. I figured, why not take Arthur for a test run and see if there's fireworks?"

"And were there?"

"Not a one."

Darby couldn't help but smile. "Well, I think you're wrong about Esme. You should come out with us one night and really get to know her."

They'd reached their floor. "I'll take a pass on that. In the meantime, start dating some boys and doing your own thing, away from her."

"Right." She thought of Sam in the kitchen and smiled. "I'll do my best."

"Thatta girl."

Stella blew her a kiss good night and padded down the hallway to her room.

CHAPTER NINETEEN

New York City, 2016

W ho exactly are we meeting here? I hope you don't think we're going to be able to expense this." Rose turned in exasperation to Jason. He'd called her a few hours ago and instructed her to meet him at an address downtown, which turned out to be a restaurant called Neo. She'd read about it in *The New York Times* a few weeks earlier, where it had been well received by the dining critic for its refreshing, offbeat menu.

"A friend of mine works here," Jason assured her. "It's part of our research." He led Rose inside, where the hostess, a doe-eyed beauty with a huge Afro, ignored them.

From what Rose could tell, the entire waitstaff had been chosen from the cream of the genetic pool, young men and women with long limbs and shiny hair. "In what way is this part of our story? Do you think Darby's working here as a waitress?"

He gave a snort of a laugh. "Now, there's an image. No, I don't think that. Did you bring the spice book?"

She pulled it out of her bag. "Yup. But I—"

"Good. Now, please give this a chance for five minutes?"

Jason whispered something to the hostess and her demeanor changed dramatically. She laid a manicured finger on his arm and gave him a warm smile revealing even, white teeth. Then she turned and wobbled away on her four-inch heels.

Very impressive. "What did you say to her?"

"Just dropped a name."

More people had squeezed into the narrow foyer and now they were pressed against one wall, shoulders touching. Chasing the latest trends in fine dining wasn't for her. Too much posing, for one thing—she hated all those hot spots where more attention was paid to the atmosphere than the food. She'd take a good juicy burger over a celebrity sighting any day of the week.

"Jason!"

The crowd waiting to be seated parted like the Red Sea as a large man in a chef's uniform strode forward. He shook Jason's hand with enthusiasm and nodded when Rose was introduced. "So glad you could come."

"Chef, you look sharp in that toque. And busy," said Jason.

"Always have time for you."

"Rose, this is my buddy Steven Hinds. Steven, Rose."

He shook her hand and led them back to the kitchen. Jason gave Rose a wink.

She refused to rise to the bait. "I get it, so you know the chef. Stop showing off."

They swept through swinging doors into the enormous open kitchen. Every surface was pristine, and the copper pots glistened under the fluorescent lights. The line cooks and sous chefs barely looked up, concentrating on the task at hand, whether searing meat or cutting herbs into slivers.

The chef directed them to a quiet corner. "Let's see your book, then."

Rose placed it on the counter, happy to see that he wiped his hands on his apron before handling it.

"This is from the fifties?"

"Nineteen fifty-two, to be exact," she said. "A man named Sam Buckley compiled it, and we're trying to find out more about him."

He spent several moments perusing the text. "Well, I can tell you this much: Sam Buckley was way ahead of his time. No one back then would dare experiment with these spices. Several were unheard of in America until thirty or so years ago. Where did this guy come from?"

"From New York City, originally. But he was abroad during World War Two. We think he wrote this after he got back."

"These are amazing blends, surprising even today. Let's try one of them and see."

He called out a list of herbs from page seventeen of the book to his sous chef, and in no time had a pestle and mortar as well as jars of fresh spices lined up in front of him.

"Nice to have someone do your bidding," said Jason.

"Like when I used to make you do my science homework."

Rose turned to Jason. "You were in school together?"

"High school. I did his homework and he fed me homemade pizza after school."

"Sounds like a fair trade."

The chef measured out the recommended amounts of each spice, mixing dried cilantro, dried kaffir lime leaves, and pepper.

"This is one of the simpler formulas." Steven mixed it with lime juice and then chopped up papaya and mango and drizzled the dressing over the cubes. "Preferably, you'd want to dry or cure the spices yourself, to get the optimal flavor. Can you imagine the housewives of that time making something like this? We're talking about the era when TV dinners first came onto the scene."

He speared a mango and offered it to Rose. The taste was frighteningly powerful at first, with a sour finish that left Rose wanting more.

"Delicious doesn't come close to describing this."

"Agreed," said Steven. "It's a complete crime this guy Buckley was never recognized for his genius."

"Any idea how we might find out more about him?"

"I think I do, actually. Jason knows I'm a pretty major food history geek, and as far as I understand it, the spice trade in New York City was handled by a single person back in the fifties—a man named Benny Kalai. He was originally from Jakarta, but had a storefront in Chinatown and a warehouse in Brooklyn, on the docks. All spices came through him."

Jason looked at Rose and smiled. "Told you it wasn't a waste of time."

She ignored his ribbing and smiled at Steven. "Thank you for letting us stop by."

"Oh, I can do more than that. Table for two coming right up." He waved at a passing waiter.

"No, we shouldn't." The thought of sitting across from Jason for a fancy dinner unnerved her.

"Are you really refusing a chef who just received three stars in *The New York Times*?" asked Jason.

Her stomach growled from hunger after the small bite of mango. "You've got a point."

They were seated in a far corner of the restaurant, away from the hubbub of the bar and kitchen, and Jason ordered a bottle of white wine.

"Are you planning on expensing this? I have to warn you, Tyler will not be pleased."

"Don't worry. Steven owes me. He would've never passed physics if it weren't for me. We won't be paying a cent for this meal."

"Good to have friends in high places." She sipped the wine, letting the citrus and tannins mingle in her mouth before swallowing. Jason was staring at her. "What?"

"Nothing." He held up his glass. "Here's to Darby McLaughlin and Sam Buckley, wherever they may be."

They clinked glasses and devoured the first course of squid with a hint of lime.

She racked her brain for something to talk about. "Tell me about growing up in New Paltz."

"You're kidding, right?"

"I'm not. As a city girl born and bred, I picture upstate as Norman Rockwell territory."

"Far from it. Couldn't wait to get out. That changed when my mother got ill and I went back to take care of her. Luckily, she wasn't in too much pain and, at the end, passed quickly. Not the type of lady to linger."

"I'm sorry, that must've been very difficult." She had no doubt her father would have expressed a similar sentiment about his own decline, if he were able to.

"What about your mother?" Jason asked.

"She disappeared when I was young. We heard she died years later from a drug overdose. My father didn't like to talk about it." The vagueness of her mother's history unsettled her, as always. Normally, she told people that her mother died when she was young and left it at that, but for some reason, Jason's story brought out the truth. She shifted uncomfortably in her chair. "What do you think of this Benny Kalai idea? I figure I'll do some digging and find out what I can about him."

"There's no way he's still alive."

"True, but maybe we can get some color around what Sam was up to back in the day."

Jason was looking at her closely; his eyes were very blue. She was struck by how masculine he was. More than Griff, who had the crisply polished appearance of Manhattan's one percent. Jason was rougher than that. And his speaking voice was rough as well. His quiet confidence appealed to her.

The dinner was more entertaining than Rose had expected. They both knew many of the same journalists, and Jason's travels around the world were astonishing in scope and detail. By the time they'd finished their dessert, they'd also finished off several glasses of wine and Rose swayed slightly as they fought their way through the crowds and out to the street.

"That was quite a surprise," she said. "Thank you."

"My pleasure." He stood facing her, unmoving.

"I should head home."

"Share a cab?"

Once again, the driver was the kind who liked to race to the next red light at great speed, then jam on the breaks. "Why is it we attract the daredevils?" Jason murmured.

The driver took a turn onto Park Avenue with no warning, sending Rose careening into Jason's side.

She laughed and righted herself. "Sorry about that."

The driver swerved into a different lane and they banged shoulders once again, but this time she stayed where she was. She liked the sensation of his muscled arm against hers. He took her hand in his. "You have beautiful fingers."

"Thanks."

The kiss was simple, easy, tasting of wine and sweetness. He didn't do anything but touch his lips to hers, ever so softly, then pull back and wait to see her reaction.

"Jason," she said. "We shouldn't."

He lifted his head, smiling. "You're absolutely right. That was awful."

The cab was nearing Sixty-Third Street. "This is fine. I'll get out here."

"Are you sure? We can drop you off at the front door."

She didn't want to explain why she couldn't go in that way, and the fire in her body was not to be trusted.

"Yes. Have a great night, and thanks again."

❧

Rose was still thinking about Jason when she tripped over Miranda in the stairwell of the Barbizon.

She'd collected Bird for his last walk of the night and was rounding the third-floor landing at a good clip when a pair of jean-clad legs stopped her in her tracks. The girl sat sideways on the top stair, one leg stretched out, the other foot resting on the stair below. Her back was pressed up against a blue-green mosaic embedded in the wall. The painted tiles might have once depicted a churning sea or a lively reef teeming with fish, but time and bleach had worn the animation away. Miranda's hair curled out prettily against the faded glaze. She had her earphones in and stared down at the screen of her phone, which was cobwebbed with cracks. At Rose's gasp, she looked up.

"Jesus." Miranda pulled out an earphone. "You almost knocked me over."

"Sorry, I didn't see you." Rose's voice was higher than normal, weak. She was trapped, and only a couple of seconds went by before recognition flickered over the girl's face.

"Rose."

"Miranda."

"What the hell are you doing here?"

"I promised a neighbor I'd walk her dog while she's away."

The tough teenager from the park had transformed back into a kid. The makeup had been scrubbed off, and an oversize blue hoodie overwhelmed her thin frame. The rims of her eyes were red, but it was hard to tell if that was from crying or a heavy hand with the makeup remover. Her left hand was dug deep in the pocket of her hoodie. Hiding something.

Miranda stared at the ball of fur in Rose's arms. "Can I pet the dog?"

"Sure." Rose knelt down and put him on the floor of the landing, where he sniffed the air before placing a tentative paw on Miranda's thigh.

"He's cute." She gave his paw a shake. "My mother won't like the fact that you're here."

Rose resisted the temptation to say that she'd been here first. "This is the last walk," she lied. "Then I'll be gone. What are you doing here?"

The girl pulled an e-cigarette out of her pocket. "You want a hit?"

"What's in it?"

"Vape. Tastes like cotton candy."

"I don't get it. Why don't you just eat cotton candy instead?"

She rolled her eyes. "Jesus. You sound like Dad."

"Yeah, I'll try it." Had it come to this? Fake smoking in stairwells with Griff's kid. Anything to keep her talking and not snitching.

Miranda swung her legs around and held up the e-cigarette. Rose perched on the stair beside her and took a small hit, then made a face as the vapor rolled over her tongue. "Tastes like cotton candy that's been dipped into a vat of chemicals."

Miranda laughed and lifted the e-cig from Rose's fingers. "You get used to it."

"How are you, Miranda?"

"Fine." She scratched at one of the tiles on the wall. It fell off easily, along with tiny flakes of plaster. "If you don't mind being mental."

"You're not mental."

"Oh, please. Like you have any idea. Don't sit here with me trying to be cool so that I won't tell them that I saw you. It's too pathetic."

She was right. Rose had lost her mind. "Look, I was trying to be nice. Your dad and I . . ." She trailed off. What was there to say?

"He dumped you. I heard."

"What did you hear?"

Miranda gave a tense smile, pleased to have the upper hand. "Look. My father will never leave my mother now. And not because of my fucked-up problems. He used you as arm candy when you were on TV. Dating a hot future anchorwoman was good for his image back then. But for the job he wants now, he has to be a family man. Griff Van Doren has large ambitions. You were just a phase. A blip."

The truth hit her with a thud. He needed his ex-wife's connections if he was going to take City Hall. Connie's family ran in the right circles, could influence his race for mayor. In ways both positive and negative.

Rose scooped up Bird and stood. "I gotta go."

Miranda let out a guttural sigh. "Don't be mad, Rose. Trust me, I'm on your side. It's better for me if they're split up. Easier to manipulate the situation, get what I want."

They stared at each other for a moment. The girl's skin was smooth, her lips so pink. She was just a troubled kid, yet Rose was standing in a stairwell listening to her as if she were some wizened old sage. Between the two of them, Rose wasn't sure who was more screwed up.

"Miranda!" Connie's voice echoed down the stairwell.

Without a word, Miranda rose and headed upstairs, her combat boots heavy on each tread. Only when the fire door slammed shut did Rose continue on her way.

CHAPTER TWENTY

New York City, 1952

The next couple of weeks passed peacefully, as Darby found a groove that allowed her to juggle her classes and hours of homework but still visit the club. She studied with Maureen and the twins on Monday and Tuesday evenings, and headed downtown after dinner on Wednesday through Saturday. Sunday was spent in bed, recovering. At the club, the first few hours were devoted to Sam in the kitchen, while Esme worked her shift. Mr. Buckley wouldn't allow Sam to experiment with the menu any further, but he hadn't raised a fit about his hijacking the kitchen, either. In the meantime, Sam was making great progress with his spice book, and Darby had promised to type it up for him once it was completed.

Even better, Sam had kissed her several times in the back alleyway. She might have allowed him to take it further, but they were never alone. The memories of being with him tantalized her as she lay in bed after sneaking into the Barbizon, waiting to drop into a dreamless sleep.

One Wednesday morning at Gibbs, her shorthand teacher called out her name. "Please report to Mrs. Tibbett's office."

Darby looked up from her desk, surprised.

"I'm sorry, why?"

"I don't know the answer to that. She'd like to see you now."

Darby stood up and gathered her books. She'd passed all her tests this week, albeit not with the high marks she'd been known for in high school. But still.

Mrs. Tibbett's office looked down on Park Avenue, one of the few two-way avenues in the city. Cars lined up bumper to bumper at the traffic lights, tearing away when they turned green, only to stop again a few blocks later. Like an inchworm with tires instead of feet. If inchworms had feet.

Mrs. Tibbett gestured for Darby to take a seat.

"Miss McLaughlin, are you all right?"

Darby coughed. "Yes, I'm fine."

"I've warned you before about your distracted behavior, and your teachers tell me that you've been having a difficult time adjusting. Is that right?"

"I did have a difficult time, in the beginning. But I'm enjoying class very much now. I think in the next month or so, you'll see I've made real progress."

"I see." She looked down at a piece of paper on her desk. "Your scores are low. Very low."

"Right. As I mentioned, I got off to a bad start. But I promise you I'll make it up. I can do the work."

"What exactly has been the problem?"

She was unsure how to continue. "It's not what I expected. All the drills. I find it difficult to concentrate because the work is . . ." She couldn't finish the sentence.

"Dull?" Mrs. Tibbett's mouth softened, ever so slightly.

Darby sighed with relief. Presumably, other Gibbs girls had experienced similar pains adjusting to the program. "I'm afraid so. It's awfully repetitive. But I'll get used it. I'm already getting used to it."

"My dear child, not every girl can be a Gibbs girl. It takes a certain can-do-it-ness. It's about serving others, not thinking of ourselves."

Or thinking *for* ourselves. Darby didn't say it out loud, just nodded.

"You may know that I sent a second notice to your mother last week, indicating that you were doing poorly. And after hearing from the other teachers during midterm conferences, we've decided that it's best if you don't finish out the year."

Darby's chin dropped. "I'm sorry?"

"You've been given many chances, but we don't want to waste our time with a girl who shows up late and half asleep, performs badly, and feels she's above the role of secretary. We think you'd be happier elsewhere."

She'd walked into a trap.

"No, you don't understand," Darby sputtered. "I didn't mean the work was dull, not at all. It's my dream to be a secretary, and you see, my mother has spent all of her savings on my tuition. I can't fail." She imagined Mother reading the letter of expulsion, knowing that none of the fees were refundable, and a cold sweat enveloped her. She reached out a hand and gripped the edge of the desk. "You can't tell Mother. I'll make it up to you, I promise. Please. Tell her that I'm still enrolled, that it was a mistake."

"I'm sorry, Miss McLaughlin. Please take your belongings with you. You are expelled."

CHAPTER TWENTY-ONE

New York City, 2016

Ms. Doris Spinner of apartment 4G gave Rose a charming smile. "We would sneak boys up all the time. The girls who worked the back elevator would keep quiet if you gave them a lipstick, or you could climb up the back stairs. There was a woman in charge, Mrs. Eustis or Ewing, I can't remember, who was intent on running a tight ship, but there were leaks here and there, no doubt about it. I lost my virginity in this building, to a boy who worked in a bank. He had a wicked way about him."

Rose waited two beats and then signaled for Jason to stop recording. The sound bite, and Ms. Spinner's interview, couldn't have gone better.

"That the kind of thing you're looking for?"

"Yes, exactly. Thank you so much for your time. And your level of detail. We really appreciate it." They'd taped several interviews that morning, and Rose was relieved to find that her relationship with Jason wasn't strained from their strange parting in the cab. If anything, they were more in sync than ever while interviewing the women of the fourth floor. Rose had spaced out the schedule so they could take their time with each one, shooting either in their apartments or in the second-floor lounge. She deliberately avoided coming up with a list of questions beforehand, preferring to allow the interview to ebb and flow like a real conversation, and the result was better than she'd expected. Tales of back-room abortions and rampant sexual harassment were tempered with stories of young love and the joys of living in an intoxicating city.

But that wasn't the least of the good news. Rose had shown up uncharacteristically late to the first interview, after visiting the New York Public Library at Forty-Second Street earlier that morning. As soon as the library's doors opened, she'd followed the grand marble hallway into a shabby room with dropped ceilings and fluorescent lights. It was a place she knew well, having done hours and hours of research there as a newly promoted assistant producer, and it felt like coming home. She always enjoyed digging up the past, whether it was for a tribute for some star who'd passed away or deep background for an investigative piece.

Even though the clunky microfilm machines probably dated back to the 1970s and scratches marred the glass viewfinder, she patiently scrolled through back issues of every newspaper in New York City from the week of October 31, 1952, including the ones that had gone out of business. She was constantly surprised at what she found: a listing in the real estate section for a two-bedroom, terraced apartment on the West Side for one hundred dollars a month; help-wanted sections divided up by gender, where women could find work as typists and receptionists while men were sought in engineering and sales positions. This was the world Darby had encountered when she'd come to New York.

A few hours in, she hit the jackpot.

After showing Ms. Spinner to the elevator, Rose returned to the lounge, bursting with excitement. Jason was packing up, wrapping a cord around his elbow and wrist with quick, sure movements.

"You did a really good job today," he said.

"Thanks. I always find the best quotes come from the least likely questions, the ones tossed off at the end, as an afterthought."

"Do we dare take a cab back? I have to say I enjoyed our ride the other night."

Remembering the few seconds they'd kissed sent a ripple of pleasure through her. Weird how a man so completely different from Griff could have that effect on her.

Griff. Over the past week, as she'd dived into the story, she'd stopped thinking about him quite as often. Instead, she'd been consumed with the narrative structure of writing about Darby and her neighbors. And she wasn't about to jump into another relationship so soon.

She needed to be clear with Jason. "Look, I just got out of something serious and it's complicated." She hated how much her words sounded like everyone else's. She'd never get away with writing that kind of cliché. "I think we work well together, and I'd hate to fuck that up."

"We do work well together, I'll give you that."

God, he was distracting. Before he could say anything else, she reached into her bag and pulled out several sheets of paper. "Here's the reason I was late this morning."

"What's this?"

"I went to the library, going through every issue of every city newspaper printed around Halloween of 1952, when Stella said Esme fell."

"The library? Serious old-school research."

"I looked for anything in the local news that might be related to our story, and not only was the Flatted Fifth mentioned, but Benny Kalai's name showed up as well." She pointed to the top page. "This was in the October 31st issue of the *New York Herald Tribune*. 'Harrowing Tales of Heroin.'"

She read aloud from the article, which included a transcript of a conversation between the police and an informant:

Q: **How old would you say the buyers are?**
A: Sixteen, maybe. I know one couple who give drugs
   to their young baby.

Q: **How old is this baby?**
A: Less than a year old. When the baby cries, they
   give him a shot of heroin to shut him up.

"My God." Jason looked ill.
"I know. Awful. But here's the juicy part."

Informant conference with Esme C., Puerto Rican
hatcheck girl at the Flatted Fifth, interviewed by
Det. Quigley.

Q: **What about where you work?**
A: Should I mention names?

Q: **Yes.**
A: Charlie Parker and Stan Getz always buy heroin.
   Same when Gene Ammons's group comes. Sonny Stitt
   when they're there, and when the Machito band is
   there, there's a lot of cocaine.

Q: Where is it sold, right in the Flatted Fifth?

A: Yes. And at Hector's Cafeteria on 50 Street and Broadway. The addicts come in, put their money down, pick up the drugs, and leave.

Q: Where does it come from?

A: A guy named Benny Kalai.

Jason whooped. "This is huge. Esme was involved in heroin."

"Looks like it. No mention of Sam in there, just Esme. And Kalai."

"I wonder if Darby knew what was going on."

"We'll have to ask her that when we see her."

"I can't wait. Speaking of which, any news as to when she'll be back? Tyler wants a rough cut and the first draft by the end of next week."

"It'll be close," said Rose. The discussion of deadlines ignited a fizz of nerves deep in her belly.

He leafed through the pages. "I wonder what happened to Kalai after this came out?"

"I had the same question. Turns out Kalai ended up in Sing Sing in 1954. Looks like it took some time to indict him. He died there ten years later."

Jason beamed at her. "Tyler will love this."

"Maids and heroin deals in the fifties? You bet."

"Right up his alley, twisted fuck."

"Makes the story more interesting, rather than the reminiscences of a bunch of old ladies."

"That's harsh. Their stories are fantastic. You know that as well as I do."

She tried not to gloat at the reversal. Jason was championing the cause. "Yup."

Her phone vibrated. The ID read ASTOR ASSISTED LIVING. She answered immediately.

"Is this Ms. Lewin?"

"Yes."

"This is Brenda from Astor. I'm sorry to bother you, but I'm afraid your father's had a fall."

Rose closed her eyes and swayed ever so slightly, trying not to panic. "Is he okay?"

The woman's answer was not reassuring. "You should meet us at Mount Sinai West."

"I'm on my way."

CHAPTER TWENTY-TWO

New York City, 1952

Darby sat down to write a letter to Mother as soon as she got back to the Barbizon. Strange how now that she'd been expelled from Gibbs, her room took on an unexpected, nostalgic hue. She'd miss the view from the window. Even the garish curtains and bedspread seemed endearing.

The door opened with a bang and Maureen rushed in.

"Darby, I heard the news."

"Right. I guess everyone at the school knows by now."

Maureen leaned over and gave her an awkward hug, then sat on the bed. "I can't believe they'd do this to you."

"It's so unfair. I explained to Mrs. Tibbett that I was really trying, but she wouldn't listen."

"What are you going to do?"

"I'm writing a letter to Mother explaining everything, saying that I'm sorry to disappoint her but that I'll go back to Defiance and work hard, pay her back in full." Esme came to mind, working one job during the day and another at night, all while going to school. "I know I can do it."

"Is there anything I can do to help?" Maureen's gaze drifted over to the open door, where two Ford girls trying on princess costumes for Halloween squealed over each other.

Darby shrugged. "I'll be fine, I'm sure. I feel bad about the money, of course, but it's probably all for the best."

Maureen nodded, her mouth slightly open, still entranced by the creatures in the hallway.

"I'll miss you and the twins."

Maureen snapped back to attention. "And I'll miss you terribly. Why don't I go to Mrs. Tibbett and put in a good word? Do you think that'd help? I know Edna and Edith will join me. They absolutely adore you."

"I doubt that would do any good. Maybe I'm not cut out for New York after all."

Without excusing the interruption, one of the Ford girls turned and beckoned to Maureen from across the hall. "You. We need your fingers. Sandra's zipper is stuck."

Maureen scuttled over and did as they commanded, holding the material together as the other girl slowly encased Sandra in a taffy-colored satin gown. After, Maureen remained in the doorway, watching them drift off without even a thank-you. Not that she needed one. For Maureen, just getting noticed by one of the giraffes was enough reward. Thanks to Esme, they no longer had such an effect on Darby.

Once she'd broken free from the spell, Maureen insisted that she and Darby be pen pals, and after Darby promised to write, they hugged a teary good-bye. Darby finished the letter, sealed it in an envelope, and placed it on top of her desk. Part of her was relieved to no longer have to pretend that she wanted to be a secretary, but she'd never let anyone down like this before. Mother's displeasure would be crushing.

A knock on the door broke her concentration. She recognized the sharp rap. "Come in, Esme."

"Hey there, *chica*. What's going on?"

She didn't bother softening the news. "I've been expelled."

Esme perched on the window ledge and crossed her arms over her chest. "It's because of me, isn't it? I was a bad influence on you."

The same thought had gone through Darby's head. What if she hadn't made friends with Esme and gotten dazzled by nights filled with bebop and Sam?

She shrugged off the thought. "I'm the one who showed up late, who failed tests. I hated secretarial school, but I liked what we did together. Anyway, I just wrote to Mother. Once she gets this and sends me train fare, I'll be on my way."

"How long do we have?" A note of desolation crept into Esme's voice.

"I don't know. A week, maybe."

"Do you really have to go?"

"I can't stay. I can't make a living here."

"Of course you can."

Darby let out a scornful laugh. "I don't think you understand. I'll never be a secretary now. It's over."

Esme leaned forward. "So do something else. Why is it so important to go back?"

"Mother spent all her money to send me here and I have to pay her back. I owe her that much. I've completely disappointed her."

"What about how she's disappointed you?"

Darby shrugged. "I don't know what you're talking about."

"She married that Mr. Saunders. It seems to me she's the one who put you in this position to start with. What if she'd taken the money and gone to school herself? Learned to be a nurse or something?

Then she could have supported herself without having to lean on a man and lightened up on you."

Darby couldn't imagine Mother pursuing a career; she was of a different generation. All she knew was dinner parties and tennis. "That was never going to happen."

Esme stood up and paced the room. "You're gonna have a career, just not the career your mother thought you would."

"Meaning?"

"Meaning we work together to get a recording contract. We can call ourselves the Downtown Dollies."

Darby squirmed. "I'm not sure that's realistic."

"Sure it is. Hell, we're just getting started."

"And how do I feed myself in the meantime?"

"We find an apartment together, something cheap. You can take up some shifts at the club as a waitress. Sam and I can put in a good word for you there. We hang on until we hit it big. Whichever comes first: me on Broadway or us together as a singing duo."

"I don't know." Even as she said it, Esme's plan was taking root in her brain. Being in New York City but not having to go to secretarial school had never figured into Darby's thinking. The two were intertwined from the very start. Maybe Esme was right. Maybe she could stand on her own two feet. She touched the envelope sitting on her desk, imagining what Mother would think when she heard of her plans. "I'm not sure if I can do it."

"Of course you can. Look at me and my papa. He was the center of my world in Puerto Rico; we obeyed him and did whatever he said and were terrified to cross him. But when I got to New York City, I had the power. I took control, did what I had to do. Now it's your turn."

"The only money I have is from our gig. And I'd have to send that to Mother, to show her that I'm planning on paying her back." She did the calculation in her head. "I don't see how I can swing it. Even if I found a job right away."

"I'll take care of that. Don't you worry about a thing. I'll take care of you."

A terrible thought sprang into her head. "You won't be doing that thing you talked about, when the men came after you, will you?"

Esme snickered. "No way. I have resources at my fingertips and they don't involve turning tricks."

Darby choked at the frank choice of words and gave Esme a weak smile. Her mind raced with a list of possibilities. She could go home, face Mother and Mr. Saunders, and lick her wounds. Or she could stay here, with Esme and Sam, and figure out another approach. One she had never imagined.

Darby picked up the letter to Mother, took a deep breath, and ripped it in half.

Esme let out a yip of delight. "That's my girl."

"I'll write to Mother and explain everything. Maybe she'll understand."

Or maybe her news would come as a relief. The household was probably more peaceful now and would remain so if Mr. Saunders could continue to pretend she didn't exist. Darby was a constant reminder of her father.

"What do we do first?" she asked.

"You're paid up at the Barbizon until the end of the month, right?" Darby nodded.

"That gives me a couple days to find us a place together. You can talk to Mr. Buckley at the club and get a job. By this time next week, we'll be two girls out on the town."

Relief poured through Darby. "I was a terrible Gibbs girl."

Esme hugged her hard, so she could barely breathe. "You certainly were."

⁂

"You're using my sink."

Darby stared at Candy through the mirror but didn't stop brushing her teeth. She'd woken up the day after her expulsion in a daze. The sinking feeling in her stomach was worse than the one she'd felt when she first arrived at the Barbizon. Kicked out of Gibbs, all the money gone. The afterglow from Esme's excitement had dimmed overnight.

And now here was Candy, claiming a sink, when there were three sinks available to Darby's left.

Grogginess at the early hour draped around Darby like a nubby blanket. She couldn't stop staring, nor did she stop brushing her teeth. Candy's hair was done up in pink sponge curlers, and a smudge of mascara marred the pale skin under one eye. The imperious set of her chin reminded Darby of Mr. Saunders when he was displeased. Her mother would do anything to make his jaw relax, whether it was pleading, teasing, or pouting.

Darby had several choices. She could scurry out of the bathroom, apologizing profusely. She could move down one sink and continue brushing her teeth.

But she'd be out of the hotel in less than a week, and Candy no longer had any power over her. In fact, she never had.

Candy stamped one foot. "You deaf? I need my sink. I have a go-see in two hours."

With a slow deliberateness, Darby turned off the faucet and tapped her toothbrush a couple of times to dry. She leaned over the sink and opened her mouth, letting the mixture of toothpaste and saliva drip out of her mouth into the basin in a thick, wet mess.

She turned around, wiped her mouth with the back of her hand and gave Candy a smile.

"All yours."

Candy's screeches followed her down the hall.

Stella poked her head out of her room. "What's going on? Another cockroach in the shower?"

"Candy's having a bad day, I guess."

Stella laughed. "What else is new. Hey, where have you been? I haven't seen you in a while."

"I got kicked out of Katie Gibbs."

Stella's hand flew to her chest. "What? When?"

"Yesterday."

Stella held out her arms and pulled Darby into them. "My dear girl. You don't deserve that. What can I do?"

An unexpected lump formed in her throat at her friend's kindness. Stella had tried to look out for her, from the very beginning. Darby couldn't get any words out to answer.

"Come with me." Stella led her up the stairwell and opened the door to the sky terrace. Back when the Indian summer was in full swing, girls in ruched one-piece bathing suits would gather on warm afternoons, but this morning all was quiet. Darby plopped down on the nearest chaise longue and looked out into the distance, where the Chrysler Building stretched into the sky, bright and gleaming. Being up so high above the city made her troubles seem less dramatic.

Darby filled Stella in the best she could, ending with a reenactment of Candy's horror when she'd dribbled in her sink. "That was fun, I have to admit."

"You're not the same girl you were before."

Darby shrugged. "I don't know about that."

"No. You're a grown-up now."

"Wait'll my mother finds out. I'll regress to an infant."

"Why?"

"No refund. She put her heart and soul into me improving my lot in life as a Gibbs girl, and I couldn't even last two months."

"What are you going to do?"

"Well, Esme wants me to work in the club and for the two of us to try singing together, like an act."

Stella squinted, whether from the idea or the bright sun, Darby wasn't sure. She shouldn't have brought up Esme's name.

Darby pulled her robe tight around her. "I wish my father were alive."

"Were you close?"

"We got on like crazy. My mother doesn't understand me at all, not that she tried very hard. We don't have much in common." The sun shone on Stella's hair, highlighting the gold strands among the auburn. "She would have loved to have you as a daughter. You're pretty and stylish, like her."

Stella fiddled with the rhinestone bracelet on her wrist. "Pretty only goes so far."

"All I know is I'm headed for deep trouble. My mother hates failure. She got so mad at my father when he got fired. Even when he was dying, she couldn't bear to be in the same room with him."

"She does sound like a pill. Why did he get fired?"

"Something happened at work. His boss said he was too nice."

"Too nice?"

"He was innocent, in a way. Trusted everyone, I guess."

"Your mother seems to have very high standards."

"You got that right." Darby sat upright and swung her legs to the side. She was done feeling maudlin. She had to come up with a plan, decide her fate. Whether it was defying her mother or managing Esme, there was no more time to wallow in self-pity. "I have to figure this out."

Stella reached over and patted her knee. "Don't think too far ahead. That's my go-to remedy in a time of crisis. Do something this morning that will make you happy."

"Like what?"

"I don't know. Pop down to the diner with me and have an egg sandwich? Buy a new lipstick?"

Something that made her happy. Darby smiled.

"Thanks. But I think I know what will do the trick."

✦

Sam took Darby's hand as they entered Washington Square Park. She'd found him in the kitchen of the Flatted Fifth, grinding spices in a mortar, and hadn't had to say a word. He saw the look on her face, took off his apron, and together they walked west while she told him the story of her meeting with Mrs. Tibbett, stopping only to buy two coffees at a corner deli.

She took a sip to conceal her delight at the nonchalant way he'd taken her hand. As if they had been together for a while and did this kind of thing every day. Like she was his girl.

"How did you feel after you found out?" he asked. He'd taken the news easily, thoughtfully, without any of the awkward gestures of Maureen or the sweet pity of Stella.

"Panic. Then relief. I was happy not to live through another eight months of secretarial accounting and pretending to answer the phone."

"Okay. So it's a good thing. What's next for you, then?" He stared over at the fountain, where a man with a guitar sat playing, surrounded by girls wearing blue jeans and tight tops that would have sent Mrs. Eustis into a tailspin.

What if she'd read this all wrong? Sam might be relieved she was out of his hair, and hoping she'd be on her way to Ohio on the next train out.

"Mother will want me to come home so she can torture me for letting her down."

"And what do you want?"

Darby cocked her head. She'd never been brave enough to seriously consider the question until now.

For seventeen years, she'd done what others wanted. Her mother had been so brittle with rage that Darby hadn't dared to speak her mind. Mr. Saunders's presence hadn't helped the situation, and she'd slowly tucked her real self inside, like a turtle being poked by a stick.

"I owe my mother a lot of money, to pay back the tuition, and I feel very guilty about that."

He looked down at her. The guitar player strummed something in a minor key and sang about lost love. "That's not what I asked you, though."

"Right, but that's a big part of it, what I should do versus what I would like to do. And Esme is very excited. I saw her in the elevator when I was on my way here. We couldn't talk for long because Mrs. Eustis got on at the next floor, but Esme said she was working on some scheme, that she had my back."

"What's Esme's scheme involve?"

"She wants me to work at the club and sing with her, try to get some gigs."

"Typical Esme."

Darby laughed. "I know, but I like the way she doesn't let anything or anyone hold her back. I could use more of that myself, I've come to realize."

"For now, leave that all be." He touched her chin lightly with his index finger. "What do you want?"

Her love of books had stayed the same, no matter if she was a Barbizon guest or a Gibbs girl. "I want to work with words, with writing. I met a girl at the Barbizon who works in publishing, and that sounded like fun."

"If you want to work with words, I have no doubt you'll make it happen somehow."

The simple conviction of his delivery brought tears to her eyes. "So you don't want me to go back to Ohio?"

"What?" He tossed his coffee cup into a nearby trash can in an easy arc. Darby did the same but missed by a foot.

"Oops." She picked it up and dropped it in. "I thought you might be tired of me hanging around and wouldn't want me working at the same place you do."

He took the scarf from his neck and looped it around Darby's, pulling her in closer to him and kissing her on the lips. "No. I don't want you to go back. But the whole point here is that you decide what *you* want. Do you want to stay?"

"Yes."

And she did. Her first decision, made on her own, was that New York would be her home. The second was that she'd find Charlotte as soon as she got back from London and charm her way into a job.

If she had to work waiting tables in the meantime, that would be fine. And one day she'd repay her mother.

"I think I know what I want," she said.

Sam didn't ask her to elaborate, just kissed her again. "And I want to watch you get it."

"Should be a crazy trip, I must warn you."

"I like crazy. Do you mind if I come along for the ride?"

She swallowed hard. "I would love that."

"Good. Because I wouldn't miss it for the world."

CHAPTER TWENTY-THREE

New York City, 2016

Rose's father had banged his head and broken a hip trying to walk unassisted, and was on sedatives and painkillers after spending several hours in surgery. The nurses and doctors warned her that the recovery would be difficult. Of that she had little doubt. Her father was a shrunken figure in the hospital bed. Jason had insisted on staying with her and taking her back to the Barbizon. He wanted to cook her dinner. She couldn't let him see where she was staying, so she conceded that he could make her a quick meal in his apartment. She'd have a bite and go home.

She expected his apartment to be in one of the modern, bland condos that were springing up like Jack's beanstalk around town, but instead he lived in a floor-through in a Gramercy Park brownstone, one of the poshest and most coveted addresses in the city.

He gave her a small glass of bourbon. "This will help."

"Do you think he's in terrible pain?"

"The doctor promised to keep him medicated and the nurse said he'd sleep through the night." Jason spoke as he stirred a pot of soup on the stove. "You can go back first thing in the morning, but for now you need to eat and get some sleep."

"My poor dad." She took a sip from her drink and exhaled as it seared her esophagus. "He used to stroll in the front door after a day at school and call out my name and insist I tell him everything that happened that day. I'd tell him all the silly details of a nine-year-old's life and he'd listen so carefully, like I was discussing state secrets."

"Try this." Jason handed over a bowl and a spoon. She tasted the soup, butternut squash with a hint of cinnamon. And something else.

"You've been experimenting with spices." She took another spoonful. Delicious.

"I have. Sam's book inspired me."

She gestured around the room, a mixture of modern furniture with a few antiques. "How did you end up here?"

"My grandmother lived here for years, and she left it to me. I moved in after my mother died."

"I had a feeling the china cabinet wasn't your pick."

He looked at it and laughed. "No."

"My father's going to die, isn't he?"

Jason didn't answer.

"He hit his head, broke his hip. How can he recover from that? I have to face the facts. That's what the doctor hinted at, right?"

"That is what he said. I'm sorry, Rose."

She was glad he was there. That she had someone near to confirm the underlying message the doctor had given her, the tone that seeped out from under the inventory of body parts and injuries.

Jason continued. "They're going to keep him on heavy sedatives, he won't feel any pain, and he won't be confused. He seemed very peaceful by the time we left, remember that."

She nodded. And burst into tears.

He came around from the other side of the counter and stood

close, wrapping his arms around her. Her head fit perfectly into his shoulder, and she wept. When she was done, he passed her a napkin to wipe her eyes.

"Sorry about that." She balled the napkin up in her fist.

The heavy weight of his hands pressed on her shoulders. She wanted to be tight against him again, to feel the body of another person with its muscles and contours. Several years ago, she'd read a book by a woman with autism who had invented a "hugging machine" that pressed against her on all sides and offered a relief from anxiety. That's what she wanted from Jason. To be enveloped and enclosed, to shut out the awfulness of the day.

She put the napkin on the counter and placed her hands around his neck.

He gently removed them.

"Have you ever covered a war and fallen into something because you felt so bad, and it made you feel good? Have you ever done that?"

He shook his head. "I don't think you're in the right frame of mind for this."

"You know what I'm talking about, though, don't you? Where it takes away some of the pain?"

"I do know."

"Then let this be that."

She pulled his head gently toward her and kissed him. He stayed very still but didn't pull away. She continued, enjoying his lips against hers, reaching her tongue out, rewarded when he parted his lips and gave a short intake of breath. Rose moved her hands to his waist and pulled him into her and he took her face in his, his tongue exploring her mouth and moving to her neck. She gasped as he teased the curves of her ears. He knew his way around a woman.

And that's what she wanted. He led her to his bed, asking if she would regret this tomorrow. She insisted she would not and knew she wouldn't. Jason was an unexpectedly graceful lover. He savored every inch of her, relished bringing her almost to the edge, then retreating and teasing her, his eyes sparkling with a delicious cruelty. His technique was unlike that of any other man she'd known, and for moments at a time she was transported. She returned the favor, enjoying the satisfied look on his face afterward.

"So there's that, then," he said, rolling onto his side to trace one finger along her belly.

"Yes." She thought of Bird. "I should be getting back."

"Are you sure?"

"I am. Thank you."

"I aim to please."

She kissed him lightly. "I bet."

She grabbed her phone and called the nurses' station at the hospital. "He's resting peacefully," she reported to Jason.

Rose slipped on her panties, turning away slightly, then yanked on her jeans. "I've really got to go. Back to real life. And we should probably lay low until the Barbizon project is finished up."

"Worried about the ethics of this?"

She sighed. "Always." If he only knew how unethical she really was.

"What happened with Gloria Buckstone?" He sat up and put a pillow behind his back, as if he had all the time in the world.

The vision of Gloria's black leather boots, which hugged the shin and ended right below the knee, flew into her head. Rose closed her eyes, remembering the look on Gloria's face as she leaned against her desk, her mouth set into a firm line. It was what had made her the star she was, her way of incorporating the coyness of a twenties film queen with the granite determination of an undertaker.

Rose's sweater was lying on the bedside table. She pulled it over her head. "What rumors have you heard?"

"Rumor has it that Buckstone set you up for a fall."

"Nothing that glamorous. The banking documents we got on Senator Madden seemed suspicious. I told Gloria we should wait to make any accusations, that they might be false."

Jason nodded, encouraging her on.

"I cared more about the facts than being first. But she didn't want to wait."

In fact, Gloria had laid into Rose when she'd expressed her concerns. Told her she was smart and capable and if she wanted to rise in the company, she'd have to be more sure of herself. Take risks. Her words had stuck in Rose's head, like an anti-mantra: "The only person who's scared is you," Gloria told her, "and it shows. If you want to report the news, you have to be the one in the driver's seat. Now, drive."

Rose looked at Jason. "Gloria mentored me, helped me make my way up. I owed her. But I wanted corroboration, a second source."

"Understandable."

"We aired it anyway, and were vilified when the documents turned out to be fake. I was asked to resign and Gloria was suspended. She pushed the story despite my doubts and then she never said a single word in my defense when we were busted. My hunch was correct, but that was no consolation."

Jason nodded. "Until a week later when the story turned out to be true. At which point you and Gloria were vindicated."

"I guess so."

Griff loved introducing her as "Senator Madden's nemesis." It was good for his image, dating a journalist who went after corrupt politicians. Or at least it had been, for a while. An involuntary shiver ran up her spine. She didn't want to think about Griff right now.

"Well, I'm sorry she screwed you. And I'm glad you're at Word-Merge now."

"Thanks."

Strange, how easy it was with this man. If anything, distance had made her see where she should have taken a stand.

It felt good to come clean.

CHAPTER TWENTY-FOUR

New York City, 1952

My darling!"

Darby's mother stood in the middle of the lobby, arms outstretched. Less than two days had passed since Darby had been expelled, and the last person she expected to come calling for her was Mother. When the concierge rang her room to say she had a visitor, she'd hoped that it was Sam. Instead, when the elevator doors opened, she was greeted by Mother.

Mother obviously hadn't heard.

Darby stifled the impulse to run into her arms and bury her head in Mother's perfumed embrace as if she were a four-year-old child. The sound of girlish laughter drifted down from the mezzanine, and she didn't want to embarrass herself in front of any other guests.

She accepted a long hug instead.

"I missed you, Darby dear." Mother held her at arm's length and studied her carefully. "The school sent a notice last week saying you were having difficulty and I jumped on a train and here I am."

Darby added the cost of the train to her ongoing tally of repayments. "You didn't need to come."

"I'm glad I did. You don't look very well. Have you been eating?

Never mind; let's pop into the café right here and I'll get some food in you."

They walked through the inside entrance to the café with linked arms. The gesture was strange and artificial, as if Mother was acting out some scene in a madcap movie. Darby slipped inside a booth near the back and fiddled with her silverware until Mother shot her one of her signature looks.

"Sorry."

"Now tell me everything."

Darby evaded the command. "How is Mr. Saunders? And the dogs?"

"All are well."

Mother called the waiter over and ordered Jell-O salads for both of them. Daddy used to say his wife could have been a Hollywood star, with her arched, plucked eyebrows, high cheekbones, and tiny nose. She neatly placed the napkin on her lap and removed her gloves. Every gesture was careful and precise, as if she were a doctor in an operating room.

"Now, Darby. What's going on with you?"

"Well, I've been struggling, to tell you the truth. With the classes, the teachers." Why mince words? Better to be quick, like pulling off a Band-Aid. "And now I've been expelled from Katharine Gibbs."

Mother's eyes closed briefly. An unnerving stillness settled over her. "Why?"

"I never fit in there. And for a while I thought I was doing all right. But the classes were awful and boring and I don't want to do that with my life."

"You've only been there two months. I spent all that money and you couldn't even be bothered to try?" The pitch of her voice rose, never a good sign. "Because you found it boring? The program takes less than a year, for God's sake. We'll go to the school right after lunch and I'll explain that you must stay on."

"They made it clear I can't go back. The letter of expulsion was mailed to you two days ago."

Mother slammed her hand down on the table, making the silverware jump. "You've wasted your father's insurance money. It's gone. There is no refund. Do you remember, when we talked about you coming here, that there was no refund?"

The waiter came with their food, two plates of wobbly green Jell-O mold in which slices of olives, celery, and cheese floated, garnished with lettuce and tomato.

"I'm sorry about the money. I'll pay you back, I promise."

"And how exactly will you do that?"

"I made a friend, a wonderful friend, named Esme. She works at a jazz club and we sang together and people really raved. Yesterday I went to the club and spoke with the owner, and he said I could start work there as a waitress tomorrow."

She didn't mention how her legs had gone liquid from fear when she and Sam had stepped into Mr. Buckley's office at the club after their talk in Washington Square Park. To her relief, he hadn't asked her if she had any experience, just told her to show up for her first shift on Saturday at five and then demanded they both get the hell out and stop bothering him.

Mother stared at her as if she were speaking a foreign language. "A waitress? In a jazz club?"

"It's what I came here for, right? To broaden my horizons."

"And this Esme, is she a student at the Gibbs school as well?" The syllables of Esme's name dripped off Mother's tongue as if they tasted foul.

"No."

"And where did you meet her?"

"She works at the Barbizon. As a maid."

Mother pushed her plate away and sat back, arms crossed. "Oh, Darby."

"You'd like her, I'm sure, if you gave her a chance. She's a lovely girl, Mother. Smart and very talented. She's going to be a famous actress and singer someday." The words sounded crazy to Darby's own ears as she spoke them aloud. She took a deep calming breath and began again. "And I have another friend, too, who's offered to help me. Charlotte is traveling right now, but she said she'd get me an interview with a publishing company when she returns. No matter what, I'll be okay. I can't tell you how grateful I am that you sent me here to live. At first I was so nervous, but now I love it. I don't want to go back."

"You cannot stay here unchaperoned. And I can no longer afford the Barbizon hotel, obviously." She wiped her mouth with her napkin, careful not to smudge her lipstick.

"Esme and I are going to get an apartment together."

"You do realize that you sound like a madwoman, don't you? Do you think you're that special? Do you realize how many girls come to New York hoping to make it big, then fall on hard times and are ruined?"

Darby flinched. "I assure you I won't be ruined. This isn't Defiance, and I'm not an innocent girl anymore."

"What on earth does that mean?"

"Nothing, not that." Well, not exactly that. "The idea of going to Katharine Gibbs was your dream, not mine. I'm not suited to it."

"So you'll work as a waitress instead? Very nice. Your father would be thrilled." Mother pressed one delicate hand to each temple and heaved a dramatic sigh.

"What about publishing?" Darby offered. "That's a respectable career for a girl like me."

"Oh, please. You don't have what it takes."

Maybe Mother was right. Darby had never held a real job. What did she know about supporting herself?

Mother's eyes grew watery and she searched in her purse for a handkerchief. "When your father died, I thought we might end up begging for help. He left me nothing but his insurance policy, with the instructions that it all go to you." As she dabbed at her tears, her mascara smudged in the half-moons underneath her eyes. Darby took the handkerchief out of her hand and gently wiped the makeup away, knowing Mother would be horrified to be seen in public looking messy. "Thank you."

"I'm sorry, Mother. I really am. I've disappointed you."

"I suppose I'm partially responsible. I've kept you safe, maybe too much so. But you aren't equipped to go it on your own, not yet. That's why I did everything I could to make this work for you. Tuition, new clothes, a train ticket, a room at the best women's residence in town. A girl like you needs protection from the real world."

"I know you meant well, and I tried to do the right thing, I swear. But in the end, the life you wanted for me seemed more stifling than safe."

"You have no idea what stifling feels like." Mother's words were acid. "And now every penny gone. What a waste. I never imagined you'd associate with the staff. A maid, for God's sake."

"I will pay you back."

"All I wanted was for you to be independent. To be your own woman. But not like this. Mr. Saunders will be very unhappy, I assure you."

"But don't you see, we want the same thing. I also want to be able to be independent, to take care of myself. Being a secretary isn't the only way to go about that. Upstairs, there are hundreds of girls, approaching the world in different ways. Your way isn't the only one."

"I don't care what the other girls are doing. I won't have my daughter working as a cocktail waitress."

Neither of them had touched the food. Mother called for the waiter and left several crisp bills on the table, her hands shaking. "Now we will go upstairs and you will pack, and we'll catch the next train home. You are done with New York City."

❦

"What on earth is this?"

Darby's mother pulled out the satin dress Esme had given Darby from the small closet in her room.

"Something I picked up in the store." Darby stifled the impulse to grab it out of her hands, to protect it.

Mother pinched the fabric between her finger and thumb. "Cheap. And shiny. Did you ever wear this out?"

"Just once."

"Well, we'll leave that one behind." She tossed it on the floor. "Help me, please. Pick up the suitcase and open it up on the bed."

Darby's heart pounded in her chest, but she did as she was told. Her life had been about following orders, whether they were from Mother or Mr. Saunders. She'd done well in school, obeyed the rules, never asked uncomfortable questions.

"Daddy would have listened to me." She spoke the words quietly, almost under her breath.

Mother's back stiffened, but she didn't stop her methodical sorting. "Don't you dare bring up your father. Not now."

Darby's voice grew stronger. "If he'd lived, he would've at least considered my side of the argument."

"You have no idea what your father would have done under the circumstances. He was not the man you think he was."

"All I know is he was sweet to me, he tried to be sweet to you, and you constantly put him down or yelled at him. Even on his deathbed you couldn't be bothered to comfort him. Nothing he could have done deserved that treatment."

Her mother turned to her, her fingers twitching. Darby knew that movement. She'd seen it in Mr. Saunders before he'd pounded his fist on the table or slapped her mother across the face.

"You think you know what goes on in a marriage? You are a child, a little girl with a big mouth. If Mr. Saunders were here, he'd put you right in your place."

The threat of violence was the final straw. She would no longer back down to the likes of Candy, Mr. Saunders, or even her own mother. "You've insinuated horrible things about Daddy since he died. I'm not going anywhere until you tell me what happened."

"You already know. He got fired. And that meant that when he died, the only thing we had was the insurance money. No pension, no savings. Nothing. Which I misguidedly spent on your education. Which you then wasted."

Darby couldn't help herself. She was picking at a dangerous scab, one she'd always left alone before now. "Why did you have a private funeral?"

"It was what he wanted."

"Or was it so that you and Mr. Saunders could get married right away, without too much talk?" Her body shook as if she were freezing cold. She had never spoken to Mother like this in her life.

Mother stood motionless. "How dare you?"

"You wanted to bury Daddy quickly and with the least amount of fuss so you could move on to Mr. Saunders. You seemed relieved. Happy. How could you?"

To her astonishment, Mother nodded. "I was relieved. I was happy. I never wanted to see your father suffer, but he brought it on himself. Mr. Saunders said it was God's will. If you must know, your father's funeral was private because there was not a soul who would have attended a public memorial for him." She placed her hands on her hips. "He was a degenerate, and word spreads quickly in a small town."

Darby's voice caught in her throat. "What are you talking about?"

"Even the doctor in town wanted nothing to do with him." A tiny bit of spittle stayed on Mother's lip. "I married Mr. Saunders quickly in order to restore our family's good name. I sent you to New York in order to spare you the shame of having people whisper behind your back, saying terrible things. Mr. Saunders protected me, protected us."

"But what were they saying?"

Mother ignored the question. "I thought you'd start a new life here at the Gibbs school, that you'd be able to move beyond the hideousness of your father's behavior. And what did you do? You've disgraced yourself, and me, even further. It's a good thing I came to fetch you. I see now that you were on the verge of ending up in the gutter. Just like him."

"But you still haven't even said what he did. What did Daddy do that was so awful no one could ever forgive it?"

Mother took a deep breath, as if she were about to dive underwater. "He was found in a compromising position with another man in a hotel in Cleveland."

Darby's mind raced. The man who held her hand and encouraged her to be herself. All those trips away. Daddy was a degenerate. A hateful word. That explained Mr. Saunders's smugness, the way the girls in high school had been so distant. Everyone knew about Daddy but her.

He liked to be with men. He liked to kiss other men. She didn't want to imagine the things her father had done; she should never have pushed her mother so far. The shame of his behavior flooded over her.

Victory gleamed in her mother's eyes. Darby looked down at the floor.

What about Esme's kiss in the recording booth? Did that mean Darby was a degenerate as well?

The kiss with Esme had been soft and full of shared desires, but not in any way sordid. If her father had kissed men like that, was that so bad? He was still her father, the man who built an unsailable boat so he and his daughter could have an excuse to escape the emotional frigidity of the house.

He had loved her, and she had loved him. And life was full of strange and unexpected complications.

With that, all doubt faded away. He would have wanted her to stay in New York, free from the small-mindedness of Defiance.

"I'm not going back."

"You're going to stay here with your little friend? You'll be cast out, like your father, I can tell you that."

"I know you spent a great deal of money on me and I promise I'll pay you back, every cent."

"You'll spread your legs, is that what you're thinking?"

The shock of the phrase coming out of Mother's lips stunned her for a moment. "No. I told you, I have a job as a waitress. I have other options. It's not the nineteenth century anymore."

The muscles in Mother's jaw tightened. "You were always a strange one. Even when you were a little girl. You rarely cooed or giggled in your crib. Instead, you'd stare at me, like you hated me. I'm your mother, so I had to take care of you. But look what's become of you. You're like your father in so many ways.

"If you stay here, you won't get any more support from me." She pointed a red-nailed finger in Darby's direction. "I don't want to hear from you, and I don't want to see you. When you have been misused and mistreated, do not show up on our doorstep to ask for help. I have struggled since your father died to make a new name for myself, and I will not have you shred that again."

"You needn't worry. I won't return."

Mother picked up her purse and turned on her heel. She stared at Darby once, a cold, bitter look that seared her like a branding iron. Then she was gone.

Stiff and sore, as if she'd been beaten, Darby leaned over and picked up the satin dress that Esme had given her, hanging it back in the closet.

She had to find Esme. More than anything, she needed to hear Esme laugh and tell her everything would be all right. That she could survive in New York without the protection of her family and the Barbizon Hotel for Women.

In this new version of her life, Darby would work hard—whether it was writing, waiting tables, or even singing. And late in the evenings, when she and Esme were done for the day, they'd double-date with their beaux, and Sam would smell like spices and fresh bread.

She'd prove Mother wrong.

CHAPTER TWENTY-FIVE

New York City, 2016

At least he isn't suffering." Rose had called Maddy from the hospital, but declined her offer to stop by. She liked being alone with her father, had just needed to hear a friendly voice to break up the stillness of the room.

"He'll fade into a deep sleep, like my father did," Maddy assured her.

"After all of his dedication to his work, his students, to me, it's so weird that this is the end." Rose sighed. "Out with not even a whimper."

"Do you think he'd rather rage against the dying of the light?"

In spite of herself, she laughed at the thought. "Probably not. He'd never raged once, even when my mother left. And better this than the ongoing chaos of his dementia."

"You sure I can't come down? I'll bring in a flask of the hard stuff for you."

Rose assured her she was fine, then hung up and stared out the window at the gray skies. He'd last a few weeks at most, and she needed to make the necessary arrangements. All his life he'd talked about being cremated and for his ashes to be scattered around the lilac bushes on the corner of Sheep Meadow in Central Park. Apparently, that was where he proposed to her mother, before life became difficult.

Rose kept vigil until the nurses sent her home to sleep. Around midnight, nervous and wired, she scanned Darby's bookshelves for something to read. A worn binding on the top shelf turned out to be an ancient copy of *Romeo and Juliet*, the cloth cover hanging on, literally, by a thread. She perched on the couch, the book balanced on her lap, and turned to the title page. It was printed in 1887, the pages mottled with time, although the gilt edging was still bright. One of Juliet's soliloquies had been marked up in pencil, the page filled with questions, comments, and stage directions. At the very back of the book, a flash of white caught her eye. She picked up the envelope and gave a startled yelp at the return address. Sam Buckley had sent it from California. The postal stamp read 1953.

Dear Esme,

I assure you I won't give up your secret, however devastating it has been to me. As you wish, I won't try to contact you again.

Sam

But Esme was dead in 1953.

Or was she? Rose's mind raced. Was the woman she'd assumed to be Darby really Esme impersonating her friend? She picked up her phone and tried to reach Jason. No luck. She left a voice mail for him to call her back right away and scanned the letter one more time.

If the slashing had been that brutal, Esme might have been disfigured enough to get away with the switch. And if Darby had been the one who fell to her death, the same reasoning applied. A grisly thought. Maybe Esme had become a new person, disconnecting herself from the drug scandal and forging a new life. But where had Darby's family been in all this? Wouldn't they have known?

According to this short letter, Esme had revealed the switch to Sam, who had been crushed by the news of Darby's death. But something was off. The whole thing felt like a bad soap opera, a scene from one of Maddy's scripts. Yet the letter existed for a reason.

Rose googled the address, but there was no Sam Buckley living there anymore. Not surprising, as more than sixty years had passed. But there was someone else she could ask. Stella had known Darby both before and after the accident. She called Stella's cell phone and left a voice mail, asking if they could meet again.

The next morning, at ten a.m. sharp, she waited for Stanley Jr. outside the button shop. As he unlocked the gate covering the entrance, she got right to the point.

"I have an odd question for you. Did you ever hear Ms. McLaughlin speak Spanish?"

He laughed. "No, I can't say that I did."

Rose nodded. "Okay. Thanks. Sorry to bother you." She turned to go.

"But her young friend did."

Rose spun back around. "She spoke Spanish to Darby?"

"She called her *Tía*. I remember that from high school Spanish. Practically the only thing I remember."

Tía. Aunt.

Not Christina or Tina. Stella had heard the girl say "*tía*."

Darby was hanging out with a young girl who spoke Spanish and called her aunt. Further bolstering the theory that Esme had switched identities.

Rose checked her phone on her way to work. Still nothing from Jason. A twinge of regret tugged at her. She'd thoroughly enjoyed their encounter at his apartment, but she'd been a needy, twisted mess that night. Bad timing all around.

Her phone rang. Stella.

"Well, hello, Rose. How is it going with Bird?"

"Just fine, Stella. More importantly, how are you?"

"I'm almost back in fighting form. I heard from Darby yesterday."

Relief poured over her. Darby or Esme, whoever she was, was safe. "Oh, yes? How is she? Where is she?"

"She couldn't talk long, and the line was crackly. Said she'd be back next Monday."

Rose swallowed hard. Less than a week.

Stella continued on. "And I have to say she was a little miffed that I left Bird in your care. She said she'd refused to speak to you."

She'd been caught. Better to play dumb. "She was reluctant, sure, but I had no doubt in time she'd warm up to the idea."

"Hmm. Anyway, she said she'll come to your apartment and collect Bird as soon as she arrives."

She could imagine the look on Griff's or Connie's face when the old lady showed up at their door, demanding her dog back. They'd send her off to Bellevue. "Maybe you should just give her my cell number instead, and I'll bring Bird to her."

"If she calls me back, I will. Apparently, she's out of the country."

"I see. Listen, I was wondering if I could come back out to New Jersey. We're on a tight deadline with the story, and I'd love to get your input on something that just came up."

"That's fine—and in fact, I think it is better we speak before Darby returns."

"Can I come now?"

"Yes, you may."

⚜

Stella waved away Rose's polite inquiries about her health.

"I want to know what you're doing with Darby's story. She doesn't know you at all, claims she's never exchanged a word with you."

Rose squirmed under her scrutiny. "Well, that's true enough. I apologize for not being clearer, but as you know, it was an emergency. I was happy to help out."

Stella pursed her lips, still not convinced.

"Did you know Darby well before her accident?" Rose asked.

"We spent some time together. Not much. We had something of a falling-out soon after she arrived. Why are you so relentless on this subject, Rose? Is it really all that newsworthy? Something that happened more than fifty years ago?"

"It's part of the story of the hotel, in my mind. The guests, the staff, whatever dividing lines existed. Seems strange she'd want to stay on, after such a tragedy."

"She had nowhere else to go, no other choices. Before the accident, she'd started coming out of her shell. It was easy to see who she might become given the opportunity. Afterward, though, it was as if she decided she'd been punished for trying to live outside her comfort zone. She withdrew again, and that was pretty much that."

"I see. Did she seem very different after she got back from the hospital?"

"What exactly are you getting at?"

Rose leaned forward. "The girl she's been hanging with, I think she called her *Tía*, not Tina. Which means 'aunt' in Spanish. I'm wondering if it's at all possible that Darby was the girl who fell, and the maid, Esme Castillo, was the one who was scarred."

Stella went white. "What on earth are you suggesting?"

"Is there any chance the two women may have switched identities? That the woman we think of as Darby is in fact Esme?"

"That is the most ridiculous thing I've ever heard." Stella's hands gripped the armrests, her fingers like talons. "Absolutely not. The poor woman has been through enough— and I won't let you repaint her life as though it was some two-bit melodrama. Why can't you just leave her alone?"

"I'm sorry." Rose had overstepped. Coming here was a bad idea. "I guess I worry about her."

"You don't even know her." Stella's voice boomed.

"I understand what it's like to be alone in the city and not have anyone to depend on."

"How dare you assume to understand Darby? To understand me? You think just because we don't have a man or children, we're fragile, bitter old ladies? Scared of being mugged or dying in our apartments and not being found for days? Is that what you think our lives are like?"

"No, of course not." Her reply wasn't all that convincing.

"Well, let me put you straight." She planted her legs wide and leaned forward on her elbows. "We aren't weak. We don't need anyone's help. We help ourselves, and we help out each other. My life is rich and full and I get to do whatever the hell I want, when I want. If I want to eat macaroni and cheese for breakfast, I do it without thinking twice. The city is teeming outside my window with life and people to watch, but I don't want to be them. I don't need to be them. I love my life and I don't need your pity."

Rose sat back, stunned.

"Don't you dare project your own fears onto me." Her nostrils flared. "I reject them. If you're lonely and scared, you better deal with it now, because life only gets lonelier and scarier, no matter how many people fill your home or your heart.

"It's up to you, sweetheart. Ultimately, you're on your own."

⚛

Jason was in the office kitchen when Rose finally made it to work. As he reached up to get a mug from the cabinet, his T-shirt rose slightly, showing off his flat stomach, pale and smooth.

He gave her a catlike grin. "Hey. I saw you left messages; it's been crazy here. Some big announcement coming down the pike."

"A new infusion of capital?"

"Don't know. Tyler's been in his office talking with men in suits all morning."

Rose filled him in on the strange turn of events, including the letter from Sam and her conversation with Stanley Jr.

Jason gave a low whistle. "Darby is really Esme? Could she pull off that kind of stunt for so many years?"

"I wondered the same thing. When I mentioned the theory to Stella, she vehemently denied it. Maybe too much so." Rose didn't go into further details, as she was still recovering from the woman's verbal onslaught. Which was well deserved, she had to admit.

"Wait a minute." Jason held up a finger. "Our conversation with Malcolm. Do you remember what he said when you asked about Esme?"

"Not exactly. That he knew she'd died, something along those lines."

"Follow me." He hurried to one of the editing suites and pulled up Malcolm's interview. He hit a button and Malcolm's face appeared on the screen.

"Who, Darby?"

"No, Esme."

"Right. They say she fell off a building and died. But I don't know much else."

He sat back and crossed his arms. "Malcolm mixes them up. And why use the qualifier words *they say?*"

"He also looks away from me when he answers." Rose took a deep breath. "Do you think he knows the truth?"

"He might, if he and Sam have been in touch."

Rose picked up her phone and tried Malcolm. Once again, it went straight to voice mail.

She left another message and hung up. "Darby's coming back into town soon, so maybe we'll get our answer."

Jason nodded. "We'll have to save it for the camera, though. Imagine the reaction shot. This could make this piece really sing."

"But if we can't see her eyes, how will we know?"

"She'll stiffen, pause, something. We'll be able to tell. As long as you get her to sit down and talk." Jason moved closer and placed a hand lightly on Rose's arm. "How's your dad doing?"

"I'm heading back to the hospital as soon as work is over. I need to be there as much as possible. Even if he doesn't know who I am."

"I'm sure he senses something."

She sighed. "Between the dementia and the sedatives, I'm hoping he doesn't sense much at all right now."

A coworker dashed into the room. "Tyler wants all of us together."

Outside his office, Tyler shook hands with the men in suits and then headed into the conference room. WordMerge employees popped up from their cubicles like meerkats, shuffling in behind him, amid whispers and stifled laughter. Rose and Jason hovered near the back.

Tyler rubbed his hands together. His pants were fashionably short and tight.

"I'm happy to announce we're exploring a new paradigm here at WordMerge." He enunciated the company name carefully, the only way to say it without sounding like you hailed from the sticks. "Our audience has made it clear what they want: short, sharp pieces that can be shared on social media. You'll be getting more details in the next couple of days, but for now I want everyone to start thinking in snappy visuals. Lists, photos, funny, smart, you know the type of thing I'm talking about, because it's what you seek out every day."

"You've got to be kidding," murmured Rose.

Jason shook his head. "I don't do snappy."

Rose raised her hand. Tyler looked annoyed. "Yes?"

"Does that mean we're no longer doing in-depth pieces? I thought that was supposed to be WordMerge's brand."

He sighed. "The financials are difficult right now. We need to take a detour, get the page views and get the advertising."

Another editor raised his hand. "What about the stories we're currently working on?"

"Keep on working."

He answered several more questions in a manner that was more vague than comforting, and closed the meeting. As Rose and Jason headed back to her desk, Tyler called them both into his office.

"Sit, sit." He motioned to the chairs opposite his desk. "I'm killing the Barbizon story."

Rose took a deep breath. "Why?"

"Too complex. So many story lines. It's not for us."

Jason spoke up. "I wish you'd let me walk you through it. There's a narrative arc you might have missed, a compelling one."

"The key source is returning to town in a few days," added Rose. "And I have reams of notes. There's a lot of gold in there."

"Reams?" Tyler made a face. "So old school. And that's the problem. If we're going to survive, we have to shift gears."

Frustration welled up. After all their work, all her digging. She imagined the looks on the women's faces when she told them their histories hadn't measured up. "Let me at least put together a rough outline for you. We've found out some shocking twists, heroin rings, identity switches. This is a killer story."

"For *The New Yorker*, maybe. Not for us."

She dug in. "When you hired me, you told me you were creating a multimedia version of *The New Yorker*."

"That was then." He turned to Jason. "I have a new assignment for you. You'll work with Cheryl on a list of top ten narcoleptic dog videos."

Jason spoke up. "I have to say I agree with Rose. The Barbizon story is good. It deserves a platform."

"Sorry. I am, really. Check in with Cheryl, please."

Rose nodded at Jason. Maybe if she could speak with Tyler alone, he'd be less defensive.

After Jason left, she tried again.

"Tyler—"

He cut her off right away. "Look, Rose, I'm sorry. I know this isn't what you signed up for, I get that. But I have to ask you to go along with this. The kids out there look up to you. If you're walking around pissed off because your story got killed, it's not going to help morale."

She sat back, stunned. "First of all, I don't walk around pissed off. I've had stories killed before and sucked it up with no complaints. I'm more worried about the shift in focus of the site. You'll be like everyone else. Don't you want to stand out? Isn't that why you formed the company in the first place?"

He bit the side of his thumb. "If you don't like it, you should just leave."

The realization of what he was doing hit her hard. Her salary, though paltry, was bigger than any other journalist's at the company. He wasn't killing anyone else's story, only hers. Because he wanted her out.

"Tyler, would you prefer it if I left WordMerge?"

"Of course not." The expression on his face remained unchanged. "Unless, of course, you don't feel you'd be happy here. You might find the work slightly tedious."

"Then you should let me go." How much severance could she get? Four months, maybe?

"Oh, no. Of course I'd never fire you." He'd probably figured out the cost of her severance as well. And didn't want to pay it. "When you first came here, I was glad. But things have changed."

Her jaw clenched. She refused to spend the few remaining days of her father's life putting up with Tyler's nonsense. "If I go, I'm taking everything to do with the Barbizon story with me."

"You can't do that, it's the property of WordMerge."

She lowered her voice, better to threaten him. "You don't want that story. I do. I get everything and I don't go to Gawker and tell them you're floundering. You know they'd like nothing better than dirt from a notorious journalist."

He went white. "Okay, fine, take your story with you. You can have it."

"Thank you." She stood, grabbed the ball that hung above his desk and yanked it so hard it came loose from its tether, then threw it into the trash can. "In that case, I quit."

CHAPTER TWENTY-SIX

New York City, 1952

Darby entered the grand lobby doors of Carnegie Hall and looked about her, confused, until a man in an usher's uniform redirected her to the back entrance. She took the elevator up to the floor where the American Academy of Dramatic Arts was located, and stepped into a hallway filled with young people her age. Some were talking loudly or laughing, others singing scales. The noise level was astounding.

She stepped over two khaki-clad men sprawled on the linoleum floor, smoking cigarettes and reciting their lines out loud. Hopefully, Darby would get a chance to pull Esme aside before the next class began. She scanned the crowd for her friend's dark mane, with no luck, eager to surprise her with the news that her mother had come and gone, that the deed had been done.

Darby opened a door marked OFFICE at the end of the hallway, where a secretary talked with a distinguished-looking gentleman who perched on the side of her desk. The secretary looked annoyed at the interruption.

"I'm looking for Esme Castillo." Darby was nervous, but all the phone lessons at Katharine Gibbs had paid off, for her voice remained perfectly modulated.

"Who?" The receptionist looked down at a list on her desk. "Is she a student?"

"Yes, she began studying here this fall."

"How do you spell that?"

Darby spelled it out and waited.

"No, I'm not familiar with that name. Hank, you heard of her?"

The man was handsome in a Hollywood way, with thick, wavy hair. He seemed to enjoy being looked at and took his time answering "No, can't say that I have. Are you sure you have the right school?"

"AADA. I know I do. She tried out last month. She's been taking classes each week."

The receptionist giggled and the man named Hank smiled. "We call them auditions, not tryouts."

"Right. Auditions."

"Wait a minute." The man froze, one hand lifted, mouth parted, as if he was teasing her or playing some kind of acting game, but then his concentration broke. "Esme Castillo?"

She breathed a sigh of relief. Of course, with so many students, it would be hard to keep track. Particularly if you were as self-aggrandizing as this guy. "Yes. That's her."

"Does she have an accent?"

"Yes. She's from Puerto Rico."

The secretary bit her lip and looked confused. "Huh."

Hank cut in. "I do remember her. I can't believe I ever forgot this." He held his hand in front of him, palm facing outward, setting the scene. "I wasn't scheduled to be on the panel that day, but Mr. Peterson was ill. This woman came in, lipstick the color of blood, shiny brown hair."

"That's Esme, yes."

"She was arresting, I'll give you that. She stood in the center of the room, wearing a dress that was quite revealing, and launched into a monologue from *Romeo and Juliet*. I tell you, I could barely understand a word the girl said. We sat there with our mouths agape."

"We don't take people with accents," said the secretary, by way of explanation.

Romeo and Juliet. Esme had left a copy of the book in her room soon after they'd met, saying she didn't need it anymore now that she'd been accepted. "She's not enrolled, then?"

Hank laughed. "No, of course not. But she certainly perked us all up after a long day. I remember her well."

Anger surged at his offhand dismissal. Esme had spent weeks preparing her speech. Only to be cut down by these buffoons. "Would she have studied with someone from the school, or anything like that?"

"No, there's no room in the industry for girls who don't know how to speak properly. Sorry, but you won't find your friend here."

⟡

Back in her room, with Mother's condemnation still echoing in her head, Darby was surprised to learn she had another visitor. Had Mother returned to drag her back to Ohio? Or maybe she regretted their harsh exchange?

Instead, Sam stood in the lobby of the hotel. Darby checked herself from running into his arms, as Mrs. Eustis was greeting some new arrivals near the front door.

"I'm so glad to see you. I was just about to head downtown to find you."

He looked around, pulled her close, his voice low. "We need to talk."

Darby requested a visitor's pass from the registration desk clerk, and led Sam up the stairs to the public lounge on the mezzanine level. A couple of the models giggled when they walked by, but Darby shot them a look that, to her surprise, sent them scampering away. To her relief, Sam didn't gawk at their long limbs and silky hair as she expected him to. He pulled her down onto the tufted leather sofa.

"My God, it's good to see you."

"What's going on?"

Sam ran his hand through his hair. "We're in trouble."

"We are?"

"Well, I am. The club, me, Esme. Big trouble."

"I went looking for Esme at her acting school earlier, but they said she never enrolled."

He straightened up. "Look, Darby. I think she's run off."

"What do you mean, run off? We have plans."

"I know this will be hard to hear, but your plans mean nothing now. I don't think she'll ever show up here again."

What was he talking about? Darby didn't like his grave tone. "What's going on?"

He reached out to touch her, but his hand fell back to his lap, as if it didn't have the energy to finish the movement.

"Sam, tell me."

"An article came out in the *Herald Tribune* today." He pulled out the paper from his jacket pocket and handed it to her. "Esme did something really stupid."

Darby glanced down. Sam pointed to the lead column and she began reading. The words swam on the page: *Puerto Rican hatcheck girl, Detective Quigley, heroin,* and the names of musicians she knew well. *The Flatted Fifth.*

She swallowed hard.

Sam ran his hands through his hair. "Esme had another side to her, one she didn't want you to see."

"What do you mean?"

"She's worked for Kalai for the past year."

Darby tried to understand why this would be a problem, but it didn't add up. "Esme sold spices?"

"Mr. Kalai has another kind of import business. He brings in heroin, other drugs on the side. He's mentioned later in the article."

"My God, Sam! Did you know all along?"

"Yes, but I stayed out of that part entirely. Kalai's a brilliant man, and he was willing to pass down his knowledge of spices to me. His sons think spices are a waste of time—they only care about the money from the drugs. So they leave me alone and manage the heroin sales under their father's watch."

If she had been on shaky footing when she woke up this morning, now the ground was crumbling under her feet. "How did you get mixed up with a man like Mr. Kalai?"

"I met him through Esme. Part of her job as hatcheck girl was to act as a go-between for Kalai and his clients."

"Why would she agree to do such a thing?"

"Money."

Darby remembered the heaps of makeup that Esme had, the dresses that materialized out of nowhere. The strange encounter at Hector's Cafeteria. "I think I saw her once, actually. Uptown at lunch. She passed off something to a man in a suit. She said he was in her acting class." She looked up at Sam. "Obviously not."

"She double-crossed Kalai, gave info to the undercover cop at the club."

"She couldn't have. She hated that guy."

"This article includes a full transcript of an informant, an 'Esme C.,' spilling secrets. Which means Kalai knows everything. He'll be after her; that's certain."

Why hadn't Esme ever confided in her? All the lies and cover-ups. Still, she deserved a chance to defend herself. Darby owed her that much at least.

"I'm sure she can explain everything, Sam. Or I hope she can, anyway—there has to be a good reason why she'd do this."

Sam blinked a couple of times. "Don't you understand, Darby? She's gone, and if she's smart, she'll stay that way. She's in serious danger now. And, by extension, so am I."

"But why are you in danger?"

"My father told me Kalai is out of control, in a complete rage. He has his sons out looking for anyone else involved."

"But you weren't involved. You just said so."

"Except that it was me who convinced Kalai we couldn't toss the cops out of the club night after night. I thought it made us look too suspicious and would end badly for my dad. But now Kalai thinks I was secretly working with the undercovers all along, that I convinced Esme to rat him out. He thinks the sting was my doing."

"I don't understand. Can't you just explain to him that it wasn't you?"

"Kalai is paranoid. He's decided I'm to blame and so I am. My father wants me to leave right now, go out to California where my brother is."

Darby's world was collapsing. Esme was a police informant and involved in the drug trade. Sam was fleeing New York City. Mother's harsh words echoed in her brain. She'd been blinded by her hopes and didn't see the danger they were all in.

Sam reached out and took her hands. A slight tremor shook his fingers.

"You're shaking," she said.

"I'm angry. I'm angry at Esme for screwing everything up for me. For us."

Darby's heart pounded in her chest, heavy with dread. "I think Esme did this for me."

"What?"

"I think it's probably a scheme she came up with to take care of me, until we're on our feet. If she got money for snitching, it was to support me. She couldn't have known that it would be leaked in the papers."

"She should have talked to me first. I could have helped. Now I have to leave and go where no one knows me. I'll have to start as a line cook somewhere, begin all over again."

She couldn't bear to see him go. "Maybe it's only for a month or two. Mr. Kalai will end up in jail, and you'll be able to come back."

"His sons won't give up the business. The money involved is too enormous. The police may get Kalai, but the organization will carry on. That's why I want you to go with me."

Her heart stopped for a moment as she processed his words. "To California?"

"Why not? We'll take the train out tonight. I have some money saved, and we'll find my brother and start a new life together."

"The two of us?"

"Yes. I hear California's great, no freezing winters and you can eat figs right off the tree."

"But what about New York City?"

"It'll always be here. We'll come back in ten years, when the coast is clear and I'm a successful chef and you're a famous writer. We'll be married with a couple of kids and we'll show them where we first met and fell in love." He took a deep breath. "I love you, Darby."

The room closed in around her. If she chose to go with Sam, she'd be a single girl, traveling with a bachelor. No chaperone.

And no more gloves. No clunky typewriter with the x key that always stuck. No giraffes.

But no Esme.

"I love you, too. I'll go with you. But I have to say good-bye to Esme first."

"You won't find her." He spoke firmly, calmly. "I'm telling you, Darby, I promise you, she's gone."

She thought of Daddy, what he might have revealed to her if she'd known to give him the chance. Esme deserved that as well. "I have to try. Can you give me some time? Not much. Just enough to nose around here a little bit. Her shift starts in twenty minutes. If she doesn't turn up, I'll leave a note for her at the front desk."

"Fine, but be careful. I'll head downtown to get my things and meet you under the clock at Grand Central in two hours. Okay?"

"Okay."

"Good." He brought his hand to Darby's cheek and smiled. "I'll be waiting."

CHAPTER TWENTY-SEVEN

New York City, 2016

After packing her personal possessions from her desk into a canvas bag—there weren't many, a mug, an umbrella, and an extra pair of high heels—Rose walked out of the WordMerge offices for the last time. The rest of the staff had no idea what had occurred with Tyler. She'd collected her things and left, as if she were only popping out to the gym.

Five years ago she'd been a rising star, groomed to take over a national anchor position one day. And now she couldn't even hold a job at a start-up. But with her father so ill, the trajectory of her career seemed an inconsequential thing, like a burned-out lightbulb you kept meaning to fix. She'd get back to it and figure it out soon enough. For now she had to focus on her dad.

Bird was eager to get outside when she returned to Darby's apartment. Or maybe Esme's apartment, really. But once they walked out the service entrance, the rain began falling in sheets. She tucked Bird under one arm, strode into the park, and planted him beneath one of the giant elm trees. The leaves acted as a de facto umbrella: large drops broke through the foliage every so often, but the worst of the weather was kept at bay. Bird found a patch of dirt of which he approved and took a long pee, glaring up at Rose for invading his privacy by watching him. She looked away. How had she got to this point, where a ten-pound dog bossed her around?

As Rose approached the Barbizon, a figure caught her eye. Jason stood underneath the awning that led to the lobby, looking down at his phone. In a smooth movement, he slung his backpack over his shoulder, and her stomach did a flip. His every move breathed of sex to her now; she couldn't help it. But she didn't want him going inside.

"Jason!"

She called out and crossed the street, almost getting hit by a cab that had veered suddenly into the left-hand lane.

Jason looked up. "I've been trying to reach you."

"Sorry, I left my phone in the apartment." She glanced back at the lobby. Patrick saw her and waved. "We've got to go around the side. Come this way."

"Wait a minute." Jason stood firm. "I just went inside and they said you don't live here anymore."

"Well, not officially. I dog-sit for another tenant."

"Then let's go in; this rain's a disaster. And we have to talk about what happened today. Tyler said you quit."

"I did. If I stayed, he would've made my life more miserable than it already is. But we have the story still, so that's good news. Come around this way and I'll tell you all about it."

He still didn't budge. "Why don't we just go in the front?"

The answer came to her in a flash. "Dogs aren't allowed in the lobby. Management rules."

"Rose!"

The deep voice was instantly recognizable. She begged silently for it to be only Griff, not Connie, but her luck had run out. The two were unfolding themselves from a black town car, wearing matching Burberry raincoats.

"Griff, hi."

"What are you doing here?" His eyes darted back and forth between her and Jason.

"This is Jason." She was unsure what else to do. She nodded at Connie, who glared back. They'd met a couple of times when the kids were dropped off, but never exchanged more than a few words.

Griff shook Jason's hand like the politician he was, firmly and with great sincerity. "Nice to meet you."

"I'm going inside." Connie disappeared, leaving behind the faint whiff of Chanel No. 5.

Jason dug his hands into his pockets. "I'll leave you two for a minute."

"Don't," Rose insisted. "Griff, I'm not here to see you; you don't have to get all bent out of shape."

"I'm not bent out of shape. Simply surprised. Did you leave something behind?"

Jason looked at Rose, confused.

"I didn't leave anything behind. I'm visiting a friend in the building."

Relief crossed Griff's fine features. "Right. The woman on the fourth floor. In that case, after you." He gestured inside.

"No, you go ahead. I have to speak with Jason."

"All right. And maybe we can make an arrangement to talk, in a week or two. Would that be possible?"

An unmistakable heat came from his eyes. Maybe it was the fact that Jason was standing close to her, ever so slightly possessive, that got his competitive juices flowing. Or maybe he'd actually missed her.

Two weeks ago, she would have loved the opportunity to bring him back into her life, in whatever way. To find their connection again. But not anymore. And her change of heart had nothing to do with Jason. Her father's decline, Stella's painfully honest rant, and the ladies' stories had made her see her life in a new light. She would be in charge from now on. As a result, the chemical attraction, the aura that encircled Griff and made him the focus of her world, had dissipated. Just like that.

"Sorry. I'm too busy."

"I see. I guess I'll see you around. Jason, it was nice meeting you."

Jason grunted in return, and when she turned to face him, she could see he was pissed.

"What exactly is going on?"

"Well, that's Griff, my ex-boyfriend. And his wife. I mean his ex-wife."

"We were introduced."

Patrick was making his way outside, and she didn't want to have to speak with him. "Follow me and I'll explain."

The walk to the service entrance and up the stairs seemed endless. Once in the apartment, she dried off Bird with a towel before he skittered over to his usual place on the couch. He stared at Rose expectantly, as if he were a tiny bearded spectator at a boxing match.

"Who lives here?" Jason asked.

The time had come to tell the truth. Now that the story had been killed, maybe Jason wouldn't be too horrified. Rose grabbed a towel from the bathroom and dried off her hair, avoiding his gaze. "This is Darby's apartment. Or Esme's. I can't quite wrap my head around who she is anymore, to tell the truth."

"You appear to be quite comfortable here."

"I've been taking care of her dog."

"Whoa. Back up a minute." He lowered himself onto the couch and exchanged glares with Bird. "First of all, why did you quit?"

She sat cross-legged on the chair. "I don't want to make stupid lists. That's not why I signed on with Tyler."

"I can understand that. But we could have convinced him to do the Barbizon piece at least."

"No, he was done with it, and done with me. I'm tired of playing games and being played."

"So what will you do?"

"I'll pitch the story to someone else. *The New York Times Magazine*, that kind of thing."

"And what about all this?" He gestured around the room. "How will you explain to your editors that you're living in a source's apartment? The *Times* doesn't like that type of thing, you know. No good news source does."

"I know. It wasn't planned."

"Obviously, there's something you're not telling me. You're taking care of her dog, yet you don't know much about her, and have no idea where she went. "

"It all happened at once. Stella Conover was dog-sitting but she had to go to the hospital, so I took over. Apparently, Darby hasn't made many friends on the floor. She's standoffish."

"Why didn't you take the dog back to your own apartment?"

"It was Griff's apartment. Until we broke up. Griff and his ex-wife, who you just had the pleasure of meeting, got back together, and she wanted to live there. He gave me only a few days to move out, and I was desperate. It's a temporary solution."

"You haven't spoken with Darby since she left, right?"

"Right."

"Does she know you've been holing up here?"

She took a deep breath. "Not yet."

He rubbed his chin. "I hate to ask this, but how exactly did you get all of your information? The book of spices, the letter, that kind of thing."

Without thinking, she glanced at the bookshelf.

"You went through her belongings?" His eyes widened with shock. "You're living in a woman's apartment, squatting. If she comes back and finds you, she could call the police. You're trespassing. And snooping."

"I wish I could explain. But I feel this strange connection with her."

"With an eighty-year-old woman you've only met in passing? That makes no sense."

"I know, none of this does." Her words tumbled out. "But I'll be out of here before she returns. I'm moving into my friend Maddy's apartment. I'll take Bird with me and leave Darby a note. When she calls, I'll explain everything. And she'll be so grateful that I took care of her dog, she'll agree to be interviewed and we'll have a truly tremendous story. And if my hunch is correct and the woman who calls herself Darby is actually Esme in disguise? Can you imagine how huge that would be?"

He took a deep breath, his broad chest rising and falling. "What about this scenario: She comes home, finds out that you have the dog, and considers what you've done is a major invasion of privacy, not to mention dognapping, and turns you in to the cops."

"I have Stella to back me up, that I helped out in a pinch. And what's going to happen to me? I'll get fired? Too late for that."

"Never mind getting fired. What about the ethics of what you're doing? What if someone did this to you? It's criminal, no question about it."

"No." She punched the word. "The story is much more than that."

"In what way?"

"It's about losing the people you love, being alone in a big city with nothing more than the four walls of your apartment to protect you. Ending up lonely and bitter with no one around."

"This isn't a Grimms' fairy tale, Rose. Darby, or Esme, whoever she is, made her choices, from what it sounds like. We don't know what she got involved in. But she wasn't an innocent. Whatever happened up on that terrace in 1952 was tragic, but not unavoidable. Heroin, drugs, informants. They were involved in some serious shit."

God, he was right. His words sunk in with a bitter force. She'd deluded herself these past weeks, crossing lines and making bad judgment calls about a series of events that had nothing whatsoever to do with her.

But there was no going back now. Rose stood. "Everything you say makes sense, Jason. But I want to find out exactly what happened. I have to."

"Why? So you don't end up the same way? A crazy old lady with no friends, living in a dingy, rent-stabilized apartment?"

It was as if the wind had been knocked out of her. "That was cruel."

He softened, only slightly. "I get it. With your father being so ill, with everything you've been going through, I understand why you might be inclined to fixate on this woman. But you shouldn't. It's not healthy. Maybe Darby-slash-Esme is off on a beach in Tahiti, sipping rum punches with her sixty-year-old lover."

"I don't think so."

"Do you think you could be overcompensating for what happened to you at the network?"

She bristled at his presumption. "No. Of course not. These are two different stories."

"Maybe. But hear me out. Before, you were afraid to go forward because you didn't have all the information."

"Yes. I waited, but the story got away from me anyway. Maybe if I'd shown some guts, like Gloria, I wouldn't have been made the scapegoat. Maybe I should have been more willing to go out on a limb."

"And so that's what you're doing here. You're being aggressive, pushing boundaries and rules in order to get the full story. But you may never have it. This old lady, whoever she is, may never tell you what really happened. Maybe the unfinished business between Sam and Esme and Darby should stay that way."

"I don't think so. I want to put the pieces of the puzzle together. For Darby's sake."

"Esme's sake."

"You know what I mean. Don't you want to find out what happened?"

"I do, but I'm not about to go breaking the law to do it. Tyler was right to kill the story."

"Tyler's an idiot. This story has legs."

"You're not much smarter than he is right now, as far as I can see."

"Very nice." Rose gritted her teeth. She didn't have to take this. She'd had enough of men telling her what to do and when to do it.

"I can't believe you don't see what a tightrope you're walking on." Jason had turned red; a vein pulsed on his forehead. "You're way too caught up in the story. Step back, take a break. And move out of here now." He held his hands out, palms facing out. "If you don't, I'm done."

"What are you saying?"

"I'm saying I don't want anything to do with this. You're digging yourself into a huge hole. You need to move out of here and get on with your own life."

If only there was a life to move on to.

⟨∞⟩

At seven thirty that evening, while reading out loud from Stephen Hawking's latest, Rose looked up to discover her father had passed away. He gave no sign, no warning, not even a raspy breath. One moment he was there, and the next, he was gone. She was unprepared for the suddenness of the ending. The nurses said he'd been doing well that day, had opened his eyes once or twice. She'd pictured his death in her imagination already: He'd shift back into consciousness, focus on her, and even if he didn't say a word, they'd have one last connection.

But that didn't happen.

Maddy was by her side not long after receiving her anguished call, murmuring all the right things. Rose fell into her arms.

"I don't know, did I do the right thing? Maybe I should have kept him in his home longer, moved in with him and found an aide to help during the day." Had he been happy at all, in the recesses of his cloudy mind? She couldn't say the thought out loud, and burst into tears.

Maddy handed her a tissue. "You did what had to be done, and he loved you dearly. Don't second-guess yourself."

"I can't help it." The full weight of his fear and confusion fell upon her with a brutal force. She didn't do enough, she let herself get sidetracked by work and Griff. Just as her mother had disappeared one day, her father had as well.

All her life she'd been terrified that her father would disappear the way her mother had. That feeling had dissipated as she headed into her teens, but she'd replayed the same game with Griff. Hoping if she said the right thing or presented herself properly, he'd never abandon her.

But they all had, in one way or another. Stella was right. In the end, she was alone. Not even Jason would bother with her, now that he'd learned the truth about her craziness.

She wished she could disappear as well, leave all the pain and solitude behind. She imagined the fall off the terrace of the Barbizon. The drop would take mere seconds. A rush of air and then a burst of pain. Then nothing. What had gone through Darby's mind during the descent? What were her regrets?

Rose's were obvious. She regretted everything to do with her father. Each decision had been made carefully, but there was no way of knowing if any of them had been correct. He'd gotten sick, he'd fallen, he'd died. The narrative arc was all there. They might have happened no matter what she'd done. But she could have done more. She should have done more.

She couldn't even remember the last real conversation they'd had, before he'd become muddled and angry. How she wished she could rewind the video of her life and watch just that snippet. To see if she'd smiled at him, or touched his hand, or done anything to show him how much she loved him.

She held his hand now, and cried.

CHAPTER TWENTY-EIGHT

New York City, 2016

Arrangements were made; kind words were said by the nurses and doctors who'd tended to Rose's father over the past few years. His normally easygoing nature had turned obstinate and changed as his disease had progressed, so it wasn't surprising how few of his former friends showed up to his memorial service. The nursing home sent flowers, as did one or two of the students he'd stayed in touch with.

His death was a shock, even though Rose had been preparing for it for a long time. The pain was surprisingly physical, as if her inner organs had liquefied and all that was left was a hard outer shell that protected a dull, pulsating ache.

After the service, she packed up her belongings, knowing Darby would be back in three days. Maddy had offered to spend the afternoon with her, but Rose wanted to say a quiet good-bye to Darby's spirit before she left the Barbizon for good tomorrow morning. She'd wait out the next couple of days at Maddy's apartment and hand over Bird without asking any further questions. Just a good neighbor helping out in a pinch, that's all. She'd miss Bird. They'd come to appreciate each other as roommates. She was sure he'd even smiled at her once when she came home. In a toothy, doggy way, but still.

She placed the small copper urn with her father's ashes on the windowsill while she tidied up. Her plan was to wait until spring to scatter them, when the lilac bushes were fragrant and thick with blooms. The winter would seem very long, but having a set period of mourning somehow seemed appropriate.

The book of spices went back on the top bookshelf where she'd found it; same with the copy of *Romeo and Juliet*. It was time to let Sam and Darby and Esme go, let them be at peace, wherever they were.

Her phone rang. Griff again. He'd been calling Rose regularly since their awkward chance meeting in front of the building, trying to explain how sorry he was and asking if they might "grab a coffee and really talk." She let the call go to voice mail without an ounce of regret. At the very least, the past few weeks had freed her from her bond to Griff. She didn't miss him anymore.

She did think about Jason, though. Which was annoying, as she had no desire to replace one man with another. Maddy had advised her to slow down and stay out of the game for a while, and she agreed. Too much had happened for her to be running into the arms of another man. No matter how tempting those arms might be.

For the first time in her life, she was free from everything. No family, no lovers, no job. Maybe she'd travel the world, write free-lance pieces from faraway places that mashed up the best places to eat with some kind of soul-searching epiphany. No, that'd been done already. Besides, she was always the type to dig in, to nest. What made Rose happiest was sitting in a comfy armchair on a rainy day, reading a good book. Crossing China by train or driving the Mongolian deserts paled in comparison. She was a homebody at heart, like her father.

Unsure of what to do next, and reluctant to go, she lay facedown on the sofa. Maybe Jason was right. She'd been living Darby's life instead of her own. Much easier to stay buried in the past, particularly someone else's past. Her phone rang again and at first she ignored it, expecting it to be Griff once again.

But it was Jason. She knew she shouldn't talk to anyone, considering the state she was in. But she couldn't resist.

He spoke quickly. "Look, I was awful to you the other day. I was angry about the story and that you quit."

Rose sighed. "You said it yourself, it was better that the story was killed. We didn't even have Darby-slash-Esme lined up; it was a disaster waiting to happen. I handled it terribly, lost my bearings."

"Maybe, but there was a lot of pressure on you. I've seen journalists lose their minds plenty of times, believe me."

"In war. Not doing a feature on old ladies. Pathetic, really."

"You and I both know it was a great story, nothing pathetic about it. And I'm sorry I said you were no smarter than Tyler. You're way smarter."

She laughed for the first time in days. "Apology accepted. I know you were only trying to look out for me."

"Hey, your instincts are great. You fell into the trap of overempathizing with your source. Happens all the time."

"But I barely even knew her."

"Which meant you were able to project everything you wanted onto her. She was a scary vision of your future, everything you were worried about turning into."

"You're quite the therapist, Dr. Wolf."

"I like that. 'Dr. Wolf.' Maybe I should switch careers."

"I'm thinking about doing the same."

"How's your father?" His voice was tentative, careful.

"He passed away three days ago. Peacefully." She couldn't say anything else or she'd burst into tears.

"Oh, Rose. I'm so sorry. Jesus. I know what you're going through, I really do."

"We had a lovely memorial, with all five of the friends he had left. Funny, it made me wonder who would turn up at my funeral." The dog looked up at her and panted. "Bird, maybe."

"I miss you."

Her heart turned over a couple of times. "I miss you, too."

"Listen, I just noticed that Malcolm is playing at Dizzy's at Lincoln Center tonight. Some kind of tribute to the old stars of bebop. I think we should go."

The chance of listening to the music live was tempting. "I thought we were going to drop the story. I'm moving out first thing tomorrow morning, just so you know."

"Where are you going?" His voice carried a hint of concern.

Perhaps he was worried that she'd be going back to Griff. "To my friend Maddy's. Should be a circus. Two kids, husband, me on a couch."

"You can stay here, if you like, until you figure things out."

"It's nice of you to offer, but I can't; we barely know each other."

"We know each other better than you think. For example, I know what the spot on your lower back, right where your spine curves, tastes like."

She shivered. "And what does that taste like, exactly?"

"Sweet, like honey."

"However tempting your offer, I have to take some time and think things through."

"You're not thinking about going back to the Ken doll, are you?"

"Not a chance."

"Good. So let's go out and hear some music tonight, all right? It's a great venue, musicians who've been around the block and will blow our socks off. Your dad would want you to try to enjoy life, right?"

The last thing he'd want was her lying around on the couch like a mopey teenager.

That much was true.

∾

"I wonder how long it's been since Malcolm performed." Rose turned to Jason as the musicians walked onto the stage to the sounds of whistles and clapping.

"That's a good question. You can ask him afterward."

The quintet was a little creaky in the joints, from the look of it, and for a moment Rose worried that Malcolm wouldn't be able to get himself behind the drum set without tripping. Once they were all safely in place, the trumpet player counted off and they launched into "52nd Street Theme."

She was glad she'd come. Instead of the typical dark jazz club, Dizzy's was located on the fifth floor of a massive skyscraper overlooking Central Park. The room was all strange angles and curves, with huge windows that soared behind the musicians. The dusky sky acted as the backdrop, changing slowly throughout the set from azure to navy. And the crowd was an eclectic bunch, ranging from large tables of Asian tourists to serious jazz aficionados who punctuated the solos with determined approval.

The musicians played off each other, laughing out loud at times. The sax player riffed on a theme that the pianist then took up, and Malcolm all the while kept up a fast beat, the bass drum underlining each turn of phrase. Malcolm's face was ecstatic with joy, and Rose's eyes filled just watching him.

As the musicians took their bows, she reached out and touched Jason's arm. "This is amazing. Thank you."

"I'm glad you came."

"I am, too." She wiped away her tears. "Sorry I'm so emotional."

"Please, you don't have to be sorry about anything."

The crowd began to filter out, but Rose and Jason ordered another round. They waited until the musicians reappeared, mingling with those who'd stayed. The stragglers all knew one another, and there was much handshaking and backslapping.

"There's Malcolm." He was walking toward an older man seated at a table in the back corner.

Jason and Rose weaved their way over. Jason spoke first. "I hate to interrupt, Mr. Buckley, but we wanted to say hello."

Malcolm's eyes registered confusion.

"We spoke at your apartment a couple of weeks ago, about the story for WordMerge," offered Rose.

Malcolm nodded but didn't say anything.

She continued on. "Anyway, the story's been killed, unfortunately, but we wanted to thank you for your time. We heard you were performing and had to come. You were terrific."

"Well, I appreciate that."

The other man slammed his hand down on the table and they

all jumped. "What story? You need all the publicity you can get, old man."

Rose explained. "It wasn't about music, really, more about something that happened back in 1952 at the Barbizon Hotel for Women."

The other man stared at her with cloudy eyes. "The Barbizon?"

Malcolm touched his arm. "Now, don't get all excited." He turned to Jason and Rose. "I'd like you to meet my brother, Sam Buckley."

Rose stared, trying to match the man's lined face and thinning gray hair with the image she had in her head of Sam as a young man. He was thinner than his brother, as if he'd been ever so slightly deflated. The purple dress shirt he wore was crisp and pressed but one size too large. His strong features hadn't been softened by age, his chin charmingly dimpled.

"You're Sam. And you're in town," Rose managed to stammer out.

"I am indeed, on both counts."

"We've been looking for you," said Jason. "It's a pleasure to meet you."

"We thought you were unreachable," added Rose, looking over at Malcolm.

"Now, who told you that?"

Malcolm crossed his arms. "His stepdaughter, Jessica, had been taking care of him out in San Francisco, and last year she got transferred to New York and brought him along. My brother's been through a lot, and I didn't think he'd be interested in your questions."

"What questions? For God's sake, I can still hear what you say, little brother. I've got glaucoma. I'm not deaf." Sam picked up the cane resting against his chair and banged it on the floor a couple of times. "My sight's not what it used to be, but I can smack you with this cane easy. I'm going back to California if you think I'm such a fragile flower."

"Fine; talk, then. I'll leave the three of you to it."

Malcolm got up and was immediately surrounded by well-wishers.

Sam smiled. "My brother is protective of me. What's this story about, exactly?"

Rose filled him in on the background, about meeting her mysterious neighbor and the interviews with the women of the fourth floor.

"But the woman disappeared before I could interview her."

"Who?"

Rose got the impression he was testing her. "Esme, who we think assumed Darby McLaughlin's identity after the fall on the roof."

He stiffened. "And how do you know about that?"

"We saw the letter you wrote to her; she saved your reply."

"She showed it to you?"

Jason stepped in. "We've also seen the book of spices. It's phenomenal, and we were wondering what you ended up doing out West, if you were able to put your recipes to use."

"The book of spices. I can't believe it's still around." He scratched his jaw. "I showed up at my brother's hotel room, on the run, and tried to forget about that damn book. Got a job in a Vietnamese restaurant and eventually married the owner's daughter, a widow. Not a bad life, until she passed away and my eyes started to go. But Jessica takes good care of me."

"I'm glad to hear that. We found the book intriguing, to say the least."

"Well, thanks. It's funny to think Esme's saved it all these years. I figured she'd tossed it in the trash."

"Maybe you can meet her, and she'll give it back to you. It is yours, after all."

He cleared his throat. "I don't want to stir up trouble. I have nothing to say to her." A fleeting look of pain crossed his face.

Rose threw a warning glance to Jason. "We don't want to upset you in any way, Mr. Buckley. But we know about Mr. Kalai and the drug ring; we were hoping you could fill us in on some of the details we're missing."

"You want to know what happened that day?"

"Well, we don't want to pressure you. But yes, we'd love to get your perspective. To try to put the pieces together."

Malcolm returned to the table. "We've got to go, Sam."

Rose pressed her card into Sam's hand. "My cell number is on there; feel free to call anytime you want to talk."

"I'll think about it." He reached for his cane and stood. "It was a pleasure meeting you both."

The two men shuffled out of the club.

Rose and Jason took the elevator down to the ground level and walked out into the night. She grabbed him by the arm and pointed. Malcolm and Sam stood by the line of taxis, arguing. Sam spoke rapidly, but he was too far away to be understood.

"He wants to talk to us. We should go to him."

Jason sighed. "No. Let them work it out; we don't need to cause any more problems than we already have."

She couldn't resist. She ran over and touched his arm. "Sam, let's go get a drink; there's a pub across the street. Please."

Malcolm leaned into Sam. "I'm telling you, you've got to watch what you say."

"Please, Sam. One drink."

"One drink," he agreed. "Maybe it's time to let go of some ghosts."

Malcolm pulled Rose aside as they crossed the street. "Take it easy on him, that's all I ask. He was a mess when he turned up in

San Francisco all those years ago. His life was going one way, and then it suddenly took a sharp turn. It took him a long time to recover."

Rose nodded. "I understand, believe me. We won't push him."

They sat at a table in the back of the empty bar, where Frank Sinatra crooned gently over the sound system.

Sam sat next to Malcolm and began to speak, staring out over their shoulders and into the past.

CHAPTER TWENTY-NINE

New York City, 2016

Darby and I had fallen hard for each other by then," said Sam. "Or at least I had fallen hard for her. She was a combination of smart and innocent, not like most of the girls who hung around at the club."

"I heard a recording of Darby and Esme," said Rose. "Darby did the harmonies, but it was gorgeous."

"Darby's voice was pure as snow. You see, when she sang, it wasn't about showmanship or glitter but about the song and the words. You were captivated when she opened her mouth. And she had no idea. Sometimes she'd put herself down, like she was some dowdy girl from the Midwest, but she was much more than that."

"What was Esme like?" asked Rose.

"That girl was ambitious, always had been. I knew she was working for Kalai; a lot of people were; it was how the system worked. But the minute she got paid to squeal, she was asking for trouble."

"What happened the last day you saw Darby?" asked Jason.

"My father showed me the article in the paper, where Esme ratted out the musicians and Kalai. Kalai was furious, of course, and word on the street was that he was after me and Esme, both. He and his sons figured I was a snitch, too."

"But you weren't."

"Didn't matter. I convinced Darby to leave with me; we were going to go to California together. By then she'd been kicked out of school. I went downtown to pack and as I was pulling my stuff together, I heard Kalai's guys come into the club downstairs. I was trapped. So I wrote a message in the spice book and tossed it out the window to one of the busboys, told him to bring it to the Barbizon for Darby." A tiny muscle in his jaw twitched. "I was taken to Kalai, where they beat the hell out of me and held me for several days."

Rose shook her head. "I'm so sorry."

"They had no mercy, none. I was locked in a room in the back of the spice shop. That's what kept me going hour to hour, trying to take my mind off the pain by figuring out what spices I could identify by smell. Until my nose became too bloody to breathe through."

She couldn't imagine the terror. "Your father must've known where you were. Couldn't he tell the cops?"

"Kalai controlled the neighborhood, and he controlled my father. When it came to a choice between the club or his son, my father chose the club. But Kalai loved me better than that in his own way. He wanted his men to punish me, but he didn't want them to actually kill me. Once he figured I had learned my lesson, he released me to my father with a warning to leave town. That same evening, my father took me to the bus depot and sent me across the country, to my brother. By then, my mind wasn't right.

"After a few months, I pulled myself together. I sent Darby a letter, explaining what had happened to me, and asked her to join me.

Esme wrote back and told me that Darby had died, that she was living at the hotel now and I should move on."

"Did she tell you what happened, about the accident?"

He didn't respond to the question. "What do you know?"

Rose had to be careful; he'd been through enough. "We think there was some kind of skirmish up on the terrace. We don't know exactly what happened, but we think Esme got slashed badly on the face, and Darby fell to her death. From that letter, along with some other pieces of evidence, we assume Esme took on Darby's identity."

"That way she'd avoid Kalai looking for her."

Rose nodded.

"They were the same size, had similar builds," recalled Sam. "Strange, to think she could get away with it for so many years."

"The letter you received must've given you quite a shock."

"It did. I had imagined her going to the club and my father telling her I'd gone away and wouldn't be coming back, not giving her any further details. The thought made me sick. So I was thrilled when I got a letter back with the Barbizon Hotel on the return address. I was sure this would be a new beginning for us. The news of Darby's death hit me hard. I never forgot her, or what we might have done together." He took a long sip of his drink. "Esme said never to contact her again; that much was easy."

"Do you think Darby slashed Esme with a knife?"

Sam shook his head. "She wasn't like that. Only if she was being attacked. Otherwise, it doesn't make sense to me."

So many unanswered questions. And in the meantime, Sam and Darby's love had been subsumed by something dark and ugly.

"Well, I'm glad we were able to talk, as it helps us understand most of what happened," said Rose.

Outside, they said their good-byes and Rose and Jason promised to stay in touch.

Sam held Rose's hand tightly in his. "It was all so long ago, but what's funny is I still dream of Darby. Just last night, in fact, I dreamed of her. That she was singing at the club and it was as if she was only singing to me. That's what it was like, watching her. Like you were the only man in the world."

CHAPTER THIRTY

New York City, 2016

Rose asked Jason to help her move her things to Maddy's after their talk with Sam; she didn't want to wait until morning. As they climbed the back stairs for the last time, she was hit by a wave of nostalgia. She was connected to the building like no other in Manhattan, even her West Village studio, even the town house she'd grown up in. Knowing that hundreds of women had walked the halls—it was a history she was pleased to have been part of, even if it was only for a few months.

She opened the door to the fourth-floor hallway. "Thanks for helping me out."

"Of course."

She put the key into the lock and opened the door.

The figure of a woman stood less than two feet away.

Rose jumped backward and let out a screech.

Esme.

Her figure was cast into silhouette by a bright light behind her, making her seem more like a dark ghost instead of a human being. When she spoke, her scratchy voice echoed in the small hallway. "Well, well, well. Looks like Goldilocks has returned."

Rose's heart pounded in her chest and her mouth went dry. "You're back."

"Indeed, I am." She studied Rose and Jason through a brown hat and veil that sat slightly askew, as if she'd quickly planted it on her head. She stepped aside and waved them in.

Rose cautiously led the way, hoping at the very least that Bird would jump into her arms, happy to see her. But he remained on the couch, panting like a lunatic, as if he were curious to see how this all played out.

Her suitcases were stacked beside the coffee table, the throw she'd used as a blanket these past few weeks neatly folded on top of the pillow she'd borrowed from the bedroom.

"You've made yourself right at home in my absence, it appears. Sleeping in my bed, drinking my coffee."

"I wasn't sleeping in your bed. Just on your couch." As if that helped.

"Are you being impertinent?"

"No, not at all. I'm so sorry about this."

"So tell me." Esme crossed her arms. "Why are your belongings in my apartment?"

"You see, Miss Conover—"

Esme cut her off before she could go on. "Yes, Stella tells me you walked Bird while I was away. And I thank you for that. But you don't need suitcases to walk a dog."

"You remember I lived right above you? Well, I had to leave my apartment."

"And why was that my problem?"

"I had to move out, but I didn't want to leave Bird. No one else on the floor offered to take him in."

"Bunch of hermit crabs. Not surprised at that."

Encouraged, Rose carried on. "So you see, I decided to stay here until you returned. Miss Conover said you wouldn't be back until Monday."

"Were you planning to make a quick escape before I came home?"

Not being able to see Esme's eyes made it difficult to connect with her, to gauge what she was feeling. "To be honest, yes. I felt horrible, doing this, but it was an emergency, because Miss Conover had to go to the hospital."

"I ought to call the police on you. I know exactly what you were up to. You wanted to find out more about what happened to me, so you made yourself right at home and went through my things." Her voice rose. "This is a complete invasion of privacy."

Jason stepped forward. "Rose's father just passed away. She lost her job, her father died, and taking care of Bird became very important to her. She was out of line, that's true, but she didn't mean to do you any harm."

"Who are you?"

"Sorry, Esme, this is Jason Wolf. He's a journalist as well."

"Jason Wolf. Quite the name." She looked him up and down before turning back to Rose. "Why did you call me Esme?"

She'd blown it. But considering there was no way this woman would ever grant them an interview, the truth might as well come out.

Rose pointed to the bookcase. "One night I took out your copy of *Romeo and Juliet*. It caught my eye, the binding was so old. It's a gorgeous edition." She paused. "And a letter dropped out."

"And you read it, of course."

The awfulness of what Rose had done hit home. This poor woman wanted nothing more than to live in peace, not have to relive what must have been the most horrific few moments of her life. No matter what she'd done in 1952 to Sam and Darby, decades had since passed. "I apologize. I wasn't thinking straight. I never should have read it. Or come in here at all."

"You got that right."

"Esme, I know what happened at the club, about the drugs, and Sam, and I wanted to know more. I couldn't help myself. Maybe it's because I'm a journalist. But it's also because I'm a woman in a tough spot, not totally unlike the one you and Darby were in. No one's here to blame anyone."

"How dare you talk to me of blame?" Waves of anger emanated from her body.

She was blowing it. "Please, for Sam's sake. He should know the truth as well." Rose was taking a risk. Either Esme would rise to the bait, or she'd close them off forever.

Esme opened her lips, but no sound came out for a moment, all of her bluster faded away. "Sam?"

"He's in town. We saw him a few hours ago. I'm sorry if that's a shock."

"A shock. Yes, you could say that."

"Can I get you some water?"

"Yes, please." Esme lowered herself into the armchair. Rose grabbed a glass of water from the kitchen and by the time she'd returned, Jason had draped the throw over Esme's shoulders. Her fierceness was gone, replaced by an overwhelming melancholy.

Rose knelt at her feet and looked up. "Please. What can I do to make this up to you?"

"Put on my record."

She knew the one Esme was referring to. She walked over to the small record player, turned it on, and, with a shaking hand, lifted the needle and placed it carefully on the edge of the revolving vinyl. The familiar recording of the two women's voices began, Esme and Darby, singing, followed by the tiny giggle at the very end.

Rose couldn't help but smile. "I heard you playing this the day we met in the elevator. It's beautiful. And intriguing. Your voices are remarkable together."

"I'm *so* pleased you think so. And now it is time for you to get the hell out of my apartment." Esme's mouth was set in a firm line, her cheeks slightly flushed.

"Okay, we'll go. I'm sorry it all came crashing down. I only started asking questions because I was worried about you. Being all alone—I get that. I'm alone now. No family, no job. I have to start again from the ground up. I'll be the first to admit my behavior here was suspect. But it's because I need to know how to do this. How to start again."

"Don't compare our situations." Esme pointed a long, crooked finger at Rose and slowly rose back to her feet. "Maybe I could have had a different life; we'll never know. Once I was marked, scarred, it was all over. I was only a shell after that, working in the back room of a button company, balancing books and paying bills, staying away from people who felt sorry for me or wanted to find out the lurid details." She paused, breathing heavily. "That's what you want, isn't it? Do you want to see it for yourself? Me as a freak?"

"Not at all," protested Rose. "I don't presume to know what you've been through."

The woman gave out a low moan. "You speak of blame. And you're right. I deserve everything that's happened to me. I destroyed lives. Including my own."

"Don't say that."

Rose's own despair was nothing compared to the years of torment her neighbor had been through. She looked at Jason in a panic, and he held up his hands. "No, we're very sorry. We're going now."

"Don't move a step. You want to see the damage? Is that what you want?"

Without ceremony, Esme pulled off the hat and veil and tossed them on the floor. What first struck Rose was the elegant line of her neck and head, like a ballet dancer's. But the slashes from the knife had brutally disfigured the upper part of her face. A thick white gash cut across her forehead like a waxy centipede, and another crossed from the corner of her forehead, down across the bridge of her nose and below the eye, stopping at the top of her cheekbone. The skin around her nose and forehead was pulled taut and looked weirdly translucent, and one eye drooped at the corner. The blade had barely missed her greenish-gray eyes, which stared back at Rose with bitterness.

Rose kept her gaze steady. She needed to reach this woman, to make her see that she was not the enemy. "What happened to you was awful. You've suffered, and we think we understand what happened. Would it help to talk to us? We won't publish anything, we won't tell a soul."

On the couch, Bird whimpered.

"You charge in here, take my dog, spread your things around." Esme grabbed the urn from the windowsill and held it up with one hand. "Redecorating, were you?"

Horrified, Rose ran over and snatched it from her, holding it close to her chest. "No, it's not like that."

"Now you know what it feels like to have a stranger manhandle your belongings."

Shame washed over her. She should have never camped out at the Barbizon after Griff kicked her out. What she'd done was unforgiveable.

"Rose, are those your father's ashes?" Jason spoke quietly.

Rose nodded.

Esme's eyes grew wide. "Her what?"

"Her father's ashes."

"Dear God." Shaking her head, Esme sat back down in her chair, mouth slack. She looked at her empty hands. "Dear, dear God."

"No, this was all my doing. I'm sorry. We'll go now." Rose stepped toward her suitcases.

"Stop." Esme thrust out her chin. "Sit. I need a moment to think."

They did as she commanded, side by side on the couch.

Rose held her breath.

"You are obviously in distress, Ms. Lewin, and I was once like you." Esme lifted her head. "I'm going to tell you what you want to know. But only because I don't know which of us needs this confession more." She took a deep breath. "You. Or me."

CHAPTER THIRTY-ONE

New York City, Halloween 1952

Darby's room was dark and quiet, a contrast to the hallway where girls in an assortment of costumes roamed, screeching with excitement as they readied for the evening's delights. A light rain had begun to fall, tapping against the window like the snap of tiny rubber bands. Darby was already packed, thanks to Mother, and in little more than an hour, she would simply gather her things and go. She'd meet Sam at the station and they would begin a new life together, someplace far away.

But first, she had to try to find Esme. She remembered when they'd met. Esme had rolled her eyes and made faces as the elevator crawled upward, while Mrs. Eustis ticked off the rules of the hotel. Darby had been terrified that day, and Esme offered a lifeline with no expectation of kindness or reward. Only a coward would abandon a girl like that when the tables were turned.

Darby tucked the recording of the two of them singing in one side of her suitcase, where it wouldn't break, and added her hairbrush and comb. That was it. She'd be traveling with a man who was not her husband, but that couldn't really be helped, given the situation. She wanted Sam to be safe, and if he had to leave the city, she would be by his side.

As she made to leave the room to search for her friend, the door opened and Esme flew in.

Darby almost fell into the bureau, shaking with surprise. And relief. "Esme."

Esme ran into her arms and they held each other for a moment. "Are you ready to hit the big time?"

"What?" Darby pulled back.

Esme's skin was shiny with sweat, her eyes wide. "I stopped by earlier but couldn't find you. Where have you been?"

"Talking with Sam. About you."

She studied Darby's face. "I see you've heard the news. The police screwed me. Royally."

"Sam showed me the article. You talked about babies being given heroin; did you really see that happen?"

Esme shrugged. "I live in the slum. Of course that's what I see."

Darby should never have assumed Esme's world in any way mirrored her own. She'd seen more foulness in her life so far than Darby probably ever would. She pulled Esme down to sit on the bed. "Why would you work for Kalai in the first place?"

"You saw those louts. I had to; it was part of my job at the club. Buckley knew it; everyone knew it. No surprise there. Why do you think the Flatted Fifth was so popular? Because it was an easy place to score. And I needed cash, in order to get all decked out and make a scene. I couldn't do it if I looked average. Glamour ain't cheap."

"Why did you go to the police?"

Esme flinched. "For you, of course. I figured we'd use the money to get an apartment. Then they fucked me. Quigley swore word wouldn't get out, but it got leaked to the papers."

"You named the musicians. You didn't think the police would go after them?"

"Everyone knows jazz musicians do drugs. No surprise there. And now I have enough *dinero* that we can hang loose until our careers take off."

Darby's heart ached for her friend. There was no way Esme could ever show herself again in New York. "You ruined people's lives."

The bravado fell from Esme's face and she stared blankly at the floor. "Well, I'm sorry for that part. But I got screwed, too. Mrs. Eustis just fired me."

"You're in terrible danger. So is Sam."

"I wonder who you're more worried about."

"Don't be ridiculous. I'm terrified for the both of you."

"We'll be fine." She glanced over at the suitcase. "And I'm glad you're packed up. I have a cousin with an apartment where we can crash until the coast is clear."

Leave it to Esme to have a backup plan. But it was too late. "I went to your acting school and they said you'd never enrolled."

Esme walked to the window, pressed her forehead against the glass. "Those idiots wouldn't recognize talent if you gave them a roomful of movie stars."

Darby had taken Esme's ambition for something solid and positive. A girl who could rise up against all odds and prejudices with her confidence. When in fact she was willing to hurt other people, betray her own friends, in order to get her way. The signs had been there all along, the nagging feeling that Esme wasn't telling the truth, or perhaps manipulating it.

Yet no matter how awful Esme had behaved, her actions weren't born of malice. She'd fought tooth and nail, never faltering when insulted by the acting school or abused by stuck-up hotel guests.

Esme had stood firmly by Darby's side since day one. She'd been a good friend and now she was in trouble.

Darby walked over and put a hand on her shoulder. "Sam's asked me to go away with him."

Esme spun around. "You can't. I need you, Darby. We make a good team. I'm sorry for what I did, but you understand why, don't you? We have to stick together."

"Keep your voice down."

"I love you so much." Her voice cracked. "I can take care of you. Better than Sam. I've worked two jobs since I got to New York, and when we needed extra cash, I came up with it."

"I was in a bind. But that wasn't right, what you did."

"It was all for you."

Darby needed to find somewhere quiet to calm her down and make her understand. If she caused a scene and Mrs. Eustis was called, they'd both be in serious trouble and Darby might miss her meeting with Sam. "Come with me."

She headed up the back stairs to the sky terrace, and Esme followed with no fuss. A cool wind blew and the stone floor was slick with puddles.

Esme lit a cigarette and sat on the edge of the wall, kicking her feet against the balusters. "We're a team, you and me. It's not fair for you to run off with Sam. Not after everything I've done for you."

"I appreciate what you've done. From the day I arrived here, you looked out for me. But now you've put Sam in danger. He has to leave the club, leave his family."

"Don't throw it all away for a man." Esme's lip curled. "That's what your mother was worried about, right? That you wouldn't be able to support yourself and be trapped by a man who was unworthy of you."

"Mother disowned me, so whatever she wants is no longer an issue. It's what I want."

"We can sing together."

"I'm not interested in a singing career, never have been. That was your dream."

Esme tossed her cigarette over the side of the building and stood. "You're making a big mistake. You'll end up like your mother, dependent on some guy you barely even know."

The words stung more than they should have. Darby remained silent.

Esme pulled the small knife from the pocket of her dress and walked over, holding it out in the palm of her hand. "Look here. I can protect you. Sam can't. He went to war and became a cook, too much of a coward to join the fight."

"Don't be silly. Put the knife away."

"I will if you hear me out first, okay?"

"Fine."

"We hide out at my cousin's for a couple of weeks until Kalai gets tossed into jail. I'll help you with your stage fright, with everything. And before you know it, we'll be famous and living in the Ritz. Or at least a cool place in Greenwich Village."

Darby took a deep breath and spoke in the most soothing tone she could manage. "It sounds lovely. But it's not safe. Sam says Kalai's sons will keep the heroin ring going even if Kalai gets put away."

"What does Sam know? I know the streets better than him."

"And on top of that, it's not what I want for myself. Mother made big plans for me, but she only did it out of guilt. I know you do it because you care about my future, because you love me. And I feel the same about you. But I can't be told what to do anymore, by anyone. I have to make my own decisions now."

Esme reached out and touched Darby's cheek. "We're a pair, re-member? You can't leave me all alone."

The misery in her voice pierced Darby's anger at their predica-ment. She remembered the gentle way Esme had helped her out of her umbrella dress when she'd been a wreck, how close they'd become. Maybe her father had had a special friend as well, one who hadn't stuck by him. What if he'd felt the same panic when his world came tumbling down around him?

"Why don't you come with me and Sam to California? We'll hide out, explore a brand-new city."

"What am I going to do in California?"

"We'll find jobs, work, make money."

"But all my singing contacts are here. I have auditions lined up for us."

"You've destroyed those contacts by talking to Quigley."

"I tell you, it's only temporary. And now I've got money. Gobs of it. You won't have to worry about a thing."

There was no talking to the girl. She couldn't see the big picture, was lost in a haze of self-delusion and dreams.

"I'm not willing to risk my life." Darby's heart pounded in her chest. "I'm leaving with Sam. I'm sorry, Esme."

She turned to go, but Esme grabbed her arm. Darby lost her footing on the wet terrace and fell into a shallow puddle, her palms stinging from the impact.

Esme loomed over Darby, her eyes blazing the color of molten caramel. "No. We're not done talking yet." She held out a hand to help her stand up, but Darby smacked it away.

"Don't be ridiculous. And don't try to stop me." The words trem-bled on Darby's tongue.

Esme took one step back, pleading. "Let's leave together, head to

Hector's for a malt. I have to explain it to you better, that's all, and then you'll understand."

Darby slowly rose to her feet, wiping her hands on her skirt. "I'm meeting Sam at Grand Central. You're welcome to come with me, but I'm not staying here in the city."

"You can't leave me!" Esme lunged for her, forgetting about the knife, which sliced into Darby's arm. Blood oozed from the wound and she cried out in pain.

Esme froze for a moment, in shock at what she'd done, and finally crumpled, tears pouring down her face.

Darby stepped forward and held Esme's face between her palms as blood trickled down the length of her forearm. "You need to get to safety, that's the first order of business. Hide out at your cousin's. I'll write to you once Sam and I are situated and you can follow us."

But instead of agreeing, Esme shook her head. "No."

Time was running out. Darby had to get off the terrace, fast. Esme's obstinacy had turned into madness.

"I'm sorry, Esme. Sam will be waiting for me." Darby turned to go, but Esme came at her fast from behind, knocking the wind out of her. Darby managed to free one hand, and drove her elbow into Esme's side. Esme staggered back against the balustrade, breathing heavily, her features contorted with rage.

"Darby?"

Darby whirled around to see Stella stepping out of the doorway onto the terrace, cigarette in hand. She wore a black cat costume, replete with a headband with pointed cat ears, and whiskers painted over her ivory cheeks. Behind her stood a pirate, who lifted up his eye patch to get a better look.

Stella stopped for a moment, frozen. "What's going on?"

Darby opened her mouth to warn her, but Esme's arm was around

Darby's neck before she could speak. Stella stayed near the door, lips in a wide O, her eyes green and huge.

"Esme, that's enough." Darby's bellow, which came from a deep, dark place inside her, caught them both off guard. She whirled around, facing Esme.

At first, Darby thought Esme had hit her in the nose and broken it, that her nose was bleeding. Pain seared her forehead and cheek. Blinded by the gushing wound, Darby lashed out, flying at her friend, unaware how close they were to the edge.

For a moment Esme was suspended, hands waving in the air, clutching at nothing.

Then she was gone.

CHAPTER THIRTY-TWO

New York City, 2016

Outside, the city was eerily silent, as if in respect for Darby's story rather than the lateness of the hour.

Rose and Jason sat quietly for a few moments once Darby finished speaking. Darby, not Esme. Relief flooded through Rose with the knowledge that Darby was the one who had survived. It was almost as if she'd come back from the dead.

Darby's face was white, her eyes watery. "I'll never forget the look she gave me as she fell backward. Shock, surprise. I didn't realize we were so close to the edge. I didn't mean to push her so hard."

"You were only trying to protect yourself." Rose's words were inadequate, but she had to say something.

Darby took a handkerchief from her sleeve and dabbed at her nose. "No. She was my dearest friend. And I killed her."

"Why did you tell Sam you had died instead?"

"When I got back from the hospital, the book of spices was waiting for me. All that time, I figured Sam had shown up at Grand Central and left without me, wondering where I was. But when I read what he'd written inside, I knew he was in trouble. I didn't want him coming back to the city to find me. Kalai's men were all over.

He would have been in terrible danger. And I couldn't imagine going out to San Francisco and facing him, telling him what I had done. I was mortified at the thought of him seeing me like this. So I told him I had died. I offered to send the book of spices back. I knew how much it meant to him, but he didn't want it."

"And you kept it all these years."

"I did. As a reminder of my shame. You see, Esme had trusted me, she'd loved me. She was a woman who struggled to rise above her station in life in spite of terrible prejudice. Not that she was perfect. She made a rash decision, not thinking of how it could affect all her friends, including Sam. But every night, when I close my eyes, I see her tipping over the side of the railing, reaching out for my hand as she falls. I look over the edge and watch her body slam into the ground. I relive it over and over." Darby let out a sharp breath. "I couldn't face Sam. I wasn't brave enough to try again."

"But it was an accident; she attacked you first."

"Intentions are worthless to me. I pushed her and she fell to her death. After, Mrs. Eustis at the Barbizon took pity on me and let me stay on, and the Gibbs school arranged for the job at the button store. Pity, for my terrible wound. There I could work behind the scenes and stay out of view. Of course, as styles changed and hats went out of fashion, I knew I looked strange, traipsing around town in my veils. But by then, I didn't care. My life was structured, orderly. I paid my rent on time each month. The world around me transformed dramatically, but I refused to. I couldn't."

Jason spoke quietly. "You never heard from your family again?"

"No. I wrote my mother, but she didn't write back. I made a quiet life for myself, working, coming home. It's more in my personality, to do the same thing day after day. Like Bird, here."

"He does like a structured regimen," said Rose.

"Thank you for watching over him while I was away."

"I'm sorry I invaded your apartment. That was terrible of me."

Darby's shoulders tensed, but instead of scolding Rose as expected, she shrugged and let out a sigh. "It's the building. I would probably have holed up in a broom closet at the Barbizon if they hadn't offered me the chance to stay on after Esme died. By then, it had become my refuge, my sanctuary. I can understand the deep pull of the place. You can shelter here when the city feels too overwhelming to bear. Sometimes I wonder if it's a living, breathing animal instead of an inanimate pile of stone and cement."

The thought was strangely comforting. Rose spoke up. "Can I ask where you've been the past few weeks?"

Darby gave a mischievous smile. "*Oui.* Montreal."

"Montreal?" Jason blinked a couple of times and he and Rose exchanged incredulous looks. Not their first guess.

"Yes." Darby pointed to the black-and-white photo on the bookshelf. "The girl I consider my grandniece was performing at the festival they hold there each year. Her international debut."

Rose stood and took the photo down. "The one who calls you *Tía.* I thought this was a photo of Esme."

"No, no. Alba loves the old black-and-white studio portraits from the fifties; she insisted on this for her professional photo. My influence, I'm proud to say. A head shot, they called it." She wiggled her fingers at Rose, who handed her the photo. Darby stared at it, smiling, and for a moment, Rose got the sense of what she might have looked like without the scar tissue. Her face was radiant, underneath the damage.

"Looks just like Esme," Darby said. "We're not related, but she calls me Auntie anyway, dear girl. Alba is the granddaughter of Esme's sister. She'd invited me to hear her sing in Canada and initially I said no, too far for an old lady like me to go. But when you showed up at my door, I figured it was a good time to hit the road, as they say. You lived in the building, I knew there would be no avoiding you. So I flew up and she took great care of me. I had the best seats, was brought backstage, went out for drinks after the gig with the band. Treated like royalty. She's a good girl."

"So you'd stayed in touch with Esme's family all these years?"

"About twenty years ago, I had sunk pretty low. It was during October, a time of year I've always found difficult. I had constant nightmares, as if Esme was haunting me. Although I had always visited her grave a few times a year, that year I went on the anniversary of her death."

"On Halloween?"

"Yes. I'd hoped to have a quiet moment to say I was sorry, but there was a group of women there, lots of commotion, in a good way. Esme's family. They were pleased to meet someone who'd known her then."

"Did they know who you were?"

She shook her head. "The hotel told them that Esme jumped of her own accord. Keeping the fuss to a minimum. This little girl was there, at the graveyard, dressed as a fairy in her Halloween costume. She played by herself off to the side, singing in perfect pitch, and I found her delightful. Over the years the family was kind to me, invited me over for dinners every so often. And as Alba grew up, I offered to pay for her singing lessons, head shots, whatever she needed."

"She's beautiful."

"Inside and out. When I was in Montreal with her I told her the truth, about who I was and what I'd done. Alba didn't care. She said it explained why I'd taken her under my wing and nurtured her. That it was my way of making it up to Esme."

"Esme would have been so proud of her," offered Rose.

"True. Esme made some terrible decisions, but she should have had a singing career, an acting career. If she'd lived, I have no doubt she would have made something of herself."

Rose stood. "Thank you for telling us all this. The story's been killed, so we won't be writing about you or Esme."

"Killed?"

Rose cringed at her poor choice of words. "The company I worked for doesn't want long stories anymore."

"And this would be a doozy, huh?"

"It certainly would." She paused. "You should see Sam again."

Darby stood as well. "How could I, after all this time? We're both doddering fools; nothing good can come of it."

"You can return his book to him," said Jason.

"Oh, you two can do that. No need for me to get involved."

"You're both in the same city after decades of being apart," urged Rose. "Please don't pass up the opportunity."

"I couldn't let him see me like this; better for him to remember the girl I was." Darby's fingertips went to her scar. For a moment she was lost in thought, lost in time. Then she shrugged. "Although I bet he's no spring chicken anymore, either."

"He's a good-looking guy, for eightysomething."

Darby let out an unexpected giggle. For a moment it was as if she were a teenage girl again. "I bet."

"Think about it." Jason's voice was calm, soothing.

"When I think about all the things we could have seen and done together." Tears filled Darby's eyes. "I shouldn't have sent that letter."

"You can tell him yourself." Rose moved closer and took her hand. "You *should* tell him yourself."

❦

"You seem more nervous than Darby," whispered Jason to Rose as they guided Darby into the restaurant.

Rose made a face, but she had to agree. They were dining with Sam and Malcolm at Neo, Chef Steven's restaurant.

Darby wore a mint-green satin vintage dress that curved around her skinny frame. A small matching hat was angled on her head, the requisite veil underneath. Jason gave Rose's hand a squeeze as the hostess brought them over to where Malcolm and Sam sat, looking dapper in suits and ties. Both gentlemen rose to their feet.

Should she make introductions? The finer points of etiquette were completely inadequate here.

Darby walked over to Sam and took his hands in hers. "Sam. My dear Sam."

Sam's eyes watered and his chin quivered ever so slightly. "You're here."

"I've always been here." She lowered her voice so it was barely audible. "I'm sorry. I'm so sorry."

Sam nodded slowly. "When I think of what you went through, my heart breaks."

"I thought I was protecting you. But I was protecting myself." She gestured toward the veil. "And I didn't want you to see me like this."

"I have to be perfectly honest with you."

Rose held her breath, unsure of what he would say next.

"With my glaucoma, you look like a 1950s pinup."

Their laughter broke the ice, and after Darby filled Sam in on what had occurred after their parting at the hotel in 1952, Sam told his story. He kept the details vague, but his voice broke in the telling and Darby reached out and put her hand on his arm, where it remained until the waiter came out with the first course.

"I asked the chef to prepare something special for us," explained Jason. "Please, dig in."

Before them was grilled octopus on a bed of arugula.

Rose observed Sam's face as he took a bite. His eyes grew wide and he quickly swallowed. "This is one of mine!"

Darby laughed like a child who'd been keeping a secret. "Jason and I gave a few of your blends to the chef, in honor of our dinner tonight. I hope you approve. This one is flavored with sea salt and fennel, with a hint of citrus."

"I knew I was onto something, but in the hands of a master these rise to a completely different level," Sam said. "Exquisite."

The appetizer was followed by a Moroccan-inspired, spice-encrusted sea bass, and finished off with ice cream that tasted of lavender and honey.

As they finished their coffees, flavored with cardamom, Rose looked around the table. Darby and Sam were in a deep, private conversation, while Jason and Malcolm were chatting about a bebop festival being held next month.

"Rose, do you have the book?" asked Darby.

"Of course." She reached into her bag and pulled out the book of spices and placed it in front of Sam.

"I thought this should go back to its rightful owner," declared Darby.

Sam opened it and leafed through the pages. He leaned in and gave it a sniff. "I can still smell Kalai's shop, after all these years. Thank you. I have one request."

"Of course."

"I'd like you to read it out loud to me. Over coffee one day, perhaps."

"It would be my pleasure." Darby patted his hand. "And now it's my turn to surprise all of you. Follow me."

To Rose's shock, Darby led them down the side streets of SoHo to an intimate jazz club, one of several new venues that had sprung up over the past few years. They trod down a set of stairs so narrow and steep that Jason insisted he walk first so Darby had someone in front of her as a guide. Sam trotted down with a renewed vigor, Rose couldn't help but notice.

As soon as they'd ordered a round of drinks, the lights dimmed and a young woman stepped into the spotlight, accompanied only by a bassist. She began singing a plaintive, deceptively simple version of Monk's "Ask Me Now," one that conveyed layers of pain and the sorrow behind the lyrics.

Rose listened closely, mesmerized. Not just by the voice, but by the girl. Esme's grandniece, Alba. She wore a simple coral-colored sheath dress with matching lipstick and her dark hair fell in waves over her shoulders. As she sang, her luminous skin caught the light and reflected it, as if she were glowing from within. She was magnificent.

No matter how she had suffered, Darby hadn't retreated from life after all. In fact, she'd embraced it. Quietly, carefully, but with dignity and love. Rose silently vowed that she wouldn't retreat either.

Jason took her hand and squeezed it. She smiled and nestled next to him, imagining the ghost of Esme hovering around the darkened room, soaking in every note and breath.

EPILOGUE

After only a couple of weeks of searching, Rose had scooped up a one-bedroom apartment on the Lower East Side, right around the block from where the Flatted Fifth used to be. Its uneven, sloping floors and blackened brick fireplace only added to the charm, in her opinion. And when the tiny retail shop on the ground floor came up for rent, Sam and his stepdaughter, Jessica, signed a lease and opened up Sam's Spice Shop. News of their magic powders spread among the chefs of Manhattan with lightning speed, and a feature story in *The New York Times* stoked demand from amateur gourmets as well.

Rose spent her days working on a book about the women of Barbizon's fourth floor, for which she'd received a healthy advance, while a floor below, Jessica filled orders in the shop and Sam played around with new spice combinations. A few evenings a week, Rose would meet up with Jason to hear about the progress on his documentary on the history of the city's heroin trade, and after he'd often stay over in her spice-infused bedroom. The arrangement worked perfectly, with time for play as well as time for work.

Every weekend, Rose would pay a visit to Sam and Darby in their apartment at the Barbizon, followed by a walk with Bird in the park, where the regal woman with the hat and the man holding a cane drew looks from passersby for their obvious devotion to each other.

The Dollhouse, once the stalwart host to thousands of girls, was now dwarfed by skyscrapers that were taller and shinier. The guest rooms were gone and so were the young ladies who had once dreamed and plotted beneath the building's Moorish arches. But every time Rose approached the building, she would stop and look up and think of them all, forgetting—for a few quiet moments—the steady stream of pedestrians who curled on the sidewalk around her.

ACKNOWLEDGMENTS

This book couldn't have been written without Stefanie Lieberman's encouragement and expert guidance, as well as Stephanie Kelly's enthusiasm and sharp eye. The entire team at Dutton deserves a huge round of applause, as do those who weighed in on early drafts, including Lisa Nicholas, Madeline Rispoli, Lindsey Ross, Jess Russell, Tamra Tuller, and Jamie Brenner.

In terms of research, I am grateful to Carol Kirn, Joan P. Gage, Olga Jiménez de Wagenheim, and Swing University at Jazz at Lincoln Center. Several books and articles provided inspiration, including *The Art of Blending* by Lior Lev Sercarz (which I first read about in Alex Halberstadt's *New York Times* article on Lev Sercarz), *Katharine Gibbs: Beyond White Gloves* by Rose Doherty, and *The Puerto Ricans: A Documentary History* edited by Kal Wagenheim and Olga Jiménez de Wagenheim.

Finally, I want to thank my dear friends Linda Powell, Cynthia Besteman, and Carrie Molay, and my family—Brian, Dilys, and Martin—for their unwavering support.

THE DOLLHOUSE

Fiona Davis

Reading Group Guide

A Conversation with the Author

An Excerpt from The Address

DUTTON

Reading Group Guide

1. When Griff returns home from work, Rose ponders if he ever wondered, as a man, "whether his face was too shiny, his hair curling unreasonably, or if his crow's-feet had possibly deepened overnight? . . . He entered the room as an agent of change, a man who made the news. Not as the pleasant-featured girl who simply reported it." Do you think her comments reflect the current climate for women in the workplace experience? Why or why not? How is this different from or similar to Darby's time?

2. Why was Darby attracted to Esme as a friend? What characteristics did Esme espouse that Darby desired? Is Esme a foil for Darby? What does Stella represent? Which one of these three characters would you rather be in the story and why?

3. What did you think of young Stella's plan to find the wealthiest, handsomest man she could? Do you think it was a mark of codependence or independence? Why or why not? Did your impression of Stella change from the 1950s to 2016? If so, how and why?

4. What did you think about how *The Dollhouse* portrays the darker, seedy underbelly of the New York City jazz scene in the 1950s? Does it still retain its glamour? Why or why not?

5. Why do you think Esme kissed Darby? Was it a sexual kiss? What did it mean to each woman?

6. Do you think Rose is justified in her skewering description of the modern start-up workplace and start-up CEO? Do you think it accurately reflects the modern culture of these workplaces?

7. Put yourself in Darby's shoes. Would you have gone back home after being expelled from Gibbs? Why or why not? What did you think of Darby's plan? How did it differ from Esme's? What do these differences reveal about their friendship?

8. What did you think of Esme in the end? What different factors of her life played into her desperate final actions? Is she a character to be pitied, vilified, or something much more complex? How did she change Darby, for better or for worse?

9. What did you think of Rose's concerns about her future after her breakup with Griff? Were they justified? Was Rose fair in how she viewed the lives of the elderly Barbizon women?

10. What do you think of the older women's lives now? Are they a symbol of feminism or a dying breed? What are the advantages and disadvantages of being one of the original Barbizon inhabitants?

11. Is Rose an accurate portrayal of the modern-day woman? Do you think Rose was too opportunistic in her desire to become a news-breaking journalist? Was she too desperate for Griff's attention? What choices would you have made in her place and would those choices have been difficult?

12. Did Rose's story mirror Darby's story? Why or why not? What differences and similarities did you notice between the two characters? How do you think each woman changed and grew over the course of the novel?

13. Several people take on different identities or present themselves to the world in a not-entirely-truthful way in *The Dollhouse.* What purpose did these identities serve and how do you think they helped or hurt the various characters in the end?

14. How do you think the presence of food and delicacies—the different textures, spices, and smells—plays into the plot and texture of the book? How does it illuminate or obscure aspects of the two time periods? What was your favorite meal?

15. What do you think about how Darby handled things with Sam after her skirmish with Esme? What would you have done? How do you think Darby's life would have been different if she'd made a different choice?

A Conversation with Fiona Davis on Her Debut Novel The Dollhouse

How did you get the idea for *The Dollhouse*? Once you had the setting, did the plot or characters come to you first?

The idea came to me when I was hunting for an apartment in New York City. My broker took me to the Barbizon 63 condo, which I knew used to be the Barbizon Hotel for Women. While there, I learned that a dozen or so of the long-time residents had been moved into rent-controlled apartments on the fourth floor when the building went condo in 2005. I was fascinated by that arrangement, and couldn't help but wonder what it was like for these women, who'd seen such dramatic changes in the city and the building over time.

I first focused on the characters and figured out who they were, what they wanted out of life, and what their strengths and weaknesses were. I'd been an actress when I first came to New York, and that method of diving in seemed the way to go. From there, ideas for the plot began to unfold pretty organically.

You did a lot of research to bring 1950s New York to life; do you enjoy the research process?

I loved doing the research. I interviewed women who'd lived in the Barbizon, read lots of books on the 1950s, and watched movies set in New York in that era. I'd been working as a journalist before I turned to writing fiction and I approached the research in the same way I would if I'd been writing an article. For example, once I decided to use a downtown jazz club as one of the settings, I signed up for a course in bebop at Jazz at Lincoln Center, which provided me with tons of material for the book, as well as an innovative way of thinking about the music behind the story and how it affects the characters.

The theme of personal fulfillment for women—in the workplace and their personal lives—is explored a lot in *The Dollhouse*. Did you set out to write a book on this topic, or did it grow from the story? What are your thoughts on how things have and haven't changed for women since the 1950s?

As part of my research, I read through women's magazines from the early 1950s and was struck by the mixed messages. They often advised women to embark on a career, but only until they settled down and married. For example, one article offered a list of the best part-time jobs for women, because working full time cut too deeply into "the satisfactions of housekeeping." I was astounded.

As I sat down to write the book, I decided to explore the idea of the two main characters being out of step with their time. Darby, who comes to the city in 1952, is determined to never marry, while Rose, in 2016, has placed herself in a rather precarious position because she was counting on a man to take care of her. For Rose's storyline, I was influenced by friends and acquaintances who were model mothers and wives but found themselves at a loss when the kids grew up or they got divorced. While women today have much greater freedom in deciding what to do with our lives, sometimes we still box ourselves in to the 1950s paradigm.

Who do you identify with more: Darby or Rose?

I love Rose's doggedness in trying to figure out what happened to Esme back in the fifties, but her questionable journalistic ethics were painful to write, even if they helped move the story forward. In terms of Darby, I wanted to capture the discombobulation that a newcomer to the city feels, as I experienced that myself when I first moved to New York, and I adore her vulnerability and quirkiness.

I also knew I wanted to write about what it's like to step onto a stage and perform, the courage and sheer obliviousness required, and making poor Darby sing in the jazz club was the answer. I think that's one of my favorite scenes in the book, and I love how much she grows over the course of the story.

Esme is such a complex character—how do you, ultimately, feel about her?

She made some very poor decisions, but in the end I root for her because she had to work ten times as hard as everyone else. As part of my research, I did a lot of reading about the Great Migration of the 1950s, when thousands of Puerto Ricans immigrated to New York City in search of a better life and were met with hostility and discrimination. Esme is talented, smart, and driven, yet she can't get a break. So I understand and sympathize with her choices and fallibilities.

How did you juggle writing two separate timelines? Did you write them simultaneously or one after the other? Were there any particular challenges that came with writing a dual narrative?

Once I had my characters set, I plotted out the two timelines before carefully weaving them together. I wrote the book chronologically by chapter as a first draft, then separated the two time-lines and read them each straight through while editing. Since there's a mystery element to the story, I found myself losing my mind every so often because if I changed the location of a clue or red herring in one timeline, it ultimately wreaked havoc with the other. Whenever that happened, I'd go and eat a block of cheese, and that helped. (Always does.) With the guidance of my terrific editor, we sharpened and focused the story so everything eventually fell into place.

Would you have liked to live in the Barbizon during its hey-day as a women's hotel? Why or why not?

Since the book has been published, I've heard from many former guests of the Barbizon Hotel who've shared their memories and stories with me. For all of them, their stay at the Barbizon marked a seminal moment in their lives, when they were declaring their independence and forging their own lives and careers, and I can only imagine the buzz of energy that flowed through the halls day and night. Even if boys weren't allowed upstairs and you had to provide three references to get a room, the restrictions and rules were just part of life, unremarkable. However, I must also consider the fact that many of my dearest friends wouldn't have been able to stay there due to the religious and racial intolerance of the time, and that would have been a serious problem.

My hope is that *The Dollhouse* will remind all of us how drastically different life was back then for a single girl in the city, and of just how far we've come. And how by examining the past, we can continue to challenge traditional assumptions about aging, identity, and what it means to be an independent woman today.

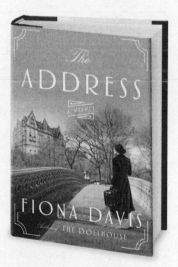

CHAPTER ONE

London, June 1884

The sight of a child teetering on the window ledge of room 510 turned Sara's world upside down.

After several years toiling as a maid and working her way up the ranks, she'd been awarded the position of head housekeeper at London's Langham Hotel a month prior. One of her largest tasks was keeping the maids in line, all young girls with hardly a shred of common sense among them. When they should have been straightening the rooms, she'd more often than not find them giggling in the hallways or flirting with the boys delivering tea trays or flowers.

That morning, she'd been called into the manager's office and reprimanded for not being harsh enough on her charges.

"You're soft. We're starting to wonder if you're simply too young for the position," said Mr. Birmingham from behind his walnut desk, which, despite its elegant spindle legs, was roughly the size of a small boat.

Having recently turned thirty, Sara didn't feel young in the least, not that she'd ever acted that way. When she'd first arrived at the Langham, she'd skipped the giddy overtures of friendship from other maids her age, knowing that she had to stand out if she wanted to move up quickly. Her coolness had paid off, and her higher salary more than made up for the lack of companionship.

But for Mr. Birmingham, who found pleasure in making the younger maids cry, Sara's self-imposed isolation wasn't enough.

He directed her to take a seat, but once she had settled herself, the perspective in the room suddenly felt off, as if something in the furniture's configuration had changed since Mr. Birmingham last summoned her to this spot—or else she was so annoyed by his request for an interview during the busiest hours of the day that she'd worked herself into a kind of nervous imbalance. Sara's employer was short and had the poor luck to have a torso shaped like a chicken egg with a double yolk. She towered over the man by several inches. Yet somehow Mr. Birmingham was peering down at her from his throne-like seat. She stole a glance at the floor. The bottom five inches of his chair legs were stained a different color than the rest. He'd had them lengthened.

When she looked back up, he puffed up like a songbird, clearly peeved that she'd noticed.

She shifted in her seat. "I'm sorry, Mr. Birmingham, I will be tougher on the girls."

"If they're difficult, give them a slap. Better yet, send them down here and I'll do it for you." He licked his lips.

Right. She imagined he'd enjoy it immensely. "Is there anything more?"

"No, Mrs. Smythe. Off you go."

She was still getting used to being called "Mrs." Strange how a single promotion afforded not only a living wage but also a new moniker that had nothing to do with her marital status, or lack thereof. No head housekeeper could be called a "Miss." Wasn't proper. The girls were still getting used to addressing her by her full name, and she had to be firmer with that as well. It wouldn't do for Mr. Birmingham to overhear them calling her "Sara." It might be the last straw in what was a very unstable haystack.

That hot June afternoon, after patrolling the halls and basement to break up any assignations, she retreated to her office on the sixth floor to double check the laundry bills. She needed a rest from shooting dour looks at the girls; her face was tired from scowling. The one window in the room was open as wide as possible in order to catch some semblance of a breeze, but the weather refused to cooperate. All day, the air had been still and humid, making the hotel feel—and smell—a little like the greenhouses at Kew Gardens. A movement from the curtain drew her up from her desk in the hopes that an afternoon thunderstorm was brewing.

To her disappointment, the sky was a hazy blue. She looked across the courtyard and there, one floor below, a flash of flesh caught her eye, a chubby arm with fingers that grasped the edge of the sill. Then another arm flailed out and did the same, followed by a head covered in golden curls. The girl sported a velvet bow at the back of her head at a skewed angle. Sara's breath caught in her chest. Surely a minder would appear at any moment and guide the child back into the room.

With some effort, the child eased her chest up onto the windowsill and stayed motionless for a second, surveying the ground below, arms dangling downward. Sara willed the child away from danger. If she called out, there was a chance she would frighten the child into pitching farther forward. But still no one came. To her horror, a foot swung up and over the sill—three limbs in all. The child was climbing up, possibly drawn to the cooler air and away from the stifling room.

There was no time to waste. Sara sprang out of her office and down the corridor, one hand clutching the heavy chatelaine of keys that dangled from her waist. She lifted her skirts far higher than was decent and dashed down the stairs, her eyes riveted on the few feet in front of her so she didn't lose her footing on the slippery marble. At the fifth floor a couple of guests stepped off the lift and she swooped by them, muttering a quick apology, without losing a beat. Then a turn left and what seemed like an eternal race to the door of room 510. No banging, it might startle the child, and at this point it didn't matter if she was barging in on anyone. Even if doing so was against hotel policy.

The key turned smoothly in the lock and she opened the door. The girl, wearing a peach-colored dress, now stood upright on the sill facing out, one hand clutching the casing. She had to be around three years old. What was she doing alone?

Walter, one of the porters, and Mabel, the floor's chambermaid, appeared by Sara's side, breathing heavily. They must have sprinted after her, knowing something was terribly wrong.

Sara put out her arms to stop Mabel and Walter from moving any farther into the room. "Shh. We don't want to send her off balance."

"Where's her minder?" whispered Mabel. "Is anyone in the bedchamber?"

"I don't know." Sara took a step into the room, walking as if the floor might give out at any point. The plush rugs softened her footfall.

As she drew closer, she realized the child was singing to herself. A lullaby about being on a treetop.

The child turned her head and stared at Sara. Her rosy lips parted and her eyes grew round.

Sara held out one hand, palm up, and began humming the same

tune softly. In response, the child laughed, but then, with the changeability of the age, her eyes suddenly filled with tears.

"Mama!" the girl demanded, then shook her head. Sara didn't dare move any farther and her muscles tensed with the effort of doing nothing, staying frozen. A breeze blew in and ruffled the girl's curls, pushing her slightly off balance. If she fell backward, into the room, Sara might be able to reach her in time to break her fall.

But instead, the little girl overcorrected, and her hand began slipping off the window frame. Such tiny fingernails, tiny fingers.

Sara lunged forward. Her hand grazed the voluminous skirt of the child's dress and she gripped as much of the material as she could, yanking hard. The girl, shrieking, flew off the ledge, inside, to safety. They hit the ground together in an awkward tangle of limbs and petticoats, the girl practically sitting on Sara's lap.

The girl twisted around and looked at Sara, blinking in astonishment. Sara was sure she'd cry out but instead the girl resumed her babbling song while reaching up with one hand to stroke Sara's chin.

"Well done, just in time," said Walter as he and Mabel gathered on either side of her.

"Do you think she hurt herself?" asked Sara.

"No, not a whit. You broke the fall. Are you all right?" Mabel scooped up the child while Sara let Walter help her to her feet. She was straightening her skirts and rubbing her hip, which no doubt would sport a large bruise by tomorrow, when a tall, thin woman appeared in the doorway.

"What on earth is going on in here?" the woman demanded, clutching the hand of a little girl a few years older than the one held by Mabel.

The name popped into Sara's head from the guestbook: the Hon. Mrs. Theodore Camden. Traveling with three children, a husband, and a small coterie of servants. Mr. Birmingham had instructed Sara that all of the Camdens' needs be anticipated, as the wife was the daughter of a baron.

Sara stepped forward. "The child was standing in the window and we brought her inside."

"More like saved her life," said Walter. "Mrs. Smythe here leaped in and dragged her back inside in just the nick of time."

The child, as if only realizing the heightened emotions of the grown-ups around her, began to wail. The woman dashed forward and scooped her out of Mabel's arms, holding the girl close. When her cries subsided, Mrs. Camden looked up, as if seeing them all for the first time.

"I thank you for your assistance, but where is her nanny?"

As if on cue, a plain-looking girl stepped into the room.

"Ma'am?" she inquired, her face scrunched up in confusion.

"Miss Morgan, where have you been? Lula almost fell to her death due to your absence."

"I'm sorry?" The girl gazed around at everyone in the room. "I popped out for only a minute, to drop off a postcard at the front desk."

"You were supposed to be here minding the children."

The child buried her head in her mother's shoulder, weeping again.

"Where is Luther?" Mrs. Camden rushed into the adjoining room and they all followed. Another child—a boy who seemed to be around the same age—lay on the enormous bed, fast asleep, his curls damp around his head.

Sara, standing beside Mrs. Camden, could practically feel the woman's fear and relief emanating from her body, like the aftershocks of an earthquake. The nanny took Lula from her arms and set about calming the girl down, avoiding her employer's eyes.

How awful if something had happened. Two little children left alone with a wide-open window; the thought was unimaginable. Sara turned to Mrs. Camden. The woman's profile was precise, her coloring fair other than thick black lashes that framed hazel eyes. Sara had encountered innumerable members of the peerage at the Langham and they all shared a common way of moving in the world, a confidence that their every desire would be met. It was rare to see one in crisis.

She sensed Walter and Mabel hovering behind them, and became protective of the woman's dignity. "Is there anything else we can do, Mrs. Camden?" asked Sara.

"No, that is all." The woman's face softened. "Thank you for saving her."

"Of course, ma'am." Sara nodded to Walter and Mabel and led the way out of the room. Once the door was closed behind them, Sara exhaled with relief.

"That was a close call." Walter rubbed his forehead with the back of his hand.

"You were spectacular, Sara. I mean, Mrs. Smythe," said Mabel.

Sara wanted more than anything to crumple onto the floor, but she couldn't allow her staff to see that.

"That's more than enough excitement for one day. Back to work. And Mabel, please remember to address me properly."

"Of course, Mrs. Smythe."

Sara turned away and strode down the hallway, grateful her quaking knees were hidden under multiple layers of petticoats and skirts.

The rest of the day, whenever Sara's mind returned to the events in room 510, her heart thumped wildly in her ribcage. What if she hadn't grabbed the child in time? What if she'd had to peer over the edge and see the lifeless body splayed on the hard ground of the courtyard below? Sleep tonight, in the damp heat of her Bayswater bedsit, would be impossible.

But there was enough to keep her busy until then. She finished updating the ledgers, and was about to head out to inspect the turndown of the guests' rooms when a man rapped on her office door. She knew it was a man from the knock's hard, hollow sound. Maids' knuckles were barely audible, already apologizing for disturbing her, but the men, whether Mr. Birmingham or a janitor, had no such qualms.

She stood and opened the door, expecting Mr. Birmingham to have made a special trip upstairs to upbraid her for causing a scene with the guests. Instead, a stranger's face peered down at her. As if he sensed her discomfort, he stepped back a pace. "Mrs. Smythe?"

"Yes. May I help you, sir?" He was clearly a hotel guest, dressed in a fitted, bespoke suit with a Broadway silk hat tucked under one arm.

"I apologize for intruding." He wiped his brow with an enormous hand. "How do you manage up here, with this insufferable heat?"

"It's a rare occurrence, luckily."

"I believe you saved my daughter Lula today. I wanted to thank you in person. My name is Mr. Theodore Camden." His accent was American, his voice a warm tenor.

Sara gestured to a chair opposite her desk, offering him a seat. He moved with an unexpected grace, given his large build. Nothing about him was handsome, by standard measures. His head was small in contrast to his broad shoulders, his eyes close-set to an irregular nose. But when put altogether, he was magnetic. She looked down and closed the ledger in order to stop herself from staring.

"I'm glad she's safe. She is all right, isn't she?" The image of the wailing girl came to mind.

"Yes. We offered her a slice of Battenberg cake and she's completely forgotten the incident." He chuckled before a brief look of pain crossed his face. "I don't know what would have happened if you hadn't gotten there in time. The twins, Lula and Luther, are constantly getting into trouble."

"Best not to think of it."

Sara was unsure how to proceed. She'd never had a hotel guest in her small office, and he was so tall he took up much of the space.

"How did you know what was happening?" Mr. Camden leaned back in his chair, his hat in his lap. He didn't seem to realize how indecorous it was to be sitting together like this, even if the door was open so nothing could be construed as irregular. It was almost as if he enjoyed it, while most guests wouldn't dream of mingling with the staff.

"I can see your hotel room from my window. I stood to get some air and saw her climb up."

"The girl was supposed to be watching the twins while Mrs. Camden was out. Needless to say, she was fired immediately."

"Well, luckily all turned out well." Other than for the nanny, of course.

"What is the ratio of staff to guests here?"

Such an odd question. "We have three hundred rooms and a staff of approximately four hundred."

"How long have you been head housekeeper?"

"This is my first month. But I've been working here in some capacity for the past eleven years."

"You know the place well."

"I do."

"Mr. Birmingham says you're highly efficient."

Mr. Camden had inquired after her. "That's kind of him to say."

"It's a grand building, the Langham. Beautifully built."

"Yes." Americans were very strange indeed. His statements and questions unnerved her. He didn't seem to be in any rush to get back to his family. Mr. Birmingham might have sent him up here as some kind of a test. "I'm happy to be employed here."

"This hotel featured the first hydraulic lifts in England. Did you know that?"

Perhaps he was the type of man who collected facts, and loved to show off how much he knew. She nodded.

Mr. Camden smiled. "I'm going on and on, sorry about that. I simply wanted to figure out a way to thank you."

"There is no need. The hotel staff does everything it can for its guests."

"You did more than that. I hope you didn't injure yourself in the process."

"Not at all."

One of the laundry girls popped her head into the room and then jumped back, startled when she caught sight of Mr. Camden.

"Sorry, Mrs. Smythe. I'll come back later."

"That's fine, Edwina."

"Edwina, my mother's name." Mr. Camden swiveled around and gave her a smile. His face beamed with delight. "Edwina, may we trouble you for some tea?"

He was here to stay. But what for, she couldn't guess. Edwina turned to Sara. Her eyes held the same faint alarm Sara's must have, but Sara checked herself. "Yes, please, Edwina."

The girl shuffled off and Mr. Camden turned back to Sara. "If I'm not keeping you from anything, of course."

"Not at all. But there is no need for further mention of the incident. All's well, as they say."

"May I ask about your background?"

"I'm not sure if that's necessary, Mr. Camden."

He turned red. She hadn't meant to embarrass him, just wanted to redirect the conversation. Caught off guard, he tilted his head and stammered. "In a professional capacity, of course. I'm quite interested in how a big place like this keeps running along day after day, crisis after crisis."

"I assure you we seldom have crises like the one today. Most of the time it's a well-oiled machine." One of Mr. Birmingham's favorite expressions. She'd never liked it, as it turned the flesh-and-blood staff into cogs in an engine, but she was uncertain how to keep the conversation with Mr. Camden flowing.

"Of course not. What would you say is the biggest problem the staff encounters?"

She considered the question. "We are a first-class hotel, Mr. Camden. We make sure that every guest's whim is answered. Sometimes that can be a juggling act, as the turnover is quite high."

"Do many of the guests bring their own servants?"

"Of course. But they still need rooms cleaned and freshened. Lady's maids and butlers have their own roles to play, separate from the hotel's amenities."

"Before this, did you work in service?"

"I did not, however my mother was housekeeper to an earl. Before this I was a dressmaker's apprentice."

"Yet you still ended up in service?"

She should never have offered so much of her own history. But something about the man's manner made her speak more than was proper. And now she'd stumbled into uncomfortable territory.

The tea arrived and Sara welcomed the interruption. Enough with the man's incessant questions. She would turn the tables, regain the upper hand. As she poured the tea, she inquired after his work. Americans seemed to enjoy chattering on at great length about their accomplishments.

He rose to the occasion. "I'm assisting the construction of an apartment house in New York City."

"You're an architect?"

He beamed. "Yes. I work for the great Henry Hardenbergh."

Sara shook her head. "I'm afraid I'm not acquainted with his name."

"He's taking New York City by storm. He's designed a place where the best families can live with elegance and privacy, sharing amenities like laundry and housekeeping. Why, we're even keeping a tailor and baker on staff. As you can see, I'm fascinated with the inner workings of places like the Langham. Who keeps it humming, and how."

That explained his interrogation. "It sounds like a large project."

"The Dakota, it's called, and it will change the way the upper class of the city live. At the moment, the elite of New York reside in brownstones, equivalent to your terrace houses, with one family per abode. The idea of sharing common space and amenities with others, as the French do, is considered gauche."

"And why is that?"

"It's too similar to a working-class tenement, where dozens of families live together in poverty and squalor."

He continued on about the new building, barely stopping for

breath, and she drank down her tea quickly, grateful for the liquid on her parched throat. Finally, he pulled out his watch. "I must go. We leave very soon, heading back to New York. I say, you wouldn't want to work at the Dakota, would you?"

Her cup clattered against the saucer. She'd looked up when he'd spoken and missed the center.

He laughed. "I see I caught you unawares. We're in need of a head housekeeper and you are obviously well-qualified. New York City is an exciting place, I promise. I could mention your name to Mr. Douglas, the building's agent."

His words came tumbling out, as if he'd only just thought of the idea. Perhaps he had. Typical American boldness. It was a ridiculous suggestion, going to another country when she had a perfectly good job here, even if Mr. Birmingham was never pleased.

"I'm quite happy where I am, Mr. Camden. But thank you for the offer."

"I'm serious." His voice and visage grew animated as he worked through the details. "I'm going to send you a formal letter when I get back, as well as fare to come over. The opening is set for the end of October. Consider the idea. It's the least I could do, after what you did for my family today. Will you consider it?"

She shook her head. He was caught up in the moment, an impulsive American like many others she'd encountered at the Langham. Too loud, too close, no sense of propriety.

"No, Mr. Camden. But thank you. Please let me know if there's anything else you need during your stay. Good day."

After he'd left, she shut the door behind him and went to the window. The one to room 510 was firmly shut, curtains drawn. Good.

She'd had more than enough excitement for one day.